The Mermaid's Purse

Praise for *Losing Gemma*:

'You can't put this book down' *The New York Times*

'Scorching stuff indeed' *The Times*

'This is authentic travel writing-cum-action adventure' *Independent*

'A page-turner' *Observer*

'A menacing study of friendship and self-knowledge' *Sunday Mirror*

'Gardner has planted clues with expertise' *Daily Telegraph*

'Tense, dramatic and surprising, this book plays on your paranoia'
New Woman

'Fast-paced and gripping' *Hello!*

'A brilliant page-turner' *Heat*

'Fast-paced, this tale grips like a vice, carrying you along until the
unexpected twist hits you square between the eyes'
South Wales Evening Post

Katy Gardner teaches social anthropology at the University of Sussex. She lives in Brighton with her husband and three children. This is her second novel.

The Mermaid's Purse

KATY GARDNER

MICHAEL JOSEPH
an imprint of
PENGUIN BOOKS

MICHAEL JOSEPH

Published by the Penguin Group
Penguin Books Ltd, 80 Strand, London WC2R ORL, England
Penguin Putnam Inc., 375 Hudson Street, New York, New York 10014, USA
Penguin Books Australia Ltd, 250 Camberwell Road, Camberwell, Victoria 3124, Australia
Penguin Books Canada Ltd, 10 Alcorn Avenue, Toronto, Ontario, Canada M4V 3B2
Penguin Books India (P) Ltd, 11 Community Centre,
Panchsheel Park, New Delhi – 110 017, India
Penguin Books (NZ) Ltd, Cnr Rosedale and Airborne Roads,
Albany, Auckland, New Zealand
Penguin Books (South Africa) (Pty) Ltd, 24 Sturdee Avenue,
Rosebank 2196, South Africa

Penguin Books Ltd, Registered Offices: 80 Strand, London WC2R ORL, England

www.penguin.com

First published 2003

1

Copyright © Katy Gardner, 2003

The moral right of the author has been asserted

Set in 13.5/16 pt Monotype Garamond
Typeset by Rowland Phototypesetting Ltd,
Bury St Edmunds, Suffolk
Printed in Great Britain by Clays Ltd, St Ives plc

A CIP catalogue record for this book is available from the British Library

To my mother

Acknowledgements

Many thanks to: Helen Osborne, Richard Gardner, Saul Dubow, Wilf Hashemi and Nina Beachcroft for their advice and support. Clare Conville is the best agent I could hope for, while the enthusiasm, faith and incisive editing of Louise Moore have made this book possible. Finally, thank you Graham for always being there and always understanding.

Preface

It was the last thing he was expecting to happen, that hazy August morning as he walked upon the beach. He was a man of regular habits, as predictable as the tides. He would wake at dawn, swing his old legs out of bed and, whatever the weather, stride down to the sea. He loved his early-morning communes with the waves, the dog barking with joy, her tongue lolling deliriously as she scampered beside him; it made him feel alive.

A quick cuppa, then out to greet the sun, just him and the pooch, striding down the hill, all the curtains in the other houses drawn. Sometimes he passed a solitary road-sweeper or a meandering drunk, but usually he had the town to himself. He liked to feel the fresh breath of sea, rising up at him at the bottom of the hill, the place still so full of space. Later, when the charabancs and day-trippers arrived it would be different: the roads would be chock-a-block, the pebbles covered in inert pink and white bodies, the screams and boom of the sea-front rides carried back up the hill on the breeze. But at the moment the place was his.

Now that he had reached the bottom he could see the listless water, still and oily against the horizon. The sky above was pastel pale. They crossed the empty dual-carriageway, then down the steps and the dog was half mad with desire, pulling on her lead and panting, her claws clicking on the concrete. Finally he leant down and let her go and she raced off, her tail waggling furiously, her eyes rolling in anticipation as she plunged over the shingle towards the sea.

It was getting hotter. The sun had almost made it over the

sea-front's Regency façade: he could feel it warming his bald patch. He turned towards the pier, stretching out and clicking his fingers as he stepped over the remains of the night before: empty bottles, the blackened embers of a fire, a limp plastic bag. Bleached flotsam lay all along the tideline: dried cuttle-fish, twisted rope, little bits of wood. He scuffed at the stuff with his shoes, only half hearing the dog's sudden, surprised yelp. There never used to be this mess, was what he was thinking. Then he looked up and saw that the dog had still not reached the water, that she had found something.

She was going almost crazy, barking and scrabbling at the sides of a fishing-boat resting on the stones. Perhaps there was food in there, or a bucket of rotting fish. As he got closer he saw some clothes discarded by its wooden base: what looked like underwear, and something else, a pullover perhaps. It would be the aftermath of some silly girl's seduction, the knickers and bra left like flags on the Sunday-morning beach to mark the conquest. He started to trudge dutifully across the pebbles, just so he could push the dog away, but she had managed to clamber inside and her excited yelps told him that what she had found was more interesting than fish. As he reached the vessel he put his hands on the rough wooden sides and peered down.

It took him a second or so to make sense of what he saw. The dog was crouched in the base of the boat, growling almost protectively over what seemed to be a bundle of bloodied clothes. He stood there for a moment, staring down at her bristling spine, thinking it must be a joke, some art-college prank. But as he shoved her firmly aside he could no longer deny it: the thing inside the boat was human. He almost cried out when he finally realized: he could feel the grief prickling the corners of his eyes, a lumpy panic accumulating in his throat. No, this was not a joke, more like a nasty dream.

He stared and stared, his heart flopping over. The wet head was plastered with a slick of dried brown blood, the eyes closed tight. Then there was the covered body, and protruding from the other end of the woollen shroud, a pair of mottled feet. It was those feet that made him jump to attention. Then, his thoughts fusing in panic, he shouted at the dog to get away and reached for the face with his hands. And when he touched it, God, it was so cold.

Many years ago he would have had a better idea of what to do. But now all he could think was that he had to get help. He was not a religious man, but as he bounded back up the beach, towards the road and gleaming buildings, he was praying.

I was seven when we found the Mermaid's Purse, that summer I never learnt to swim. Mum spotted it first, with her gannet's roving eye. Clambering over the Cornish rocks she plucked it from the foam, carrying it gently back to me in the palm of her hand like the treasure it was. It was such a small, precious thing, no more than a few inches long, with trailing seaweedy strings attached to the shrivelled leathery pouch. She handed it to me and I ran my finger over its cool, sea-washed surface. Neptune must have left it there: that was what I thought. There must be pearls inside.

But there was more than that, much more. So when she lost her temper and tossed it back into the sea, I ran to save it from the encroaching waves. After that I gripped it tightly in my pocket, all the way home. It was my secret, that I had it still. It was something she would never know.

I

Take nothing for granted: it's one of the first rules of academic endeavour. Distrust your assumptions, dig deep beyond them to discover what lies beneath. And remember, what your informants say and what they actually do are often not the same.

Take Matt, an excellent illustration of the latter principle. A true leftie, ardent supporter of equality, teacher of politics, professor-in-waiting and author of three well-received volumes on welfarism and the state: my lover and companion of the last ten years. Matt reads the *Guardian* women's page without sarcastic comment; he frequently assures me that my career is equally important to his. And yet if one studies Matt's behaviour the gap between ideology and practice is all too clear.

His current body language is a case in point. I am standing in the middle of the room considering it, trying to remain objective as I pretend he is merely a research subject. He has retreated to the balcony. His back is hunched against me, and he has lit a fag, cupping his hand around his face and away from me as he takes deep, furious puffs. My face is hot with the realization of his anger; my chest feels tight. I had not expected it, for what he said was different, but evidently Matt is highly displeased by the recent turn of events. One has endlessly to look beyond the surface: social behaviour is not always what it seems. It's a perspective I've been teaching for years, perhaps a lesson I still have to truly learn.

What has happened is this. I have accepted a post teaching history in Brighton, something we both agreed I should do.

Matt has spent the last three days helping me move in to my new flat and now he is fed up. I should have anticipated this reaction, should have known him better. Because what Matt really, really wants is for me to stay in London and for his career, not mine, to come first.

So, right now, I have to win him back. I step over one of the many piles of books that cover the hideous brown deep-pile carpet and move in a kind of nonchalant on-purpose shuffle towards the balcony. I am hoping to catch his eye, for there to be some kind of unspoken communication that will instantly negate the angry words we've just exchanged. But he is refusing to play ball, still smoking sulkily and glowering at the road. I see that it's been building all day, this scene, and without understanding what I was doing, I gave him the perfect opening. And now, as always, I shall be the one to make peace.

'Don't be pissed off,' I say. 'I mean, it doesn't really matter about the mirror.' He shrugs. I take a deep breath. 'I'm sorry I said you were a prat.' *I just wasn't expecting you to drop it like that*, is what I want to add but, after ten years of Matt's moods, I know better. Instead, I take another step towards him, so close I could almost reach out and lay a hand on his sweaty T-shirt. 'I know this is difficult for you,' I say gently.

'We should have hired a removals company,' he mutters. 'I need to be working. This has taken all week. And then before we know it it'll be term again and I'll be fucked.'

I pause. There is fucked as in disaster, and fucked as in mildly inconvenienced. Matt is referring to the latter, for all that will happen is that he won't now send off his latest journal article for a couple more weeks.

I've made it to the narrow balcony, with its peeling wrought-iron balustrade and dried-out plant pots. Standing behind him I put my arms round his belly and try to hug him. His scent is of tobacco and exertion and our washing-powder, so deeply familiar that it's like opening the front door and smelling home. Beyond the shiny tops of the cars, I can see the sweep of the communal gardens down to the sea, and then the wide strip of blue water, flecked with distant boats. The sun is about to set into a Turneresque orange smudge over the pier. In the trees opposite, a huge, chattering flock of starlings is starting to roost. Matt stands stiff and unresponsive, still not looking at me.

'I just don't understand why you have to move everything lock, stock and barrel. It's not as if there aren't trains.'

'Well, just look at the view. Isn't that a good enough reason?'

We both know that I am not being entirely honest, but for now this seems to soothe him. He chucks the dog-end over the balcony and turns, reaching out and putting his big hands round my face. Dr Hughes, with his great burden of ambition and impatience, and all his hidden insecurities. He's put on weight over the years, his hair's gone grizzly around the temples and frown lines have appeared at his mouth, but he's still handsome, still my love. Ten years ago when I was still a student I thought I would never need anyone else. Wandering aimlessly in the library stacks or later, gazing at the pile of scholarly texts I had picked out, I would whisper his name, like a spell that could protect me from the malevolent outside world. Matt, my protector: he guided me from postgraduate muddle to well-received Ph.D., coached me into my first post, even helped me with my book. More importantly, he became my family. And now, as I look into his face, his eyes are suspiciously moist.

'I'm not leaving *you*,' I whisper. 'I just need to take this job.'

He shakes his head mournfully and then his hands are reaching up inside my top, feeling for my bra-strap, like they owned it. And the funny thing is that, even though I know

7

that all I need to do to comfort and make him happy again is to let myself be pulled on to the floor with him, I gently push him away and step to one side. 'Let's bring the last boxes up,' I say.

After he's gone off, grumbling, to catch the train, I roam around the flat. Despite Matt's protestations I've brought little with me from London, just a few suitcases of clothes, my books, some basic cooking stuff and the futon we had stored in the loft. As I keep telling him, I'm not *moving out*, I'm simply renting a place I can stay in during term. I originally had a tiny Virginia Woolf-like garret in mind, a room of my own, where I could work and think and be alone. But somehow I've ended up here, a first-storey flat in a dilapidated garden square, with a vast sitting room, french windows opening on to the rusty balcony, grand albeit crumbling plaster ceilings and original Regency fireplaces that the Stoke Newington crowd would kill for. There's an L-shaped bedroom with stained-glass windows where I've unrolled the futon, a tiny second bedroom where I've shoved my PC, a dark bathroom at the back, and a corridor kitchen, both questionably decorated with flowered tiles and scuffed cork lino but otherwise inoffensive.

Now that Matt has departed and I am alone, I can feel the rhythms of the place reasserting themselves, like water smoothing after the disturbance of a splashing stone. From the stairwell at the back there's the sound of dripping; when I turn the taps on, the pipes clank. From outside there are cars and the communal chatter of the massing evening starlings. Above me, it sounds as if someone is pacing across the floor. There's a burst of muffled music – 'A Whiter Shade Of Pale' – then silence.

The place smells musty, as if it has been shut up for too

8

long. I've thrown open the windows, but the carpets are so old and every surface covered with a thick, ancient layer of dust that it would take days of cleaning before I might impose a different array of scents. Not that I shall be doing much cleaning. Back in London it is Matt who fusses around the house with the duster and scrubs the kitchen floor. No, now that I am alone I intend to do next to nothing, for what I crave, with a passion that has astonished me with its force, is the opposite of our London domesticity: takeaway food, minimal housework and uncluttered space. I shall unpack the books, and stack them by the wall. At some stage in the future I may buy a cheap sofa; I have a wooden table for the computer, which I shall position adjacent to the french windows, and a couple of folding chairs. I am not anticipating many guests, however, for I shall be spending most of my free time in London. That was the deal. This flat is for convenience, nothing more.

It is almost dark. The birds have quietened, and in the street below the cars' lights are on. If I stand at the far end of the balcony and crane my neck, I can glimpse the neon sparkle of the pier, its disco beat still rumbling. I find my cigarettes and pull up one of the chairs so I can sit out in the cooling evening air. It's nearly the end of the summer: darkness is coming upon us more quickly, the air has a sharpness to it, a hint of damp leaves and storms to come.

My bare arms smart with sudden cold. I need a cardigan, but now that my feet are positioned so comfortably on the railings I am unable to move, transfixed by the unexpected tranquillity of the dusk. Over the trees, at the bottom of the gardens, the strip of sea is now so pale as to be almost translucent. The dark hulk of a ferry moves slowly across the horizon; if I listen carefully, I can hear the drag of waves on the pebble beach.

Matt will be almost home by now. After he gets in he'll

9

cook something comforting: his famous shepherd's pie, or pasta, perhaps. He'll eat it straight from the dish, glug down the remnants of last night's wine. Then he'll unclick his laptop and return to his article. He hates being alone so huddles under his work, as if it were a comfort blanket. He thinks I'm deserting him, but he's wrong. I still love him, still want to spend my life with him, but recently something in me has started to shift. I can hardly explain it, not to him or to myself.

It's just that right now I need to be alone.

2

I'm not naturally an assertive person. Nor am I particularly extroverted. I never rise to my feet during academic conferences to pose long-winded, self-referential questions; I dread the idea of being interviewed on Radio Four. I'll say something too lightweight, I think, or get into a muddle. Matt says I lack confidence: it's the perennial female problem.

I do, however, love to teach. Give me a lecture podium and a herd of nose-ringed, dreadlocked twenty-year-olds and my inhibitions fall crumpled around my feet, like stepping out of constricting clothes on a sweltering summer's day. Right now I'm sitting in an overcrowded seminar room on the fourth floor of Block D in my new place of employment, gazing around at the variously polite, attentive and – in a few cases – barely conscious faces of my new charges. It is the first day of term, and ten minutes past nine.

There are fifteen of them in this group; next week another hundred will face me in the lecture hall. The early-autumn sun is falling through the window and on to our tables in warm wedges of dusty light. The place smells of worn institutional linoleum and plastic chairs, chalk, and the frightful muddy tea I have just discovered inside my polystyrene cup. The room is filled with an expectant hush. The students have stopped chatting and shuffling their papers, the door has been closed, and now they are staring at me, waiting for my first words.

I take a deep breath. I can feel the familiar adrenaline rush of a new term, the mass of words forming in my head, the slight shake of my hands as I put my cup down.

'Hi,' I say, and my voice sounds more concertedly cheerful, more confident, than normal. 'Welcome to this course on historical method. My name is Cass Bainbridge and I'm going to be teaching you this term. You already have the reading lists, I think.'

They nod slowly, waiting to be impressed. My pulse is slightly quicker than normal, but I am good at hiding the tremor of nerves behind the glaze of my smile. This third-year course is what the curriculum refers to as 'interdisciplinary', and since the students on it are doing a variety of degrees, many have never met before.

'So, first let's introduce ourselves, and then we'll start thinking about some key questions and themes.'

As they tell me their names I scan the room. They seem to be a representative sample of the student population, at least for the soft-centred humanities. Currently facing me are ten young people with piercings somewhere on their faces: a bloke with such weighty studs in his ears that the lobes are elongated, like a Masai warrior's, who has just told us that his name is Andy, two middle-aged women, both ex-nurses, and a handful of pretty girls with names like Emma, Nicole or Natalie, all with the requisite baggy jeans and nose-rings. There is also a young guy sitting at the back whose name I have already forgotten and who so far has not smiled once. His books are arranged in a neat pile in front of him and, as I talk, he is leafing through the reading list and frowning, as if discovering a host of elementary mistakes.

Finally we have reached the last person in the room. I stop writing names and put down my pen. If I was more organized I would have the printed list of all these particulars, supplied to me by the university registry, but typically, I have misplaced it. By now most of the students are thumbing through their reading lists; a couple have started to yawn.

Too much clubbing and too many drugs; whatever they have been doing the night before, nine in the morning is always a terrible time for a class. I used to empathize, but increasingly I have little sympathy. They're here to learn, to be inspired and challenged, not to spend their three years getting laid, taking in nothing but cheap alcohol and narcotics.

Or perhaps I'm just getting old. To the left of the room is the low hum of chat. I stare disapprovingly at two of the Emmas who flush, and are instantly silent.

'Right,' I say, stretching out my arms and clicking my fingers as if I was the calmest and most relaxed tutor ever to pace the corridors of Higher Education. 'Objective historical fact. Is there such a thing?'

The room stirs, there is a tangible collective sigh and then silence. It's a huge question and no one wants to be the first to speak. I look around at the group, biting my lip and waiting. Please, I am thinking, don't be NSHers, not my first ever class at this place: it would be too depressing. NSH: the silly, secret code I used to scribble for Matt in essay margins when I was still finishing my Ph.D.; Matt already had his London post by then, and I used to help him with his marking. 'No Sodding Hopers'. The students who make the academic heart sink: the ones who read nothing and have even less to say, who write dreary, dreadful essays that reduce every inspirational lecture or stellar monograph to a series of limp statements, their original meaning and intention drained from them like blood from a corpse. They attend their classes in a fog of incomprehension and laziness, leave with undeserved 2:2s and make me want to weep. And somehow, they always seem to be bunched in the same seminar group, the way that sleepy woodlice huddle under a single stone.

I can bear it no longer. This stultifying and increasingly fraught silence is not the way to start the term. I am just about to say something encouraging, to lead them kindly towards my point, like shy Shetland ponies towards the junior jumps at a gymkhana, when there is a cough and the guy at the back of the room says quietly: 'Most people believe there is, but obviously every narrative about the past is going to be subjective to a degree. I mean, once you've got beyond the verifiable hard facts, the stories that bind them together are going to depend on who's telling them.'

It's a clever answer, spoken with the disdainful tone of someone who believes the question to be clunkingly simple. I glance down at my list and recall that the young man's name is Alec. He's a handsome lad, tall and slim with short dark hair and brown eyes hidden behind his frameless specs, but something about him is different from the other students. Perhaps it's his apparent self-possession and air of slight arrogance: he has the impatient, slightly irritated look of an older man who finds himself stuck in a room of giggling teenagers. Now he's staring down at the table, still frowning, his shoulders stiff. I have not yet managed to make eye-contact with him.

'Thanks, Alec. That's useful. Can you say more about these "hard facts"?' I clear my throat and he stares at me impassively, obviously not wishing to bother with such a boring question.

'Can anyone else answer?'

'Well, there's carbon dating, which is a scientific fact,' somebody ventures from the back. 'And there are records, stuff that's been written down, so you can check things against that. Like the Doomsday Book, or records of births and deaths . . .'

I'm nodding enthusiastically. 'That's right, and some of this course is going to be concerned with those very sources. But do these make "history" –' I wiggle inverted commas in the air with my forefingers to signal that what I am referring

14

to is a construct '– any more objective? Is what we're concerned with just a matter of finding out what really happened?'

'People are always going to argue about what really happened, depending on their agenda.'

I nod, signalling at the dreadlocked girl who offered this comment to continue. Now that the discussion is taking hold I can sense the room relax. Perhaps they are not going to be NSHers, after all.

'It's all, like, relative. That's the point. There are no facts, just constructs.'

This is from Andy, who is leaning back in his chair with his arms folded and smiling, as if he were a genius. Like many students who do not wish to think too hard he seems to have latched on to post-modernism as the clever answer to everything.

'So the Holocaust,' I say, smiling at him sweetly, 'was that just a construct?'

He blanches. There is a pause, and then one of the young women sitting on my right says, 'Of course it wasn't. Millions of people died in the Holocaust and there's hard documentary evidence of it. Only Nazis and lunatics would dispute that. I mean, isn't that the point of history? To find out what actually happened so that people can't, like, screw around with the facts?'

As she finishes speaking, she smiles, pushing her frizzy blonde hair out of her eyes and blinking humorously. Her accent is hard to ascertain: estuary English, but with a dash of something northern. She is dressed like the other young women in the room: jeans, trainers, the obligatory nose-stud and a baggy skateboarder's sweatshirt, but I get the impression she is not part of the Emma-Nicole-Natalie crew. As I regard her, she folds her arms and grins impishly. On her pad I can see that she has written the title of the course, followed by my name, and then, neatly underlined, the question 'Is history objective?'. Like many girls of her generation her handwriting is small and rounded: conventional, unsurprising.

'True,' I say. 'But does that mean that good history is just a matter of detective work, or is there more of an interpretive element to it? Alec, did you want to say something?'

He is leaning back in his chair, holding his pen aloft as he waits to speak. He seems bored.

'The post-modern perspective clearly has ridiculous implications. But that doesn't mean we shouldn't pay close attention to who is saying what and why. It's fairly obvious just looking through the most basic historical texts that there can be many different versions of the same history.' He says this in the languid tones of someone who considers themselves too clever for such a basic discussion but in spite of his imperious manner the other students are glancing appreciatively towards him.

'Thanks, Alec,' I say smiling blandly. 'That's great.'

He sits back again, his eyes flicking towards the window.

'I don't get that, to be honest. I mean, going back to the Holocaust, people died: fact. How can there be different versions of that?'

This is from the girl with the frizzy hair again, her cheeks slightly flushed. I glance down my list and see from my notes that she told the group her name was Beth Wilson, that her major is gender studies and that the reason she is taking this course is so that she can 'explore her own past'. I beam at her reassuringly. 'Say more.'

'I mean, why do you want to argue about the fact that all those people were gassed?'

She stops, giving a self-conscious little laugh. She is not particularly pretty, but the freshness of her face, her large eyes and soft skin give her the appeal of a fluffy young animal.

I squint back at her, wondering if it was a good idea to introduce such an emotive topic so early in the course.

Alec is shaking his head, jiggling his foot so vigorously that it hits the rucksack of the guy next to him. 'That's completely missing the point.'

The vehemence with which he says this makes the girl blink. She looks at me beseechingly so I give her a little wink, as if to say: 'Don't worry. You're doing fine.'

'Look, this is a good start,' I announce. 'The main point is that we need to be reflective about the different conditions under which historical accounts are constructed. That's why as well as being quite practical, in that you're going to consider different historical methods and even conduct your own individual historiography, I want you to be continually questioning how history is made, and who makes it.'

With the exception of Alec, who has pushed aside his notepad, the students scribble furiously in their pads. It is always pleasant to be taken so seriously. I stretch out my legs, wiggle my toes in my shoes. The term has started.

An hour later my new students are packing away their notepads and spilling out on to the corridor. I gather up my things, keen to be back in my tiny new office with its cartons of unpacked books and unread memos. I am hungry, my stomach rumbling for sandwiches and cake, my spirit longing for silence.

'Dr Bainbridge?'

I turn to find that Holocaust Girl is standing behind me. She has pulled a stripy woolly hat over her yellow hair, making her look like Worzel Gummidge's pretty younger sister, and is clutching her books to her bosom.

'Hello, there.'

She pauses, then says breathlessly, 'I just wanted to tell you how much I enjoyed the class.'

'Great!' I am not really concentrating, thinking only of food and emails, wanting to deal with her quickly then get away.

'I thought it was really, really clever of you to make that Andy bloke confront the political implications of what he said. I mean, what type of person would want to deny genocide?'

I raise my eyebrows. 'I don't know if he was doing that exactly.'

'It's so refreshing to go to a seminar where people actually seem to care about things. Now I feel all inspired.'

'Do you?' I smile at her, the compliment warming me like a glug of mulled wine. Hoicking my bag on to my shoulder I walk through the door.

'I'd really love to know more about your research,' she says, trotting alongside me. 'I mean, all it says in the prospectus is that you're an expert on post-war family history.'

'It's on exactly those issues we were talking about in the class, about whose versions of history get heard and whose don't. My Ph.D. was based around the oral histories of women growing up in the East End during the war and their attitudes to family life. The book's on the reading list.'

'God, it sounds *fascinating*.' She pauses, glancing through an open window at the campus below. Although it is already October, the sunshine is still warm; outside Block D, students are sprawled on the grass as if it were high summer. 'Do you think I'd be allowed to do something like that for my course project? I mean, I was thinking about looking at my own family history. Is that the kind of thing you want us to do?'

'It's exactly the kind of thing you could do. But you need

to think about some kind of angle, not just the collection of genealogical details.'

Her face goes blank, as if she is momentarily stumped. We have reached the staircase leading to the second floor and I stop, signalling that I am not expecting her to follow me to my room. She seems a lovely girl, but I want my lunch.

'I was thinking,' she says suddenly. 'We could set up a discussion group, or something. I mean, besides the class. If you have time . . .'

I squint at her through the late-autumn sun. If this is what all the students are like here, I am going to have to adjust my expectations. Back in London only the keenest did any reading, let alone lobby to set up extra-curricular groups. And despite my deep desire for refreshment and a break, her enthusiasm is infectious, for now I am nodding and smiling back at her. 'What a brilliant idea. I've got an office hour tomorrow at eleven. Why don't you come and see me then? We can discuss it.'

She grins back at me, revealing a row of stained front teeth. Perhaps she's a heavy smoker, although with her youthful clothes and plump, eager face it seems unlikely. 'Wicked.'

Pulling her bag over her shoulder, she stands aside as I turn towards the staircase. I am just about to put my foot on the first step when I remember something. 'What was your name again?'

'Beth.' She taps her foot, nodding at me. She has that American habit of making a statement sound like a question. 'Beth Wilson?'

Dear Mum
I can call you that, can't I?

I've been thinking about you a lot lately, don't ask me why. So this is my decision: I'm going to write it all down in these letters to you. You'll probably never read them, I know. It's my own private therapy.

What things should I tell you about me? I'm a student — in my third year now. Perhaps I look like you, perhaps not. Whatever, I don't expect you'd know me if we passed on the street. I'm a hard worker, always have been. I wouldn't say I had a heap of friends. I don't like partying, don't do drugs or clubs or suchlike. A lot of people say I'm old for my age, but that's not how I feel. What I like is to sit in the library, lose myself in the words and ideas. Sometimes I'm there all day and when I re-emerge the daylight seems harsh, the other people scurrying across the campus alien.

Oh, and I like the sea as well. It makes me feel like it's OK to be alone.

How about you? What do you like to do?

3

Back at my office a sheaf of notes is stuck to my door: apologies for missing the class, pleas for appointments, a memo concerning a meeting this afternoon, which I had forgotten about. I have only been here for a few days, and am already submerged under an avalanche of administration, the emails popping up like burger orders at McDonald's each time my attention is diverted from the screen. Outside my door the place is heaving, the corridors filled with first-years swarming around the noticeboards, the air stiff with nervous excitement. Poor buggers, the first week is harder for them than for me, with their pristine notepads and desperate attempts to find friends, and almost palpable teenage fear. I can hear the strained pitch of their voices outside my door as they pass: the overly loud swearing and forced congeniality of freshers trying to make an impression.

My induction to the university has been more genteel. So far I have had polite mugs of coffee in the canteen downstairs with three of my colleagues, and lunch with our genial, ageing professor, who kept calling me Kerry and belching softly as we munched our stale sandwiches. The rest of the history faculty I have yet to meet: they are either off doing research or buried in lectures, tutorials and bureaucratic chores. I keep telling myself to relax, but I have had new-girl nerves all week, my stomach jumping queasily at the merest provocation, my head throbbing by the end of each day. I had a perfectly acceptable teaching post in London. I had a flat, and a long-term partner and a much-tended bonsai tree, which no doubt he will neglect to water in protest at my absence. I was contented, settled; there was no reason for all this disruption. And yet it was what I wanted.

I stare at my screen, scrolling past all the boring-looking messages until I reach one titled 'Long time no hear'. It's from Sarah, my oldest friend.

Just a quickie to say hi. Haven't seen you for absolutely yonks, so wondering what you're up to . . . Saw Matt the other day in Sainsburys. He looked a bit morose, but I didn't have time to go and say hello, mainly cos Poppy was having a massive tantrum, the little s*d. Traumas aside, life here remains great. Pops is talking so much now, even reciting the alphabet. Yesterday she put her fat little arms around my neck and told me that she loved me. And she's not even two! You really don't know what you're missing, Cass. You'll have to tear Matt away from his books and get a sperm donation ASAP. Anyway, can't chat – she's just waking up from her nap. Lots of love – we'll talk soon, OK?

My hand hovers over 'reply', but I cannot think of a suitably light-hearted message. The trouble is, there is so much to say and none of it feels emailable. I run through the possibilities, frowning at how much I suddenly miss her.

Dear S.
Lots of news. Have moved out of happy conjugal home to spooky seaside flat for life of solitude. Don't ask why!!!! Love and kisses, C

Or:

Sperm donations currently unviable due to complete change of direction in personal life. Ring for further information (evenings only).

What I need to do is talk to her in person, but these days it's increasingly difficult to exchange more than a few meaningless platitudes: *I'm fine, he's fine, it's fine.* It's time, that's the problem. Sarah likes to call in the middle of the day when Poppy is napping, but that's when I'm at work. And when I call her in the evenings I invariably get the answerphone. The last time I got her in person we chatted for about a minute before Poppy grabbed the receiver and cut me off. In the intervening months there has been a trail of emails and answerphone messages, but no direct communication. And now I have moved down here, and she doesn't even know.

I carry on scrolling, past a pile of deadly-looking messages marked 'Curriculum restructuring', then suddenly see one with no title but the sender: M.Hughes@uni.ac.uk, and my heart lifts a little. I double click the mouse, hoping for an affectionate reprieve.

So how come you get the car? That's what I thought as I sat in frigging East Croydon last night for over an hour. Some half-wit throws themselves at a train a mile up the line, and it means I don't get home until after midnight. So next time, you come to me, OK?

Hope you're enjoying your 'independence'. Is that what this is all about? Matt

So he's still upset. I swallow, reread the message then hit 'reply'. No doubt he did not intend it to sound so aggressive, but the message has made me feel as if someone has punched me only half jokingly in the stomach.

Hon [*I write*]. Sorry you had a nightmare journey home. Of course I'll come up to London on Friday. I'll call later. Love you, C

I press 'send', imagining my words flinging themselves towards him through the ether. He'll read them quickly, his mind still immersed in his article, the delicately constructed argument, the point he has been working towards and which he is saving for his final, concluding section. Then he'll delete me without replying, letting me stew in my own juice, all those silly games he likes to play.

There is so much to do. For a start, I should be opening, reading and acting upon the pile of memos that is already spilling over my office floor. And then there are the files from the postgraduate admissions office, the painstakingly filled-out forms and statements of proposed research that I should be reading and commenting upon, but which I shall leave to fester at the bottom of the pile until I have had at least three emails and one urgent phone call from said office. There are about twenty first-year personal tutees to meet and greet, and an induction meeting of MA students to attend in ten minutes. And finally there is the lecture course I should have prepared over the summer but which, until now, I have left unconsidered and unwritten and which starts next week.

But I am not going to panic. No. What I am going to do is put my feet up and eat my lunch.

Yet just as I start to peel the clingfilm from my chicken-tikka roll, there is a bang at the door and before I have had time to shout, 'Yes!', a thirty-something man walks into my room as if he owns it.

He is quite handsome, in a ruffled academic way, with heavy-rimmed Harry Hill specs, jeans and a zipped-up black cardie. His blond goatee, sandy eyebrows and macho swagger make him look like a twenty-first century Viking. He seems to be laughing, although whether this is at the spectacle of me with my sad little lunch surrounded by the debris of academic life in my stuffy boxy room or some previous joke is unclear.

'Well, hello there, Dr Bainbridge. Welcome to the first day of term!' He says this loudly, standing with his legs apart in the middle of the worn acrylic carpet, chuckling. His sandy hair is cut brutally short, possibly in an attempt to disguise impending baldness, and he has a large nose and the kind of eyes that disappear when he smiles. He is regarding me with the supreme confidence of the alpha male in his place of work. I already know who he is. His name is Julian Leigh and his office is next to mine.

'Hi,' I say, and put down my roll. It's good to see such a cheerful, encouraging face.

'Had a productive start?' He is glancing at the paper flotsam on the floor, his lips twitching.

'Yeah. Kind of.'

'Met any punters yet?'

'Yeah.' I'm nodding at him and, even though I'm still not sure what the joke is, have started to laugh.

'Did they charm you with their intellect?'

'Erm . . .'

'Who've you got?'

I stare at him, trying to remember all the names. 'The guy with Masai ears . . . Andy Dubow?'

He groans and claps his hand to his forehead. 'Thick as two short planks but thinks he knows it all. Heading for a third.'

'Uh-huh. That was the general impression. Um, a couple of older women, Mary and Ellen, or something? . . . A girl called Beth?'

He pulls a face and shakes his head. 'What about Alec Watkins? Thin guy with glasses? He'll keep you on your toes.'

I remember the way the boy frowned at my reading list, the irritated jiggle of his foot. 'Is he a problem?'

Julian pulls a face. 'Only if you make him one. Got a straight first in every paper he took last year.'

'I thought he seemed good.'

'Mmm.'

There is a brief pause and I feel unaccountably embarrassed. Julian is still looking at me, as if waiting for something more.

'So,' he says. 'How's the seaside? Where did you say you were living?'

'Queen's Square.'

'Charming sea views.'

He seems to be teasing me, but I am momentarily stumped for a witty retort. 'Yes, it's nice.'

'You're living there . . . alone?'

He has stopped chuckling and, for the briefest of moments, a look almost of anxiety passes across his face. Jesus, *he's chatting me up*. I swallow, glancing down at my unringed hands. 'Well, kind of,' I say, and ridiculously, I feel my cheeks turn schoolgirl pink. It does not bear analysing, but I do not want to tell him about Matt.

'Kind of?'

'I share a place with a friend in London.'

To hide my crimson face, I look down, smoothing my skirt unnecessarily with my hands.

'Your flatmate?'

This is the point where I should be correcting him, telling him that my friend is not exactly a flatmate, more like a long-term partner, but for some reason all I can do is move my head up and down, like a nodding dog on a car dashboard.

'So, you're enjoying the university?' he says, and unaccountably laughs, as if he was asking if I enjoyed some hilarious hobby, like extreme ironing. The way he keeps glancing at my tits is making me feel more and more uncomfortable. 'Not worried about being jumped?'

My face twitches. What is the man *talking* about? Is this another joke? 'Jumped in what respect?' I say, grimacing.

'Ooh, you know, all those dark campus corners. Not good places to walk around alone at night.'

'Aren't they?'

He gives his lips a salacious lick. 'We had a student attacked outside Arts B last term.'

'Really?'

'And another girl was raped in the woods by the car-park over the summer.'

He says this with what sounds like lascivious glee. By now my face has gone into a spasm of twitching, like someone with a mild neurological disorder. Wishing only to change the subject, I blurt, 'How about you, do you live alone?'

'*Tout seul.* Got a divorce last year and moved down here.'

And he is smirking at me again, clearly reading my questioning of his living arrangements as a sign of romantic interest. I ought to inform him quickly about Matt, but cannot think of how to backstroke the conversation without plunging into even deeper currents of miscommunication. Anyway, now it is too late for he is glancing at his watch and moving towards the door. 'Jesus!' he mutters. 'I'll catch you later, Cass. Maybe we'll go for a walk – or we could meet up and have a drink.'

I swallow hard. 'I don't—' But before I have had time to finish he is waving and slamming the door loudly behind him.

Some time later I stand in the women's toilet and gaze into the mirror. An overweight, almost middle-aged woman stares back. I must have been mistaken about the tone of Julian's questions, I tell myself, for besides Matt nobody has fancied me for years. And even if Julian *was* flirting, is this something I wish to encourage? I was enjoying our conversation, almost starting to flirt back, but then, bizarrely, he was joking on about girls being attacked. No, I tell myself. His is an attractiveness that slides too quickly into something less palatable, like a fruit that looks juicy and delicious at first glance but turns out to be slightly off.

I no longer much enjoy looking into mirrors, I realize despondently. I have the same round face, the same green eyes and thick black hair, the same snubby Celtic nose and plump lips as always, but these days there's a new, barely noticeable sag around my jowls, and I keep having to pluck white hairs from my temples, my new geriatric tiara. I'm fatter too, even more so than I was as a teenager, when I would starve myself to the point of fainting just so I could fit into a Miss Selfridge size sixteen. Nowadays I have taken to wearing loose, hippie-dippy dresses over elasticated trousers and clogs rather than the tailored trews and stacky boots I used to favour. There is no denying it: I am, inescapably, *a woman approaching her late thirties.* Many of the women I interviewed in the East End were grandmothers by my age.

I push my hair out of my eyes and put on some lipstick, my feminist hackles rising at the dreary direction of my thoughts. To hell with it, I refuse to get depressed. So I discovered a grey pube yesterday evening, but who gives a toss? Would a man care? I'm not that bad. I still have nicely rounded, strong legs, which remain browned from the summer and, unlike Sarah, my tits are perkily buoyant. 'Love handles', that's how Matt refers to my flabby bits: 'Come here, Sexy, let me squeeze those curves.' And, of course, fat does not negate good looks. I'm what has been described as handsome.

Perhaps a bit of lipstick was all I needed, I think, smiling back at myself determinedly. This is how I present myself to the world: a cheerful, comforting, positive woman, wholly at one with herself. I bite my lips, smudge in the lipstick and, raising my eyebrows at myself, go back to work.

4

It is late afternoon by the time I leave the university. I climb into the old Beetle Matt keeps insisting we trade in for something more grown-up, and start the drive home. As the day has progressed the sunshine has dimmed and the sky smudged and darkened, the descent into autumn increasingly irreversible. Now a dark grey ridge of cloud hangs forebodingly over the horizon and, as I put my key into the ignition, a splash of rain lands on the dusty windscreen. I edge the car out of the campus towards the dual-carriageway that leads into the centre of town. From somewhere not far off I hear a roll of thunder. The sea will be green-grey now, all nervous and frothy, stirred up by the impending storm.

I am numb with exhaustion, drained by the effort of being nice to strangers all day. I do not want to see anyone or talk to anyone or do anything. I am driving back to my empty flat, where I will sit very still and very quietly, all by myself. I put the car into third, step down on the accelerator and, just as I am about to pull into the rush-hour traffic, there is a bang on the side of the car, and I am swerving to one side, screaming, 'Shit!' and stamping my foot so hard on the brake that the Beetle hops forward, then jerks still, like an injured rabbit.

I have hit something. Behind me, the queuing cars have come to a standsill, and a middle-aged woman in a black raincoat is running along the pavement and stooping down, peering under my car. I pull open the door and stumble out. I can feel the wet splatter of rain on my forehead, smell the heady chemical reek of spilt petrol. My heart is pumping so violently I can hardly breathe.

It is a cyclist. I can see the tangled metal wheels of the bike protruding from under the boot, and there, lying slumped on the kerb – oh, Christ – is a body. It's a girl: I can see her hair, flopped over her face, and the scuffed denim of her jeans. For a few seconds everything slows down: I am stepping over the kerb and leaning down and saying, in a voice that does not sound quite like mine, 'Are you all right?' In the road other vehicles are slowly slooshing around my stationary car, the occupants gawping at the scene. At the sight of their prurient faces, I think I might be sick.

'God, I'm so sorry,' I am saying. 'I had no idea you were there.'

And then, miraculously, the girl is sitting up, looking around, pulling herself to her feet and I see that the person I have knocked over is Beth Wilson, the student from my class.

'*Hi*,' she says breathlessly, and as I put out my hand to help her up she grins at me with something almost like relief. Suddenly she is standing on the pavement, brushing mud from her jeans and looking at me almost expectantly. I keep shaking my head, repeating, 'I didn't even know you were there . . .' as if this somehow exonerates me.

Next to me, the woman has her arm round Beth's shoulders. A small crowd is dawdling on the pavement, too English to stop and stare blatantly, but curious none the less. The rain is more soaking now, the fine spray falling like a veil. Thunder rumbles around us.

'Shall I call for an ambulance?' the woman says, and I see that she has pulled her mobile hopefully from her briefcase and is fiddling with it, trying to get a signal.

Beth smiles at me reassuringly. 'No. No, it's OK. I'm fine. The car didn't even touch me.'

'But what happened?'

'I dunno. I guess I must have just slipped. Like, in the rain?'

Relief trickles through me. I take a deep, stabilizing breath, trying to remember the yoga classes I was rarely organized enough to attend. 'You mean it wasn't my fault?'

'No, it was me, my wheel hit the kerb.' She laughs.

'What about your bike?' This is from the woman, who is now peeking dubiously under my car at the tangled spokes. I sense her eagerness for drama, her undefined antagonism towards me, and wish she would move away.

'Oh, *that*.' Bending down, Beth yanks it out from under the Beetle. Considering the bash she must have just had on the hard Tarmac road, the shock as she felt herself toppling under my car, she seems remarkably calm. We regard the remnants of her bike in silence. The front wheel is badly bent, the saddle ripped. Eventually she leans it against a lamp-post. 'I'll have to wheel it home, I s'pose,' she says.

'No, you mustn't. You're not walking home.' I put my hand on her shoulder. 'I'll drive you. It's the very least I can do.'

'Yeah?'

'Yes, absolutely. I insist.'

She wipes her wet, oily hands on her jeans. 'Cool.'

Almost immediately she is at the passenger door, pulling it open eagerly and climbing inside. The car is so crammed with old newspapers and disgustingly aged takeaway cartons and empty Coke cans that I have to clear a space on the front seat for her, chucking the debris over the ripped head-rests into the back. There are still three boxes of books there, stuff I have yet to unpack. She sits perched on the front seat, her feet touching a bag filled with CDs, her bottom sharing space with a pair of velvet curtains I inherited from my grandmother and, for some reason, lug from place to place, although I never hang them.

'Sorry about all this crap.'

'No, really, it's fine.' She grins, clearly delighted to be

getting a lift. We sit motionless in the steamy interior of the car, our faces dripping, our hair laced with droplets of rain.

'What about your bike?'

She snorts. 'No one's going to want it now, are they?'

Another murmur of thunder, as yet no lightning.

'So, where to?'

'I don't mind.'

'Where do you live?'

'Just drop me at the sea-front,' she says breezily. 'It's near there. I'll walk it.'

As she says this she puts her hand up to her nose, wiping at it absent-mindedly. It is bleeding very slightly, I notice, with a jolt, and now there is a smear of brown blood on her cheek. I reach into my pocket and pass her a tissue. 'Your nose is bleeding.'

'Oh, right.' She dabs at it, hardly seeming to notice.

She seems tense: clutching her rucksack so tightly that the white bones of her knuckles are showing through the skin, and not looking at me. Possibly she is in delayed shock from the accident. I pause, then say, 'Tell you what, how about I take you for a coffee or something? Just to check that you really are OK.'

This seems to do the trick, for her face lights up. She is very young, probably only nineteen or twenty. 'Wicked.'

I switch on the ignition, push the car into gear, and we pull away. We drive for a while in silence, up over the Downs, in a long, splashing line of rush-hour traffic. It will be dark soon and the street-lights have already been turned on. I am thinking that we will go down to the sea-front and find the sort of café where they serve strong tea and slices of Mother's Pride and don't mind how long you stay. I have a heap of work to do, but the girl has just been knocked under my car: it will have to wait.

She is clearly enjoying herself, lolling back in the Beetle's saggy upholstery and giggling as I recount my famous story about the day I got half-way through a lecture on the history of British sexuality before I realized that my audience consisted of first-year engineering students hoping to attend a talk on thermodynamics. I keep glancing at her, to check that she's not about to collapse or have some kind of post-traumatic fit, but her eyes are bright, her cheeks pink.

'So, are you enjoying university?' I ask. It's one of my standard opening gambits. That, and 'How do you think the course is going?'

'It's great. I mean, it's just such a change for me.'

'Because?'

'Well, you know. I just love studying, all the books and sitting in the library and that.'

I stare into the passing headlights until they blur. I am not wholly concentrating on what she is saying.

'And Brighton's meant to be a great place for night-life,' I say vaguely. 'There are lots of clubs and so on.' I don't know why I add this since I have not been to a club for years. Perhaps I want her to see that I'm *in touch* with the world of bright young things.

'Yeah, I *love* all that. Clubbing and stuff.'

We have reached the other side of the hills and are rolling through the rain towards the sea. Beneath me I can see the neat rows of council housing that border the city, and out on the water, the distant, bobbing lights of a fishing-boat.

'I was thinking about what you said in the seminar, about how we make our own stories up? That you can bend the facts how you want them?' Beth suddenly says. 'I mean, is that really what you think?'

I frown, trying to focus my thoughts. 'Well, yes, to an extent. Clearly, two people can have different versions of the same event, and that's something historians have to remember.'

'But what about when they have the *same* version? When they both feel the same thing at the same time? I mean, like, what about when people fall in love?'

I glance at her, only just able to stop myself snickering. She has totally missed the point. Or perhaps she is just more suggestible and imaginative than most, like a child who spots faces in the sky when everyone else sees clouds. 'I don't think that's really relevant.'

'Why not?' She has folded her arms and is smirking at me challengingly.

'Well, for a start, we're talking about academic endeavour, not emotions.'

'And the two things aren't connected? Doesn't emotion change everything?'

'I guess it does, but—'

'So I'm right!' She laughs, punching the air in triumph. I would say more, but suddenly hear the comic jangle of my mobile. Matt has set its dial tone to 'Rudolf The Red-nosed Reindeer', the rotter, and despite my earnest perusal of the blasted thing's instructions I cannot change it. As I pull it from my bag, I see that it is him calling. 'Hi, darling.'

'Hello, my buxom beauty.' His voice is upbeat and cheerful, the sulk forgotten. I had not realized how much his silence hurt, but now relief powers through me, like unzipping a pair of overly tight trousers after a long and arduous day.

'What's new?' I say airily. With Matt, it's always better not to refer to previous disagreements, lest the peace is ruptured again.

'Just wanted to hear your voice.'

'I'm in the car, giving someone a lift.'

'Oh, yeah? I'd like to give *you* a lift.'

'Sounds interesting.'

Out of the corner of my eye Beth is staring dreamily through the steamy window.

'I'd better not chat now, though,' I say. 'I'll call you later, yeah?'

'OK. *Ciao.*'

Then, typically, he turns off his phone before I can slip in the last word. It does not matter. I am so pleased that his anger has passed that, as I press my foot down on the accelerator, I hum a little tune.

We have reached Marine Parade. It's more windy down here than it is in the hills where the campus nestles, and the car rocks slightly, buffeted by the gusts. I park and, bracing ourselves, we run through the slanting rain towards a greasy spoon to the east of the pier. I don't mind the sea when it is stirred up in the storms like this, the ice-cream boards flapping, the sea-gulls riding the wind like surfer boys. Abandoned by the tourists and foreign-language students and vanloads of Sikhs up from Southall, it is something else entirely. Churned up and disturbed by deep, secret currents, it's unconnected with memory and regret.

When we reach the café I yank open the door, gasping with relief, and we are instantly engulfed by the warm blast of cheap cooking oil and stale fags. The place is empty. There are ten or so Formica tables with wooden chairs and tin ashtrays and, above the counter, a blackboard advertising 'full breakfast' for £2.50 and tea for 75p. They have bits of wrapped-up cake and stale-looking scones, sausages and chips for three pounds and an array of dog-eared sandwiches.

A saggy man in an apron is leaning over the counter, smoking. His belly is so fat that it is virtually resting on the stained surface, his grey hair greasy. He eyes us with dull resignation: perhaps he was hoping he could shut up shop and go home. I order two teas, a snack-pack of digestives for Beth and a KitKat for me. I will stay for fifteen minutes, I think. Then I really *must* go back to the flat and write

35

the first lecture. Gripping my tin tray, I walk slowly towards the table by the front window where Beth is already sitting. That morning it would have given a direct view to the beach and sea, but now all we can see is rain splattering the dark glass.

I grapple with my plastic chair, which has got stuck under the table. Beth has placed her chin in her hands and is looking expectantly at me. 'Need a hand?'

'No.' I give the chair a final tug and it shoots out, jolting the table and spilling my tea in a steaming puddle over the Formica. 'Sod it!' I laugh at her apologetically. 'I don't know why I'm always so clumsy.'

'You don't *look* clumsy.'

'No?'

'No way. You look really *together*.'

I pull a face. The truth is that while other people seem in admirable control over the material objects that tie them to the world such things have been constantly slithering from my grip all my life. Childhood treasures smashed, vital keys misplaced, best dresses torn. 'Little Miss Muddlefoot,' my mother used to call me. 'She's always in a mess.'

'I mean, isn't that what doing history is all about?' Beth continues. 'Being careful with the facts?'

I look up at her, surprised at the insight. 'Yes, I guess it partly is.'

'So perhaps that's why you're doing it professionally.'

I would like to say more, but am increasingly bothered by the sense that something is missing. Something very important. I reach down beside my feet and discover that my battered leather rucksack is not there.

'My bag!'

This is typical Cass behaviour: I am always putting things down and wandering away in a haze. I can clearly recall picking up the bag after I had parked, so perhaps I left it by the side of the road when I locked the car. I start to castigate myself for my obvious stupidity, but am distracted by Beth's happy smile.

'It's OK.' She leans down and produces it, like a rabbit from a hat. 'I picked it up for you. You left it on the bonnet of your car.'

'Thanks! Now you see what I mean?'

She shrugs good humouredly.

Suddenly we both speak at the same time.

'I—'

'So, do you—'

She reddens and gives her small, choking laugh. 'Sorry!'

'Do you enjoy gender studies?' I continue.

'Oh, God, yes. It's like, great.' She says this so definitively that I cannot think of anything else to ask.

'Jolly good.'

She blows on her tea, then slurps it noisily, wiping hair self-consciously from her eyes and glancing up at me. I reach into my bag for my cigarettes. I have started to plan the lecture now, my mind wandering from Beth to the list of questions I shall open with, the case study I shall use to illustrate my main point.

'I was meant to go to Harvard,' she goes on.

I can't find the buggers. I am still not entirely concentrating, groping around in my bag, wondering if I've left them in my office.

'I passed the interview and everything. And I had a place at Cambridge, too. I was going to study law. I was in the top ten per cent of A level results in the country.'

I have given up the quest for fags and am focusing on her properly. She is leaning across the table and gazing at me, her arms folded. I nod at her encouragingly, having slipped into my attentive-teacher mode. It is quite sweet but completely transparent, this naïve attempt to impress.

'What a high flier!' I say, trying not to sound too patronizing.

But if she registers the irony in my voice she does not show it. 'The thing was, when it came down to it, I couldn't stomach it. I mean, all that mega-success that the parents want out of you. So I decided to come here instead. Against my mum and dad's wishes, I might say.'

'Good for you, to follow your heart.'

I snap off a finger of KitKat, peel away the silver paper. Perhaps I am giving the wrong impression of my place of employment. 'Of course, we wouldn't like our students to think of this as a soft option, either,' I start. 'I mean, we may not be in quite the same league as Harvard—'

But Beth interrupts me: 'Was that the same for you? You know, parental pressure pushing you into academia?'

'Christ, no. Rather, the reverse.' I pop the KitKat into my mouth and take a gulp of tea, sucking the liquid through the chocolate biscuit. It's a disgusting habit, which Matt loathes, but deprived of my fags I cannot help myself.

Beth is still gazing at me wonderingly. She has not touched the digestives. 'How do you mean?'

'You don't want to know.' I chuckle and take a final swig of the tea. This is not a line of enquiry I wish her to pursue.

'So, you followed your heart, too,' she says, 'and did the thing you wanted to do. That's so cool.'

I glance at her, then stand up.

'I ought to get home,' I say, rubbing my hands.

Beth pushes away her chair and rises too, grinning eagerly. 'I'm going down to the beach to look at the waves,' she says. 'I was swimming in it this morning. You'd never believe it from looking at it now, would you?'

I cannot prevent my involuntary shudder. 'Not for me, I don't think.'

'It's still quite warm.'

'It's not the cold.'

The question I see forming on her face does not make it to her lips. She picks up my bag and hands it to me, presumably in case I forget it again, then leads the way to the door.

It has stopped raining. We part outside the caff and Beth hurries off towards the shingle, the nylon fabric of her kagool flapping, like a bird trying to take off, as she leans into the wind. As she disappears into the misty dark I force my thoughts back to my lecture. Perhaps I should try to find my slides of Bethnal Green in the Blitz and open with those, or broadcast a snippet from one my interviews. Whatever, tonight my work cannot be avoided.

Yet now that I have located my car, climbed inside and closed the door, I am unable to move. In less than an hour my good mood has dissipated, and now I feel flat and dull, like a promising day that has unexpectedly clouded over. All it would take is for me to switch on the ignition and drive away, but I am frozen, my hands folded uselessly round the key, my legs resolutely crossed. Outside the windscreen, just a few hundred yards or so, the waves are crashing on to the pebbles. I can hear the drag and roll of the stones, the suck of the frothing water. I should not have come down here, should have insisted on dropping Beth wherever it is that she lives, then gone straight to my empty flat and my laptop. And now I am stuck, shivering, in the driving seat of my chilly Beetle, the helpless victim of my own malaise.

Beth may think me 'cool', but I'm a fake. It is true that I have a doctorate and have published a well-received monograph on the oral history of rationing and family structure in the East End, 1949–50; I give lectures, hold classes, even get invited to participate in austere, scholarly conferences. But ever since I finished my Ph.D. I have had the inescapable sense that I know nothing and that one day the depth of my

39

ignorance and general incomprehension of the world will be discovered.

'An expert on families, what a joke.' I say this aloud, my voice surprisingly vehement. The very cool Dr Bainbridge: that same woman whose own family has all but disintegrated, whose brother lives on the other side of the world, whose father is dead and who has not spoken to her mother for years, despite the begging birthday cards she receives from her. 'Please get in touch,' she writes, in her small, spiky hand. 'It would mean so much.' And before I can stop myself I picture her: not now, but as she was when I was small, with her curly black hair and the polka-dot dress she wore to parties. Back then I thought her as beautiful as the angels. I would snuggle in her lap, trace my finger across her soft, powdered cheeks towards her glossy pink lips. I never wanted her to go out, and would try to hang on to her and stop her moving, but always, without fail, she would lift me up and deposit me firmly back on the floor. '*Clinginess*,' she called it; a trait she hated.

And suddenly I remember the sensation of water going over my head, the sharp pain in my sinuses, my panic at the murky, suffocating depths. Then I would bob up again, arms flailing, half screeching for help, half gulping at the air, and she would be there, her feet placed firmly on the sandy bed, laughing at me. 'Don't be so soft!' she'd tease. 'What are you going to do when I make you take the armbands off?'

I sit up straight, shaking the thoughts from my head, like those last clinging drops of rain. So what if I have experienced 'problems' with my family? That doesn't disqualify me as an expert on family history. I'm an academic, not a student counsellor; there is a huge difference between what one knows intellectually and the cloudy, shifting substance of what one knows emotionally. And even if the haranguing critics who inhabit my thoughts are constantly telling me

40

how little I understand, I am so well defended with my reading lists, carefully thought-out arguments and meticulously researched sources that no one need ever find out.

I start the cold, juddering engine, yanking angrily at the gear lever. It is time to go home.

5

It does not take me long to reach Queen's Square. I park the car and hurry towards number sixteen, my building. The road is filled with what were once generous Regency town-houses but is now distinctly down on its luck. Surely it was not quite so sordid when I viewed it. This evening it is a mess of spilt bin-bags, rusting bikes chained to railings and soggy mattresses deposited on the basement steps. With the exception of the end building, which is decorated with a gaudy rainbow and has a large banner hanging from the top-floor windows, announcing DEFEND YOUR RIGHT TO SQUAT, all of the houses are converted into flats.

Number sixteen is perhaps the tattiest on the road, the peeling exterior paint grey with age, the window-frames rotting. I leap up the steps, groping for my keys. They are not in my pocket, nor in the front section of my bag. I laboriously start to empty it of its crumpled contents: a handful of coppers, a squashed postcard I meant to send to my brother for his birthday six months ago, two unopened bills that arrived this morning, my purse and a large bundle of university files. But no keys. And the front door to the flats is huge, heavy and locked.

I stand back from the porch, wondering if anyone else is in. Despite having been here for nearly a week I have not met any of my neighbours. Sometimes I hear the bang of the front door and footsteps on the stairs, or catch the whiff of incense in the hall, and yesterday, as I picked up my mail, I had the distinct feeling that someone was standing behind me. But as yet there are no faces to match the list of surnames taped next to the bells by the front door.

The second- and third-floor windows are in darkness, but there are lights behind the net curtains of the ground-floor flat. Stamping my feet with cold I push my finger on the buzzer. There is a long pause, then I hear a click, followed by a burst of static. 'Yes?' It is a woman, her voice muffled by the ancient intercom.

'Hello? I live in the flat above you. I'm locked out.'

Silence. Through the thick door I hear shuffling, a bang and then the door opens two inches and a face peers out. 'Hi,' I say. 'I live upstairs. I've lost my keys.'

The door swings open. My neighbour gazes out at the street, her hands anxiously pulling at a flap of loose skin on her neck. Before I have had time to censure my thoughts the shameful phrase 'mutton dressed as lamb' flashes into my mind. She is in her fifties, possibly older, and wearing Lara Croft camouflage combats, which should be baggy but pinch at her thighs, and stacky Buffalo boots. On top she has a long sleeved T-shirt, pulled up over her podgy tum to reveal a pierced belly-button. Her face is grey and baggy, her thin fingers covered with heavy silver rings. She has dyed black hair, tied back with bits of purple rag into pigtails that sprout from her head like Buddhist prayer flags.

'I've seen you,' she says, nodding unsmilingly. 'You're in Jenny and Doug's old flat.'

I step into the draughty hall beside her. It's a depressing sight: the flock wallpaper peeling, the red carpet so dirty it is almost brown, its swirly pattern resembling coils of dried blood. Underneath a tarnished mirror there is a rickety wooden table covered with bills to long-gone tenants, flyers for double-glazing, Help the Aged bin-liners and out-of-date telephone directories. The place smells of stale cooking and damp.

43

'Hello,' I say, holding out my hand. 'I'm Cass.'

She takes it, holds it limply in hers. 'Welcome, Cass,' she says. 'You'll probably keep bumping into my clients in the hall.' Her voice is deep and husky, the grainy tones of a heavy smoker.

I nod dumbly, unable to think of an appropriate response. Through the open door of her flat I can glimpse purple walls, then a doorway hung with a glittery curtain of beads. The place pongs of incense. There is a long pause and then she says, 'I do tarot too, if you're interested. But mostly it's just the astrology.' She still does not smile, just keeps staring intently at me, as if trying to make out my aura.

I am so tired and talked out by my day that I just simper mutely.

'I can hear you walking about above me in the late hours.'

I grimace at her. 'Oops, sorry about that. These walls are so thin.'

'Oh, no,' she says, with a little laugh that sounds more like a gurgle. 'I don't *mind*. It's a comfort to hear life up there.'

I don't ask her to elucidate. All I want is to get into my flat, switch on the computer and start on the lecture. But, dimbo that I am for losing my keys, I'm still locked out.

'I'm going to have to call the managing agents or something,' I mutter, 'so I can get through my door.'

She gazes at me, then gives her lips a little lick, like a lizard hoping to catch a fly. 'I've got spare keys,' she says slowly. 'Jenny always kept them with me.'

She turns and shuffles into her flat, returning a few minutes later with a large crystal key-ring. I follow her up the stairs and she opens the door, then hastily stuffs the keys back into her pocket. From the way she is lingering on the top step I deduce that she is hoping to be invited in.

'Fantastic!' I say, as the door swings open. 'Thank you so much!'

She stares at me for just a second too long. I must appear prim and unfriendly, but I am desperate to be rid of her.

'My name's Jan,' she says, 'and you're definitely a Cancer.'

Then she turns and stomps back down the stairs.

The funny thing is, she's right.

Finally I am alone. I step through the door into the flat, feeling like an impostor. This morning I threw open windows, filled the place with the reassuring, everyday traces of my presence: coffee, burnt toast, lavender soap. But in my absence the flat has reasserted itself and now all I can smell is its malodorous, mournful scent, the damp walls and the stuffy, dusty carpet. The place has been empty too long.

I walk into the sitting room, pushing on the light and looking across the room at the piles of books, my laptop still nestled reproachfully in its case by the wall. The room feels emptier and larger than ever, the french windows stretching high up to the stained, stuccoed ceiling, the nasty woodchip wallpaper covered with pale patches where pictures once hung. When I first saw the flat, back in early September, sunlight had gushed through the windows and I hardly noticed the peeling décor. But now, under the sallow glare of the electric bulb, the sense of abandonment is unavoidable. Someone must once have installed the fake chandeliers and velveteen pelmets with hope and purpose. They must have pasted up the mock-Regency stripes in the hall with a sense of improvement, chosen the mud-green bathroom tiles with a modernizer's zeal. But that was surely many years ago. Whoever was last here clearly cared little for their surroundings.

I wander into the centre of the room, wondering what Doug and Jenny were like. The only remnant of their tenure that I have discovered so far is a mildewed postcard from the Gambia, curled behind the bidet. What pictures once hung on these walls? What furniture left such deep indentations in the deep-pile carpet? I stand by the windows, unsure what to do next. Yes, there is the lecture to write, but all day I have been spurred on by such a frantic onslaught of activity that now I am alone I feel cast adrift, unable to do anything but linger at the windows, gaping out at the blackness. The wind has picked up again and the wooden shutters are shaking and rattling as if possessed.

What I shall do is make some coffee, have a biscuit. In the kitchen I put the kettle on, do a little dance to warm myself up. It is arranged in an L-shape: a narrow corridor, leading up some steps to the cramped sitting area, which was described as a 'breakfast bar' in the rental details. At the end of this there is a sliding glass door and a small roof terrace, connected to the pavement below by a rickety fire escape. Seeing the phone fixed to the wall reminds me that I was going to call Sarah. I should be opening up the computer and typing 'Week One: Methods in Oral History', but all day I have been longing to speak to her and now I am going to take my chance.

I grab the receiver and press in her digits. She picks up almost immediately. Her voice is breathless and slightly irritated, as if she has been interrupted from something important. 'Hello?'

'It's me.'

Pause. Perhaps she no longer recognizes my voice. Then something in her seems to relax and she breathes, 'Hello, stranger, haven't heard from you in *ages*,' just like the old Sarah whom I am yearning to talk to. I am just about to tell her about how everything in my life has changed and I am now living in a dilapidated flat by the sea when she shrieks. There is a dull thud, presumably of the receiver being dropped. I can hear muffled toddler screams in the background.

46

I hold the receiver away from my ear for a while, my eyes roaming the kitchen. I shall not be doing much cooking here. The oven is truly unpleasant: a greasy wreck, the plastic coating peeling off around the knobs. On closer inspection those tiles, with their flower motif, are covered in a slippery layer of grease. I put the receiver back to my ear and hear Sarah's voice singing: 'Poor Poppy, Mummy loves you,' over and over, a maternal incantation to the God of small children. After another long gap, I hear Sarah say, 'Why don't you go and watch Bob, sweetie?'

Then, suddenly, she is back. 'Christ, sorry. Pops just fell over her trike.'

'Oh dear.'

'I *think* she's OK. I mean, she's not got any obvious bruises. But it *is* upsetting to fall over, isn't it, Popsy? Yes! Bob will fix it!'

I grip the receiver grimly. I never imagined I could feel so resentful towards a two-foot-high person whose only words are 'Bob' and 'Gimme' – or, indeed, that Sarah could be so endlessly distracted. Yet ever since Poppy was born there has been a noticeable shift in our friendship. I picture my once-glamorous friend at the other end of the line. She will be wearing a fleecy top and a dreadful pair of leggings. Her erstwhile pretty hair will be flopped over her face and she will have a little stain of Poppy's snot on her shoulder. The last time I visited her Poppy screamed the entire time. And Sarah – whom I once loved for her wit and intensity – was glassy-eyed, stoned with exhaustion and an obsessive interest in Poppy's every utterance, which I found hard to share. All in all, the visit reminded me of my emotions when, one weekend with Matt, we unintentionally passed the site of the hotel my family used to stay at in Eastbourne. The place had been almost entirely pulled down: all that remained were two crumbling walls, and a section of the roof; the entire west wing, where there had been a bar and David and I used to play billiards, was reduced to rubble. What I felt, as I stared at the large sign in the drive, which proclaimed, 'An Exciting New Development of Luxury Flats', was shock, grief, and a strong desire to get away as soon as I could. It is not, of course, that Sarah and Poppy constitute a derelict building, yet my emotions on both occasions were remarkably similar. As I watched Poppy clamber over Sarah's lap, and registered the way her gaze kept shifting from my face, back to her daughter, as if pulled by a magnet, I finally understood that the days of freedom and irresponsibility, when we could stay up all night laughing and talking over a bottle of wine, or even jet off for girlie weekends to Barcelona or Paris, had come to an end. At some time, without consulting me, my best friend had forged ahead and changed everything. And I was left standing in front of the redevelopment sign, feeling bereft and misplaced.

'So,' Sarah says, composing herself, 'how are you?'

'Fine. Yeah, I'm good. I've moved to the seaside.'

'Poppy!' she calls. 'Don't touch that!' There is a long pause, presumably as she takes care of Poppy. Then finally she returns. 'What were you saying, Cass?'

I suck at my lips, feeling my face pucker with childish jealousy. 'I've moved to the south coast.'

She is silent for so long that I wonder whether she has disappeared again. I imagine the phone dangling from its wire as she fusses around Poppy, my tinny, tiny words reverberating unheard into her kitchen wall. But she is still there. 'The sea?' she says eventually. 'I thought you so famously hated the sea.'

'It's not about the sea,' I say slowly. 'It's this job, the one I told you I was applying for.'

'Oh, you got it. That's nice . . .' She sounds far from convinced.

'Yeah, it's good.'

'I guess it *might* be a sensible move,' she ventures. 'What does Matt think?'

'He's fine about it.'

Another pause. The trouble is, she knows me too well to allow obvious lies like this to pass. To fill the silence, I add, 'It's actually really nice to have a break from London. You know me, Sarah, I'm a country girl at heart.'

'Are you?'

'Spent my entire childhood roaming rural Hertfordshire.'

'Did you?'

'And the job's much better, too . . .' I trail off. I have the uncomfortable sensation that she is about to say something I do not want to hear. 'Anyway,' I say, with fake jauntiness, 'how are you?'

'Well, I was fine until about a minute ago, but to be honest I'm gobsmacked. I had no idea you were going to actually *move.*'

I swallow. Sarah has always been devastatingly honest with me. It's one of the reasons I love her. 'It's only temporary,' I say lamely. 'And I'll be coming back at weekends.'

'But you never told me you were moving!'

She sounds so wounded that my chest goes tight. She is right to be hurt: the one-liner emails and failed attempts at returning her calls have been a poor show for a best friend.

'I'm really sorry,' I say, fighting back the urge to pretend it's all a silly joke, 'but we haven't had a chance to have a proper talk for months. If we had, I'd obviously have let you know.'

She hesitates, then says, 'I'm going to miss you. Not, of course, that I ever see you, these days, even in London . . .'

Her voice is filled with such feeling that my breath catches. 'You can come and stay. Poppy would love the sea.'

I am trying to appear cheerful but this last statement sounds somehow dismissive, as if I don't care how she feels. She sighs, and I feel something cold pass across me, an intimation perhaps of how much my life has changed.

'We need to talk,' she says. 'I feel like I don't know what's going on with you any more.'

Another cold clutch at my heart. 'I know——'

Somewhere in the distance I hear a crash and then another toddler screech.

'Oh, God! Not again, Poppy! Look, Cass, I'm really sorry, but I'm going to have to go.'

I am unable to speak. I was expecting a quick chat with Sarah to cheer me up, but now I can feel the hot swell of approaching tears.

'Look, I love you, Cass,' she says. 'We'll talk soon, OK?'

'OK.'

And then she's gone.

The moment I put down the phone, it rings again, its tone strident and accusatory, as if the person on the other end is fed up with waiting. I pick it up quickly, hoping that maybe Poppy's accident has been dealt with and Sarah has returned to me. 'Hello?' At the other end, I hear two long tones, signalling ring-back. Then there is a click, and down the end of the line the sound of breathing. 'Hello?' I say, to whoever it is. 'You did call back on my number?'

But there is no reply. Instead the phone goes dead. I hold it in my hand for a moment, considering people's rudeness, then put it down. Leaning against the sink I locate a packet of Jammie Dodgers, stuffed between a packet of tea-bags and a jar of sugar. What I need is a nice sugary snack. Stuffing one biscuit after the other into my mouth I am just about to move purposefully towards the sitting room and my laptop when the phone is ringing once more. I grab it, spluttering biscuit over the mouthpiece. 'Yeth?'

Nothing, just silence. Perhaps it is a mobile going out of range.

'Hello?' I enunciate, wiping the crumbs from my chin. I am sure someone is there. I grip the receiver more tightly, listening for breathing. 'Well, bugger off, then,' I whisper, and hang up. Yet the moment I put it back it starts to ring again. I let it bleep two, then three times. I'm feeling distinctly rattled. When I pick it up I say curtly, 'Yes?'

For a moment I think it is the silent caller again, for there is a pause, followed by an intake of breath. But then a voice says, 'I've been trying to call your mobile for the last two hours,' and with a rush of relief I realize that my caller is Matt.

'Have you? I didn't hear it.'

'You've probably lost it again,' he says, and I imagine him smiling slowly back at me. Despite his attempts at plaintive complaint he sounds jocular, his tone only slightly chiding. '– And then the phone was engaged.'

'Sorry. I was chatting to Sarah.'

'How's full-time motherhood? What's little Poppy up to?'

'It's all going fine,' I say hastily. 'How about you?'

'All the better for talking to you.'

He's using his flirty voice, warm and teasing. I smile, my body relaxing at the reassuring tone. When we are here, in this sunny place, it's easy to forget his stormy side: the unpredictable tempers and rampaging jealousies that flare up when he feels unloved. We can be how we always were: long-term lovers or, as Matt would have it, 'partners', our roles secure – Matt, the experienced and confident Reader in politics, and Cass, his girl. No game plan, no pressure, just the comforting companionship of two shared lives.

'How's the house?'

'All the tidier for not having you here.'

'I'm not that bad!'

51

He laughs.

'Did you get my email?'

'Yup. And the answer is that I'm off to Vienna next week for the European Network conference, remember? Then I'm going to steam ahead and finish the 'State and Society' article, so there isn't much point, really, in you coming all the way to London. I'll come and see you the week after that. I'm writing it down for the first week of November. OK?'

It is just as well he cannot see my face, for I am grimacing with what feels oddly like relief. His announcement means I shall not see him for nearly a month. With the exception of a two-month research trip to Washington seven years ago, we have never been apart for longer than four or five days. This is new terrain, a situation I had not anticipated: it had never crossed my mind that we would not see each other at least every weekend. Certainly, I had not expected us to have to make formal arrangements with diaries and personal organizers, like newly dating yuppies. The unexpected freedom makes me feel strangely elated.

'So?' Matt is saying. 'Aren't you going to tell me how it's gone?'

'It's good. I met my first bunch of students this morning, and there've been meetings all afternoon. And now I'm milling around in this crappy old flat wishing you were here to keep me company.'

The moment I say this I know I have made a mistake. Down the phone I can sense him tense, his expression clouding.

'Well, sorry. You made your bed,' he says curtly. 'If you want me around to keep you company then don't endlessly prioritize your academic ambitions.'

'Don't be ridiculous! I haven't gone to Edinburgh. It's only sixty miles from London!'

'Yeah, but somehow it feels a lot further.'

I do not like the way he says this. I bite my lip, my eyes welling. 'What do you mean?'

'Oh, come on, Cass. You know.'

My hands are getting sweaty. 'You think I should have stayed in London,' I say slowly.

'I don't want to get into this over the phone.' He is using his dealing-with-irritating-students voice: brokering no objections, cold and horribly closed.

I plough on, aware of the dangers, yet unable to stop myself. 'Get into what?'

'Stop playing games with me, Cass. You know what.'

I swallow, unable to respond. In the end I choke, 'It isn't going to make any real difference.'

'Yeah, sure.' And then, as usual, he puts the phone down on me.

After I have calmed down I stand by the french windows, looking down on to the road below. It has stopped raining and patches of deep blue appear from behind the racing clouds, sometimes the odd star.

Things used not to be like this. Matt and I were once so happy: he was my saviour, my provider of security and comfort and unquestioning affection. I lean against the window-frame, closing my eyes. I am standing in a draught and the wood vibrates slightly from the rush of air. I was a penniless postgraduate when I first met him, sharing a large, chaotic house in Holloway with five other students and living on tuna sandwiches, fags and instant coffee. Most of my time during those early days was spent struggling to transform my rambling research notes into something coherent. I had ideas, lots of them, and had read copiously on the civilian experience of wartime Britain, post-war occupational structures and gender relations. But when I tried to connect this great fish-stew of debates and data to the old women whose stories I had heard, everything I wanted to say fell away. I felt lost, frustrated by my inability to do what was required. Then one Saturday evening, after a day spent trying to write a single paragraph, I remembered I was meant to be having dinner at a friend's. I arrived late, had not even bothered to change. And there he was, sitting at the end of the table with a spliff in his hand, holding forth about Foucault and the end of organized politics, his pet subject. When he saw me he stopped talking, made space for an extra chair and poured me a glass of wine.

It's a cliché, but it was as if we had known each other for years. We spent the entire evening discussing our work, rudely oblivious to the people on either side. When I described my East End ladies, he listened with an empathy that far surpassed my supervisor's, and when we shared a taxi home later that night I followed him unquestioningly into his house. We took it for granted even then: we were a couple before we had so much as kissed.

I bite my lip, remembering how good things were. We have been together for so long, our domestic routines and habits ground so deeply into my psyche that, until a week ago, I hardly noticed they were there. Now that they have gone I feel cut adrift, my single state more bracing than I could ever have imagined. We were in the comfort zone, every part of our lives mapped out. It was utterly un-demanding, like lying in a warm bath with a copy of *Heat*. We worked at the same university: him with his readership and me in a variety of exploitative temporary posts; our house was cosy, painted in bright, warm colours, the walls covered in pictures we'd bought together, the shelves packed with our numerous books. Most evenings he would cook as I sat and listened to him talk about his day; we would drink a bottle of wine, then go to bed with our books and each other. Sometimes we would eat with friends, all of them in couples now, most with children. Saturday mornings we'd do Waitrose, then a walk on the Heath or an afternoon film; Sundays he'd work, or we'd go for a leisurely brunch with the papers. We rarely fought, any abrasive edges between us smoothed by long acquaintance. Or, rather, I had learnt the great female art of accommodation: I would nurse him out of his insecurities and humour his tantrums. I was used to them, took it all in my stride. I loved him, loved our life together, still do not understand why I had to go and spoil it all, come here and be alone.

I shudder, stepping back from the window. Why have I started thinking about him in the past tense? Nothing has finished. This is just a phase, a short interlude while I add to my CV. And, anyway, we both knew that we could not always remain so blissfully unfettered. There was the Life Cycle snapping at our heels, like some bad-tempered dog that needed to be endlessly fed with change and readjustment. You've been doing this for too long, it was snarling. Cass is thirty-five, Matt nearly forty. You need to *get on with your lives*.

It should all be so easy, just as it has been for Sarah, and almost all of my other friends. And yet rather than embrace the changes, which everyone expects, I am tugging in the opposite direction. For some reason the Waitrose trips started to pall, the once convivial evenings with friends to feel oppressive. It was as if I was watching myself playing a part in a dull, predictable TV drama. Increasingly, what I wanted to do was lean over and turn myself off.

I blink in surprise at the thought, for I have never quite articulated it like this. I must be exaggerating. *Everything is fine.* Matt and I are merely going through the ten-year doldrums. The reason I have come to Brighton is because, for the first time in my career, I was offered a permanent post, not because I wanted to leave him. I trace my finger absentmindedly across the dusty radiator. It is true that lately we have been squabbling too much but this is only because he resents the change in direction. He thinks it is unnecessary and, if one accepts the view that life is a series of stages that one is duty-bound to pass through, he is right. What I should be doing, right now, is nest-building with him in London.

But sod it. I'm not some earth-mother type, with a brood of infants sucking at her bosom as she kneads her home-made organic bread. And if he really thinks about it, Matt isn't the kiddie kind either. The only reason he's started to fantasize about having children is because Josh, his oldest friend from his wild Manchester postgraduate days, has just had a baby. Ever since they met on the Heath and Josh had the comatose tot strapped to him in a sheepskin sling and was rhapsodizing about his joyous new life, Matt has felt left out. But the fantasy doesn't involve serious input. He expects to carry on exactly as before, give or take the odd papoose-carrying stroll with his friends on a Sunday afternoon. No, I decided, as I watched the kid posset a little puddle of sick on to Josh's collar, the person who will be doing all the work is me.

And, once again, I am filled with the anger and alienation that increasingly stalk our relationship. I shake my head, as if to loosen the mouldering emotions that have clogged up inside. Down there, beyond the gardens, over the road and past the pebbles, the sea is churning. Sarah was right to be nonplussed by my news: what am I doing in this place, which scares me so?

I move away from the window, bilious and unnerved.

Dear Mum
This is a dream I had last night. I get it a lot, and it seems significant.

I'm on the beach, and there you are, standing on a ridge of stones, staring out at the waves. It's not really you, of course, but the person I imagine you might be. It was high summer, just like it always is. In the background I could hear the screaming of kids splashing in the sea, the electronic beep of the slot machines. There were people everywhere, spread out across the beach in happy family clusters: fat dads and snoozing mothers, children screeching in the surf. Above them, the scavenging gulls circled in the warm Channel air.

But you did not notice any of this. You just stood there looking out, as if waiting for your ship to come in. Your long hair was golden, your billowing silk dress blue; I think your feet were bare. When you turned I saw my own features, reflected in your face.

And then, as I was waving and calling out your name, you turned and started running across the pebbles towards me. I sat there, paralysed with joy and terror. Finally, I kept thinking. Finally. But then, when you were almost upon me, I realized that you were not looking at me after all, but past me, at something I could not see. And even as I was holding out my arms and shouting at you to stop you were gone.

Do you have dreams? And am I in them?

6

I was not always afraid of the sea. When I was a child, our annual seaside holidays were as woven into family life as our neat suburban house, or the woods at the back where David and I played Wacky Races on our bikes. In retrospect, the preparations and planning for this trip were often better than the event, which by the time I reached the ambiguous pre-teenage years had become increasingly tarnished and dull. By then I longed to be like other girls in my class, whose more adventurous and better-off parents would swan off to Majorca or Corfu. *Boring!* I would groan. *Not Eastbourne again!* But when I was younger, I still thought of the British seaside as a place of magic and adventure, where ice-cream vans were parked on every beach and the sea was always sparkly blue.

The evening before we left, David and I would help Dad load up the Rover, filling it with suitcases and bags of raincoats and wellington boots and the old rubber dinghy, which, on arrival, he would painstakingly inflate with his bicycle pump. On the coffee-table in the lounge, he would have spread out his 1971 *Roadways of Britain Atlas*, his route already carefully planned. In less than twenty-four hours, we would think feverishly, we would arrive at whatever draughty holiday cottage they had rented, or the shabby south-coast hotel where we habitually stayed, which – at least on our first visit – appeared to us the ultimate in consumer heaven, with portable televisions in our room, baskets of toast at breakfast and sachets of shampoo and soap in the bathroom. Later, I would lie awake in our bedroom, listening to David's steady breathing as my tummy jumped with anticipation. In the drive below my window, the Rover waited, its engine poised for action, its suspension weighed down with our collective dreams.

And then morning would come and we would take our places in the vehicle, driving through the quiet Home Counties roads of our not-quite-a-village backwater towards the highway. My memory of what must be about ten trips to varying locations has been compressed into one totemic journey: Mum and Dad in front, bickering over directions and when to stop for lunch, and David and I squeezed up in the back with our toys and comics. As the hours grew interminable, we would become increasingly crazed with boredom and too many of Dad's Glacier Mints from the glove compartment. There was no M25 back then, so it was down the A1, through the urban sludge of the North Circular and into the endless suburban sprawl of Purley Way. Then, just when we felt we could stand it no more, the car would cut loose and head for the coast, like a city dog spotting a distant rabbit and dashing ecstatically across the fields in pursuit.

And, finally, the sea. In my memory, this was always glimpsed over the crest of a hill, a glistening band of blue, framed in my imagination with a metaphoric rainbow, like a scene from the *Wizard of Oz.* We would cheer then, pinching ourselves awake; Dad might even stop the car, lean over and give Mum an unaccustomed peck on her cheek. We had two, sometimes even three weeks ahead of us. No school, no grumpy childminder hired to 'watch' us in the mornings while Mum answered the phone at the local surgery and, best of all, the constant presence of a father who would morph from a grey-faced and silent presence at the dinner-table to an energetic builder of sandcastles, organizer of tickling contests and champion belcher.

Even Mum would relax. 'This is where I really belong,' she would say reproachfully, sighing and looking out at the water wistfully, as if her marriage to Dad and subsequent life in land-locked Hertfordshire was a penance, forced upon her by the cruel, uncaring whim of her overbearing husband. As she was always reminding us, she had been born in Dorset, and grew up by the sea. It was true that she always seemed happier when close to it. I can picture her now, sitting loose-limbed in the sun, her cardigan spread over her burning knees, humming jauntily as she filled rolls with Sandwich Spread or wrote messages for us in the sand. She was a good swimmer, better than Dad, and at the end of every day would rise and let her towel fall on to the sand as she headed for the bobbing waves. She never screeched at the cold, or made a big show of splashing water over her arms like the other women on the beach, just plunged straight in, swimming away from us in a straight line, until her head was a distant speck. I loved her then, for her strength and disdain of danger.

How many holidays were there like this? Probably no more than two or three, and all before I was ten. After that came the summer when Mum forced me to try to learn to swim 'properly', without armbands, and I acquired my terror of drowning. 'Ridiculous child,' she would mutter, under her breath, as I increasingly refused even to dip my toe into the water. 'Just jump in and do it.' As was the case with Mum and I, we were both quick to up the ante. Before long I was refusing even to change into my swimming-costume, while she was threatening darkly to leave me in the hotel. Yet despite this later experience, the sun-filled seaside holiday epitomizes something about my early childhood: a time of grace, perhaps, when we were all at our best and did not know how much would soon be lost. And even though, as each year passes, those memories become less easy to

60

distinguish, the colours and contours fading into sepia sameness, there is one that still stands out. It returns to me each time I think of my mother, and each time I now stand on my balcony, overlooking the sea.

I must have been seven or eight and, unusually, Mum rather than Dad was helping me to build a sandcastle. We were in Cornwall this time, not Sussex. I remember golden shell sand and jutting rocks, a Neptune's cove of shady pools and hidden reefs. Unlike my father's constructions, which, given his profession as a surveyor, unsurprisingly involved regimented cities of perfect towers produced by David's bucket, this creation was more fantastical, a Mervyn Peake folly with wiggly turrets and a collapsing, water-logged moat. I had spent most of the afternoon scouring the tideline for décor: we had covered the balustrades with seaweed, limpet shells and gull feathers, and now I was roaming the slimy pools on the edge of the beach, with their prickly pink urchins and skating plankton. Mum, too, had temporarily abandoned the castle and was wandering in the surf, her face dreamy, her pockets filled with shells. I have no memory of the whereabouts of David or Dad.

'Look at this!'

Turning, I saw that she was striding purposefully across the beach, cupping something precious in her hands. When she reached me, she smiled and crouched on the sand, opening her clasped fingers to reveal what at first I imagined to be an ancient leather purse, the relic of a shipwreck. Spiky tendrils were attached to each corner, to be tied on to a pirate's belt, perhaps.

'Do you know what it is?'

I shook my head. She did not often talk to me like this, so seriously, as if we were accomplices in an adventure.

'It's a mermaid's purse,' she said gently. 'A dogfish will have laid it, or a shark. It's full of eggs. It's got washed up in the current.' She picked it up by one of the strings and handed it to me. 'It might even have a baby inside.'

I held the thing in the palm of my hand, staring hard. I wanted to say something that would please her, but was not sure what that might be. She was so unpredictable, apt to laugh dismissively at my comments, or lose her temper and flounce away. Looking back now, I suppose she was unhappy with the way things had turned out.

'Can we look?' I whispered.

'Let's see.'

Holding out her hand for me to take, she stood up and we walked solemnly back towards the sea. The tide was coming in, flooding across the sand and rocks in swirling rivulets. As we squatted by the strand-line it lapped playfully at our toes, splashing up and over our bare legs. Reaching into the back pocket of her shorts, Mum produced the penknife she kept for picnics. 'It's probably empty,' she was muttering, furrowing her brows as she dug into the tough skin of the pouch. I stared at the thing, willing this not to be so.

And there, as she pulled away the top of the purse, a tiny embryo wriggled, pale yellow and slimy, my baby fish. We gazed down at it in awe, mother and daughter, our hands entwined.

'Incredible,' she breathed, and I could feel the warmth of her fingers squeezing mine, the sudden excitement in her pulse. 'I've never seen that before!'

Cupping the purse silently in her palm she blinked at me in the late-afternoon sun. By now I was imagining the baby fish growing into an adult under my loving care: my own pet dogfish; a breed obviously more cuddly and intelligent than most. I could keep it in my bedroom, I thought enthusiastically; I could get an aquarium. Smiling back at her, I said the first thing that came into my mind: 'Can we keep it?'

The calm wonder on my mother's face vanished.

'Don't be silly,' she snapped, shaking away my hand. 'It would only die.'

'We could put it in a tank and feed it seaweed,' I mumbled feebly.

'They don't eat seaweed.'

'Mum, please!'

But now I had ruined it: her expression shrank back into its normal set-upon weariness, and she was frowning in irritation. 'No.'

'But I could look after it!'

'It's non-negotiable,' she said, looking curtly away from me as her fingers closed over the egg sac. 'Don't even think about having one of your tantrums.'

And before I could stop her she had hoisted herself up. For a moment I thought she was going to search for a safe place to put the purse, where at least the tiny soft thing inside might have a chance of surviving, but then I saw her arm swing back over her head and she lobbed it into the foaming swill. Brushing the sand off her hands, she turned sharply away from the waves and jogged back up the beach, out of reach of my clamorous wails.

Or have I remembered it wrongly? Was this, in fact, just a dream? I can feel the cold sand under my feet, hear the suck and splash of the waves, even the raucous cries of the gulls, but then I sit up and see that I am not in Cornwall, but have simply fallen asleep on the worn carpet by the windows. I must be more exhausted than I knew. My mouth tastes fetid, there is a pool of spit on my chin where I have been dribbling.

And now that my eyes are properly open and I am returned to reality, I realize that I am not alone. The room is dark at its outermost edges, but the centre of the carpet is washed with a pool of callow yellow light from the street-lamp opposite. And surely, over there, in the blackest recess by the door, I can hear somebody breathing. Standing, I start to walk unsteadily across the room. The breathing has stopped but in the darkness the door has just trembled shut.

'Hello?' I whisper. 'Who's there?'

But, of course, there is no answer, just the dull sound of poisoned blood thumping in my temples.

7

'What are life histories?' I pause and look around the lecture theatre, trying to appear authoritative. I am leaning against the podium in an effort at informality but am having problems with my hands, which for the past few minutes I have been gripping piously in front of me, like those of a novice priest. Folding them tightly over my bosom, I take another breath.

'Life histories are primarily concerned with recording people's spoken recollections of the past, or what today are often fashionably referred to as their "narratives". These are by their nature less formal than the meta-narratives of mainstream history, the grand tales of kings and statesmen and wars, which make up school history texts. For some, life histories are therefore inevitably more subjective.'

I stop, more for effect than to study my notes: I know exactly what comes next. I click on the overhead projector and the transparency I prepared in haste ten minutes ago echoes me mutely: *What are life histories? Are they important?* Rising in steep rows in front of me are over a hundred students, some staring at the screen, some jotting notes in their pads. I do not recognize any of my seminar group. I scan the room, failing to locate Beth's face in the darkness. Suppose she suffered a delayed reaction to falling under the car last week, I think, and is currently lying alone in some dingy bed-sit, having sunk into a coma?

Squaring my shoulders and sucking in my tummy, which is bulging more than it should over the waistband of my linen trousers, I take a deep breath and continue.

'There is, for example, the worrying problem of memory. We may be able to check formal accounts of history against secondary sources, but the stories people tell about the past are often less verifiable. Memories are profoundly unreliable: how many of us have not listened to the muddled recollections of elderly relatives?'

I look up, forcing myself to smile. It's always better once I've got into my stride.

'And what about the things we think we remember, which are only indirectly related to actual events? Photographs, for instance, or videos, can be both useful and distracting aides to memory; they can peg us into a mistaken terrain. For a good many years, for example, I believed that the young bridesmaid in a photograph of a family wedding was myself. I could remember the fabric of the dress she was wearing, the smell of the bouquet of roses she held. I was there at Cousin Milly's wedding, I remembered it all. Only many years later was I told that the little girl was not actually me but another child of similar colouring and build. At the time of the wedding I had not even been born.'

Finally I spot Beth in the front row, deep in concentration as she notes down what I have said. My relief at seeing her causes me to chuckle aloud, as if what I have just said is quite witty. Folding the top corner of my notes, I pause for a second, then plough on.

'Once we conclude that all accounts, whether formal or informal, need to be put in context, we need not worry so much about these problems. What we need to practise is the art of interpretation . . .'

It is almost eleven o'clock. I have ten minutes left to finish the lecture and circulate a handout of main points and key readings, which I printed off in considerable panic this morning. I draw to a close and, sensing the change in tone, my audience put down their pens, shuffle their feet in expectation of movement. My voice sounds husky from last night's cigarettes. I hope no one has noticed that the trousers I am wearing, the only clean ones I could find, are torn at the gusset from sitting down too heavily after breakfast.

'Right,' I say as I turn off the projector, 'that's it for today. See you next week.'

And now they stand, grabbing their coats, leaning over the benches and calling out to each other, a mass exodus of young people moving towards daylight, slinging their bags over their shoulders, opening cans of drink and shoving food and fags into their mouths. I survey the rapidly emptying room for familiar faces. The ex-nurses are standing together at the back, Andy Thickow has disappeared and Beth is still bent over the bench, making laborious notes. Perhaps she senses me watching her, for she glances up and gives me a little wave.

'Dr Bainbridge?'

I jump, then turn to find Alec Watkins hovering behind the podium. I am so unused to hearing my title that, for a ludicrous moment, I believe he is teasing me. Most students address me by my first name, and even when telesales girls ask, 'Is that Miss or Mrs?' I am never quite pompous enough to put them in their place by answering, 'It's *Doctor*, actually.'

'Yes?'

'Can I have a quick word?'

'Of course.'

He has a slight stoop, as if ashamed of his height, and does not return my smile. Instead, he purses his lips and stares down at his feet, which in sharp contrast to the ubiquitous student trainers are clad in the type of soft-soled lace-ups my father might have once chosen. I have the sinking feeling I get whenever I sense that a student is about to lodge a complaint.

'It's to do with the course,' he says, and my belly takes a dive. I should be more like Matt, who takes criticism as a challenge, chuckles at the rude comments he occasionally reads on his course-evaluation forms, and is generally too confident to care what students think of him, but I have yet to rise above the petty concern of wanting terribly to be liked. And, of course, while Matt's position is tenured, I am currently on probation.

'What about it?' I flash him a warm and welcoming smile, still hoping to win him over. As he peers back suspiciously I notice that he is gripping his hands tightly in front of his chest and feel a spurt of pity for his gauche manner. As a child he probably sat at the front in class and put up his hand to answer every question; the sort who regularly got roughed up by the tough boys. As I linger questioningly in front of him, my papers clutched to my chest, his face turns beetroot. He turns his head away from me, mumbles something, then quickly shakes his head, as if trying to erase it.

'Sorry?'

'No, it's OK. It doesn't matter.'

'What did you want to say?'

There is another long pause. Despite my good intentions I am becoming increasingly irritated. With a small sigh, I glance impatiently at the exit.

'Look,' he says suddenly, 'I've written this.'

He stops, fumbles in his rucksack and produces a cardboard folder covered on one side with a large coffee stain. I have the impression that this was not what he intended, that it is a stalling device. 'Here,' he pushes it into my hands, 'it's my essay for week three.'

'Great! But it might be better to give it to me when everyone else hands theirs in on the due date. Otherwise it'll get into the wrong pile and, knowing me, I'll go and lose it.' I laugh lightly.

He regards me gravely, refusing to be cajoled. 'I'd rather not.'

Reluctantly I take the folder from his outstretched hands. Still he does not move. I try to edge towards the door, but he is blocking me. 'Was there something else?'

He swallows, eyeing me petulantly. 'It's just that I'd like to come and see you,' he mutters. 'In private, if at all possible.'

'Fine,' I say, nodding at him to signal that I intend the conversation to end. Perhaps I am being unfair, but his ponderous and overly stiff manner are not attractive, and I am anxious to be rid of him. 'My office hours are on my door.' With this, I turn decisively towards the lecture-theatre door, leaving him standing alone in the large, empty room.

When I get outside I take a deep breath of the cold air. Inside, it was stiflingly stuffy, but out here it is a beautiful autumn day. Yesterday's rain has cleared and, through the campus buildings, I glimpse the poster-paint blue of the sky. Yellow and red leaves are scattered over the concrete walkways, the road splashed with puddles. I love this time of year: after the undefined yearnings of the summer heat I settle back into myself once more, greeting the change in the weather with a surge of excitement and purpose. I turn right, heading for the cafeteria in Block D. Not wishing to think any further of my uneasy exchange with Alec, I focus instead on the extra large chocolate brownie and *latte* I intend to buy there. I plan to return with my hoard to my office, close the door and consume them with utter dedication, letting the chunks of cake melt in my mouth as I sip at the bitter coffee, then licking the crumbs off my lips. I hope very much that no one disturbs me, but this is not because I'm ashamed of over-indulgence. Rather, I like to give good food my full attention: it's a reaction against all the diets my mother enforced on me – the tasteless iceberg lettuce and dried-up fish, the ban on sweets and cakes, the way she would weigh me at the end of every week, frowning in dissatisfaction at her lumpy daughter. Is it so surprising that I have not stood on a weighing-machine for twenty years?

Yet when I reach my door I see that my little feast will have to wait, for Beth Wilson is standing outside.

'Hi!' I put the coffee on the floor and fumble for my keys. Typically, I never found the originals so these are the spares, the ones I was going to give to Matt. 'How can I help?'

'OK.' She takes a breath. 'Two things, and neither will take a moment. The first is that I really, really enjoyed the lecture. Everyone afterwards was saying how good it was.'

'Really?' I stare at her in surprise. My impression had been that it was serviceable but dull.

'The second thing is that I've just started going through some of my family papers and I really think it's going to make a wicked project. I was just wondering if I could talk it through with you some time.'

'Of course. But maybe not now.'

'Tomorrow morning, then? First thing, like, a breakfast meeting?'

'Fine!'

And unlike Alec, who is so sub-Asperger's that he has no idea of body language or when to leave, she simply gives me a thumbs-up sign, and turns in the opposite direction. I can hear her singing chirpily to herself as she skips back down the corridor.

Five minutes later, the brownie is history and Julian Leigh has barged into my room. Today he's wearing a tight-fitting T-shirt and stressed denim, showing up his muscular physique; as he leans in at my doorway he keeps cracking his knuckles, as if preparing to beat someone up. He must work out regularly, I think, as I regard his self-satisfied expression. No doubt he flirts with all the prettier students.

'Looks like you've had quite a morning!'

I turn away from the computer where I have been trying to compose Lecture Two, and smile at him with relief. Perhaps it is the absence of Matt's puritanical zest, but recently the only thing about work that I have found easy has been its avoidance. 'How so?'

'Well, you've got your cardie on inside-out. Or is that a new fashion?'

Twisting round, I see the Hennes label of my sparkly black cardigan sticking up, a flag in celebration of cheap clothing. 'Bugger.'

'It's actually rather fetching.'

'Oh, shut up.'

He laughs. Despite myself, I am glad that he has dropped by. Perhaps I have misjudged him, I think, as I rearrange my clothing. It is true that last week he made some decidedly odd comments about women being attacked, but perhaps it was a failed attempt at irony, the same way that in their embrace of the unsayable, otherwise intelligent people who eschew political correctness can sound like bigots.

'What've you been up to?' he says nonchalantly.

'Third-year methods lecture. I wrote it in about ten minutes flat this morning.' I do not add that I have been up since six, worrying about it, for it is decidedly uncool among university lecturers to admit to labouring too hard over something as supposedly effortless as teaching. But I have always had a tortured relationship with my work. I survive in a state of almost permanent denial, hoping it will go away, then discovering that inevitably it has crept up behind me and is baring its fangs, ready to bite: hence the sleepless nights, the dawn panic and scribbled notes.

'Impressive!'

Unsure whether this is meant sincerely, I give him what I hope is an enigmatic smile. 'Let's hope they didn't notice,' I say.

'It's highly unlikely.' He looks around, raising his eyebrows in what I take to be feigned shock at the mess my room is in. At his feet lies Alec's folder, which has already dropped on to the floor. He nudges it with his toe. 'Essays already?'

'From the creepy Alec Watkins.'

The moment I say this, I wish I could take the comment back. There is, after all, no rational reason why I am experiencing this antipathy towards Alec, but it plopped unprompted from my lips.

'How come he's creepy?'

I shrug defensively. 'He just gives me the willies, that's all.'

'The *willies*?' Julian grimaces in apparent distaste, presumably at my use of such a childish phrase, and I feel myself blush. What made me say that?

'It's just that he's so serious and keen,' I mutter.

But rather than ridiculing me, as I had anticipated, Julian chuckles sympathetically. 'Well, that's probably true. They're *all* too bloody keen. They have to take out huge loans to get here so they want to make sure they get value for money. When I was a student I avoided lectures like the plague and wrote about one essay a term. Spent the rest of the time off my head.'

I blink at him. I am thinking of my own experience, the endless days I spent in the library, the nights I stayed up smoking and drinking peppermint tea and making notes. If I ever got less than an A, I punished myself with more nights of study, not allowing myself a single night off. It was only later, after I met Matt, that I relaxed and the grip of work eased. But perhaps Julian is so clever that he did not need to study. 'Really?' I say flatly. 'So how come you ended up with a Ph.D.?'

'Sacrificial offerings to the gods.'

'Ah, yes, those.' I'm trying and failing to strike the right jokey tone. It is typical of someone like Julian, who has *upper-class male* stamped all over his sculpted features, to pretend that his scholarly qualifications simply fell into his lap. At least Matt, who like me attended a state school, readily admits to how hard he has had to work to get where he is. Julian has folded his arms, no doubt considering me hopelessly priggish.

'I know I'm being facetious,' he says, 'but there has to be a time when one goes a little wild.'

I look at him, imagining his background. It isn't difficult: educated, arty parents, a large book-filled house somewhere in North London; a posh day school, a place at a liberal Oxbridge college more or less guaranteed. At university he would have been the sort of young man who terrified me in my first year: ebullient, confident to the point of arrogance, happy to sneer at someone from a Home Counties comprehensive whose only experience of wine was Liebfraumilch and had 'done' neither Asia nor Africa in their year off. By my finals this fear had ossified into rigid dislike. I had joined the Support the Miners Action Group by then, and had moved on from the turned-up Princess Di collars and A-line skirts of the early eighties, my doomed attempts at fitting in, to Doc Martens and dungarees. And now, even though we are meant to be grown-up, I can feel a tremor of the old antagonisms pass through me. I fold my arms sullenly, trying to avoid the inevitable direction of my thoughts, but it is too late. People like Julian always end up on top, I think resentfully. By now most of his peers will be in the media or the law; a sprinkling are academics, another couple in the diplomatic service. In a few years' time, it will be people like them who run the country. And when he talks about going a little wild, he has no idea at all.

'Yeah,' I say, deadpan. 'I guess you're right.'

'Didn't you?'

'What, go wild as a student?'

73

'Yup.'

I shrug, no longer able to avoid the image of myself aged fifteen. My faded Goth dress, with the long black fringe, cowboy boots, and that studded leather bracelet, which was so heavy it made my wrist sore. Long, lost days spent in my bedroom, listening to Black Sabbath and glugging cider, when my mother thought I was at school.

'No,' I say tartly. 'Sorry to be boring. When I was a student I was just a total swot.'

He stands back, looking me up and down appraisingly. 'Somehow I very much doubt it.'

And now *I* very much want to change the subject. 'Well, perhaps you shouldn't make assumptions,' I say curtly. 'You haven't got a clue what I'm like so don't start pigeon-holing me, OK?'

I glance quickly down at the floor, embarrassment surging through me. Julian's mouth is hanging open. For a moment we stare at each other, both red in the face. My anger has quickly drained away, and I am left with a residue of mortification. I want to apologize, to laugh off my unwarranted outburst with some witticism, but I know that if I open my mouth to speak I shall burst into tears.

'Don't worry,' Julian says quietly, and although nothing has really happened, I sense him pulling back from me, wondering if he wants to be friends after all.

'I have absolutely no intention of that whatsoever.'

8

But I have done the wild stuff. Yeah, I've been there. During the winter of 1979 I was filled with rage, with desires and energies I could not control. I hated my parents and my teachers, wanted to kick out at everyone. In almost every way, I was hell-bent on becoming a full-time juvenile delinquent.

In retrospect the foundations for this superficially startling change of direction, from well-behaved, top-of-the-class pupil to school truant, imbiber of narcotics and Bad Girl, had been laid much earlier. Somehow, in those ambivalent end-of-childhood years, I had stopped pleasing my parents. Or, more precisely, I had stopped pleasing my mother. I don't know what she wanted of me: a slimmer, less obtuse and 'easier' child, certainly; one who did not, as she put it, 'always kick up a fuss'. Perhaps she just wanted me to be more like her: lean, purposeful, unflinching. She certainly hated me whingeing: by the time I was ten or eleven the slightest complaint would whip her into a furious tirade, so I learnt to shut up. Perhaps my demands simply reminded her of how little she was prepared to give.

Yet once I became a teenager this murky, shapeless dissent turned into something more tangible. Ever since the third year I had found school increasingly tedious. Rather than listen to the drone of lessons, I preferred to sit at the back of the class doodling love hearts and the names of bands in my exercise books. My small gaggle of friends and I had been experimenting with the heady mixture of nicotine, cider and vodka-and-black for some time by then, hanging out in the only pub that would serve us and snogging almost any interested male. We were virgins to the woman, but so, too, were we dedicated to the pursuit of what we dubbed 'experience'.

But it was that winter that events accelerated. Some time between beginning the fifth year and Christmas, I stopped attending school altogether. By then I had met Billie and her crowd, a group of older kids who initiated me into their impossibly glamorous world of petty crime and heavy metal. Hanging out at Billie's place, we would drink, smoke endless packets of Benson & Hedges and wander into the town centre for a little light shoplifting. I hid the eye-liners and Motorhead albums I procured under my bed. If they had discovered them, my parents would have been stunned. From time to time we snorted the speed that Billie's nineteen-year-old boyfriend had scored, cranking up the volume on the record-player and head-banging to the guitar riffs. I thought I was invincible, that nothing mattered, not now or ever.

I stare at my keyboard, try to concentrate on the memo I am writing. I should be working, not wasting time reminiscing. And yet now that I have started I cannot force my thoughts back to the present. Julian's innocent comments have unleashed a slurry of memory: thick, claggy stuff that, whenever I let my defences down, engulfs me in an avalanche of regret. I do not want to think about this. I am meant to be *at work*. I stare resolutely at the screen, forcing my thoughts to shape up. In the last minutes six new emails have appeared: something from Alec asking if he can confirm the time of our meeting, an internal memo regarding campus security, and various postings on forthcoming workshops – Queer Politics; The Semiotics of the Post-urban Landscape; Feminist Pedagogy; Into the Twenty-first Century. None of them currently makes much sense.

It seems such a long time ago now, over twenty years,

such a very long time, but I have never forgotten a single detail. Christmas 1979, and we were piling up to the Odeon in Peckham to see the new band everyone was raving about: the Dreadheads. If I close my eyes I can picture us cramming into the stuffy, steamy train, three girls and two boys sharing a bottle of vodka and chain-smoking as if their lives depended on it. Hunched in the corner, we'd smoked a spliff in the piss-splattered, broken-windowed station waiting room. We claimed not to care if we were caught. We thought we were so hard: teenage warriors from the 'burbs, brave and free.

God, it was laughable. I can see myself, already drunk as we crowded the train, the deliberate swearing, the raw bravado. When I closed my eyes, leant my head against the misty-wet window, my thoughts would tilt, sliding away from reality into buzzing illusion. Life was good, the possibilities endless, a voice inside sang. It did not matter about Dad. It was all a lie.

It's no good, I give up. I need to be outside, to be walking quickly, with the air rushing in my face. I grab my jacket and stomp out of the room, pushing past the students milling in the corridor.

When I get outside I start to jog across the campus, my baggy trousers catching between my legs. Across the playing-fields, past the car parks, there is woodland followed by a breathtaking sweep of hills. I haul myself inelegantly over a stile, breathing in the damp, mossy smell. Wet leaves carpet the path, a soggy tribute to summer's end. I trample on, aware that mud is splashing my legs, but not much caring. It is the season of fungi, of squashy toadstools and the rotting carcasses of tree-trunks. My heart pumps with exertion, my chest hurts. I keep gulping at the air, telling myself to calm down, yet now I have started I cannot stop thinking about that evening, all those years ago. I thought I had it under control, yet at a chance remark from Julian I am cast deep down again, hurtling back in time to the person I used to be. The Night of the Dreadheads, that's how I remember it. The night everything started.

November 11, 1979, aged fifteen. We were on the train, the vodka finished, our words loud and slurred with excitement and intoxication. Then we were there: spilling into the beery fug of the venue, past the touts and the T-shirt sellers, the hordes of leather-jacketed head-bangers, their stringy hair falling across spotty faces, the rock chicks with thigh-high boots and thick Cleopatra paint around their eyes. I had been to local gigs before: events held in church halls and youth clubs, where the lights were turned on at eleven and mums and dads waited in their cars outside. Yet this was different: this was Rock and Roll. A group of Hell's Angels had pushed past us in the foyer; I had to stop myself staring at a guy who had the word HATE tattooed across his forehead. The place had an edginess to it, the sense of a fight waiting to break out.

The noise was so loud it made me want to jump and kick and scream. There was a support band on the stage, lads no one but the most dedicated students of the *NME* had heard of. I could just about glimpse them, bent over their guitars, with their ripped jeans and long tendrils of hair swinging over their faces like corn, waving in the wind. The boys wanted to go to the front, so we started to push into the jiggling, tight-packed crowd, spilling people's beer and treading on their toes as we tunnelled through. I was so drunk by then that I kept stumbling, my vision doubling and blurring as if I were in a hall of mirrors. I was almost at the front now and was dancing, my head thrown back, my eyes closed. The others had been eaten up by the crowd long ago, and all around me bodies were pressing in, a surge of sweating youth, squashing ever closer to the stage. The guy on my left, whom I had been grinning drunkenly at, had his arm round my waist and we were moving together. I could hardly see his face but I can remember the warmth of his hand, placed under my top, the whiff of spliff on his denim jacket.

Enough! I do not need to think about this. So much time has passed; it no longer matters. I turn right, dabbing at my eyes with the back of my hand. I will reach the bottom of the hill, I decide, then head back. The path ahead turns sharply, narrowing as it enters an area of overgrown bushes and brambles. I stride towards it, taking in deep, refreshing breaths of the chilly early-afternoon air. Through the trees, a diffuse, watery sunlight filters to the muddy ground.

I enter the tunnel of bushes, trying not to notice how the sun has disappeared behind the thick canopy of vegetation. I am surely too rational to be reacting like this, but the simple physical facts of absence of light and woodland give me an unexpected jolt of anxiety. The path is rarely used, and nobody knows I am here, I note nervously. Behind me there is a scuffle of activity in the leaves, a squirrel, perhaps, or a bird, nothing more ominous. Yet it is enough to make me start and turn hastily, the prospect of a countryside ramble no longer so appealing. I want very much to be back in my small, safe office.

I start to walk back along the path. I did not realize how far I had come, but now, as I peer back through the trees, the buildings down the hill seem very small. Moving more quickly, I brush carelessly past the overhanging bushes. Behind me, I have just heard the sound of breaking twigs. I am obviously being silly. A grown woman should be able to walk in the woods in the middle of the day without fear of attack, especially someone as hefty as me. Yet my breath is catching, my heart pumping fast. I am sure of it now: there are footsteps, coming up fast behind me.

It will be a dog-walker, nothing remotely threatening. I start to jog down the path, my breath huffing. In a few moments my fear will seem ridiculous, I keep telling myself: silly Cassie, embarrassing herself again. But now the person behind me is running, moving swiftly closer with what feels like deadly intent. I can hear the footsteps, pounding the muddy ground, even the panting of male breath. Then suddenly he is upon me, crashing round the bend, and as he collides into me I am sent hurling into the bushes.

'Jesus!'

For a moment all I feel is smarting pain in my right knee and across my face. I have landed more or less face down in a puddle, and already can feel the water soaking through the cuffs of my jacket and the knees of my trousers. A thorny branch, which has scratched my cheek, is stuck in my hair. My assailant, who for a second landed on my back, has leapt backwards, as if struck by electricity. When I open my eyes I see trainers, white socks and dark hair creeping up muscled ankles. I stagger to my feet and turn to face my attacker, for clearly there is little point in running away. If only I could recall the details of the women's self-defence classes I took in my twenties. What did they say? Something about shouting loud expletives in our assailants' faces?

I am facing a young man, dressed in a navy tracksuit. His face is sweaty and red and he is wiping muddy hands through his short brown hair. His face is so familiar that I can feel a bubble of recognition forming in the front of my mind, almost ready to burst.

'I didn't expect anyone . . .' He trails off. He is staring at me hard.

'Why are you following me?' I gasp.

'I wasn't. I was just going for a run.'

I eye him suspiciously, my fear curdling into something more like anger. Now that I have taken in the tracksuit and running shoes, his explanation seems to make sense. 'Well, you should bloody well look where you're going!'

But he does not apologize, just keeps his eyes fixed on my face, a long, steady gaze, like a fox waiting outside a rabbit-hole. I clear my throat but, besides a stream of obscene curses, have nothing to say. The jogger's silence and watch-fulness are unnerving.

'Where are you going?' he asks.

But I have already backed away from him, and am shrugging with fake nonchalance and walking as fast as I can back up the path. My arm is throbbing and my knee hurts, but I plod on, both self-conscious and scared, hoping that he will not see the extent of my discomfort.

When I reach the first bend I dare myself to look back. I am expecting the path to be empty again, to be able to laugh at myself for being so silly, but the jogger is still standing there glaring at me. That's when I realize who he is.

It is Alec Watkins, without his glasses.

9

It is the night after my woodland encounter with Alec that the next incident occurs. As usual, I spend it alone, oppressed by the sense of tasks left undone yet too jittery to settle down to work. It is partly the flat that makes me feel like this. Something about it makes me anxious in a way I cannot fully explain. I feel as if I am intruding, as if someone else – the real occupant – is about to walk in and demand an explanation. Even the smallest sound, the creak of floorboards above or the rattle of pipes, makes me jump. The evenings are the hardest. In the morning, when the sun pours through the rusty french windows and I can hear the everyday sounds of cars and people walking on the pavement, the call of the seagulls cruising on the breeze, I am able to reassure myself. I have made the right choice, I say. This is a fine Regency flat, albeit somewhat run-down: a place of potential style, with oodles of what estate agents refer to as 'period features'.

Yet after the light has faded and I am left to rely upon the dull glow of the dusty electric bulbs, I am not so sure. I stare up at the flaky rosebuds and fish that decorate the cracked plaster ceiling. I do not want to say it, for it will fatten my unease into something tangible and real, but the place gives me the creeps. If only I could grow accustomed to the constant tapping of the radiators, the strange gurgles from the back wall, which, Matt would be sure to state with patronizing, manly certitude, are only the drains. Every time I hear the front door slam I tense, waiting for the footsteps on the stairs to reach my door. And at night the constant groans and sighs of an old building settling make the hairs on the back of my arms bristle. It is as if my body is on full alert, waiting for something to happen.

But it isn't just the flat. This nagging sense of foreboding is also linked to the phone. Every evening now it trills at me at regular intervals of about ten minutes. Yet whenever I pick it up there is silence. Or, rather, what I hear is the quiet breathing of the person at the other end. And when I dial 1471 all I am told is 'The caller withheld their number.' I have grown so unnerved by this nightly performance that I have acquired an answer-machine and switched it to 'instant pick-up'. Merely passing the damn thing in the hall, with its evil, flashing box, announcing the ten or so blank messages I have received that evening, is enough to make my stomach churn.

It is in this frame of mind – restless, with an anxiety I am unable to pin down, lonely but unable to pick up the phone and call home – that I take a bath and go to bed. I will move, I decide, as I pull the covers over my head. Find somewhere smaller and in better order in the centre of town. I had romantic aspirations, but coming here was a mistake. On the other side of the shutters, I can hear the faint drag of the tide. The beach and its shingle repel me, yet I am increasingly pulled back to it, the way the moon drags the tides. I fall into a doze, the events of the day blurring at the edges. I picture the lecture theatre and the woods and Alec's face. Then, mercifully, my mind goes blank.

I wake with a start. I have been dreaming muddled, fearful scenes, and for a few moments lie with my eyes closed, trying to pull myself back into reality. I was running through a wood, pursued by someone – a man, whose face I never saw but whose pounding feet grew ever closer. I kept trying to go faster, but I was mired, my legs refusing to work. And then, just as he was almost upon me, the trees disappeared and I was standing on the edge of a cliff. Far below, the pale sea stretched smoothly into infinity. On the horizon a solitary liner slid slowly past.

The vista filled me with such dread that I cried out. Perhaps it was this that woke me. On opening my eyes I see the dim outline of the fireplace, the empty walls and thick velvet curtains that hang over the stained-glass windows. The digital face of my watch flashes 3:05.

I roll over, trying to clear the images from my mind. It must be the after-effects of the dream, for I feel irrationally rattled, like a little girl who has woken from a nightmare and still believes there is a monster under her bed. Perhaps I should switch on the radio, hear the reassuring lullaby tones of an all-night DJ. I fumble for my cassette-recorder, but just as I am about to turn the dial, I hear something else: a knock and then a bump from the direction of the kitchen. I stiffen, feeling my guts clench. There it is again: a banging, shuffling sound, coming from the flat roof outside the sliding door in the kitchen. It must be rats or the pigeons that huddle grumpily by the fire escape. Whatever, I am now so alarmed that, besides cowering under my sheets, the only course of action is to investigate. I swing my feet to the floor, then creep out of the bedroom and along to the kitchen.

The fuggy orange glow of a street-lamp illuminates the hall. I can make out the front door, the saggy shape of my jacket hung over a peg, and the flashing answer-machine, which informs me that since falling asleep I have received six new messages, all presumably from my ghostly caller. As I stand in the half-light, my threadbare gown draped round my naked body, ears straining for sound, I am overcome with a terror so raw that I can hardly breathe. It is the night that is doing this to me, I keep telling myself, that and being so alone. In a few hours, when the dawn takes over, I shall laugh at how scared I was by the gull or cat that is almost certainly making the noise.

I take another step, my teeth chattering. From the kitchen I have just heard another thump. Perhaps I should phone the police. Forcing myself to continue, I move stealthily down the corridor and into the narrow room. At the other end, the steps lead up to the so-called breakfast bar, then the windows and the flat roof. Like the hall, the kitchen is washed with a dull light from the street-lamps, the half-hearted darkness of city nights.

The large sky beyond the windows is purple and sickly-looking, bruised by the urban glow. I take a hesitant step towards it, my heart pounding. The windows are locked, I keep telling myself. Even if there *was* someone on the roof, they could never get in. But as I put my foot on the first step I suddenly shriek.

There is a man on the roof, staring in at me. As I looked up I saw a figure leaning by the edge of the window and, for a fraction of a second, the outline of a hooded face peering through the glass. But then, before I could be sure, he stepped away. And now, as I stand gasping on the step, he must be beating a hasty retreat down the fire escape to the pavement.

I am going to be sick. I stand, frozen on the step, riding the nauseous swell. It *must* have been a mistake. I keep staring at the window, wishing to reassure myself that the man has really gone, but am not brave enough to climb the steps and investigate. Perhaps he was an opportunist thief, a junkie probably, who, noticing the fire escape, hoped for an open window.

But however prosaic I attempt to be, I cannot erase the image of that face looking back at me through the glass. And now, as I try to move my quivering legs, I realize that I must have been standing in the same position for over a minute, and my hands are clasped to my mouth as if to stifle a scream.

I move woodenly back down the steps, trying to think it through rationally: (a) he was a burglar who has been frightened away, or (b) I imagined it. But now I find that I am racing to bolt and double-bolt the front door, for what I really believe is that he is a bogeyman of unimaginable horrors who is currently creeping up the stairs towards me with a bloody axe held behind his back.

I am on the verge of tears now, my trembling hands struggling with the dead-locks at the top and bottom of the door. I keep stopping to listen for more sounds, holding my breath and willing my heart to quieten, but there is nothing, just a plane heading for Gatwick, the occasional passing car.

And now that the locks are secured I sink to the floor, my back to the door, my shaking fingers reaching for the phone. *Please answer.*

Matt picks up immediately, for the phone is right by our bed.

'Yeah?'

He sounds groggy, disoriented, as I suppose anyone would who is woken at ten past three in the morning. 'It's me!' I screech. 'There was someone on the flat roof by the kitchen! He was staring in through the windows!'

'Whassat?'

'I could hear someone, and then I went into the kitchen and there was a face!'

I imagine him pulling himself up, flicking on the bedside light, forcing himself into wakefulness.

'Hold on, Cassie, calm down,' he says slowly, and as I hear his familiar voice, still blurred with sleep, I long to be with him now, snuggled up in our Ikea bed with its linen duvet and oversized pillows. It was madness to leave him and, right now, I can no longer remember why I did.

'Was this just now?'

'Two minutes ago! And now I don't know what to do!'

There is a pause. Perhaps he is stifling a yawn.

'Have you called the police?'

'What can they do now? He's run off, hasn't he?'

My voice is rising again, the distress I was trying hard to keep corked seeping unstoppably out.

'And you'd have to spend the rest of the night waiting for them to turn up, too . . .' he adds, almost too reasonably.

'But supposing he comes back?' I can feel sobs accumulating somewhere in my throat, a great wave of them, waiting to break.

'That's hardly likely,' Matt says gently.

'Is it?'

'Look,' he says, after another brief pause, 'are you really one hundred per cent sure that you saw someone?'

'Well, I think I did. I heard these sounds. I thought perhaps it was a cat—'

'But did you take a really good look at this person?'

'No! I mean, the face was there just for a fraction of a second. And then he was gone.'

'So how did he get up there?'

'It's that stupid fire escape, why can't you—' I stop mid-sentence, a speeding car slamming on its brakes: I am about to screech at him to shut up. I cannot bear any more questions. I want to yell. Just take me seriously!

But, oblivious to this, Matt pushes on: 'So you would have heard him climbing down, then running along the pavement, wouldn't you?' he says, in his reasonable, grown-up voice. 'If he had been scared away . . .'

'I didn't hear anything,' I mumble.

'Because you know what this reminds me of . . .'

But he does not need to finish, for I have just remembered it too. Four or five years ago, when he was away at a conference, I woke convinced that there was someone downstairs in our house and, in a panic, dialled 999. The subsequent police search yielded nothing but my own red-faced apologies. There was no one hiding under my bed or in the cupboard, as I had imagined, and no sign of a forced entry. I had imagined the whole thing, there could have been no other explanation.

That I have only just recalled this shows the extent of my shame and how vehemently the memory has been repressed. And now that Matt has begun to question me like this, my memory shudders with doubt, like an old banger with a blocked exhaust. There *was* a face, wasn't there? Or could it have been the moon, glimpsed through parting clouds and refracted through the glass? And the sudden movement I saw, by the edge of the window, perhaps that was an animal, rather than a human prowler. It does indeed seem odd that there was no clang of the ladder as the man climbed back down, or a rush of footsteps retreating down the road.

'Do you think I imagined it?' I whisper.

'You *do* get jumpy sometimes, Cassie. That's all I'm saying.'

'Perhaps you're right,' I reply weakly. I feel like a little girl, being stroked and soothed.

'Look,' he says, in his let's-fix-it voice. 'You've got all the windows and doors locked, right?'

'Right.'

'Then try to forget about it for now. Tomorrow you can see if it looks like someone's been trying to get in. But now you need to go back to bed.'

'OK, Daddykins.'

'There! You're feeling better already, aren't you?'

'I suppose so.' I attempt a smile. 'Yes, I am.' I pull myself up, feeling our conversation draw to a close. He has done his best to reassure me, treated me kindly and not snapped at being woken up, but I feel more alone than ever. 'I'm so sorry to wake you up,' I say. My pulse is normal, my voice steadier. I am cold, in need of my bedcovers.

'I'll call you again tomorrow morning, OK?' he says gently.

'Matt?'

'Yes?'

I was going to tell him that I still loved him, but then he gives a little sigh, and I swallow it back. I know what the sigh signifies, *Silly old Cass, in a muddle again,* and as I picture him putting down the phone and turning back to the bed it is as if he is hurtling unstoppably away from me, into the vortex of our separation. And however much I do not want this to happen, I am unable to stop it.

'Thanks,' I whisper.

10

I give a cry of confusion and sit up. I was dreaming about the cliff again, and now somewhere, from the other side of the door, I can hear a buzzer.

I am in Brighton, safe in my bed. My terror at being pursued, the vista of the sea beneath the cliff and the rushing of air in my ears were a dream. Yet now that I flop back against the pillows, I also remember that something unpleasant – I cannot yet recall what – took place last night. I gaze round the room, struggling to clear my mind, but like damp cobwebs, my muddled dreams cling on. What was it that scared me so? I grope on the floor for my watch, see that it is nearly nine o'clock and suddenly remember: there was a face, staring in at me from the roof in the kitchen.

There it is again, the buzzing sound. Pulling my dressing-gown around my shoulders I stumble blearily into the hall. Someone, most likely a Jehovah's Witness or an ex-convict with a bagful of second-rate dusters, must be downstairs pressing the bell to my flat. Yet before I can press 'talk' on the intercom, I see the outline of a head appear in the frosted-glass of my front door. For a shuddery moment I picture the face on the roof and my throat constricts, but then I hear a soft female voice say, 'Cass?' and, reaching for the lock, I pull it open.

To my inordinate relief, the person standing on the other side is Beth Wilson. She is holding a bunch of pink and purple stocks in one hand, a rattan bag in the other, and regarding me cheerfully.

'Good morning!' she chirps.

I stand aside, both surprised and pleased. I have no memory of arranging a meeting with her here this morning, and would normally be irritated by a student's unexpected arrival at my home, especially so early. Yet right now there is no one I would rather see. I look into her bright, smiling face, and feel myself relax a little: a youthful female presence, and lots of bright talk of work is just what's required.

'Your neighbour let me in downstairs,' she burbles, as she undoes her denim jacket and strolls into the sitting room. 'I've got all my papers and stuff with me . . . I don't know where to start with it all so it'll be good to get your views.' She stops. 'You did mean to meet up here rather than at the uni, didn't you?'

'Er . . .'

She spins round, clamping her hands to her mouth in a parody of embarrassment. 'Oh, God, you didn't, did you? You meant in your office. Duh! Beth Wilson, you are a *prat*!'

I chortle, walking behind her into the sitting room. I remember something about a meeting, but she is right that my intention was that it should take place in my office. 'Don't worry about it,' I say lightly. 'I should have made it clearer. Anyway, it's probably just as well you've come to me because, as you can see, I've overslept.'

Early-morning light falls to the ground from the french windows in spinning, dust-filled columns. It is more pleasant to hear a carefree young voice in the flat than I could possibly have anticipated. I have been spending too much time alone, I think dourly. It is loneliness that is making me so jumpy.

'Hey,' Beth is saying, 'this could be really nice!'

'Hmm. *Could* being the operative word.'

As my student casts her critical gaze around my new home I am uncomfortably aware of how squalid it must appear: the piles of books and papers, the empty plates on long-abandoned dinner trays, the dreg-filled mugs that increasingly cover the mantelpiece. I have always strenuously denied it, but perhaps Matt is right after all: he *does* do all the housework. And now, along with the keys, I've lost my mobile. Why am I always in such a muddle? At least in London I have Matt and his domestic systems to keep me in order: the conveniently placed hooks for keys; the phone numbers stored on our mobiles and PC; the lists of Things To Do that he would scribble on the kitchen blackboard. But since I have been here I have increasingly succumbed to the demons of chaos.

'I've brought breakfast,' Beth says brightly, setting her bag down in the middle of the room. 'All we need is some coffee.'

I grimace: all I have is an almost empty jar of instant. Matt is the coffee-maker in our house, obsessively measuring the quantities of grains and water in our percolator as if the production of good coffee were rocket science. If he could see the contents of my cupboards, he would be dumb-founded. But, hey, I remind myself, Beth is a *student*, not the ever-critical Matt.

'Here we go,' she says, squatting on the floor and pulling items from her bag. '*Pains au chocolat*, some yummy warm bread, freshly squeezed orange juice and some mangoes they had going cheap.'

'You shouldn't have gone to all this trouble,' I mutter. Despite the eager gurgling of my stomach, her extravagance is misjudged. It is I, the tutor, who should be providing the food, and she, the student, who should be gratefully receiving it: the unexpected rearrangement of our roles makes me feel uncomfortable.

'Give me a break!' She gives me a cheeky smirk. 'This is the undergraduate equivalent of bringing Teacher a shiny red apple.'

I laugh, reaching for one of the pastries. So what if she's overdone it?

'Well, I'm horrified that you've caught me in this terrible old dressing-gown. I really ought to get dressed before you start telling me about your work.'

She gives me a long, appraising stare. 'The colour really suits you.'

'Get out of it!'

I leave her in the sitting room and, gobbling a second *pain au chocolat*, go to get changed. When I return five minutes later, with two mugs of tea, two plates and two glasses for the orange juice, she is standing at the mantelpiece, arranging the flowers in an empty milk bottle. The food spread on the carpet has not been touched.

'Do you have a vase?'

''Fraid not.'

'Never mind.'

I watch her fussing with the flowers, which have already filled the room with their sweet fragrance. Unlike her esteemed tutor, she obviously derives satisfaction from domestic order.

'So how did you know where I lived?' I ask. She has finished with the flowers now and, after scrutinizing the marble mantelpiece, decides on the best spot and carefully sets down the bottle.

'Your secretary told me,' she replies, turning with a smile. She is wearing baggy jeans, which sag over her hips, and a tight little jumper that shows off her small round breasts. Her hair is tied back and she has smudged some colour round her eyes.

I blink at her. '*Did* she?'

'Yeah, she was, like, totally cool about it. You don't mind, do you?' She looks at me inquisitively, cocking her head to one side like a small garden bird, then pads across the room and sits down beside me, folding her hands in her lap as she watches me reach for another slice of bread. Well, I might say, I don't really *mind*, but I am a little surprised at Maggie's relaxed attitude. In my old place, students were viewed in rather the same light as the British state views asylum-seekers: they knew they had to let them in, but they were to be held at arm's length, dealt with during office hours and by the most lowly officials, certainly not made friends with and invited home. But perhaps Maggie's happy dispensing of my home address is a sign of a friendly, open institution rather than the sloppy administration it would signify in London.

'No,' I say. 'I don't mind at all. In fact, it's rather nice having someone here, cheering the place up.'

She grins like a little girl receiving praise. 'Don't you like living alone?'

'It's fine . . .' I hesitate. The urge to confide is impossible to resist. 'I guess it's just that sometimes it can get a little creepy.'

'Creepy?' She eyes me, waiting for more, and suddenly I am unable to stop myself.

'Last night I even thought there was someone staring at me through the window.'

I give a hearty guffaw, already feeling better: now that I have spoken the words they sound ridiculous. But Beth's eyes widen and, like me on the kitchen steps last night, she places her hand over her mouth.

'Oh!'

'There wasn't really anyone there,' I say lightly. 'I'm sure I just imagined it. Isn't that stupid?'

'But you saw someone?'

'No, of course I didn't. That's just it. I had a bad dream and imagined it. It was probably just a reflection of the moon.' I am on the verge of forcing out another loud guffaw but stop, ashamed at exposing myself like this.

Beth stares at me empathetically, her eyes round and bright. '*God*. Isn't that what happened to that girl?'

The way she says this makes the goosebumps rise along my arms. 'What girl?'

'You know, that girl at the university? Where she woke up in her study-bedroom and this guy was, like, standing in the corner of the room, staring at her?'

I was about to take another bite of the bread, but the crust remains unchewed in my rigid hand.

'He got in through the window,' Beth adds. 'While she was asleep.'

'Jesus,' I whisper. 'What happened?'

Beth shrugs. 'It was a while back,' she says, 'but I think she was killed.'

I gaze at her, my mind stalling. At last I move my hand to my mouth and put some bread inside it. I masticate it mechanically, wishing I had never told her about my prowler.

'Aren't you going to have some of this delicious loaf?' I eventually manage to say.

She shakes her head apologetically. 'I'm allergic to wheat.'

'Oh dear!' I grimace at her, no further comment to make.

'Don't worry,' Beth says. 'I never have breakfast anyway.'

'Good God. You must be mad.'

Finally the tension is broken. For no real reason we both laugh, relieved to have changed the subject.

'I'm not really supposed to have dairy, either,' Beth adds, taking a tiny sip of tea.

'Blimey.' I chomp my food self-consciously; I feel like someone on a nudist beach who has enthusiastically stripped only to find that everyone else has kept their clothes on, claiming that sunbathing causes cancer. It is lucky that Matt is not here for, like homeopathy and macrobiotics, people's alleged food allergies are apt to elicit from him a fit of ranting that makes him sound like an intellectual Alf Garnett rather than an urbane academic. It's what he terms 'the new irrationality' and it drives him into a slathering state of fury: otherwise intelligent and educated people's fervent belief in something he judges to be only one step up from applying leeches to feverish skin, or forbidding menstrual women to milk the cows.

'It makes one very lethargic, you know. I mean, all the toxins,' Beth is saying. 'You really should try cutting them out. It isn't so bad once you get over the first few weeks. If you like I'll come and cook you a vegan, wheat-free meal.'

'Crikey.'

'No, really, you'd love it.'

I hope my face does not register my total absence of enthusiasm. Like Matt, I have always loved to eat all the meat, cream, butter and cheese that life has to offer. In fact, when we first met we made three solemn pledges to each other, our anti-wedding vows. The first was that we would never call each other by cutesy pet names; the second that we would always leave the washing-up until the morning after; and the last was that any food in which health rather than taste was the main objective would be banned from the kitchen.

'So,' I say, wiping my mouth and setting down my plate, 'what about this project?'

'It's about women's history over the twentieth century,' she says, reaching for her bag. 'I mean, I know it's a bit early in the term for thinking about our projects and everything, but I got so inspired by the seminars.'

I sit back, folding my arms. Inspiration is not a term usually used by my students. 'Why don't you just tell me what you want to do?'

'Right.' She takes a breath, gathering her thoughts. 'It's a bit like your research. I mean, I know I couldn't do anything as good as that, but I was thinking of interviewing all the women in my family about how they thought women's position in society had changed over their lives. Like, my

96

gran and her sister? They both still live in Yorkshire, where my mum comes from. And then, there are these papers . . .' She rummages in her basket and pulls out a folder. 'These letters were written by my great-grandmother to her husband, during the war. She was a nurse, based in London?'

'Fab.'

She is still rootling around, her fringe flopping over her forehead. She has pimples there, I notice, which she has carefully disguised with foundation. The makeup does not fit with her otherwise tomboyish appearance and I wonder if she is aware of how much the tan-coloured foundation stands out against her pale skin.

'There's a whole wad of them. All about the bombing and how it was for her. She had small children, too.'

'They sound fascinating,' I say, genuinely interested. 'I'd love to see them.'

'It's just amazing how women lived, isn't it? I mean, my grandma really held her family together. She would never have said she was a feminist or anything, in the political sense, but she was so, like, strong. That's what I want to capture.'

She has stopped searching for the letters and sits back, gazing at me with shiny eyes. I have just remembered that, however inappropriate the setting, I am meant to be teaching her. It's odd, but she has the knack of making me forget that she is the student and I am the tutor.

'You'll have to do some reading on feminist historiography,' I start. 'I'll give you a bibliography once we're back in my office.'

'God, that would be so brilliant.'

'No letters, then?'

'I must have left them at home. Beth the Prat strikes once more.'

'It would be good to set your own historiography down with comparative work –' I go on, but she interrupts me.

'Is that something you've considered? Writing about your own family?'

'Er, no.'

'How so?'

I swallow back the unpleasant smarting emotion I get whenever I am asked about my family. A part of me would like to tell her to mind her own business, and if we were sitting in my office I might say something brusque about getting back to the point, but here in my sunny flat such a response seems rude. 'They're all dead,' I say, and feel my face swamp red at the childish lie. Dr Bainbridge, the eminent academic, making up porkies in front of a student. *Completely pathetic.*

Beth's eyes open wide. 'Oh!'

I want to grab the words out of the air and stuff them back into my mouth, but it is too late. Opposite me, on the dusty carpet, Beth is regarding me with wonderment. 'So you're an orphan, then?'

I am overcome with shame. Supposing she discovers I have been lying? How will I ever explain? And then, before I can stop it, I picture my mother's letters, folded away in a wad among my books. I have never answered a single one. But neither have I thrown them away.

'Let's think more about some key readings,' I blurt, desperate to change the subject, but Beth ignores me.

'How did they die?' she whispers. 'Was it a car crash, or something?'

I give her a limp smile, my mind crowding with half-truths. Even the part of it that is not a lie I rarely speak of. Yet here I am, opening my mouth and saying, 'My dad died of lung cancer when I was fifteen.'

How is it that a simple statement of fact, a row of words arranged one after the other, can evoke such powerful emotions? I smile unconvincingly, trying to make it sound as if it no longer matters.

'How *terrible*!'

'Silly bugger smoked a packet of Player's a day, so it was hardly surprising.'

I am reaching for her folder, my lips still rigidly upturned. I would have done almost anything to avoid it, but now I am picturing Dad that Christmas his illness got the better of him, sitting propped beside the TV, coughing so hard he retched, as Bruce Forsyth's Christmas special blared in the background.

'Now let's go back to thinking about this.'

But she is like a terrier with a dead rabbit: she refuses to let go. 'And your mum?'

'Similar scenario.'

I pick up the folder, open it and gaze at the contents, but all I see is Dad's grey face. 'It's a long time ago,' I say briskly.

'How incredibly sad.'

She studies me with such sorrow that I'm afraid she is about to burst into tears. 'It's not a big deal. Not any more.'

'No, it is. I know what it's like.'

I look up, surprised by the change in her voice. She squares her shoulders, and tips back her face so that I cannot avoid her eyes, then speaks in a low, confidential voice. 'I don't usually tell anyone this. But I don't have any real family either.'

I scrutinize her features, which she is trying hard to control, hating myself even more. How terrible that my cowardly lying has propelled her to confess her own intimacies. 'But your mum,' I say hopefully, 'and your grandma?'

'Not my own. They just foster me. That's why I have to be careful with this project, you know, not to alienate them in any way.'

'Oh, God, yes. Of course . . .'

I wish she would stop, but she continues talking, her voice low and matter-of-fact, as if she was explaining something mundane and unimportant.

99

'I've only been living with them for a couple of years. In the family before, I had to be taken away because the dad became abusive.'

'Jesus!' I goggle at her. *The poor girl!* I cannot think what to say, just want desperately to reach out and squeeze her hand.

But suddenly she is standing up and brushing imaginary crumbs from her jeans. 'It's not a big deal,' she whispers, smiling bravely. 'I wish I hadn't brought it up. I mean, Sue and John are really great. They give me what affection they can, and that's enough for me. Their own daughter was killed in a car crash, so I'm kind of helping them with the grieving process?'

'But that must be so difficult for you . . .'

'It's cool.' She shrugs. 'That's why I don't like to move out of their house? I mean, what with all the loss they've had and stuff. I know everyone else at uni is having a ball sharing houses and everything, but I like to stay close to them. That's another reason why I'm studying here, not at Harvard.'

'They must be incredibly grateful.'

She gives me a sad smile. 'I don't know if they'd see it like that. I mean, I'm the grateful one. At least there's someone I can think of as family now, even if they're not officially fostering me any more. I'm, like, way too old?'

She stands in the middle of the room, looking towards the french windows and the sea beyond. Our short meeting seems to be at an end. Since I have nothing useful to add about her foster-parents, I am about to wind up the session by instructing her to come and get the bibliography from me at the university when the phone rings.

'Oh, God! Where's it gone?'

I jump up, trying to locate the cordless handset among the detritus. Whoever is ringing has provided me with a welcome excuse to end our awkward exchange. Yet as I glance round the room, I see that Beth already has it in her hands and to my slight surprise has already pressed 'talk'. Just as earlier, when she arrived with my breakfast, my thoughts run along cross-cutting tracks: I am annoyed at the presumption of an intimacy, or equality, that is not supposed to exist between tutor and student, yet at the same time I don't really mind. In fact, it's quite sweet that she feels so relaxed.

'Cass Bainbridge's place,' she says, winking at me. Then: 'She's right here.'

I take the phone from her, pulling a face, which is supposed to put her gently in her place but most probably makes me look as if I have wind. I am expecting it to be Matt, calling to check that I am OK. 'Hello?'

'Cass? It's Julian here. Julian Leigh?'

My heart does a strange little jump. 'Julian!' My voice sounds high and girlie, presumably in embarrassment at the way I snapped at him yesterday. 'How are you?'

'I'm good, but I wanted to say I'm sorry if I upset you yesterday.'

This is not what I was expecting. Since the first day of term I have had him down as cocky, the kind of guy who habitually drives too fast, flashing cars into the slow lane as he does business deals on his mobile. Certainly I was not expecting an apology for a miscommunication so subtle it could not even be termed a row.

'It's fine.' I take a deep breath, hoping that Beth is not listening. 'I'm sorry too. I was tired and grumpy.'

He pauses. I get the impression that he is nervous, for when he next speaks he stammers slightly. 'I just feel we've got off on the wrong foot and I want to make it up to you. I know I can sometimes go over the top, joking around and everything, especially when I'm, er, "keen to impress".' He gives a strange, strangulated laugh.

'Right . . .' I say slowly.

'So, I was just wondering . . . if you'd, er . . . like to come out with me some time. I keep trying to call you, but you never pick up.'

I catch a glimpse of Beth's face. As she meets my eyes, she puts her hand on her stomach and pretends to retch. It's odd, because I'd assumed that Julian was popular with students. Yet the moment she does this, my emotions switch from a pleasant warmth at being asked for a date to a swamping shame that I am considering agreeing to it. She is right, I remind myself. He's so awkward with me, as if he harbours a secret perversion.

'So it was you last night?' I say coldly, remembering the incessant, almost obsessive ringing, but not quite believing he could sink so low.

'Was it? I don't know.'

'It's just that someone keeps calling, then putting the phone down.'

'Not guilty.'

No, I think, he is obviously not that mad.

'We could go for a walk or see a film . . .' he adds hopefully, but I have already made up my mind. It is time to be honest.

'I don't know,' I say, turning slightly so that Beth cannot hear. 'The thing is, I'm in a relationship.'

'Oh!' He sounds surprised and somewhat affronted, as if I have just whipped off my dress to reveal that I am a man.

'But I'll see you later, at work, OK?' I say hastily. And before I have to hear any more of his disappointment, I put down the phone.

11

After Beth has gone I sit by the window. I do not have to teach until after lunch, and now can barely energize myself to move, far less clear up and drive to work. I keep thinking about those letters, the ones I have secretly kept, and how I lied about my family. When I move, I find myself standing and walking hastily to my bedroom, where I jerk open the top drawer of the stripped-pine dresser in the corner and pull out a heavy book buried under my socks and pants.

It is a 1929 copy of the *Complete Works of William Shakespeare*, given to me by my grandfather on my eleventh birthday. I hold it in my hands, feeling the battered red covers, crumbling at the corners, and the embossed golden lettering. For a moment I gaze down at it, my fingers stroking the wedge of gold-edged pages. My grandfather was awarded it at school, and inside the cover is a yellowed plaque, written in careful copperplate: 'Heathview Boys Preparatory: Presented to Alfred Bainbridge, First Place in Latin Examinations, September 1930'.

I have not read the contents; that is not the point of such a book. My A level Shakespeare was gleaned from a series of cheaply produced paperbacks, over which one could guiltlessly scribble notes in the margins and underline speeches with green marker pen. Rather than constituting the sum of its contents, this book is one of those artefacts I described in my lecture: an aid to memory, part of family history, an object to be passed down over the generations. I turn the first few pages, glancing at a coloured portrait of

Shakespeare looking amused, then let the book fall open in the middle, where the letters are stored.

There are four altogether, plus the one from David. I have not looked at them for years: it is enough just to know they are there, the door shut, but the key not yet thrown away. As I pull them out, unfolding the thick wodge, my hands are trembling.

The letter from David is not so hard. I must have read it at least five or six times, but despite my good intentions – such as the unsent birthday card in my handbag and various half-hearted attempts to find his phone number – I have never replied. I peer at the address, imagining what his home is like. A low white house with a veranda and a neat front lawn in a street somewhere in Sydney, the sunlight white and relentless, the sounds of water-sprinklers and kids playing. There'd be birdsong too – what do they have in Australia? Kookaburras? And, in the evening, the low chant of crickets. Unlike me, David's escape has been happy, and non-confrontational: in contrast to his unruly sister, he has always played at being the good, well-balanced son.

'Dear Cass,' I read, my eyes skimming over sentences I know by heart. 'How are you?'

As you can see, I've moved. I've got a new job, working for a big IT company, with a whacking salary and all the perks (you should see my car, this year's BMW!). It's all a bit of a step up from the Sunblest factory, ha ha. So we've finally taken the great leap from our cute flat near the harbour to a four-bedroom house in the 'burbs. The other great news is that Clare is expecting. Baby's due in the spring . . .

Izzy will be three by now, I think grimly. There may even be a younger sibling. I stop reading, skipping the bit where he writes: 'It's been a while now since we've heard from you. Mum said she heard you on the radio, talking about your East

End women. So we know you're still out there somewhere. It would be good to hear your news . . .'

At the end he has written, 'all the best, David', rather than the 'love and kisses' I had remembered. How typical that he should sign off like that, as if it were a note to a colleague or a barely remembered acquaintance. I let the letter rest on my lap, gazing unseeingly at the neat script, the way he has printed his name in capitals, as if to jog my memory. The letter evokes a weary combination of sadness and guilt, the double-headed monster that accompanies me wherever I go. I should have written back, of course I should. I kept intending to, but with every month that passed it became increasingly difficult to know where to start. After this letter came the card announcing Izzy's birth, then nothing. I suppose he is in a huff that I have not responded to his overtures. He can find out easily enough on the web where I work, so must know that I have received his letters. Perhaps he is angry; he must at the very least feel hurt at my rebuttal. What, I wonder, does he tell himself about why I am behaving so badly? What does he remember?

After the summer when we found the Mermaid's Purse, there were no more holidays by the sea. Something had happened, for Mum started working full-time at the surgery, and her face assumed the harassed quality that I associate with those later years: worn and tired, her eyes distracted. We moved, too, from a more generous house overlooking the village green to a boxy, Barratt Homes two-bedroomed thing in one of the 'closes' that were increasingly spreading around the edge of the village. In retrospect, I think Dad must have lost his job around this time, for I remember him being at home more than usual, picking us up from school and cooking us our tea while Mum was out at work. Unlike her, he never shouted at us about the food we spilt around our plates or forbade us to put our elbows on the table: he was soft as rancid butter, she would say, returning late and cross, and surveying the wrecked kitchen.

I loved him that way. After my bath I would climb on to his lap, and we would read together: *The Hobbit*, the Narnia books, Jennings and E. Nesbit. He would play with us for hours too, while Mum soon grew impatient and bored by the childish complexities of our fantasy games, the goodies and the baddies, the precariously constructed camps and secret codes. What I suppose constituted a lack of drive in the adult world made him a good parent to my clingy, insecure eight-year-old self. He should have been the mum, I remember saying, and him laughing, but in a way that made it obvious it was not something he wanted to hear. He was not a twenty-first-century house-husband. In the 1970s they had yet to be invented, at least among the provincial lower-middle classes. He should have been the provider, not Mum, and 'babysitting', as she scornfully referred to it, was women's work.

But our closeness was not confined to that brief period of unemployment. Ever since David's birth it had been Dad and me versus David and Mum. I suppose that's the way it goes: the new baby demanding the mother's attention and, almost by default, the older child ending up with the father. Yet rather than being temporary, in our case it was a pattern that, over the years, became increasingly established. Mum had always made it clear that she preferred David's company to mine. He was a 'terrifically easy' baby, or so she endlessly told people, quite the opposite of her *first*. Where I was squally and unsettled, David was placid and content; where I demanded more milk than her body could provide, she breastfed a blissful David until he was almost one. Where I refused to walk, be potty-trained or to sleep through the night, David approached each developmental hurdle just as he was to approach his later life: with ease, confidence and accomplishment. He was always so 'laid-back' – that was the received wisdom in our family. And, in contrast, I was always so difficult.

Or, at least, that is how I remember it. But I am enough of a professional to know that memory is a self-obsessed, moody beast; it chooses what it wants from the past and moulds it to its own narcissistic concerns. And these days I no longer communicate with anyone whose own memories might hold mine in check. I refold David's letter and as I open the Shakespeare to tuck it back inside a Christmas card falls out.

Merely looking at the writing chills me, but I cannot stop myself picking it up and opening it. On the front is a blodgy picture of a robin, probably painted by someone with special needs; it's the sort of charity card my mother would buy in bulk then stockpile at the back of her desk. *Merry Christmas!* Underneath the cheery greeting, she has written in small, tight lettering: 'I hope this finds you well. Please send me your new address, if you have moved. Love from Mum.'

How did she expect the card to reach me if I had moved? Or did she know from David that I was still working at the University of London, and write this as a coded rebuke? I reread the message, then rebury it in its literary mausoleum. Joining it there are other, longer notes, mostly giving David's news. One recounts in detail the funeral of a cousin of hers whom I don't think I ever met, another describes a garden in the West Country she had recently visited. Her letters are impersonal and blank, telling me virtually nothing about herself. And then, about two years ago, they stopped.

After a while Dad had found another job, but it must have been less well paid than the first, because there were still no holidays and Mum kept on at the surgery. I moved from the village school, where I had known the name of every pupil and spent most of my time doing 'projects' on horses, to a large, rough comprehensive in town where we were streamed and had proper lessons on chemistry and geography, and homework was set. I hated it at first, not because the work was too demanding but because the place scared me, inhabited as it was with teenagers in stomping great platforms and feather-cut hair who smoked in the toilets and tripped up the first years. It was the early days of punk, and some of the older girls painted their eyes with heavy black kohl, like adolescent Cleopatras, and wore safety-pins in their ears. I was still several years away from my own transformation from overweight village 'snob' to rebellious third-year, so my predominant memory of the first year is of cowering terror. The main thing was not to get noticed, but already someone had written 'Fatty' on my school bag, so things were not looking good.

It was during this year that the arguments with Mum started in earnest. Dad had been sucked back into the male world of work, and would not return until late, and suddenly it was just Mum, David and me, bickering over tea. Or, rather, David would sit quietly at the table, eating, and Mum and I would scream at each other. The issue that stood increasingly between us was her desire that I should lose weight. But after skipping lunch because I was too scared to pass the fourth-year bullies on the way to the canteen, by tea I was ravenously hungry. And so, at home, I hoovered up whatever I could. By the time I was twelve I was over ten stone and Mum had a diet sheet pinned to the fridge. No chips, no butter, no ice-cream, no cakes and no chocolates. No matter that I was now spending my school-dinner money on Mars bars and crisps from the ice-cream van that loitered like a drug-dealer outside the school gates. No matter that, like Mum, I was naturally tall and what she would term 'large-boned'. The fact was she wanted me to be different from the way I was.

There was one time in particular, which I still think of. For some reason that I cannot remember I had come home earlier than usual, perhaps I had got a lift with someone's mum rather than waiting for the bus. Whatever, Mum and David were clearly not expecting me, for as I dumped my bags by the door and stomped into the kitchen I saw a spread of forbidden foods laid out before my younger brother, like offerings before a deity. He had chocolate éclairs, French Fancies and doughnuts. Even more heinously, he was tucking into a plate of chips, which my mother had clearly just cooked.

So the apples and cottage-cheese sandwiches were a charade! Behind my back, my little brother was eating like a king, while I was being starved. I stood on the threshold of the room, gawping at them like the Little Match Girl. David and Mum looked up sheepishly, but not apologetically enough. I felt as if I had caught them plotting murder rather than eating an early tea. Eventually I whispered hoarsely, 'Can I have some?'

But my mother had already leapt to her feet and was clearing the table of its illicit contents, sweeping the cakes into a Tupperware box (so *that* was what she kept in those boxes!), and scooping David's plate away.

'Don't be silly, Cassandra,' she replied. 'You know it's not allowed.'

'But I'm *hungry*!'

'There's plenty of bread and butter, and I got you some nice apples.'

'But David's eating it!'

At the mention of his name my brother frowned and forked some more chips into his mouth. A splodge of ketchup had landed on his jumper, and his mouth was smeared with grease, which he now wiped on the back of his sleeve. He was six and obsessed with the Brio trains that he spent all afternoon driving into elaborate crashes. At that age we hardly spoke to each other, much less played together. Our interaction consisted mainly of brief but violent skirmishes with pillows or fists, which invariably resulted in me being sent to my room and David getting a cuddle from Mum. I was nearly twelve, so I suppose I should have known better than to beat up my baby brother.

What my mother said next is something I have never forgotten. Even now, as I try to put myself in her place and imagine what I would do with an overweight and bullied twelve-year-old girl, the words stick in my gullet. 'David,' she said, very slowly and deliberately, 'is different from you. And that is why he is allowed to have food that you are not.'

I should have grown out of these playground emotions. I should not feel this hot clutch of jealousy over a plate of chips. I should be able to laugh it off, put it in perspective. Why is that not possible?

Dear Mum

Here are some things about my history (but not what I'd say in class).

After you left me, they put me in foster care, then eventually arranged for me to be placed in a home. I wasn't a cute little baby by then, but a truculent four-year-old, not the kind of prospect that many adoptive parents would want. Apparently I was an unsettled kid, always screaming and fussing and waking in the night. The various people who looked after me did what they could, but I have never had a home, not like the ones real families have.

I hope you would not be ashamed of me. Despite my shaky start, I have always done everything I was asked. I've been a good child, passed my exams, kept away from trouble. I find it hard to trust or make attachments, it is true. And sometimes I am overtaken by a rage so powerful I want to hit out at something, cause someone else this pain. And when the blackness comes upon me, all I can think is: what did I do to make you reject me?

So, it's my birthday today! But you already know that, don't you?

12

It is Week Five, the deepest league of term, where the choppy waters that lap the harbour of Week One have receded into the distance and the calm lagoon of the Christmas vacation is not yet in view. However tumultuous the journey, there is no alternative but to toggle up one's oilskins, take a grip on the helm and proceed onwards.

Not, of course, that I am Ellen MacArthur, just another stressed-out academic, with too much work and too many students, who is trudging wearily towards Week Ten. That's when the students depart, leaving in their wake a residue of paperwork: reports to be written, term papers marked, miscellaneous bureaucratic forms filled out, until the Neverland of the vacation arrives. But that is still many weeks away. It is the middle of November, I have only taught half of Historical Methods, and am currently trapped in a faculty meeting, which, although it has progressed for most of the morning, still has five major items remaining on the agenda: barren bluffs to be scaled before the downhill race towards Any Other Business.

I am playing dead. I would not have dreamt of such behaviour in London, where I entered vociferously into debates concerning university policy, lobbed on-the-ball questions to the speakers at academic seminars, even cheerfully set up sub-committees on exam procedures. Yet for some reason, ever since I arrived here, my calmly considered opinions have evaporated and my confidence shrivelled.

I lean forward and start another doodle on the corner of the agenda. A cartoon monster currently covers most of

Item One, his bulging eyes protruding over the list of Apologies, his knobbly knees obscuring the note of congratulations to Dr Ruth Brown, who has recently had a baby boy. The side margin is covered with untidy spirals; a row of shoes decorates the bottom. It's juvenile behaviour, and I hope no one has noticed. I look up, trying to concentrate. Chairing the meeting is Bob Stennings, the dean of Social Sciences. He's a large, cheery chap: a geographer, whose speciality before taking on the deanship was the development of water resources in sub-Saharan Africa. Today he is crumpled into a checked shirt, corduroys and a knitted tie. As he stands and starts to talk at length about library resources I picture him as a colonial boffin in baggy khaki shorts, knee-length socks and walking boots. My mind wanders, a dream-like trance descending as my colleagues drone on. If each of them was an animal, I wonder, what would they be? Jenny Montgomery, the acerbic twenty-something young star of the history department, who has just made a witty remark concerning student admissions, is easy: a Siamese cat, smugly licking her paws. John Stanley, the weary head of graduate studies, is, without doubt, a crab, scuttling around the place with his popping eyes and bow-legged gait; Bob Stennings is obviously a Labrador. And Julian? I gaze in his direction, and realize that all this time he has been surreptitiously watching me. For a split second our eyes meet, then he looks away again. What animal would *he* be?

This play-dead strategy is one of diminishing returns. Every time Stennings asks for a volunteer to do something I fold my arms and stare resolutely at my wide lap. But now he is trying very obviously to catch my eye, and I can no longer avoid him. 'What do you think, Cass?'

I pull myself together, sitting up and returning his enquiring glance with what I hope appears as a bright and professional smile. I do not understand why I am behaving like this: I may be chronically untidy with a tendency towards mess, but until the last few weeks at least, I have always been an enthusiastic and obliging workmate.

'It's hard to say,' I chirp, trying to recall what the hell he was talking about, 'but I think in principle at least it seems a good idea.'

This seems to satisfy him. Around the table people nod and the meeting moves on. I turn the page of the agenda, determined to stop doodling. We are on Item Six, a lengthy document produced by the university management on campus security. The gist of this seems to be that because of various incidents in other universities – a girl raped in Oxford, a lecturer assaulted in Leeds – students and staff should have ID cards.

'Let's just go the whole hog and do strip searches before lectures,' Julian is saying. 'I mean, the first-years might be planning to hijack Contemporary Theory and the Other and drive it into Senate.'

There is a ripple of laughter, a dissenting cluck of disapproval from Madge Wernski, the frighteningly humourless American convenor of Social Policy, who is sucking her teeth and folding her arms across her vast bosom. From the disapproving looks she has been giving Julian since the beginning of the meeting his laconic, anti-PC posturing is not to her taste. Yet Julian is on a roll: 'Or how about police searches for faculty? Check none of us has any previous convictions for drug-trafficking or child porn. Heaven help us, we might corrupt the students.'

'You guys may poke fun, but it's no laughing matter to be raped,' Madge Wernski snaps. At this the assembled faculty, who were collectively slumping ever lower into their chairs and tittering at Julian's facetious remarks, gulp and sit up, rearranging their expressions.

'I mean a girl was violently *attacked*, not in some other

place but right *here*, only last term,' Madge hisses. Her neck is covered in crimson blotches, I notice, and as she glowers at Julian, her eyes flash dangerously. 'These ID cards are important. It's vital that we protect the women in our institution.'

Around the table people are nodding.

'So shall we approve the motion?' volunteers Bob Stennings.

Everyone's hands shoot up, and the meeting moves on. I now have my elbows on the table and am resting my chin on my knuckles, smiling at my assembled colleagues in a parody of attention, but remain unable to tether my thoughts to the matter in hand. The recollection of the girl being attacked has struck a discordant and unwelcome note, and now I am suffering from nervous palpitations. If only I could relax, but my thoughts keep cantering in all directions. I turn the page, staring unseeingly at a long memo headed 'MA Periodic Review: Ways Forward'.

I should take a break, I think, go to London and see Matt. But our communications have become increasingly distant and strained. My visit to London was postponed, another planned trip by him to Brighton cancelled because he said he had flu. And now, whenever I start to dial his – our – number, something stops me. He never listens, that is the problem. Were I to tell him of the various incidents that have taken place over the last few weeks his main objective would be to prove me mistaken, a silly little girl with her knickers in a twist. The phone calls, which now follow a predictable pattern, kicking off at about six p.m., then stopping at half past eight, he would dismiss as a nuisance, the disappearance of my mobile and my keys as meaningless, and the thing that frightened me most as daffy old Cass 'getting in another muddle'.

It happened last Wednesday. I came home late after the

departmental seminar and, climbing the stairs to my flat, saw with a shock that my front door was ajar. I was sure I had locked it when I left in the morning. In fact, as I pushed it open and stepped inside I could clearly remember slamming it shut as I had hurried out.

My immediate thought was that I had been burgled. But as I nervously explored the flat I could find nothing missing. My CD player remained in the sitting room, my purse – which contained its full complement of credit cards – lay on the mantelpiece. And the Shakespeare – which I was suddenly desperate to locate – was still hidden under the underwear in my bedroom drawer. The only thing that was different, and thinking of it still makes my guts tighten, was my laptop. I had not worked on it the evening before, I am positive. In a rare fit of tidy-mindedness, I had stored it away in its case by the door. But now, as I tiptoed into the kitchen, I saw that it was lying on the table, its screen unfolded and switched on, the screen-saver spiralling into different shapes.

I did not have the courage to discover what lay beneath the spirals. Perhaps it was foolish, but I leapt up the kitchen steps, pulled the plug out of the socket and turned the damn thing off. Since then I have not been able to open it.

Did *I* leave it there? I am sure this is what Matt would assert. What other explanation could there be? Yet although I have not told him any of this and he has not been given the chance to respond, I am, I now realize, increasingly irked by his inability to take my fears seriously. I know I am not being fair, yet the insurmountable anger, the sense that I need to break away, remain.

Finally the meeting ended. I have returned to my room, and am huddled among the ever-growing piles of papers on my desk. Since this morning, four new emails have appeared. I look over them with jaded languor.

Hi, Cass. Is it OK if I come and see you very briefly this afternoon about today's seminar presentation? I promise I shan't take up much of your time!
Love from Beth

I press 'reply', thinking of last week's seminar. Besides Alec, whose grudging explication of the week's texts was nothing if not comprehensive, Beth was the only person who had done any reading. The others blushed and shuffled their feet when asked what they had done. Natalie had read a book, which was 'quite thick and had a green cover'. Oddly, she could remember nothing of the contents of this. Andy claimed flu, the others a rash of essays, due in for their Contextuals course. In another mood I would have ticked them off, or even refused to continue the class, but their lethargy was contagious. Leaning back in my chair, I peered at them with a jaundiced eye. 'Let's just break into groups and discuss the lecture.'

At this they slumped even further over their desks, a few actually groaned. Alec tutted, turning with haughty resignation towards his neighbours.

I felt a kick of shame at that, for up until recently I had been proud of my teaching, but now it seemed that only Beth was excited at the prospect of such a discussion. She must have seen my expression for, glancing across the room at me, she winked sympathetically. Forty minutes later, after the class had sat in their groups in virtual silence for twenty minutes and we had staggered through a dismal plenary session where I repeated part of the lecture, the students filed out gloomily and she was the only person left behind.

'I couldn't believe they didn't do anything!' she muttered, as she helped me rearrange the classroom furniture. 'It must be such a nightmare when everyone's so lazy. And then they wouldn't even talk properly about the lecture!' She shook her head sanctimoniously.

I gave her a tired grimace. I had been teaching all morning and had a headache. 'Well, not everyone. At least you and Alec are hard workers.'

At this, she merely chuckled, picked up her bag and books and stepped lightly towards the door. 'Can I come and see you later, like, at about four?'

But I had forgotten! Remembering the guilt-inducing note I had found on my door (*Oh dear, I must have missed you, never mind, love and kisses, Beth*) I type, 'Fine!' press 'send' and move my cursor down the line.

To: All faculty
From: Central admin
Re: Campus Security
As has already been reported in the press this morning, a student was attacked last night in the woodland by the Arts Building car-park. In light of this, and previous incidents, the university urges students and staff to be extra vigilant . . .

My heart lurches. Pressing 'delete' I move hastily to the next message.

Cass,
We need to discuss marks for the second-year methodologies assessments. As you know, the deadline was passed last week.
Bev Cope

Yikes! I had not realized I was so behind. And my co-examiner is Bev, a professor in Critical Studies whom I have yet to meet and who is famed for her crazed efficiency. I glance around the room, trying to locate the essays, and find that most have fallen behind the back of my desk. I shall have to mark them now, before this afternoon's seminar. Gazing back at the screen, I open the most recent email.

Dear Dr Bainbridge
I was wondering if you had marked my essay yet? It is now over four weeks since I gave it to you. As you know, this is the maximum amount of time which tutors are expected to take over their marking (as stated in the student handbook).
Regards
Alec Watkins

This last missive causes an unpleasant plunging sensation in my tummy. It is as if Alec were the tutor, ticking off his unruly student. My throat constricts. OK, so I have passed the deadline, but how dare he write to me like that? Without thinking, I hit 'reply'.

I shall mark your essay when I have the time. I might add that I do not like the tone of your email!
Cass Bainbridge

I press 'send', my hands wobbling furiously. Never before have I written such a curt email to a student. Friendly and approachable, those are my main attributes. I may not be a world-famous scholar, but I have always made a point of treating students with humane empathy rather than the dismissive arrogance of many of my more successful colleagues. Yet something about Alec turns me frosty and impatient. The way, for example, that he sits at the back, staring snootily out of the window, or jiggling his foot in irritation when the others try to speak, sets my teeth on edge. He always seems so critical. It is as if he has come to my seminars and lectures, sampled my wares, *knows* that I am not good enough and is just waiting for the right moment to attack.

Calm down, I tell myself. Alec is simply an awkward young man needing feedback. What I need to do is mark the bloody things and get both Alec and Bev Cope off my back. Placing the cursor over the last two emails, I press 'delete' and suddenly a fourth message flashes on to the screen. There is no title, just the name of the sender: *loveankisses@juniper*. Not thinking about what I am doing, I slide the cursor over it.

The message opens instantly.

I am in your thoughts
I am in your dreams
When you call for me, I shall not be where you THINK.

What *is* this nonsense? A circular? As I gaze at it in perplexity, I see that it is addressed solely to me. And there is an attachment too. And although I know I should not open it, that it might contain a virus and my irresponsible actions bring the entire campus to a standstill, I cannot stop myself. Clicking 'open', I gaze expectantly at the screen. It will be some joke, or maybe something Matt has sent, a way of ending the stand-off.

The computer hums and buzzes, chewing over the new information. As a box appears over the text of the message, a grainy image appears. I am expecting a cartoon, or perhaps joke pornography, with the heads of political leaders pasted on to a rutting couple, the kind of thing that often circulated in my last place of employment. What I find myself looking at, however, is a close-up of a face. The forehead is the first part to appear, framed by some fuzzy dark hair. Then there are eyes, and . . . *Christ!* My hands fly to my mouth in shock. It is a photograph of me.

For perhaps ten seconds I scrutinize the picture, my heart fluttering. The photograph is just of my face, no background or any other clue as to where I might be, or even what I am wearing. But it must have been taken recently, because those lines around my eyes have only appeared in the last few months. I am smiling, and have a slightly smug expression, like an updated, middle-aged version of the *Mona Lisa*. Swallowing heavily, I press 'delete'. I do not want to think about who might have sent it.

I turn away from the computer and, kneeling on the dusty acrylic carpet, scrabble around on the floor to retrieve the essays at the back of the desk. The email must be a student joke. All my colleagues have probably received the same thing. Yet, as I finally sink into my chair and stare at the opening paragraph of the first essay, I cannot shake off the sick, sinking sensation.

Sod it, I'm not going to think about this any longer. Around fifteen papers lie piled in front of me. Nearly all of the students have chosen to answer the first question on my list: *Discuss the relationship between the methods of historiography and historical content.*

I start to read the first with dutiful concentration. Turning the page, I gaze at the rounded, slightly childish handwriting. As I have always maintained, we lowly academic proletariat who are not able to command research grants large enough to save us from the rigours of teaching could save a great deal of time if we assessed our students' essays simply by the handwriting. Why bother ploughing through all five or six pages if all you need to know is on the first page? Neat and small, with short paragraphs, usually means a 2:2. The large, loopy stuff, with lots of crossings-out, is often a third; the very mad scribbles are more tricky, for they are either a fail or a first. The Higher Education Board for Teaching Standards may not approve of my methods, but from my brief perusal of this it is a mid-2:1. I reach the end of the paper, write some encouraging comments and useful pointers at the bottom and move on.

By the time I have reached essay number ten, two hours have passed and my eyes are swimming. Finally I reach Alec's piece. Typically this gives nothing away for it has been written on a word-processor. Clutching my red pen like a knife, I hold it critically over the opening paragraph. To be honest I am hoping that it will be terrible. But as I read, I feel an ambivalent mixture of pedagogic pleasure and juvenile jealousy. I was hoping that Alec might turn out to be one of those students to whom Matt, charming as ever, refers as 'all fart and no follow-through': the sort who are happy to spout lyrical in seminars, but cannot put an argument down on paper. But this is clearly not the case. As I continue to turn the pages, I see that it is one of the most sophisticated undergraduate papers I have ever read. He has clearly studied everything on my reading list, plus some erudite articles and books of which I was unaware. In fact, the level of argument is so elevated and his historical and philosophical knowledge so wide that the thought of him sitting through my lectures and participating in the mostly fumbling seminar discussions makes me cringe.

Swallowing my pride, I reach the beautifully argued concluding paragraph, and scribble: 'A+. This is truly brilliant. You have clearly been thinking very carefully about the issues we have covered so far and have added your own original contribution to the debate. I am extremely impressed.'

Taking a breath, I put down his paper and pick up the next. I am hoping Alec will not complain about the brevity of my comments, but his paper was so comprehensive that I can think of no improvements. Perhaps my compliments will pacify him and he will contribute to the seminar in a more positive manner. It's possible, but not probable. Glancing down at the pages I now hold in my hands I see Beth's rounded, girlie handwriting. 'What is feminist about doing oral history?' I read. Unlike Alec's paper, I want this to be good.

The essay does not disappoint. Beth writes fluently and with some verve, and although her argument is deeply familiar, I chuckle at the way she turns round the arguments of mainstream historians: 'Rather than checking oral histories against "established histories" for veracity, why not reverse the process, and check the latter against the former? This would surely undermine the power relations so deeply embedded in mainstream historiography'.

An excellent point, well made, but something about it bothers me. I tick the margin, wondering what it is. But before I am able to draw out the thought, the phone rings.

'Bev Cope here,' barks the voice at the other end. 'Look, I'm running between lectures and am off to the States tomorrow. Can we do these marks over the phone?'

I can feel the colour drain from my face. 'I'm just finishing a meeting with a student,' I lie. 'I'll call back in five minutes.'

Ten minutes later, having skim-read the rest of Beth's essay, plus Andy's, which luckily was only two pages long, I have agreed twelve marks with Bev. To my relief she showed no interest in discussing the content of the papers and our marks were almost identical. I enter them on the Examinations Office form, sign it, and fling it into the postbox in the departmental office. I should have given the marking more time, but hopefully no one will notice. Recovering from my unexpected burst of activity I am trying to galvanize myself to call Matt, when there is a bang on the door and Beth walks in.

I haven't seen her since last week's seminar, and she looks thinner, her face harried and strained. For a second I think there is something wrong, guiltily remembering the note she pinned to my door, but as soon as she sees me her expression lifts. 'Hiya!'

'Hello, Beth. I've just answered your message.'

She blinks, as if trying to remember what I am talking

123

about, then shrugs. 'Oh, God, don't *worry*! I know you must be up to your eyeballs.'

'So, what's up?'

She lingers in the doorway, her bag slung round her chest. She seems more shy than she is in the seminars, her expression uncertain and nervous, as if seeing me out of context has thrown her out of kilter. 'I just wondered if you'd like to come and have coffee with me, or something,' she mumbles. 'I mean, if you've got time . . .'

I look down at the essays, then out of the window at the golden autumn afternoon and suddenly yearn to be outside, the sun warming my face, in the company of somebody sweet and undemanding.

'OK, that would be lovely.'

Outside we find a bench and settle ourselves with the flask Beth has miraculously produced. There's a carrot cake too, which she has made herself. I swallow the moist orange slices greedily, slipping my hand into the waistband of my Maharishi pants to make more space. All this comfort eating has increased my girth by at least an inch.

It is a beautiful day. Above us, the trees have turned yellow and the air has a chilly bite, a hint of the winter about to arrive, but I could spend all morning sitting out here, sunning myself in the weak November rays. Around us, students drift happily towards their classes; I can hear the campus crows cawing and, far off, grass being mown. The sound reminds me of childhood summers: Dad with the lawnmower, David and I running in and out of the sprinkler.

'I hope you didn't do all this for me,' I say, as I lick the crumbs from my fingers. Next to me, Beth is nibbling on a tiny slice, like a little mouse.

'Oh, I love cooking. I do it all the time. It's not a hassle.'

'Well, it's delicious.'

She crumbles the cake between her fingers, wiping it from her jeans on to the grass. She has toyed with it in a pretence of eating without actually swallowing a mouthful. 'Am I keeping you from your work?'

I shake my head. 'To tell you the truth it's a relief to have a break. I've been marking essays and it's made me go a bit cross-eyed. Your classmate Alec Watkins took it upon himself to remind me that they're due back.'

I am being unfair, I know, for it was Bev Cope who jump-started me into the marking, but I am struck by a decidedly unprofessional urge to share my irritation over Alec. Beth's hand hovers over the last of the crumbs; she is still looking down, but her lips twitch into a small, pleased smile. 'He can be a bit of a pain, can't he?' she says, looking up at me. Her eyes are sparkling.

'Oh, he's *fine*,' I say, already trying to back-pedal. 'I guess he just always seems so critical . . .'

I would like to add more, but stop myself. I should not have hinted at my personal animosity towards Alec: after all, Beth is another student, not one of my colleagues. I am about to change the subject, when she adds: 'He's actually a bit of a weirdo. I mean, he spends his entire life in the computing room fiddling around.'

I raise my eyebrows archly. 'Fiddling around?'

She splutters with laughter, splattering tea over her lap. 'Not *that*!' She digs me in the ribs with her elbow and puts her hand over her mouth like a little girl caught saying rude words.

'What sort of fiddling are you referring to, then?'

'It's all these emails he's always doing. Then if you so much as walk past him to get to the printer he shouts at you to go away, like maybe he's writing ransom notes, or on some child porn site he doesn't want you to see.' She wipes at the spilt tea with her hands, her eyes suddenly serious. 'He really gives me the creeps.'

I pull a face, there being no obvious reply.

But she has not finished. 'It's quite embarrassing, actually. I mean, it's not just the way he is in the computing room. It's, like, the way he's acting about your course too.'

I grip my plastic cup, now paying complete attention. Perhaps I should be hastily changing the subject, for I am sure I will not like what I am about to hear, but I cannot stop myself swallowing and saying, 'Like what?'

Beth smirks. Of course she has no idea of the depth of my paranoia.

'Oh, you know,' she says lightly. 'All these things he's been saying about you and the course. I've been trying really hard to tell everyone not to listen, but he's very good at getting his views across.'

The words pierce my skin like arrows. I feel myself turn cold and then hot. 'What do you mean?' I am trying to hold it steady but, humiliatingly, my voice has gone all wobbly. 'What things has he been saying about me?'

'Just this and that. Silly stuff, really.' She laughs dismissively. Perhaps she is wishing she had not brought the subject up. She certainly can have no intimation of how pathetically insecure I am. Finally she says, 'Just about how it's really badly thought out and boring. He seems to think he could do it a whole load better.'

Her light, almost mocking tone makes it clear she does not take him seriously, but this is of little comfort. It is just as I suspected, I think, despair sinking deep into my belly. The cleverest student in the third year has seen through me and is now spreading the news: Cass Bainbridge does not cut the mustard. I feel as if I have been punched in the face; numb with the surprise of a violent ambush, the bruising already smarting. I try to swallow, but a large lump is lodged

126

in my throat. I should not care so much about Alec's opinion, and yet I do, desperately.

'Don't worry about him,' Beth says coolly. 'Pardon my French, but he's a wanker.'

'And what does everyone else think?'

I look into her untroubled face. To her, none of this matters much.

'Oh, God,' she says, sniggering. 'Who cares? Listen, Cass, your course is great, don't worry about it. Alec is just a prat. He just thinks he's superior to everyone.'

I nibble my lower lip. 'I suppose he can be a little annoying . . .' I mutter.

'He gets on everyone's nerves! Do you know what I call him? Android Alec!'

Despite myself, I titter into my plastic cup. Beth is right, I think, the humiliation of hearing second-hand criticism already subsiding. He's just a twit. 'Not Smart Alec?' I say faintly.

It is not remotely funny, but the puerile comment makes me feel a good deal better, especially when Beth splutters with laughter.

'Well,' I say, finally allowing my bruised feelings to override my professional judgement, 'at least I've got *some* nice students in the group.' I give Beth's knee a little squeeze and stand up. The flow of students moving towards Block D has increased, the ebb and flow of the day marshalled by the magnetic pull of the lecture halls. Beth rises too. We have only been sitting out here for ten minutes or so, but during that time I have become unintentionally in league with her, the two of us against the Smart Alecs of the world.

'Yeah,' she says, giving me a wink. 'And you don't ever need to worry about what *I* think.'

I give her a little look. OK, Missy, so I've let my guard down. Don't push it. But from the broad grin she flashes back, its subtleties are lost. As we turn towards the staircase I half expect her to take my hand and skip along beside me: Look, everyone! Cass is *my* friend! But naturally she does nothing of the kind, just trills, ''Bye,' then lollops away from me across the grass.

13

And now it is three fifteen and, despite my good intentions, I am ten minutes late for the seminar. I have my notes, I have the pile of marked essays, I have some handouts concerning feminist methodology. I am clutching a rapidly cooling Styrofoam cup of coffee in one hand and have my papers, bag and room keys in the other. I feel outrageously nervous, my tummy twisting in knots as I take the stairs two at a time. I was aware that the course was not going brilliantly, but Beth's comments have confirmed my worst fears. And now there is a real likelihood of a student revolt, with Alec, pitchfork in one hand, revolutionary treatise in the other, at the helm. I should take some form of drastic action, but feel so depressed at Beth's unpleasant news that my brain keeps short-fusing into a circuit of defensive counter-attacks. *When I was a student I always did the reading. This lot never do any work; all they do is complain.* Now, as I approach the room I can hear a low murmur of voices. Are they discussing my failings? Booting the thought rudely from my mind I push open the door, scattering my handouts over the floor and dumping the rest of my baggage on the table. I have been doing this for years: it's so silly to be undermined by just one student.

'Sorry I'm late, folks . . . Yeah, thanks for picking them up, Beth, just hand them round.'

I sit down heavily and look around the room, which has instantly hushed. Ten faces gaze back at me. To my surprise they are not filled with critical contempt, but attentive respect. Perhaps Beth was exaggerating, I think, with a small surge of hope, perhaps everything is fine.

'So, we'll just wait for Beth to sit herself down and then we'll get started . . .'

I stare around the table. I know everyone's names now, and am getting an increasing sense of their personalities, of the various alliances and enmities involved. Nicola and Emma, for example, are best friends, but do not like Andy Dubow, who is forever interrupting them with his clunking interventions. The ex-nurses always sit together, but say little unless directly asked. They, too, are apt to exchange glances when Andy speaks. Alec talks to no one. At the moment he is lolling in his chair at the back of the room, leaking dissatisfaction from every sullen pore. As Beth pushes past him to an empty seat he glances up and frowns. She pretends not to notice, her head tossed back. Yet as she flops herself down, spreading out her books and groping for something in her bag, she shoots him a glance that seems almost triumphant. As their eyes meet he looks away, scowling, and muttering something under his breath, and I am struck by something I had not considered before: *There is something going on between them.*

The thought is oddly reassuring. Leaning back I take stock of the class. Despite the unseasonably warm weather the heating has been turned up high and the room is hot and fuggy, like a car in summer with its windows up and dogs inside. Redundant coats and jumpers are draped over the backs of chairs; library books are heaped on the table. I clear my throat, smoothing out my notes.

'Right,' I say. 'First off, here are your assessed essays. Sorry for the delay.'

I shove the papers across the seminar table towards their owners. When I get to Alec's, I hand it to Natalie to pass back to him, but she merely hands it on to Beth who grabs it eagerly. Turning it over, her eyes lingering over what I have scribbled on the back, she pushes it slowly towards

Alec: *This is truly brilliant* . . . As he waits for his paper, he has picked up what looks like Beth's essay. Chewing his lip, he glances at it contemptuously, then chucks it back on to the table. I force my lips into an insipid smile. 'Alec, that was *fantastic*. One of the best undergraduate essays I've ever read.'

His shoulders twitch and something comes into his face that I have not seen before: relief, perhaps, even joy. Then he locks it away and is snatching the paper from Beth's hands, turning it over and studying my comments. Perhaps my flattery will butter him up a bit, I think miserably. Beth, meanwhile, is bent over her own essay, which she has now retrieved from the table. I thought she would be pleased by my encouraging comments and the A minus she received for her efforts, but her cheeks and neck are covered in purple blotches.

'Are you OK?'

She turns and glances up, giving me one of her one-hundred watt smiles. 'Fine, thanks, Cass.'

'Right, let's get on, then.'

I glance down at my notes and remember that she is due to give this week's presentation. Thank God it's not Alec's turn: he would use the opportunity, no doubt, to sabotage the entire course with a savage attack on everything that has gone before. Forcing from my mind the image of Alec standing at the lecture podium pointing to an overhead projection entitled *Historical Methods: the Philistine Practices and Elementary Mistakes of Dr C. Bainbridge*, I turn to Beth.

'So, would you like to kick off, then, Beth? You were going to give a work-in-progress report about your project, weren't you?'

Smiling sheepishly, she stands. The others have stopped perusing their marked essays and are opening their note-books, looking over to her expectantly. From the seminar room next door comes a blast of laughter. It's one of Julian Leigh's classes and, from the evidence that seeps through the thin partition wall, they are having a great time.

'What I want to talk about today,' Beth announces to the class, 'is my project on Feminist Voices Across the Generations. Or, perhaps I should say, *Herstory*.'

She giggles, clearly pleased with the pun. In fact, it's one of the more tired clichés of revisionist feminist history, but I guess, to her novice eyes, it seems clever. Folding my arms, I lean back in my chair. It's important that I focus.

'Both Cass and I are excited about what I'm planning to do, which is basically to interview all the different generations of women in my family about their attitudes towards feminism and the different position of women in society throughout their lifetime.' She picks up her notes with a flourish, and continues, 'But first, I want to say something about methods. When collecting oral histories, it's very important to understand the link between *narrative* and *identity formation*.'

She enunciates these last phrases slowly, allowing her peers time to write them down. Allowing my eyelids to droop a fraction, I brood on Alec. What exactly does he dislike about my course? I thought it was a reasonably solid and interesting resumé; certainly, I never had complaints when I taught it in London. And, anyway, who the hell does he think he is? Beside me, Beth is still speaking: 'As fellow historians have noted for some time, we need also to take careful note not just of what people say, but what they leave unsaid . . .'

From the back of the room, Alec gives a derisive snort, no doubt at the pomposity of *fellow historians*. Perhaps the gravity that Beth is attempting is a little foolish, but all the same I shoot him an annoyed glance.

'It is the gaps and silences that are significant, as much as the content and dominant tropes of informant discourse.'

Like the students, I, too, should be taking brisk notes,

thinking of comments to make about the presentation, but the room is so hot that I can feel my eyes sliding shut. Perhaps I should ask Alec to stay behind after the class and explain himself, I think testily. Or perhaps I should be brave and get the group to give me a spontaneous evaluation of my teaching so far. I could announce I was holding a 'trouble-shooting session'. Then I could meet their complaints head-on. I could set up a student–teacher task force and we could redesign the course, according to their specifications. Is that not something which the Council for Higher Education would deem commendable?

The idea of this makes me feel even more exhausted. Staring blurrily at Beth, I start to wonder if I should perhaps retrain as an aromatherapist, or something to do with food – an organic farmer, maybe? I could keep goats, make my own bread . . .

'. . . in many societies, for example, women may feel that particular issues, such as politics or religion, are the domain of men –'

'Excuse me? Can I interrupt for a second?'

My eyes jerk open: at the back of the room Alec is jabbing at the air with his pen. He must also be affected by the warmth, for his forehead is shiny. Next to him, Beth has stopped talking and is glowering at him with frigid disdain. Attagirl, I think, don't let him put you off.

'Can you leave your questions for after the presentation?' I say frostily.

He frowns grumpily. 'Well, I could . . .'

'Good. We'll have a question-and-answer session at the end.'

I nod at Beth to continue, but Alec interrupts me. 'The thing is,' he says, half rising from his seat, as if propelled upwards by anxious energy, a human rocket aimed at my course, 'what I wanted to say was that I thought you might all like to know that rather than taking notes on what Beth is saying, the class might just as easily go to *Society and History*, volume twenty-one, July 1999. She's quoting the introductory article, almost word for word.'

He stops, his face puce. The room has become so quiet that through the partition wall I can clearly hear Julian say: 'That is the *very* contradiction I put to you, and which Derrida has framed so eloquently.'

Next to Alec, Beth has frozen mid-position, like a child playing musical statues. The other students have stopped writing and are sitting back, regarding her with renewed interest. I clear my throat. I need to say something quickly, to show that I am still in control, but I don't know what. One of the main problems is that despite marking the introductory article to *Society and History*, volume XXI as essential on the course bibliography I have not read it. Rousing myself, I survey Alec with what I hope appears to be knowledgeable surprise. 'What makes you so sure?' I say acidly.

He has sat down now, and is patting a pile of papers lying on the desk in front of him, his lips pursed disapprovingly. 'I've got a photocopy of it right here in front of me. I've been following the points one by one. She missed the bit about comparative research, but we're currently on page four, paragraph two.'

At the back of the room Andy whispers something and his neighbour, a nondescript 2:2ish bloke in combats and trainers, snorts with laughter.

'OK, thanks.' I regard Alec coldly. 'It's nice to know that someone's paying attention. Clearly Beth needs to be a bit more explicit about her sources.'

'You can say that again.'

This time several people laugh, but Alec does not smile. I fold my arms across my bosom and nod at Beth to continue. 'Next time, give the reference to your sources, Beth,' I say soothingly. I want to make it clear to everyone that all she is guilty of is a careless oversight, not the heinous academic crime of plagiarism, of which every first-year student is warned within their first week of university life, and which carries the ultimate penalty of course failure. Something, however, is irritating me, a thought buzzing at the back of my brain, like a trapped bluebottle. 'Now, perhaps, you'd like to go straight to the discussion of your project?'

But Beth does not respond. Instead, she remains standing by the table, glaring at Alec. Her hands flail by her sides as if grasping for an imaginary sword with which to strike down her assailant. The room is silent, filled with an unnatural hush that, with every passing second, is becoming heavier and heavier, a huge black cloud, about to burst.

'Beth?'

At the sound of her name Beth turns to meet my eyes.

'Yes?'

I am about to repeat my request that she should continue when the bluebottle breaks free. I give a physical start, my fingers tingling with shock. *That* was what was so odd about her essay! I *knew* it was familiar, but what I failed to notice was that, with the exception of a few embellishments, the original author was not Beth, but *me*! I gawp gormlessly at her, my mind scrabbling over each paragraph: *Rather than checking oral histories against 'established histories' for veracity, why not reverse the process, and check the latter against the former?* No wonder I thought it was clever! I wrote it in the introduction of my own thesis! How could I be such an utter fool?

'Why don't you just go directly into the description of your project?' I mumble weakly. I am feeling so humiliated and humbled that I want to crawl under the table, whimpering like a wounded animal. I read the essays too quickly and was too eager to give Beth a generous mark, I see now, with an inner howl of self-reproach. I shall have to call the dreaded

Bev Cope, explain my mistake and discuss what disciplinary procedures to take. Like everyone else who gets to hear of it – and it will surely become the juiciest joke of the term – she will consider me a complete imbecile. For while failing to spot plagiarism may sometimes be forgivable – for example, when one is marking the work of students in another course, as Bev Cope has just done – failing to spot the plagiarism of one's *own* work is akin to a doctor failing to spot that her patient is dead.

Beth takes a deep breath, and looks around the class. The colour is returning to her face, the crisis passed. 'I'm sorry,' she says evenly. 'I know I was basing the introduction on that article. I just wasn't sure about giving references. I didn't know it was all such a big deal.'

I gaze at her. My mouth is filled with clay. 'That's fine,' I say. 'But can you come and see me after the seminar? There's something else I want to discuss with you.'

Another big, bright smile. 'Yes of course, Cass. It would be a pleasure.'

An hour later she is waiting outside my office, leaning happily against the wall and humming, as if she does not have a care in the world. As I approach, she waves expectantly. I give her a queasy grin. I feel as if something large and poisonous is blocking my windpipe. Not wanting to look her in the face, I fiddle unnecessarily with my keys, eventually push the door open and stumble inside. I spent the remaining thirty minutes of the seminar in a state of badly concealed panic at what I was trying to convince myself was a simple 'oversight', but which will without doubt turn me into a faculty laughing-stock. Luckily, the other students were so agog at Alec's attack on Beth that they were oblivious to my glum, dumb state. We spent fifteen minutes discussing Beth's plans, another ten on questions I wanted them to focus on for the next week, and I ended the class ten minutes early. As soon as I could get out of the door I legged it to the office in the vain hope that the assessed-essay marks forms had not gone off to the Examinations Office. But of course the outgoing-mail tray was empty, and my plan for a quick rejigging of Beth's mark dashed.

'So,' I say, as Beth perches on the edge of the seat opposite mine, 'I think it's time we had a talk.'

She beams at me, still not getting that I am upset. 'I'd really love that.'

I look down at my trousers, distractedly pulling at a loose thread from one of the seams. 'It's about your essay,' I blurt. I can feel my heart working faster. It's ridiculous, but it feels as if it is me who is letting Beth down, rather than the other way round. Until the seminar I had almost forgotten that she was just a student: not only had she confided in me but I in turn had begun to confide in her. And now, with what I am about to say, all that will be blown out of the water.

'I'm so glad you liked it,' Beth replies. 'I was worried about what you would think.'

I look into her face. I suppose I should feel angry, but she is smiling at me so innocently that she must be unaware of her crime. 'I actually gave you the wrong mark,' I say slowly. 'I'm afraid I'm going to have to ask you to give it back so that I can alter it.'

As I say this, she leans forward, her face puzzled. 'How come?'

I take a breath, trying to steady my voice. 'Because, as you are surely aware, you copied the whole thing directly from my thesis. I knew it sounded familiar, but only realized during the seminar. It's partly my mistake for not spotting it earlier. But you know the rules: you have to cite all your secondary sources, otherwise it's looked on as plagiarism. So now I'm afraid I'm going to have to fail it.'

I was expecting a sense of relief after this purging, but the expression on Beth's face makes me feel worse rather than better. She seems mortified, her eyes round with shock, her lower lip quivering. She is so pale I wonder if she is about to swoon.

'Oh!'

'You must surely have known?' I say. I did not intend it, but my voice is sharp with disapproval. For God's sake, I want to spit, how dozy do you think I am? 'Perhaps you're still not sure about how to use secondary sources,' I continue, 'although by the third year I find that surprising. You must surely appreciate how bad it looks.'

'Of course,' Beth whispers. 'I know.' To my consternation, she drops her head into her hands.

'Why did you do it?' I say, more gently.

She has started sobbing now, burying her face in her hands with great shuddery breaths. A part of me wants to reach out and give her a reassuring hug, but something else holds me back: anger, perhaps, for making me look so foolish. When she looks up, her face is wet, a drip of snot dangling from the end of her nose. Wiping it on the back of her sleeve, she whispers, 'It's just a stupid cock-up. I promise you, Cass, it was a mistake.'

'But how? Surely you know what's expected?'

'I think I must have given you the wrong draft of the essay,' she says. 'I wrote it out like that, without the sources and stuff, just to help me get things straight in my head. Then I wrote another version, which was the one I should have handed in.'

She stops, still moving her head to and fro, and sniffing. I stare at her, sitting so small and vulnerable in my battered office chair. I want to believe her but am not sure it is possible.

'Honestly,' she says. 'I promise I'm not making it up . . .'

'So where's the other version now?'

At this she starts to sob again, her shoulders heaving with despair. 'I thought it was the old one! I threw it in the bin! I can't believe I've been so stupid!'

I would say, 'Nor can I,' but, given my own less than intelligent behaviour, it seems somewhat hypocritical. Instead I continue to gaze at her, trying to decide what to do.

'What will happen to me?' she asks.

'I don't know,' I say slowly. 'The problem is, the essay is part of your assessed coursework, which, as you know, goes towards your final degree. And now I'm going to have to get the mark back and change it.'

'So will I get into trouble?'

'I'll certainly have to tell the dean.'

A bubble has formed between her lips. As she exhales it pops, leaving a glistening thread of saliva on her chin. Her shoulders give another heave and she sighs, so heavily that it sounds like air rushing out of a punctured tyre. 'Oh, God!'

'Look, you'll probably just have to write the essay again. It won't be that bad.'

'But it will go on my records?'

'I'm not sure. I suppose not, if we can convince them it was a genuine mistake. It will probably depend partly on what the other examiner thinks. Possibly we'll have to send it to the external.'

For a moment I think she is about to start crying again but instead she gathers herself up, sitting straighter and looking into my face. 'Please, Cass,' she whispers. 'I know I've cocked up, but I was in a real state last week, I just lost it. I mean, I don't want to bore you with what was going on and all that, but I wrote out the essay as a first draft, and then, like I said, I must have handed in the wrong version. There was all this shit going around and I wasn't concentrating properly. I didn't mean to hand it in like that. It was just a stupid mistake.'

I regard her grubby face. Her mascara is running in dark tracks down her face, making her look like a surreal clown. Still twisting the thread in my fingers I lose patience with it, and snap it off. Outside, the feeble winter sun has gone and the campus is settling into darkness. I am increasingly overcome by a thick, smothering fatigue.

'You'll have to write it again –' I start, but Beth does not let me finish.

'To be honest, Cass, I can't concentrate on anything right now. That's why I've got into this mess. It's just all this other stuff going on, and if I get into trouble here it'll be the final straw, I know it will –' She stops, her voice rising dangerously.

I lean over and take her hand. She looks up at me appealingly.

'What's been happening?'

'It's my so-called parents. They've been really letting off about everything. There's all kinds of shit flying around, and I think they're just using me as an excuse, like the fall-guy, or whatever? And last week, when it was all going on, I couldn't think of anything else.'

'I see.'

'Please, Cass, just this once, let it pass. I promise you, I'll never do anything so stupid again.'

I stare at her small, smeary face, her red eyes and unruly hair, and think of how I am going to have to call Bev Cope and the exams office, how I am going to have to get the marks sheet back, and report my mistake to the dean. I think of how I have been in this job for only five weeks and already one of the cleverest students has a campaign against me. I think of my risible performance in this morning's meeting and the pile of untended administration that is taking over my room, like summer weeds. I think of the fact that my position here is on a probationary basis, and how much Matt would like me to fail. And then I do something that in London I would never even consider: I put my hand out and lay it on Beth's elbow, and hear myself say, 'OK, then, Beth. Just this once, I'll let it pass.'

14

And still the day is not over, for there is the Post-Colonial Narratives workshop to attend, due to start at five p.m. I skipped it last week, pleading a cold, and since I was plainly hale and hearty this morning, today my attendance is obligatory. I button my coat and scurry across the campus towards the lecture theatre where the talk is being held. It is being given by Professor Maurice Salsberg, an eminent historian with a chair in California and I am late. Hurrying down the steps that lead to Block A, my feet crunch the leaves. Five hours earlier I was revelling in the warm sunshine, but now that the sun has gone my breath puffs white. The campus is less crowded than before: rather than streaming towards their classes, the students I pass are walking in the opposite direction, eager to be away.

When I reach the lecture-theatre door, I pull it open and, shutting it gently behind me, creep along the back row. The place is packed, the lecture already started. In the front row I can see the back of Jenny Montgomery and Julian's heads; a little further along, Madge Wernski is crushed beside a distinguished-looking South Asian man with frameless specs and a goatee. It's a good turn-out. There must be over forty postgraduates here, I calculate, and another twenty or so lecturers. Although I informed my methodologies group about the series at the beginning of term, so far only Alec has been in regular attendance. Now, as I take my place on the bench, I see that he is sitting two rows down.

Wrinkling my brow, I peer at the overhead projection which Professor Salsberg is gesturing towards. I cannot recall the title of today's talk, but during my research I relied closely on his internationally famous monograph *Subaltern Voices: Othering and the Discourse of Exclusion in the New Global Order*, so am keen to see him in the flesh. He's an intense little chap in his late forties, with a close-clipped beard, deep blue eyes and a Californian tan. Dressed in jeans and a button-down shirt, the uniform of the forty-something male academic, he has just made a weak joke about the state of British trains, and the audience is responding with polite laughter.

I unscrew the top of my pen and write his name and the date on the pad of paper I have brought with me. Salsberg is saying something authoritative now about the theoretical background to his work: Bromich's classic analysis of late-capitalist kinship structures, Foucault's work on mental asylums, *naturally*, and then the huge canon of post-structuralist theory that we will, *of course*, be familiar with. My colleagues nod knowledgeably. To my left, the door has just opened, and an apologetic-looking Beth has shuffled in.

She slides in next to me, removing her rustling coat self-consciously. The only person who glances round reproachfully, however, is Alec. I am half expecting him to place his finger over his lips and mime a 'Sssh', like a devout worshipper in a church full of naughty children, but as his eyes focus on Beth, he merely scowls. As I watch him turn disapprovingly back to Maurice Salsberg, I remember something that turns me cold. *He saw Beth's essay.* I had not thought of that before, but now I recall the way he picked up her paper, glanced through the densely written pages, then chucked it back on to the table in apparent disgust. He is so well read and so suspicious that it's perfectly possible he clocked that she had copied my work. And he must surely have noticed the mark I gave her, too.

Shivering, I clutch my pen tightly and methodically copy what Maurice Salsberg has flashed up on the projector: *Lost*

Lives and Stolen Voices: the Anglo-Indian Children of the East India Company, 1750–85. Yet despite this façade of studious concentration I am not listening to a word, for my thoughts have snagged on a loop of worry and regret. I should never have agreed to let Beth's essay through, I can see that now. It's true, she was in a terrible state. And it's also probably true that her mistake was genuine, for what would she gain from such easily detectable and blatant cheating? Yet now that she is no longer snivelling before me in my office, I cannot remember why I was so lenient towards her.

Supposing Alec did indeed notice that the essay was copied from my work? He could go to the dean, or even the vice-chancellor, and then how would it look? In explaining myself I would have to choose between two options, both highly undesirable. The first, that I did not notice she had copied my own work, would make me look a fool; the second, that I had noticed but let it through, would mean that I was complicit in her cheating, an unheard-of transgression of my pedagogic role. Feeling sick, I gaze hazily at Salsberg. He is standing in front of the overhead projector, so that his shadow is magnified on to the screen, and saying something in a pious voice about a story he is hoping we will allow him to tell. It's a tale of lost childhood, one of racism and terrible cruelty. And crucially, at least as far as this humble speaker is concerned – he crosses his hands over his chest and falls silent for a moment, as if he were a motivational speaker rather than a revered scholar of British colonialism – it is a case study *par excellence* of the ways in which the state has silenced, nay, literally *erased*, the histories of the dispossessed. Next to me, Beth sighs, cupping her chin in her hands.

OK. What I did was somewhat unconventional, but on a moral, humane level it was the correct course of action. Beth puts on a brave front, but the girl is in a mess. Does it really matter that she forgot to cite her sources? The essay she threw away would probably have only got ten or so marks less than the one I marked, which constitutes a tiny fraction of her degree result. And if Alec does blow the whistle, I shall revert to Position A: embarrassed ignorance. Determined to put the whole matter from my mind, I force my attention back to the lecture.

'I'm basing this on a series of papers I dug up at the British Library as part of another project on Anglo-Indians,' Salsberg drawls. 'Of course, we hear nothing from the actual children. They're not even given names, just listed as dependants under their fathers' titles. But what we can gather is that, over these ten crucial years, a surprisingly large proportion of Anglo-Indian descendants of the imperial administrators were systematically abandoned, either in India or the streets of London, after being taken from their mothers, shipped to England, then abandoned again by their so-called English families.'

I have started to perspire. This focus on children is new to the professor's work: his most famous book was concerned with the relationship between colonial administration and the representation of history, so this is not what I was expecting. In the hushed lecture theatre, his voice has a staged, dramatic quality: the guy is clearly accustomed to commanding total attention. Virtually nothing is known about the circumstances under which these children were sent to England, he tells us, stroking his beard quizzically, as if puzzling over a game of chess. What we do know from *painstaking* research, in which yours truly carefully pieced together fragments of letters, records from certain charitable institutions working in East London, and a *really awesome* account from John Taylor, an eighty-year-old Anglo-Indian living in Hackney in the late nineteenth century, is that many children were sent by their fathers to England, possibly for welfare reasons, but on reaching the country found their

English half-families to be less than enthusiastic in their reception. Abandoned around the docklands of London and Liverpool, many simply perished. Others were picked up by charitable missions and, like John Taylor, spent their lives as servants, pedlars and tramps. Yet research into the papers of the families concerned – and he has been able to trace a few of the children listed as passengers in Calcutta ships – shows that these children have been all but expunged from their collective memories.

He stops, looking around dramatically, then struts to the podium, which is slightly too high for him, and lays his hands upon it. 'We'll come back to this small matter of erasure,' he says, 'but in the meantime, let's return to John Taylor. What we've got here is an old Anglo-Indian guy, parentage unknown, who's categorized in poorhouse records as a vagabond. Yet, extraordinarily, his life history was recorded by one Mary Dunbury, probably a missionary working with the London poor . . .'

He turns away from the podium, his voice rising gleefully: 'What I've salvaged is a long account of the old guy's memories of a pauperized childhood, living on the streets of East London. He also refers to earlier memories of what appears, from the names, to be Bengal. Naturally, one of the problems is to what extent we can extrapolate from such memories.'

Naturally. I close my eyes, letting the words lap around me.

'Let us consider a little further this idea of memory as construct. How far can this take us? Isn't one of the problems that history just gets refracted back at us, a series of distortions in fairground mirrors?'

Around me, people are murmuring in agreement; some are simply listening, while others jot down notes. I twist my pen in my fingers. If memory is construct, then who am I to think these thoughts? It is, after all, part of what I have been teaching all term, but right now it seems a disingenuous academic conceit. It is easy enough to declare in a lecture that all we know of the past is distorted, but if that is really the case then how do we know who we are? And what would the eminent Californian chair of Cultural Studies extrapolate from *my* memories?

Having made his point, Salsberg is describing in more detail the recollections of old John Taylor. I, however, can no longer listen. So our stories are a web we weave to catch ourselves in. Yet sometimes the images are so strong that I feel as if I can reach out and touch them. Could it be that they are only constructs, woven by myself? David and me, sitting on the bathroom floor with towels around our shoulders as Mum picked through our hair for nits; tea on our laps in front of *Blue Peter*; the bread and milk with sugar she gave us when we were ill. And later, her gloved hands pounding on the steering-wheel, 'I've had enough of this!' and the way her eyes went red but she did not cry. And the triggers, which hurl me back. The sickly sweet smell of the brown bottled pills, for instance, which lingered in the house for months; spilt beer, cracked plastic cups, and the way the brown velour curtains were drawn against the night. And all those months later, 'Love Will Tear Us Apart'; the unbearable stench of dried fish.

And then the other thought, the one I have been fighting against since the humble Salsberg started his tale of cruelty, racism and dispossession. Can people really be expunged from the past? Or do their traces always reappear? At this, I gasp and rise from my seat. Suddenly, and very urgently, I have to get out of there, because I can no longer breathe. As I grope for my coat, the room tips, my focus blurring. Perhaps it is the stuffiness of the lecture theatre – I am desperate for the cold November air. Yet as I stand, Salsberg stops mid-sentence, and I can feel fifty or so expectant pairs of eyes fix me in their sights.

'Yes, madam?' Salsberg says loudly. 'You have a question?'

I gape at him. My breath is coming in shallow rasps, my ears are filled with what sounds like the pounding of waves. The entire audience is staring at me, waiting for some clever remark, or learned question. 'No,' I reply eventually. My voice sounds weak and waif-like, I can hardly breathe. 'Please excuse me.'

And then, pushing past Beth, I free myself from the narrow benches and stagger through the swing doors.

15

The moment I am outside I feel better. I lean against the cool concrete of Block A for a minute or so, luxuriating in the silence. When my breathing has steadied, I zip up my jacket and start to move towards the car-park. I must be coming down with flu. That would explain why I am now so cold and shivery.

I walk swiftly across the empty campus. Part of the recent discussion on campus safety has concerned the woeful state of security lighting around the university grounds, and now I appreciate why. Away from the buildings and main thoroughfares, and on this moonless night, the smaller paths lead into funereal black. Wishing the place were not so deserted, I turn left, hurrying along the concrete walkway that leads to the main car-park. The security guards who lurk here, plastering the windscreens of illegally parked cars with reprimanding stickers, have clocked off, the students, whom I passed an hour earlier, vanished. It could be midnight rather than just after six. On the other side of the trees I can hear the roar of the dual-carriageway. I swish through piles of dead leaves, walking faster. I can barely see where I'm going.

Ignoring my mounting anxiety, I reach the end of the walkway, and take a right down the steps that lead to the car-park. Somebody is coming up behind me. I can hear the soft squeak of rubber soles on the concrete and instinctively turn, but they must still be far behind, for all I can see is the outline of the walkway walls and, two or three hundred metres away, Blocks A and B lit up in the gloom like ocean liners. It is, of course, perfectly reasonable for someone else to be making their way to the car-park. There is nothing to worry about. Humming loudly, I pace along the bays that this morning were filled with cars, but have now largely emptied, like a mouth with its teeth punched out. From the sound of the footsteps behind me, the other person is proceeding in the same direction. I keep glancing over my shoulder, but still can see nothing. Clutching my car keys in my fingers, I stride ever faster towards the end of the car-park, where I have left the Beetle perched on a narrow ridge of grass beside a row of bushes. I should have arrived earlier this morning and grabbed the optimum spot by the well-lit road.

I wish to God the person behind me would veer off in the other direction. With every second that they remain so close I am growing more alarmed, but now am too scared to turn round and confront them so can only march as fast as possible towards the sanctuary of my car. My heart almost bounding out of my chest, I search wildly in the darkness for it. It sounds as if the man is right behind me. I am sure I can hear breathing and then, very distinctly, comes the scrape of shoe against Tarmac. I keep telling myself not to panic, but a yell of terror is lurking in my throat, waiting, at the merest provocation, to burst from my mouth.

Finally I spot the Beetle. Leaping towards it, I force the key into the door. As soon as it clicks open I dive inside and push down all the locks. As I jam the key into the ignition and press my foot down hard on the accelerator, the car skids half-way up the grassy bank. Mud splatters the windows, the wheels whirring angrily.

'Bugger!'

Yanking the car into reverse, I jerk it back on to the Tarmac, only now remembering to turn on the headlights. Finally I am in the right position. I engage first gear, forcing myself to slow down. As the Beetle's lights sweep the empty car-park, I am almost crying. But, of course, it is just as I suspected. There is no one there.

When I get home I go straight to the kitchen, plonk my bottom on the steps, and gorge a whole bag of doughnuts, which have been waiting seductively in the bread-bin since the weekend. I eat so fast I barely taste the soft, sugary dough, stuffing them into my mouth with shaking fingers. By the time the bag is empty, jam is dribbling down my chin and my hands are covered with grease. Then, as if the two evils might cancel each other out, I smoke three cigarettes in a row, still hunched on the steps, trying to get a grip.

I am turning into a neurotic wreck. And I am also getting too fat. Unbuttoning the top of my trousers, I stub out the last fag on my plate and stand up decisively. I am going to do what I do every evening at about this time. I am going to listen to my answer-machine messages.

The machine is skulking in the hall, winking at me ominously. Fumbling for the 'playback' button, I swallow uneasily. There have been so many strange calls over the last few weeks that I cannot escape the sense that, like dropping a net to the bottom of the dark oceans, the machine may have trapped something nasty.

Message number one is not, as I expected, from my ghost, but from Sarah.

'Me here,' she says, in an odd voice. 'Look, are you OK? I just got your text message and it's made me a bit worried. Can you give me a call?'

She sounds weird: worried, but also formal and slightly patronizing, as if I am a junior at work or her au pair. I have no memory of texting her, so she must be mistaken, but I do not feel strong enough to ring and ask what she means.

151

For the next few messages there is just the usual silence, the sound of breathing and then a click. Then, on message six, there is something else, a low muttering. It goes on for a minute or so, then cuts off. Perhaps the caller is on a mobile that has gone out of range, or Poppy has pressed the buttons on Sarah's phone without her noticing. Whatever, the sound makes my skin creep. Messages seven, eight and nine are just clicks as, once more, the phone is put down.

Bleep. The messages have come to an end. Standing, I wander nervously towards my bedroom. I do not want to dwell on the way the phone is still given to sporadic bursts of evening ringing. Perhaps I should just pull it out of the wall. When I reach the door I peer in despondently. I have allowed the place to become increasingly untidy over the last few weeks. I take in the wreck of my unmade bed, the detritus of teacups, magazines, half-read books and empty pizza cartons that constitute a week of evenings alone. Dirty clothes are strewn around the place, each garment marking my dazed approach to bed: last week's Maharishi pants are still sprawled near the door where I dropped them; a shirt, plus an unappealing collection of vests and tops, is draped over the chair. The bed is surrounded by a week's worth of worn pants and bras, cast aside at the pillow's edge, like bathers' clothes on the beach. Even I am forced to admit that the scene is disgusting.

I close the door. I should tidy up but, without Matt to spur me on with his own domestic diligence, I cannot be bothered with it. I shuffle back down the corridor and pick up a stack of old newspapers, which has accumulated by the wall. The spare room is next door. I shall shove them in there.

I open the door, step inside the tiny space and peer through the gloom at the removal boxes Matt and I placed there at the end of the summer. Dumping the newspapers on top of one of the boxes, I push further into the room.

There is a built-in wardrobe at the back, I notice. I come in here so rarely, and barely registered it on my earlier incursions.

Running my hand along the wall I progress across the room. Perhaps I could store some of the books in it, even turn it into an office. Now I see something else: at the top of the walls, above the pastel pink paper, there is a faded frieze of hopping bunnies. It looks as if it has been stencilled by hand, a patchy DIY job that is now accumulating dust and spiders' webs. I shall have to paint it over, I think, and throw open the wardrobe doors.

It takes me a second or so to focus properly on what I see inside. At first it seems to be a pile of wooden railings, stacked up like bars in a prison cell. Peering through them from the other side is a dismembered head. I blink at it in fleeting shock, then realize that it is simply a baby's cot stored on its side. Reaching through the rails, I pull out a large Cabbage Patch doll – my dismembered head. It smiles goofily into the dusky room: yellow wool hair and painted red cheeks caught in the shine of the hall light. It feels slightly damp. I drop it back inside the wardrobe, where it lands next to a child's night-light, decorated with pictures of Humpty Dumpty. So the room was used as a *nursery*. Doug and Jenny must have had a child. I close the doors, feeling unreasonably annoyed. They should have bloody well cleared out their stuff.

And then the phone is ringing again. I have had just about enough of this. I rush into the hall and grab the receiver ferociously. 'Yes?'

There is a pause, then a female voice says, very faintly, 'Cass?'

'Speaking.'

'It's Beth.'

I exhale with relief. It sounds as if she is in a bar, for I can hear the hum of voices in the background, a distant musical beat. It's a bit bloody late to ring now, Missy, I think, this had better be good.

'Beth! What's up?'

There is another long silence in which I can make out the rattle of glasses and the occasional burst of laughter. Something is wrong, I think, something has happened.

'I'm fine,' she says. 'I'm calling from work.'

'From work?'

'This stupid bar.'

And now I am sure she is crying, for I can hear her sniffing, the laboured intakes of breath. I have had such a long day, but as I remember our conversation this afternoon, my exhaustion lifts off me and I am returned to the Cass I like: caring and kind, the tutor students turn to. 'Are you still there?' I say gently.

'Cass?' she whispers.

'What is it?'

'I'm so sorry to bother you like this. I couldn't call earlier because I had to do my shift and now it's so late . . .'

'It's not a problem. Just tell me what the matter is.'

'Please, Cass, can I see you?'

'Sure, but what's happened?'

'I've –' And now her voice breaks, tears taking over. 'Oh, God, Cass, they've chucked me out.'

16

The bar where Beth works is a large, beery establishment on the sea-front, tucked under the guano-splattered arches. This is not the fashionable end of town, where the front is lined by clubs and arty boutiques, but the wrong side of the pier: a stretch of boarded-up cafés, dogshat pavement and dripping mossy pillars that face an abandoned crazy-golf course and a row of tarpaulined fairground rides. A little further on is the place where I took Beth for tea on the first day of term.

As I approach it I can hear the thud of dance music, sense the heaving, sweaty crowd inside. The place seems to be alive, a pulsating animal exuding its hot, steamy breath into the night air. Perhaps it was once an Edwardian tea-shop, but now the grand picture windows have been boarded up and covered with posters for gigs and DJs, and the reinforced-steel doors are guarded by black-coated bouncers with head-sets. They stare at me impassively as I hurry towards them, their jaws working gum.

Beth said she would be standing outside, but there is no sign of her. It is almost closing time, and groups of young people drift on to the pavement and out across the wide boulevard of the sea-front road. The November night air is icy: the revellers huddle together, pulling their jackets tightly around themselves. I look closely at their faces, peering into the dark in the hope of locating Beth. They glance back dismissively, summing me up with the quick flick of their eyes: too old, not part of the scene. I am not properly dressed for such a bitter night either. I scoot across the road: I need to return as soon as possible to the shelter of my car. In fact, I should not be here at all – I should be snuggled up in bed, not out on a mercy mission. I glance up at the perfect silver circle of the moon, the red glow of the city sky. The truth is, I welcomed the excuse to escape from the flat.

And then I see her, crouching on the pavement; her head is cradled in her arms as if she is asleep, her hair flops across her knees. She must be freezing: all she is wearing are baggy jeans and a short-cropped T-shirt, *de rigueur* student garb. She is sitting directly beneath a large ornate street-lamp, and in the unnatural light her skin looks mottled and blue. As I cross the road she looks up. Her eyes are swollen and red, her cheeks puffy. As she sees me she smiles with relief and stands up shakily. She must be very alone, I realize, as she steps out of the light. Why else would she be forced to turn to her university lecturer in her hour of need rather than her friends? The thought swamps me with pity and I stride faster, my throat constricting.

When I reach her I put my arm round her shoulders and guide her back across the road. 'I'm sorry I'm late. I couldn't get the car to start. Are you OK?'

She nods. 'I shouldn't have bothered you like this, but I couldn't think of anyone else to call . . . I just about got through my shift, and then it suddenly hit me.'

'Don't worry about it.'

She is very cold, her skin chilled and lifeless. As my fingers graze her arm I notice how thin she is too. At the university she disguises it with her skateboard gear but tonight I can feel the fragile outline of her ribs, like a tiny, injured bird's. She needs feeding up, ladles of nutrition spooned into her the way Sarah feeds Poppy. As she leans against me she is shaking with deep, intense tremors.

'You never mentioned before that you worked in a bar,' I say, trying to get her to talk.

'It's a shit job.'

'It must be really hard doing that *and* your degree.'

'How else am I going to get any money?'

I lead her back to the car, thinking how much student life has changed since my day when even the upper-class types, who went beagling and wore straw boaters at May Week cocktail parties, were given a grant. Beth remains silent, staring ahead at the moonlit sea and the sparkly neon lights of the pier. After a while I stop my chit-chat, and slide off my heavy leather jacket, place it round her shoulders. I want to wrap her with blankets, feed her hot whisky and honey.

When we reach the Beetle she slips into the front seat without a murmur.

'Do your foster-parents know where you are?' I say, as I lean over her lap and pull her door closed. It is not perhaps the most tactful question but I want to establish whether she has really been thrown out or if she has run away. She turns, glaring at me with shocked eyes. Finally, there is some colour in her cheeks. 'They're not my parents!' she hisses. 'They just made that blatantly clear!'

Bunching her fist over her mouth, she gives her head a violent shake and glances away from my searching eyes. I switch on the engine and start to drive back along the dark sea-front. I suppose I should be irritated by her refusal to tell me what has happened, after I have so kindly volunteered to pick her up, but I have spent so much time alone over the last weeks that my main emotion is relief. This is a role I am comfortable with, kind, caring Cass, not the paranoid person who gets spooked just walking through a car-park. And if there is ever a person who needs support, it is Beth. She remains hunched in the front seat, her face tight with misery, her fingers digging into her jeans. When I pull up outside my flat, she gives me a dejected glance and whispers, 'You could always just take me to the station. I mean, I don't want to be in the way.'

'But where would you go?'

'I don't know.'

Her voice is pitiful, as if rejection is something she takes for granted.

'For God's sake, girl,' I cry, giving her arm a cheery squeeze, 'don't be so ridiculous! Stay with me tonight and tomorrow we'll sort out something else. OK?'

Once we get inside I fuss around the place, making coffee, retrieving my warmest woolly from the still packed bags I have shoved into the corner of the bedroom, trying to get the imitation coal fire to light. Beth sits cross-legged on the floor in the sitting room, cradling a mug in her white hands. Swamped in my jumper, with her sunken face and trembling shoulders, she looks about ten years younger than the exuberant young woman I have grown accustomed to: a little girl alone.

'So,' I say, sitting down next to her, 'do you want to talk about it?'

She pulls a face and sips the coffee. 'It's so late,' she mumbles. 'You must need to go to bed.'

'It's fine. I can never sleep anyway.'

I reach out and brush her shoulder lightly with my hand. What I really want to do is wrap my arms round her and give her a big hug. Yet the moment I touch her, she flinches. After a while she mutters, 'I should never have let myself believe they were my family.'

I pause, then ask gently, 'What happened?'

'Oh, you know, all the usual shit. Of course I can never live up to their *real* daughter, it's impossible.'

'What did they want you to do?'

She gives an indifferent shrug, as if it were no longer relevant. 'Just be less like me and more like her. A bloody angel. Always top of the class, brilliant at everything, blah blah blah.'

'That must be so hard for you.'

Another snort. Suddenly she seems much older, her face shrouded with an anger I have not seen there before. 'Yeah, well, they're not my parents. They never were and never will be. I'm just like you, Cass, I'm all alone.'

She stops, putting her head in her hands, her fingers digging into her bushy hair. As the jumper falls away from her arms I notice with a shock that they are covered in red and purple marks, the beginnings of bruises. When she looks up her face is blank. 'It's my fault,' she says, and her voice is toneless, as if she were reciting directions or a shopping list. 'I always make the same mistake, my whole life.'

There is a long pause. I reach out and take her hand decisively, holding it in mine. She looks up, and our eyes meet again. 'Look,' I say, 'are you really sure they don't want you around any more? Perhaps all you need is to talk it through with them.'

It sounds so lame, the thoughtless sort of thing someone who likes to brush other people's problems under the carpet would say. I am instantly ashamed, but Beth does not give me the brusque reply I deserve. 'It's gone beyond talking,' she says quietly.

I hold her cold fingers between my palms, concentrating hard. Just as when we had breakfast at the beginning of term, her story makes me feel ashamed. At least I had a good start, a mother and father and brother of my own; there was never any question that I did not belong. No, it was much later that it went wrong.

'There's been other stuff too,' Beth is saying. 'I should have taken the hint years ago and got out. It's just like in all the other places.'

'The other places?'

'Yeah, you know, the other foster-homes. But I was in this one the longest, so I've been hanging on, you know, hoping.'

She stops. As I gaze at her unlined skin, pale eyes and unwashed hair, I am filled with such sadness that I feel weighted down by its vast bulk, almost pinioned to the floor with grief. 'Hoping that they'd love you more?' I murmur.

She can see it in my eyes, I am sure, this great longing that I usually cover up. Why should it always matter so much? Why can I never escape?

'Yes,' she says slowly. 'That's exactly it.' She peers at my face, so intent and serious, as if trying to discover what lies behind it. Then, suddenly, I am turning my eyes away and clumsily standing. I feel unaccountably flustered. She has seen something that I did not know was so easily exposed.

'I'll change the sheets for you,' I say, lumbering towards the door. 'You can sleep on the futon in my room.'

An hour later I am alone again, standing aimlessly by the windows. Beth has had a bath, drunk some tea, and is in the bedroom, tucked under my duvet. I am meant to be sleeping here but it is useless even to try so I hover around the flat, unsure what to do. I feel like an overblown balloon, about to burst with a devastating bang. Beth's presence draws out something in me that I have tried for a very long time to keep hidden. Is it her intensity? Or simply that she reminds me of myself? I pace around the place, trying to relax. As I look back over the last few weeks, this scene now seems oddly inevitable, as if I was an unwilling actor in someone else's plot. Yet I am unable to say exactly whose, or where the plot is leading.

I wander back into the bedroom. Snuggled under the covers of my bed, Beth sleeps. Padding quietly to the side of the futon, I squat down beside it, so that my face is almost level with hers. Her head is resting on her folded hands, her expression one of tranquillity. With her golden hair, long eyelashes and pale skin she resembles one of the Victorian angels overlooking the dead in Highgate cemetery, with their crumbling stone harps and trailing ivy. I should not be doing this, but now I am reaching out and placing my fingers on her cheek, tracing them down the smooth skin towards her pink lips. What would happen if I pushed my face even closer and brushed them with my own?

I jump up, horrified. Where the hell did that come from? For a moment I stand, stock still, in the middle of the bedroom, my eyes closed as I try to pull myself together. *This girl is your student, simple as that. Nothing is happening here that is to do with you and nothing is going to change. The past is over. Turn round and walk out of the door.*

But it is too late. I have climbed aboard this train, with its ripped-out seats and unintelligible graffiti, and whether I want to go there or not, it is going to deliver me to my destination.

'Please, just leave me alone . . .' I whimper, as I turn and rush towards the kitchen in search of chocolate. But even as I locate my stash of Mars Bars and, tearing off the wrappers, stuff one into my mouth, I am hurtling down through the thick sediment of all those years, no time to come up for air.

17

November 11, 1979. The Dreadheads had just performed the second song of their set, and I was more drunk than ever. This was not the knowing intoxication of someone who is familiar with the signs, but the headlong free-fall of an innocent. So, wasted as I was, I tipped my can of beer to my lips and, despite the spinning sensation, so soon to tip into nausea, I kept dancing. If I close my eyes and forget where and who I am now, I can see myself in picture-perfect detail: Cass, the fifteen-year-old, with her fringed purple hippie top, jeans and cowboy boots, the heavy eye-liner around her eyes and pudgy face. Little Miss Piggy, my mother had started calling me by then. She took my weight personally, could not stand the implied weakness. I, in turn, used it as a tool with which to prod her into the confrontations that increasingly formed the content of our relationship. By then the little girl who built sandcastles on the beach had disappeared. Probably I knew it already back then, but over the intervening years it had been confirmed: my mother would never give me what I wanted. And now, rather than try to wheedle some attention from her, an exercise akin to pulling a reticent limpet from a rock, my tactics were more aggressive.

So perhaps that was why I was friends with Billie, whom she loathed; perhaps that was why I was at that gig, which she had forbidden me to attend; perhaps that was why I was drunk. It would certainly be convenient if I could blame her. Similarly, the intervening years would have been easier to bear if I truly could remember nothing of what happened that night. But the truth is, it is all starting to come back.

The Dreadheads' set had just begun, but by now I was so inebriated that if, rather than a heavy-metal band, a herd of cows had been thrashing the guitars up on the stage, I doubt I would have noticed. I had been separated from Billie and her gang for over an hour, but I did not care. I was near the front of the venue, and dancing hard. Today the memory fills me with shame, but my predominant emotion was one of extreme satisfaction at how cool I must appear: a rock-and-roll chick, dancing free and so sexy. I must have been moving pretty exuberantly because people kept turning round, not, presumably, to stare with wonder at the beautiful wild child I was imagining myself to be but to have a laugh at the fat teenage girl who had so clearly lost it.

There was one guy in particular, who kept smiling at me in what I assumed to be admiration. I grinned back, beckoning him to join in. It felt good to be the centre of attention for once, to be practising my as-yet-untested sexual prowess. Wiggling my hips, I think I might even have given him a salacious wink. Laughing, the man broke free from his mates and stepped in front of me. He was not an adolescent, like the lower-sixth boys I was accustomed to with their bum-fluff and acne, but an adult, perhaps in his late twenties or early thirties. His long hair flopped limply on his shoulders and he was wearing a Motorhead T-shirt, which stuck to his chest in damp patches. For a minute or so we boogied good-naturedly together. The Dreadheads had just finished 'Hot Rod Chick', the crowd hooting for more, and I could hear the opening chords of 'Lady Of The Night', their only attempt at melody. Around us, people were flicking on their lighters, and swaying sentimentally to the synthesized organ. I stopped dancing, trying to steady myself as I surfaced momentarily. I needed to find Billie, I was thinking. I should try to push back through the crowd.

Rolling biliously, like a yacht in a storm, I staggered towards the neon exit sign, which flashed at the back of the hall. I needed very badly to get some air. In fact, I was going to be sick. I pushed past the bouncers on the door and stumbled into the cold night air, the pavement tilting nauseously towards me. I could taste bile in my mouth, my legs were giving way. There was an alley just on the other side of the doors. Pressing my hand over my mouth, I toppled towards it.

I was more sick that night than I have ever been, before or since: outside the Odeon, then in the ladies', as Billie – whom I had literally bumped into on the steps – splashed water over my face, trailing back on the train as the gang teased me about the state of my clothes, and back home, in the blessed quiet of my bedroom. It served me right, my mother said, as she stood over my inert body the next morning. She had told me not to go, warned me about drinking too much, and now I had puked all over my bedroom carpet, and she was damn well not clearing it up. She tugged back the curtains so that the bright sunlight hammered into my eyes, then stood over me unsympathetically, her hands on her hips. Didn't she have enough to contend with? she was saying. How could I be so selfish?

Downstairs, I could hear Dad call her name.

After Mum had stomped back down the stairs I lay on my bed, staring at the ceiling. I was desperate to block the events of last night from my mind. All I could allow myself to think was that it was time for everything to change. I had thought them so cool, but now I despised Billie and her crowd, with their pathetic allegiance to head-banging bands that no one other than the educationally challenged could take seriously. They might believe that their leather jackets and bandannas made them appear hard, but the truth was that they were losers. Last night, for example, Billie's boyfriend had been wearing jeans that were virtually flared. And the wispy beard he was sprouting from his spotty chin was an embarrassment. I had assumed him to be the silent, intense type, but now, as I recalled the only exchange I had ever had with him, in which he had told me that Motorhead were 'fucking nutters, yeah?', a comment that was presumably meant as praise, I saw that in fact he was the silent, stupid type.

They had laughed at me when I reappeared at the Odeon, even though I was shivering so violently I could barely speak. And they had continued the piss-taking all the way home, waving hamburgers and opened cans of Special Brew under my nose to make me retch. And now I hated them and everything they stood for. I did not want to be like those idiots any more, I thought, as I stared listlessly at my posters of Led Zeppelin and Black Sabbath. Billie was already on probation for nicking a bottle of cider from the Co-op and by my age had dropped out of school. In fact, if one took away the shop-lifting and drinking – activities I was finding increasingly empty – her company was beginning to pall. She acted as if she was a great wit, but what this amounted to were snide or sarcastic asides and a great deal of swearing. Whenever I said something clever she would look at me blankly, then accuse me of being a snob. She bored me, I realized.

So that was the end of that, I decided, as I rose from my death-bed and tore the posters from the wall. No more heavy metal, and no more Billie.

I thought it was all over, you see, that I could simply will it away. What I had yet to grasp was that it had only just begun.

*

When I next open my eyes the sitting room is half lit by an overcast dawn. I sit up, blinking at the unfamiliar gloom. The sparkling autumn sunshine we have been enjoying has ended: this morning the sky outside is grey and stormy – I can hear the wind banging at the windows, feel the shudder of the battered walls. My watch tells me it is five to eight.

Something bad happened the night before. I reach behind to rub my back, struggling to recall what. I am chilled, my shoulders stiff and bruised from a night on the sofa. Suddenly I remember Beth: her mistaken plagiarism, the way she was waiting for me outside the night-club, and the strange things that made me feel. And now she is here, asleep in my bed. I touched her cheek, I remember in mortification, almost kissed her lips. Christ!

I struggle to my feet and shuffle towards the door, thinking that I need to pee and get changed. Today, everything is going to be different: no sluttish mess, crisp efficiency in the workplace and, above all, *no reminiscing*. For a start, I tell myself schoolmarmishly, I need to do something about my appearance. Looking down I see that I have slept in the crumpled clothes I pulled on to rescue Beth and my hair is a tangled mat. As I reach blearily for the door handle I resolve to shower and change, then eat a healthy, life-enhancing bowl of muesli – not, of course, that there would ever be such a thing in the flat. My hand is just about to close round it, when I give a shriek of alarm. In my dozy state I have only just noticed that a figure is huddled up by the wall.

'Jesus *Christ*!'

But it is only Beth. She is sitting cross-legged, my duvet draped around her shoulders, her hands in her lap. God knows how long she has been there, watching me.

'Hello, Cass,' she whispers. 'I didn't want to wake you.'

I take a deep breath. My heart is hammering wildly. 'You

gave me a shock,' I say, trying to laugh, but failing and instead producing a ragged gurgle.

She smiles shyly, fixing me with her eyes.

'How are you feeling?' I croak.

'I'm OK, I guess. I've just had Alec on the phone.'

'Have you?'

'He said he was going to report me for what happened yesterday in the seminar.'

I blink at her. What the hell is *wrong* with the guy? Or is he alluding to the essay?

'That's ridiculous,' I say hoarsely. 'He doesn't know what he's talking about.'

She smiles hesitantly. I do not want her to see how angry this news has made me.

'You really don't need to worry about Alec,' I say soothingly. 'I'll sort him out.'

She shrugs. 'To be honest, it doesn't really matter what he does. Not now I don't have a family any more.' Her lower lip is twitching.

'What about a bedsit in town?' I say, pulling myself together. 'Or maybe the university has some sort of emergency accommodation. I'm sure we can sort something out for you.'

She looks away, bunching the duvet with her hands. 'I suppose you think I'm pathetic still living with them, don't you? I know I should be able to carry on alone but I just can't . . .'

'Beth, I don't think you're pathetic.' I give her a reassuring smile.

She blinks at me, opening her eyes round and large like a little lost kitten. 'I can trust you, Cass, can't I?' The way she says this makes it sound as if there is something else she has not yet told me.

'Of course you can,' I say. 'I'm one hundred per cent here for you.'

She pauses, taking this on board. How many other people is she able to trust?

'It's just that I don't want you telling any of the other lecturers about my family and everything. I like to keep it all private.'

I squat down and take her hand in mine. 'I'm not going to gossip about you, Beth, I promise, but your situation isn't anything to be ashamed of either. I mean, this isn't your fault, is it?'

'Isn't it?' she whimpers, looking despairingly at her bony hands. 'Sometimes I think it's all because of me. That they don't love me, I mean.'

I have to make a conscious effort not to sigh with impatience. How could she possibly blame herself? Whatever happened in her childhood, it can hardly be her fault. No, I think, with a nasty swoop of self-hatred, it's never the children who are to blame.

'It's just ghastly luck,' I say gently. 'I mean, I obviously don't know the exact circumstances, but there's probably little you could do to make them choose you over a daughter who died.'

She clutches her arms around her waist.

'Perhaps we should fix up for you to see a counsellor,' I continue. 'There's a free service at the university, you know. I think you'd find it really useful. Remember, they're trained and will be used to helping people facing similar issues to yours. It might be just the thing.'

She does not reply. I want to help her, but feel defeated. 'Beth, listen.'

I place my hands round her face and move it firmly so that she cannot avoid looking at me. For a moment we are silent, staring at each other with an intimacy for which I was unprepared. What does she know about my past? To her, I am just an older woman in a position of responsibility from whom she needs support. If she knew the truth, how would she feel about me?

'Whatever happens,' I say slowly, 'I shall be here for you. So just trust me, OK?'

Looking solemnly into my eyes, she nods. 'Of course I'll trust you, Cass,' she whispers. 'I'll do whatever you want.'

18

A storm is approaching, the air heavy and threatening. As I drive to work along the clifftops the leaden sky is filled with dark hydra heads of cloud moving in fast across the sea. The wind has swept away my previous resolutions. I feel weighted down and oppressed, unable to contemplate the chores I promised myself this morning that I would complete. I turn on to the campus and park the Beetle, battling to close the door against the buffeting wind. This time, I am leaving it close to the main road.

I cross the car-park and walk swiftly across the concrete walkway. The paths leading to Block D are mushy with leaves, and flurries of wet paper keep blowing into my legs. Everyone I pass has their collar up and their hands deep in their pockets, their bodies bent against the wind. The days of lolling on the campus meadows in the mellow autumn sun seem distant.

I hurry up the steps. I have drunk two mugs of coffee, eaten some toast, even showered and changed my clothes, as per schoolmarm instruction, but I still feel horrendous. My brain is fuzzy and disoriented, my belly quivers; it is as if I have not slept for days. But it is not so much my physical state that is making it so hard to hold up my throbbing head and call a cheerful 'Good morning!' to Maggie, our department secretary, who has just skipped past with a wave. No, more than my exhaustion, it is the swelling dread that has been growing in intensity all morning. I feel as if I am attempting to wade through sinking sand: the ground seems solid enough, but any minute now I shall put my feet in the wrong place and be sucked hopelessly down. Mostly, it has to do with Beth and her stupid essay. Despite yesterday's efforts, this morning I am unable to justify allowing it through. If it were anyone else, Andy, for example, or the skittish Natalie, I would not have hesitated to report their misdemeanour to the exam board. And yet with Beth it seems so much more complicated. I should not allow myself to become personally involved with my students, I know, yet the events of last night have opened up something in me that I had almost forgotten, like caustic soda poured down a long-blocked drain.

I walk into the building, heading for the canteen. There I am planning to demolish a quick brownie or two before my class but, as I soon discover, the place is crammed with people. The nine a.m. lectures have just finished, and the queue to be served stretches down the corridor. As I stomp past, I glance around distractedly. Why the hell am I so anxious? Is it just Beth's essay, or something more? As I remember the strange email and phone calls, my stomach jumps nervously. I look across the room, praying for a friendly face, but there is only Julian, who is slouched louchely at a table with a group of postgraduates, and Bob Stennings, who is sitting by himself reading the *Guardian*. What I need, I realize with a little slosh of self-pity, is Sarah, with her urbane scepticism and nose for nonsense. I want to describe to her what has been happening, my words reducing events to the sum of their parts: an odd email; a series of crank phone calls; two students, one for whom I do not care at all and one for whom I may care too much. Then I would hear her comforting snort of derision at the suggestion that all may somehow be connected, her brisk remonstration that I should get out more.

Forget the brownies, I decide. I am going to call her right now. Even if she is with Poppy, we'll arrange a time to talk.

Yet as I retrace my steps towards the corridor, my office and the phone, a figure suddenly steps out of the queue in front of me. 'Dr Bainbridge?'

I grimace with displeasure, for it is Alec. He is clasping a pile of books to his chest and simpering as innocently at me as if he was Little Boy Blue.

'Yes?' I snap, my mind fusing into an abusive tirade. Why do you have it in for Beth and me? I want to yell. What the hell is going on?

He pretends to look confused by my unfriendly response, swallowing and rubbing his hand awkwardly through his hair. 'I . . .'

'What is it?'

'I wanted to talk to you about yesterday's seminar . . .' He trails off.

I glare at him, remembering his self-satisfied expression as he fingered the *Society and History* article, his obvious pleasure at scoring a point. Get off my back, Laddie, I want to shout, I'm not in the mood for your whingeing. Instead, I suck at my lips. 'I'm glad you've brought it up,' I say, 'because I think you owe Beth an apology for the way you've behaved.'

He blanches, goggling at me with his mouth hanging open. Gradually, his face – to the roots of his hair – turns scarlet. Down the line, the waiting students have quietened, picking up on my disapproving tone in the way that a flock of birds in the trees might swoop on seeds, scattered far below. I can sense them turning to watch, the expectant hush of a crowd eager for scandal. 'That's not the way I see it,' he says coldly.

'Isn't it?'

'All I did was point out that she wasn't citing her source,' he adds, with a sneer so slight – a small lifting of the upper lip – that I nearly miss it.

'*All* you did?' I snort. 'That, plus all your threats. I think you need to consider the effects of what you do on other people.' There is more that I could say, but it is better that I stop. His face rigid, Alec gives a quiet yelp of affront. I turn away from him, not wanting to witness any more. All around us, people are straining to hear. 'What are you looking at?' I hiss, picking out a young woman with coffee-coloured skin and spiky blue hair for my attentions. 'Mind your own bloody business.'

She gapes at me, then glances quickly away, cowering closer to her aghast friends. Alec's face is pale with rage. The books still gripped in his slim, young man's hands, he pushes his way through the throng and marches out of the canteen.

Rather than making me feel better, this exchange has left me tremulous with spent emotion. I want to get away as quickly as possible, but the queue is now so long that it has doubled back on itself and to escape I will have to pass through a crowd of jostling students, all of whom have witnessed my outburst. I have behaved badly, I think, the sour regret already flowing fast and furious. Professional and sensitive student relations? Somehow I think *not*. The only possible course of action is to pretend that nothing unusual has happened. As I look desperately around the canteen for somewhere to sit, I see that Julian is waving me over ebulliently, and I cannot possibly ignore him.

'What was all *that* about?' he says, with glee. 'It looked as if you were giving everyone a good ticking-off.'

I can feel his eyes lingering on me, for just a second too long, and am suddenly aware of my appearance. I dressed so quickly this morning, and the end result is somewhat bedraggled, to say the least. As Beth locked herself into the bathroom, I threw on the first garments I could locate: an old corduroy skirt that pinches at the waist, and a baggy bobbly jumper that should, many long seasons ago, have been consigned to the Help the Aged bag. As I glanced in the mirror my main impression was of an eccentric overweight woman whose wardrobe was procured from the 10p pile at a church jumble sale.

'Just a minor student-welfare issue,' I say, forcing myself to sound breezy and sitting down next to him. I do not want to be here, but it seems my only option. I am hoping that no one will notice how my hands are shaking.

'You're quite scary sometimes, you know,' Julian says.

'Am I?'

'You seem nice and warm and everything, but underneath your friendly exterior you're *dangerous*.' He glances at me playfully.

I gaze back at him, perplexed. All I can think is how little I trust him. 'What did you say to old Alec?' he goes on. 'He looked as if he was about to burst into tears.'

'Well, that's his problem.' I try to grin, but it turns into a toothy simper.

'Why's that?' One of the postgraduates frowns at me, then leans back in his chair and starts to roll a cigarette. He's a hairy bloke, with bushy ginger sideburns and a leather jacket with the words 'Fuck Capitalism' emblazoned on the back.

'It just is,' I say, still trying to smile. I know his sort well: the type who sits on every faculty–student committee going and comes to each meeting armed with a long list of complaints. If he thinks I am going to discuss Alec with him, he is mistaken.

'Has he been showing you up in class, Cass?' Julian says, nudging me mischievously. 'He's got a reputation for being cleverer than most of his tutors, you know.'

I stare at him wildly. Has Alec been complaining to Julian about my teaching? Are they somehow *in league*?

'Nah, he's cool,' the Fuck Capitalism postgraduate says, with a shrug. 'He lives in the bedsit upstairs from my girlfriend. He's a good geezer.'

'So what's the problem?' says Julian.

I shift uneasily. I would do almost anything to be somewhere else, but I am pinioned to my chair by my dread of walking back past the queue. 'Nothing's the problem. We just don't get along, that's all.'

There is a long, loaded silence. The assorted postgraduates gaze at me, waiting for more. I look down at my hands, twisting my rings. I can sense Julian sizing me up. His jocularity seems to have disappeared; when I glance up he looks away, frowning. For a second, my suspicions evaporate: *He is just trying to be friendly.* But then he looks me up and down and says, 'Are you all right?'

This is meant as a put-down, I am sure. 'Of course I am,' I say, bristling. 'Why shouldn't I be?'

'Well, you just seem slightly flustered, I guess.'

'I'm fine.'

He raises those sandy eyebrows of his, making it clear he does not believe me. Then he looks away.

Alone in my office I make a pretence of examining the top layer of papers on my desk. I have been teaching all afternoon and now I feel drained, utterly emptied of joy or purpose. Today's seminar did not go well: the students were reticent, gazing at me warily. I filled their silence with largely meaningless gabble, waffling on about public records while they avoided my eye. When I snapped at somebody for not doing the week's reading, meaningful glances were exchanged. They must all have heard about my outburst by now; probably saw it for themselves in the canteen. The whole department will be gossiping about me, I think dismally. Perhaps Julian is right: I am losing it, and everyone has noticed.

I feel so alone. I thought I needed solitude, but it seems that I am unable to function without the comforting buffers of other people's company. And I am obviously more dependent on Matt than I thought. I picture him sitting at the table in the kitchen at home, the newspaper spread before him as he chuckles at some ridiculous story he's discovered on the inside pages. Despite his huge intellect he loves trash, bless him. I should be there now: I could be pottering around our cosy London kitchen, getting lunch. Then later, if we grew bored of work, he would come up behind me, put his big arms round my waist, and we'd go upstairs.

What is happening? We have been so closely intertwined for the past ten years that I know his habits as intimately as my own. Yet now we are apart and can no longer even speak to each other without the rapid slide into bickering and blame. I close my eyes, picturing his face, imagining his hand around mine as we stroll on the Heath, then suddenly sit up straight.

That was what started it. I have just remembered the walk on the Heath we took with Josh and his baby. Yes, I'm sure I'm right: things started to go awry when Josh's new girlfriend got pregnant. He was meant to be Matt's wild friend, from his Manchester days, with whom he would stay up all night drinking, a confirmed hedonist, with a late-youth taste in clubbing and narcotic indulgence. But then he had fallen in love with a sweet young hippie called Miranda and everything changed. Over the next months the loved-up couple had become pregnancy fanatics. Her food restrictions, her disavowal of medical interventions, her raspberry leaf tea, we heard about it all. But while I mentally gagged each time they came over, sitting close together so that Josh could place a hand proudly on Miranda's bump, Matt listened to their reports from the fertility front with eager, gleaming eyes.

'Christ, they're dull.' I sighed, as they departed after a particularly gruesome evening. 'Imagine what it's going to be like when the baby arrives.'

But rather than laughing in agreement, as he would once have done, Matt turned on me with a force that left me white-lipped and silent. 'For God's sake, Cass,' he hissed, 'you've had a face on you all evening like you're sucking lemons. What the hell's the *matter* with you?'

Or am I mistaken? Perhaps Matt was just pretending to be fascinated by Miranda's eventual three-day labour; perhaps his dewy-eyed enthusiasm for the resulting wrinkled alien was feigned; perhaps he had just insisted that *he* should take a turn in carrying the baby during our walk to be polite. Perhaps he has not really changed. With renewed resolve to set things right, I pick up the phone and dial the number of our Stoke Newington house, holding my breath. When he answers, I will announce immediately that I am going to move back to London and commute. Then I will tell him about the creepy phone calls and the email. His hearty scepticism will blow it all away, like the wind through a cobweb.

But I get the answer-machine. I do not leave a message, just put the phone down. I drop my head into my hands, sighing and rubbing my scalp, as if this might dislodge my gloom. I am not usually like this, I am Cass Bainbridge, a cheerful, calm woman who always assumes the best of everyone. So why do I increasingly feel drenched with alienation, so bitter and angry?

Perhaps I just need to get a proper night's sleep. I push the papers on to the floor and rest my head on the desk, the scratchy wood grazing my ear. The computer hums and buzzes. Outside, I can hear the whoop and laughter of students spilling from their lectures. The day is becoming increasingly windy: the tree outside my window keeps batting the pane with its branches; through my half-closed eyes I can see the dark clouds moving fast across the sky.

Dragging myself upright, I prop my elbow on the desk and stare at the computer. I should call Sarah but do not have the energy. As I click on to the email programme I wait for the list of unopened mail to appear. I might at least try to clear my in-tray. When I looked this morning I had twenty unread messages; by now I will have at least another ten. For a second or so, the screen is blank as the programme downloads. Then, as the messages start to appear, I read, 'You have 159 new messages.' Jesus, talk about IT overload! Pursing my lips, I squint at the screen as the flashing icons pile up.

The first thing I notice is that the new messages are identical. Sometimes this happens, the message-writer hitting the 'send' button twice by mistake. But for so many repeated messages to appear it must have been deliberate. Then I see the address of the sender and the subject, and freeze: '*loveankisses@juniper*. Subject: YOU'.

My stomach plunges. As I stare at the long line of messages, I keep telling myself it is unconnected, another random prank. Yet I cannot clear the image of Alec's furious face from my mind. Could he be behind this? The first email was sent at 10.09, just a short while after our confrontation in the café queue. The next arrived thirty seconds later, quickly followed by another, again and again and again. As I recall Beth's description of his odd behaviour in the university computing room, the explanation makes increasing sense. Perhaps he uses a different address when he wants to send something unpleasant. It's the kind of thing a computing nerd would relish.

And now I must face whatever it is he has sent me. I click 'open', flinching as I wait for the message to appear. I am half expecting a monster to reach out of the computer and grab me by the throat, but what I see instead is a single line:

I know.

I gaze at the screen, mesmerized. What does he mean? How can he know? Clicking with increasing desperation on 'read', I scroll down the messages, hoping to find further clues. But it is the same message, *I know*, over and over. Then suddenly I remember. *Jesus!* It is exactly as I feared. He is talking about Beth's essay! He saw she had copied it, and is now punishing me for reprimanding him in the canteen queue with this thinly veiled threat. I place my hands on my hot cheeks. What a mess.

I cannot bear to open the rest of the messages. Pushing heavily on the 'delete' button, I erase them one by one. By the time I have finished I feel light-headed, my thoughts skittering in every direction, like a flock of frightened birds. He could report me, I keep thinking. Is this a blackmail attempt? Suddenly I have to get out of the office. I push back my chair with a clatter and rise to my feet.

19

Beth must have been looking out for me: as I climb the stairs she is waiting at the door of the flat. Her hair is brushed and tied back in a plait and she has changed from the jeans and clubby top into a long red dress, which – I notice with a start – belongs to me. Despite recent events, her face is merry.

'Welcome home!' She does a little whirl in my dress, which is hugely big for her, swamping her small frame and making her look like a little girl dressing up.

'You don't mind, do you? I was getting so cold.'

I shake my head. It was too small for me, anyway, and it is good to see her happy.

'And wait until you see this!' She takes my arm and leads me across the hall towards the sitting room. She opens the door with a flourish and steps aside. 'Tra-la!'

I walk through the doorway and look around in bemusement. The place has been transformed. My books, which were lying strewn over the floor, have been placed upright and arranged with precision around the sides of the room. All the other litter – the old newspapers, empty bottles and dirty clothes – has gone. The windows have been cleaned, the carpet Hoovered. A fire is burning in the grate, and placed bang in the middle of the room is a brightly coloured rag rug.

'I found it in the cupboard in the other room,' Beth says, when she sees me staring at it. 'I thought it went nicely with the colour scheme. Now all you need are some pictures.'

'What have you done with my washing?' I say weakly. The truth is that, bereft of my mess, I feel strangely disconcerted.

'In here.' Grinning, she takes me by the arm and leads me towards the bedroom. To my amazement the floor has been cleared of clothes, which have been washed, ironed and hung in the wardrobe.

'I did the laundry,' Beth is saying. 'I mean, you work so hard, and I had nothing to do all afternoon, so I thought it would be helpful.'

I cannot think of anything constructive to say. I should be pleased, for she has clearly been trying hard to do the right thing, but she has misjudged the situation. She has seen my dirty knickers, I think, with a rictus of embarrassment, been through my things. I continue to look around the room, trying to keep my face free of emotion. I feel like a *Changing Rooms* participant whose beloved interiors have been replaced with the nightmarish schema of her worst enemies. On the mantelpiece, a bunch of dog-daisies sits in a milk bottle, and on top of the freshly made bed she has placed the Cabbage Patch doll from the box room. Unable to control myself, I lean over and pick it up. 'This isn't mine,' I say tartly. 'It belongs to the previous tenants. It needs throwing away.'

'Aah. But it's so sweet.'

'Well, why don't you have it, then?'

I push the doll into her hands and stalk out of the room. I need to be alone, if only for a few minutes. I stomp across the hall, scuffing at the carpet with my feet. Beth has merely been trying to help, I tell myself; by many people's standards – Matt's, for example – it would be positively ill-mannered of her to laze around all day and do nothing. In the kitchen I stand by the shiny oven, eyeing the crockery stacked neatly by the sink, the still hideous but now gleaming flowery tiles. She has even arranged the empty jars by the window, pushing them into a geometric line. On opening the fridge, I see that my stock of TV dinners has been joined by a box of tofu, various leafy and presumably organic vegetables, a large carton of soya milk and a packet of disgusting-looking vegetarian sausages.

'I thought I could cook you that vegan feast tonight,' Beth says quietly. I turn, to find her standing behind me. 'That is, if you're hungry.'

I nod silently, not sure how to respond. I was under the impression that I was looking after her, but our roles seem to have been reversed. Objectively she is right, the flat *did* need to be tidied, yet I feel taken over, my space invaded.

'All this,' Beth gestures at the kitchen, 'it's just, like, my way of saying thanks. I mean, you came out in the middle of the night. You didn't have to do that.'

I turn. She is hovering anxiously on the threshold of the kitchen, doing the enquiring bird gesture with her head. Unlike me, she's a homemaker, the sort of young woman who delights in nest-building. Dealing with my domestic chaos was probably a task she enjoyed, so why begrudge her it?

'It's fine,' I say, at last smiling without straining my facial muscles. 'It's really sweet of you.'

'I'm sorry if I've overdone it . . . It's just, you know, my way of controlling stuff. Tidying and that?'

She folds her arms apprehensively across her chest and I curse myself for my churlish reaction to the doll and not thanking her more effusively. 'No, really,' I say, taking a deep breath. 'It's lovely. Thank you.'

She beams at me. 'I knew you'd like it.'

I busy myself with the kettle, reaching for mugs and tea-bags.

'Mine's a herbal,' she says, as I open the cupboard and peer inside. In place of my instant coffee there is a box of camomile tea and a jar of something dubious called barley cup. 'All this food must have cost you a bomb,' I mutter. 'I ought to give you some money.'

'Nah, it was nothing.'

'But how can you afford it?'

She shrugs. 'I've got the bar work.'

'But that can't bring in much. Do you have a grant as well?'

'Oh, yeah, all that kind of thing.' She has turned away and is fussing at the impeccable taps with a cloth, humming softly under her breath. Perhaps she has an alternative source of income, something she is ashamed of. In my last teaching post I had a student who spent the nights pole-dancing to subsidize her tiny grant.

'Oh, by the way,' she says suddenly, 'I found your phone.'

'My mobile?'

'Under a pile of clothes in your bedroom.'

For the first time since arriving home, I am genuinely pleased. 'You angel! I've been looking for that everywhere.'

She drops the cloth into the sink and swings round to face me. Without thinking, I blow her a kiss, and she beams, a little girl receiving praise. Once again I am struck by her loneliness and desperate desire to please. On the ledge behind her, the kettle bubbles into a fury.

'So,' I say, trying to choose the right words, 'how are you feeling today?'

'Better.'

'Made any decisions about what you're going to do?'

She frowns. 'What is there to decide?'

'Well,' I say carefully, 'you need to arrange some accommodation. That is, if you really can't go back home.'

For a while I think she might not have heard me: she picks up the kettle, pours water into the mugs, seems to be concentrating on something else. Then, very slowly, she turns round and I see something I had not expected in her face: a trace of anger. 'I thought I explained last night, Cass,' she says quietly. 'I can't go home. They've chucked me out.'

'So you need to get yourself fixed up with something else –'

But she does not let me finish. She is shaking her head to and fro, and gaping at me in anguish. I fold my arms, my heart sinking. I want to help her, but it is all getting too complicated. And if Alec is about to accuse me of helping her to cheat, it would look even worse if she was staying here. But her face has lost its colour, her eyes are distraught.

'Please!' she begs. 'I can't think about it any more! All I want is to stay here with you, where I'm safe.'

I regard her thoughtfully, trying to formulate an appropriate response. What is she talking about? Why should she not be safe? I no longer understand what this is about. All I know for sure is that something has changed, and now my insides are tying themselves in knots.

'All right, then, stay tonight,' I say slowly. 'That's fine. But tomorrow we need to think –'

But I am interrupted mid-sentence. I stop and turn towards the front door. I have just heard a key in the lock.

20

Matt strides into the hall, dropping his bags proprietorially on to the floor as the door slams behind him. I peep out of the kitchen. He looks different: in the weeks since I have seen him he has lost weight and has had his usually shaggy brown hair cut short. With his beefy shoulders and square jaw, he looks like a squaddie. In one hand he is holding his laptop, his ever-faithful friend, and in the other a large bunch of lilies. 'Cass?' he calls, and already he is moving impatiently towards the sitting room.

I glance at Beth and hurry quickly out of the room towards him. His unexpected appearance has knocked me off balance: my heart is fluttering with nerves and inexplicable guilt. He *will* understand about Beth being here, I tell myself. He cannot, after all, turn up unannounced and expect me to drop everything.

'Hi,' I say, trying to sound happy.

When he hears my voice he swings round, grinning. 'Cass! My lovely girl!' He places the lilies in my arms and takes a step back, peering into my face expectantly. 'Go on, then, take them.'

He looks so different that I feel disoriented, struck less by the warmth of recognition and more by a cold blast of alienation. Is this really the man I have been living with for almost ten years? 'Christ, you look rough,' he says jovially. 'In need of a good seeing-to, no doubt. Why don't you come over here and loosen your corsage *avec moi*?'

He must be joking. It would be like having sex with an acquaintance. Trying hard not to frown, I place the flowers

185

gently on the floor and step away from his embrace, shocked at my feelings. I should be overjoyed at his appearance, not as if I have been rudely interrupted. 'You should have told me you were coming.' I wanted this to sound as if I were chiding him affectionately, but my voice is tight with irritation. If only I could simply give him a hug, but as he steps away from me, it seems impossible, like accosting a stranger on the street and throwing my arms round them.

'I thought you'd like a surprise.' He studies me quizzically. Like him, I must look different. I have put on so much weight, for a start, and he is bound to comment on it. But rather than the appraising stare I am cowering from, he is gazing at me lovingly.

'You keep not returning my messages,' he says softly, 'so I just thought I'd jump on the train and come and see you. I've really missed you. It's been too long.'

'Right.' I need to say quickly that I've missed him too. But all I am able to muster is, 'You should have given me some warning.'

And now his expression is changing, his eyebrows knotting and his mouth turning down. 'Christ, Cass,' he says curtly, 'we haven't seen each other for bloody ages. You might at least pretend to be pleased.'

The bruised disappointment on his face, which he is fighting to conceal, makes me want to weep. *He loves me*, I think. And then, before I have had a chance to block it out, another and far more disconcerting sentence burns through my mind: *I am going to hurt him*. 'You've been so out of touch . . .' I whisper. If I concentrate hard enough, perhaps I can force these thoughts away. 'You didn't ring or anything.'

'Of course I bloody did,' he mutters sulkily. 'I left about a hundred messages on the mobile.'

'I lost it.' He keeps staring at my face, clearly not believing me. We seem to have got beyond the point where there is anything to be gained from trying to convince him. I pause, gathering the strength to force my voice into friendly warmth. 'Anyway, it's good that you're here . . .' I take a step towards him, put my arms round his neck and attempt to kiss his freshly shaved cheek, but he steps to one side, his expression frigid. There is a bottle of champagne tucked into the side of his bag, I see, with a sharp pang: he must have been expecting a celebration. For a moment I think he is going to forgive me: his expression eases and he almost returns the pressure of my hand, but then his eyes widen with what I can only interpret as disgust, and he snaps, 'Who the hell are *you*?'

Turning, I see that Beth has followed me from the kitchen and is now standing in the hall, gazing at us. I do not know how long she has been there, or how much of our exchange she has overheard. 'She's one of my students,' I say sooth-ingly. I am clicking into calm-Matt-down mode, smoothing his ruffled feathers and cajoling him out of the temper I can see gathering force, like an oncoming storm, on his face. I take a step back smiling with false cheer. 'Beth, meet my partner, Dr Matthew Hughes,' I say brightly. 'Matt, this is Beth.'

I am hoping they will shake hands, the situation changing seamlessly from blatant hostility to friendly formality, but Matt puts his hands into his pockets and nods at Beth cursorily. 'Here for a supervision, are you?' he says dismis-sively, flicking her away with his hand as if he were a Victorian patriarch and she a scullery-maid.

She glares at him, her face darkening. 'I'm living here,' she says.

Matt's eyebrows shoot up his forehead, Beth simpers, and I gasp, both in amazement at her presumption and horror at Matt's certain reaction. He is goggling at her, then turning to me, his eyes wide. 'You've acquired a *flatmate*?'

'She's just been here for the night,' I say hastily. 'She urgently needed somewhere to stay, and –'

'Cass has just invited me to stay tonight as well,' Beth puts in unhelpfully. Then – or perhaps I am imagining it – she gives me a discreet nod of triumph, as if to say, That's put him in his place.

'Oh, has she?'

Folding his arms, Matt glowers at me. I swallow hard. If only I had known he was coming down tonight I could have prepared myself, got my reactions right.

'Kind of,' I mutter. Then to Beth, I add, 'Beth, could Matt and I have a moment alone, please?'

For a second her face changes into something unreadable. Then she says, 'No worries,' and turns on her heel.

'What the hell is going on?' Matt snarls venomously, as the door closes behind her.

His face is furious and for the first time since he has walked through the door I feel myself stiffen with indignation. 'Calm down. She's a student who needs help, not my lover.' As I say this I remember the odd feelings I experienced while watching her sleep and feel myself flush.

But Matt does not notice. Instead, he nods sarcastically. 'Well, *that*'s a relief. Once again everything is put on hold so that you can help some pathetic little waif you've managed to dig up.'

Now I'm getting really annoyed. He knows nothing about what has been going on, and yet he obviously believes that it is perfectly all right to come charging into my flat whenever he chooses and take control. I thought we were moving in synchrony but, clearly, it has taken only a few short weeks to become derailed. 'You don't know anything about her,' I hiss. 'She's in a hell of a mess. She's fallen out with her family and had nowhere to stay.'

'And since when have you been running a women's refuge?'

'Oh, for God's sake!'

I start to move across the room, away from him, but he grabs me by the wrist, pulling me back towards him. 'Don't walk away from me, Cass!'

I prise his fingers from my wrist, take a deep breath, and say, as evenly as I can, 'I'm not walking away from you, but I don't want to stand here and be shouted at. Especially not when we have an audience.'

'OK, then,' he says, picking up his coat from the floor. 'Let's go out.'

Matt strides across the road and paces towards the square gardens, his face set. As I scuttle after him I feel as if I am about to explode with bubbling, boiling resentment. Does he expect me to trail after him like a lap-dog, begging for his forgiveness? And what exactly am I supposed to have done? He flings open the gate and starts to stomp across the lawns, down to the tunnel that opens on to the road, and then the beach. I can smell salt and the earthy aroma of muddy grass. A hundred metres or so further on, traffic chunders past relentlessly. To the west I can glimpse the spangly lights of the pier, then the spreading urban mass of the city. The wind is glacial.

Finally I catch up with him, grabbing his hand in a final attempt at reconciliation. He faces me, a little boy in a temper because his evening has not gone as planned. I had forgotten he could behave like this, but now, without even trying, I am slipping back into the well-worn grooves of our relationship.

'Where do you want to go?' I say, smiling composedly as if we were simply strolling towards the sea for a night out. It's worth a try: give him a bit of time to expiate his rage, then pretend nothing has happened.

'What are you *talking about*?' he growls. 'I don't want to *go* anywhere.'

I ignore this, forcing myself to remain calm. 'Then let's go back to the flat. It's ridiculously cold out here.'

'That would be fine. Except that you've invited half the student population to keep us company.'

'Come on.'

He glares at me contemptuously and is just about to continue his long march to the sea when suddenly he turns to me again. 'Just tell me one thing,' he splutters. 'Did you do this deliberately?'

'Do what?'

'Invite someone to stay so that you didn't have to be alone with me.'

I goggle at him. Is he really so paranoid? 'That's preposterous! I had no idea you were coming! And she's only staying one night!'

I expect him at least to hesitate at this, but he does not miss a beat. 'Tell her to go somewhere else.'

'She hasn't *got* anywhere else.'

'Oh, yeah? And since when have you been her mummy?'

I resist the temptation to snap back, *Not half as long as I've been yours.* Instead, I shake my head mournfully, try to retrieve his hand. My hair is flapping in my face, freezing air gusts through my thin jumper. 'Look, sweetie,' I say, trying to pacify him, 'let's go back to the flat. If you don't want her there, I'll find somewhere else for her to stay. It isn't such a big deal.'

'You *always* do this,' he says petulantly. 'Just when we most need to be together, you find some loser to mollycoddle.'

He stands sullenly in front of me, scowling. I should be taking him in my arms, pushing Beth to the back of my thoughts, but I cannot stop thinking that in the brief time we have been apart he has turned into a stranger who no longer knows anything about me. How could that have happened so quickly? Then he lurches forward, grabbing my waist clumsily and pulling me towards him. I am so surprised that I almost trip, falling against the scratchy warmth of his duffel coat before righting myself and stepping back hastily. The thought is so terrible that I want to push it violently away, but now it has lodged in my mind, a banner headline: *Don't touch me.*

'What are you *doing*?' I stutter. 'Just get off!'

He turns away sharply, stumbling over the molehills and thistle-spiked grass towards the sea. And in the split second that I glimpse his stricken face I know that he has read my thoughts. 'Matt! Wait!' I shout, and run after him.

By the time I have caught up with him he has reached a thicket of bushes and trees, just before the gate. It has started to rain, a light sheen that brushes our faces, wetting our lips with cold spray. Matt is breathing heavily, wiping the moisture from his cheeks. 'What's going on, Cass?' he says quietly. 'What's all this about?'

I swallow. I do not like the seriousness of his voice, the intensity in his eyes. It fills my belly with a spreading, indigestible dread. 'There's nothing going on. You know that.'

'Do I?'

I shrug, faking nonchalance. I do not want to be having this conversation. I want to flick an invisible switch that will erase the last hour, return us to the comfort zone. But Matt's eyes are red and his forehead is riven with lines I have not seen before. 'Come back to London,' he says. 'We could get married . . .' He chews his lip and his voice drops to a whisper: '*Have a baby.*'

The moment he says it, I know for sure it is this that lies beneath our rift, that barely visible hairline fracture, which is now cracking into an abyss. It was such a small thing at first, his unspoken desire: a surprising spurt of envy as he watched Josh with his baby, a fleeting emptiness as he eyed the buggies in Clissold Park. But, allowed a crack of light, it has gathered strength, pushing us unstoppably apart, like ivy pulling at bricks. And now, as I stare back at Matt, whose eyes are fixed on my face with an intensity he normally reserves for his computer screen, I realize something else. Our relationship is over.

I shake my head mournfully. 'I can't,' I say. 'I'm sorry.'

'You could commute down here,' he continues intently. 'It doesn't mean you would have to give up your job. We could share the child-care. Look, please, Cass, at least say you'll think about it. I mean, neither of us is getting any younger, and you'd make such a lovely mum . . .'

But I am stepping away from him, unable to bear it any longer. My socks are too thin and in my inappropriate slip-on shoes my feet are stinging with cold. My face is soaking wet, too: the rain is dripping into my eyes and down my neck, a drenching, miserable shower.

'I need to get back,' I mutter. 'See if Beth's all right . . .'

The moment I say this his face changes, the burgeoning enthusiasm swept away by disgust. '*If Beth's all right!*' he yells. 'Jesus, woman, what on earth's the matter with you? I've come all the way from London to propose, and you're fussing about some fucking student!'

For a moment I am unable to reply. He is both right in his response yet also utterly wrong. I wipe the hair from my face, trying to marshal my conflicting emotions. There is an alarming look in his eyes. 'I didn't know you were proposing,' I say, fighting to keep control of my voice. My insides are twisting into knots. I want to rewind the whole scene, back to the bit where he walks through the door, still so optimistic. Perhaps, through a series of clever deflections, I could have avoided this. But now we are hurtling headlong into a confrontation I can no longer escape.

'Well, I am.' An imploring expression flickers over his face.

I have a horrible sense that he is about to fall on to his knee and produce a sparkling ring in a little black box. And now that it is unfolding before my eyes, I see that this is a confrontation I have been struggling to avoid for ten years: the bit where things get serious and I am forced to reveal the truth. 'I'm sorry,' I say. 'I don't want to get married.'

He flinches, but still does not take his eyes from my face. 'Why not?'

'I just don't.'

I am surprised at the calmness with which he absorbs this. Perhaps he always knew I would refuse. He stares down at the dark grass, scuffing the mud with his foot. For a mad moment I think that everything is going to be all right. When he looks up, he says quietly, 'It's to do with your family, isn't it?'

I am not able to take my eyes away from his. I swallow tightly. *Too dreary to discuss*, I would quip when he first asked about them. Then, later, when he insisted I tell him more, I would bring out the one photo I have kept, of us on the settee at home, the Christmas before Dad died. I'm sitting slightly apart from the others, scowling and pink-haired; Mum and Dad are holding hands, the hypocrites; David is looking down at the floor. It's the last photo taken of us together. *That's the way it goes*, I would say, when pressed. *Some families enjoy each other's company and others don't. So, please, can we drop it now?*

'I love you,' Matt says suddenly.

This declaration is such a surprise that my mouth drops open. Ever since we first met we have made a point of avoiding what we would scornfully refer to as 'sop': no Valentine cards, gushy songs or heartsick declarations. But Matt's eyes betray no discernible trace of irony, so perhaps all this time he has been humouring me, pretending to dislike sentimentality while secretly harbouring a passion for pink teddies and red roses.

'I'm sorry, Matt,' I say faintly. 'I just want to be alone.'

For two or three seconds he stares directly into my eyes, not with the moony passion of a rejected lover but more in a spirit of enquiry, as if he might discern things there that he had not hitherto understood. 'Why are you so afraid?' he says quietly.

I am not able to reply. Then something in his face seems to sag. I want to reach out for him, put my arms round his shoulders and hug him better, but already it is too late, for he is trudging quickly away from me, back across the garden.

By the time I return to the flat, he has gone. I push open the unlocked door, registering that the hall is empty with an uneasy mixture of regret and relief. He has taken his bags and the champagne, I note, as I step on to the rug; even the lilies have disappeared. The flat feels vast, a hollow, echoing cavern. A few minutes ago the place was filled with our angry voices. Now all I can hear are the distant disembodied sounds of Jan's TV and cars in the street below. The shut-up, stagnant smell has returned, too.

I turn towards the sitting room. I do not know what to feel: my conflicting emotions keep cancelling each other out and I am left with a wobbling, vertiginous disorientation. Is this the end of our relationship? I suppose it must be, but my mind refuses to take in such a blunt, hard fact. I wander distractedly through the door, drifting towards the draughty windows, where I stand, gazing vacantly out. I do not know whether or not I want to catch one last glimpse of Matt, disappearing down the street.

There is no sign of Beth. I stare down at the restless trees, dimly watching a tin can rattling on the pavement below.

Jesus, I keep thinking, *what is happening?* Matt is my man: despite his foibles and my inability to say the words aloud, he is the love of my life. And now this stomach-wrenching, terrible scene. He came with flowers and champagne to *propose* – like some daft Mills and Boon hero, balancing on one knee with a diamond ring nestling in a bed of red velvet. And I threw it back in his face.

But it is not what I want, is it? The idea of marrying him, of prancing down the aisle in a frilly dress to become *Mrs Hughes*, is ludicrous. I always assumed he felt the same, but perhaps this is what he has been moving stealthily towards, his sniggering at the overblown weddings of our friends a foil. Clearly, I do not know him as well as I thought. And, I think, as I move away from the window, he does not really know me. Perhaps our cosy coupledom has always been a charade, a convenient place to hide.

I shiver, only now noticing how cold I have become. Downstairs, the white noise of the TV has stopped. In its place is a hollow knocking, which the TV must have disguised. I stop moving, listening hard. The sound is coming from the direction of the kitchen, and as it increases in intensity my body tautens, as if sharp screws of anxiety are being tightened inside me. I turn away from the window and walk across the floor, my fingers tingling. It must be the wind banging something against the window.

I reach the sitting-room door and clasp the handle. The noise started as a faint rapping, but now, from the other side of the flat, it sounds as if something – or someone – is battering hard against a pane of glass. I am trying to remain calm, but cannot stop myself picturing a dark figure standing on the flat roof, his fists pounding against the sliding doors. *Go away!* I beg. *Please leave me alone!*

But the noise grows louder. I hover on the other side of the door, my slippery hand closing around the handle as I summon the courage to open it. The window is locked, I tell myself. No one can get in. Yet as my fingers clutch at the handle, I cannot prevent the nightmare refrain repeating itself, over and over. *The prowler has returned.*

I can hardly breathe, the adrenaline buzzing through my veins like a class A narcotic. I cannot allow myself to be terrorized like this, I keep thinking. I have to do something. My hands are shaking so violently I can only just get them to work, but finally I tug at the handle, turn it and step decisively through the door.

The moment I do this, the noise stops. I stand disoriented in the dusty hallway, gasping for air. There is nothing left to hear, just the theme tune to *EastEnders*, which Jan must be watching. And now Beth has appeared, dishevelled and bleary, at the bedroom door, my duvet wrapped round her shoulders. I goggle at her, dazed. For some reason I had assumed she had left and now I am finding it difficult to click back into the person I was before Matt arrived.

'Hi,' I say vaguely, trying to remember how to behave. 'I thought you'd gone.'

She shakes her head dreamily. Her eyes, which seem larger and darker than before, are fixed on my face.

'What was that noise?' I ask. 'Was it you?'

'What noise?'

'It was coming from the kitchen, as if someone was banging on the window.' I want to say more, but stop, not wishing to appear hysterical.

Beth stares at me for a minute, then shrugs, letting the duvet fall to the ground. She is still wearing my dress, which crumples like a heavy velvet curtain around her thin legs. 'I was having a little snooze.' She steps over the duvet and moves towards the kitchen. She does not seem surprised that Matt has gone. As she slopes down the corridor, she turns. 'Do you want me to go out and look?'

I shudder, too cowardly to see it through. It was surely a hallucination, my inflamed memories that summoned up the noise, nothing else. 'No, it's fine. I must have imagined it.'

'I'll make a start on the dinner, then,' she says, and disappears into the kitchen.

Dear Mum

Sometimes I feel as if I need you so desperately I don't know what to do with myself. I've been thinking about that a lot lately, how to stop these feelings. How, I ask myself, can I really need someone who to all intents and purposes no longer exists? I do not even know your name or anything about you. If we passed on the street, I would not recognize you; you certainly would no longer recognize me. But when you come to me at night and touch my cheek with your soft, smooth hands I long for you to be real. Surely, there must still be some indefinable threads that hold us together, a genetic trace we share? Do you, like me, love the wind against your face, but hate the summer heat? Do you suffer from headaches and insomnia? Do you have good strong legs, but a restless disposition? Who are your family and where are you from? You are my history and my home, you see. And without knowing who you are I have nowhere to go.

It's when I think that that I wonder if it isn't just need I feel, but something else. Something more like hate.

2 1

After we have finished Beth's nut roast I sit by the french windows, gazing towards the sea. The storm has been building all day, and now, as the windows tremble at the wind, the first raindrops are splattering the glass. I slump against the wall. Beth must have retreated to the bedroom for there is no sign of her. Perhaps she is upset by my taciturn appearance. I tried to be sociable over dinner, but was so shocked by the row with Matt that I could only manage a few ragged sentences. He wanted to marry me, but I refused, I explained, surprising myself that I could tell her even this much. I don't actually want to talk about it. I did not do her vegan feast justice, either. Dolefully regarding the food piled upon it at the end of the meal, she picked up my plate and silently scraped its contents into the bin.

But whether or not Beth is offended is hardly my most pressing concern. It is too late to say anything to her this evening, but the truth is that I want to be alone. I rest my head on my knees, refusing to give in to tears. I deserve this to happen, I think, for what Matt wants is perfectly reasonable. Why could I not have responded as he hoped? I should have wilted into his arms and whispered, 'Yes'. I should, like most childless women of my age, yearn for a baby. It should be the next stage of my life, the next big thing.

I picture Sarah, her little girl sitting on her lap. Perhaps it might seem that I am jealous, and that is why it is so increasingly difficult to talk to her. But the reality is more complicated. It is not that I want what she has, or even that I am jealous of Poppy for taking her away from me, although perhaps there is an element of that. No, it is that Sarah's success reminds me of my failure. How do all these women do it? They make it look so easy and natural: the squadrons of Sarahs and Mirandas, spooning mush into their infants' soft wet mouths; the armies of women carrying their tots on their hips as they march towards the sandpits of the western world. All those woman-hours spent hacking at the coalface of Quality Time, their lives sacrificed at the altar of childhood, they terrify me. I see them every day, pushing the fat-faced toddler lords in their carriages, or carrying them on their backs, like imperial rajas. And I know that for all my prestigious academic achievements they have a knowledge that I do not possess: they know how to love.

I sit up, trying mentally to shake away the memories that have settled around me, but they are as unavoidable as nuclear dust. Matt is better off without me, I think despondently. What he needs is a nice postgraduate, a cheery, rosy-cheeked sort, who will readily defer to all his opinions, read everything he writes and think him utterly marvellous. They can settle down in the outer ring of London, get a big house with a garden and produce copious offspring. But if he believes that I am such a woman, he is quite wrong. Surely he has noticed how studiously I avoid children. Ever since we became lovers I have been paranoid about pregnancy. Babies are yuck, that's what I've always said. All that pooing and dribble, all those sleepless nights – what a bore.

But as I sit slouched by the window, I know this to be a lie. For, increasingly, I feel an emptiness so deep and dark I know I shall never fill it, this vast burden of what I do not have and what I need to give. *Why are you so afraid?* Matt asked, and I was unable to reply.

I stand abruptly, searching round the room for my bag. When I locate it sitting neatly in the corner, I unzip it, dig deep inside and produce my battered old Filofax.

There, I have it. I ease it from its plastic folder and pull the photograph out of the back, unfolding it and holding it on my knee. It is so old, and has been folded and refolded so many times that the crease marks are in danger of quartering the picture. Christmas 1979, six weeks after I went to see the Dreadheads. *My family, photographed by Uncle Bob.* I stare down at the grainy image as if I might find the answer I need inscribed on the faces. But we just gaze gormlessly back. There is Mum, her long hair cut short and curly, with her treacherous arm round Dad's back. There is David looking bored, and there is me with my punky hair-do. Dad is smiling as if everything was normal. It was Christmas Day, but no one was in the mood for celebration.

I trace my finger over the paper, examining my plump, cross face. In retrospect I can see that my unfortunate hairstyle and doughy cheeks gave me the appearance of an oversized iced doughnut. I had cut my hair brutally short and dyed it pink only a few days earlier, a defiant V-sign at the head-bangers. After that, I ritually burned my entire record collection in the imitation gas fire. David and I watched solemnly as the vinyl discs twisted and reared in the heat, melting into sticky lumps that clogged the grate and elicited a screaming fit from my mother. I still had not recovered from the alcohol poisoning of the week before. I lit endless cigarettes, just to annoy Mum, but they made me feel worse. In truth, all I wanted was to go to bed.

But none of this much mattered or, indeed, was noticed by my parents. For by now something far more frightening than my new-found purity had moved centre-stage. They had told us on Bonfire Night, as we sat silent and shocked on the sofa, the suburban night exploding with the pop and fizz of other families' fireworks. We would not be attending any Guy Fawkes parties that year, Mum announced, for there was something we needed to know. I remember staring back at her wan face, my mind stalling. It must be that they were splitting up, I thought with a surge of excitement. And that meant that Mum would get David and I could go and live with Dad.

But it was nothing to do with the state of their marriage. Dad was sick, Mum said, her voice shaking. It was related to his cough; he'd had tests done, and it did not look good. As she said this, her eyes went hazy and Dad reached out and took her hand, a rare gesture of affection. I stared numbly into the imitation gas fire, the one I was soon to destroy with my Saxon and Motorhead LPs, listening to the hiss of the flames. He was terminally ill, Dad continued. 'It' would probably not happen for a while; it might be years rather than months. But he had been forced to go on sick leave from his surveying job, so there would be an immediate drop in income. And eventually Mum would have to stay at home from the surgery to look after him. We might even have to move. At this point he looked across the room at the front windows, closed against the pyrotechnics of the night by the new pink velour curtains that he and Mum had recently purchased. Whatever happened, he went on, we would have to be brave.

But I did not feel brave: I felt hideously let down. I was too young to lose my father, I wailed inwardly. And there was *no way* I could be happy living with just Mum. But after their rare display of emotion on Bonfire Night, the subject was shut tightly away. Dad grew quieter and more withdrawn, spending most days in front of the TV, while Mum's mood fluctuated between forced calm and badly repressed hysteria. Something horrible was about to happen, but none of us dared acknowledge it.

The days shot past. David went to school, I played truant and Mum and Dad continued to lead their separate lives. Dr Death – the lugubrious senior partner at Mum's surgery –

was ringing regularly by then, and visiting too. I couldn't work out why Mum had to whisper into the phone to him for so long, or so late at night, or the reason for the swift kiss I once saw him give her at the door. It must be to do with Dad's illness, which by now was rapidly taking him over, I decided. Anyway, Dr Death's comings and goings were of little interest to me, for it was becoming clear that Dad was far sicker than even his consultant had predicted. By the first week of December he was sleeping on a camp-bed downstairs; by Christmas a community nurse was bringing him morphine. I spent most of the holidays asleep in my room, my lethargy so thick that it was as if I, rather than Dad, was drugged.

By Easter he had been moved to the hospice. I can remember him lying on a large metal bed, surrounded by machinery. The place was Catholic: there were crosses every-where and, just round the corner from Dad's cubicle, a tiny chapel, with thick lozenges of stained-glass for windows, where I suppose we were meant to go and pray. I hated the visits, which were contorted by a hideously awkward jollity. Each time was worse than the last. I could not think of anything to say, and once he had ribbed me for the zillionth time about my pink hair and weight gain, he would lapse into an apologetic silence. Sometimes he would cough so badly he could no longer breathe. Then he would put the oxygen mask over his face and we would glance away, ashamed at his lack of control, until the fit had passed and his shoulders relaxed. He seemed lost to us, already unreachable.

The trouble was, everything about him was so different. For a start, he was very thin, his skin stretched so tightly over his bones that it seemed bruised and cracked. And he wasn't wearing his usual pyjamas, either, but some thick blue ones that must have been acquired especially for the hospice. He was unexpectedly absent too. Sometimes, when I was in the middle of talking, his eyes would slide from my face and I would realize that he was no longer listening.

My main memory of these visits is the feeling of intense embarrassment. Of course we knew what was about to happen, but we were still children, we did not know how to handle it or what to say. So when we were not at school or visiting him, we just carried on as normal. David would spend whole days kicking a ball against the garage wall, and I would lie upstairs on my bed, staring at the walls. I could not shake off the lethargy that had descended so thickly. Now, instead of playing truant from school, my absences were legitimated by the messages my mother would write: 'Please excuse Cassandra from school this week. Her father is suffering from a terminal illness and she is very upset, experiencing nausea, headaches, etc.'

I was hungrier than ever, too, all attempts at dieting successfully resisted. No wonder I was getting so fat, Mum would remark, as she watched me down another plate of cakes; she had never seen anything like it. She would hold me in her gaze, critical, bemused, not a little impatient, then her eyes would dart away and she would forget the question she was about to ask. As for me, I was weighted down, depressed, almost unable to get out of bed. At school, the other girls treated me with cautious interest. I had been the fifth-year hell-raiser, the troublemaker at the back of the class who inspired universal admiration and fear for her disdain of authority. Now I was back, and in a different role: the object of pity, a case study in how low the mighty fall. When I hung up my coat I could hear them whispering about me. *Poor Cassie Bainbridge. Did you hear about her dad?* Then, a little later: *Have you seen how much weight she's put on? Apparently her mum is having it off with some doctor. You'd have thought they could wait.*

Dad died on 21 April, the day after David's birthday. We knew it was coming, had sat holding his limp hand the day before and eventually been sent home by the nurses to our cold, boxy house where we drank Horlicks and avoided each other's eyes. They gave the time of death as 3.05 a.m., told us he had not roused from his coma, and gave the cause of death as carcinoma of the lung.

Two months later I had finished my O levels, Mum was openly dating Dr Death, and I had put on two stone in weight.

'Hi, there.'

I turn round with a start. I have been so deeply immersed in my memories that I had forgotten about Beth. But now she is leaning in the doorway, looking morosely across the room at me. Not wanting her to see the photograph, I stuff it hastily back inside my bag. 'How ya doing?' I say, forcing my voice to sound breezy. 'I thought you'd gone to bed.'

'I'm OK, I just wanted to see how *you* were.'

I shake my head, trying to appear calm and collected. It's sweet of her to ask, but I am unable to give her any more details.

'I'm *fine*,' I say. 'Just sitting here daydreaming.'

Beth takes a step into the room, shivering at the draught. 'Had any more thoughts about where you're going to live?' I say, trying to hold my mouth in a smile.

She must not have heard, for she does not answer.

'I've just remembered something,' she says, fixing me with her eyes. 'About that noise you heard?'

'Oh, yeah?'

'I don't know whether or not it's relevant, but maybe you ought to know?'

I nod slowly, pulling myself back to the present. It seems a long time since I stood by the door, too scared to open it. 'Go on,' I say apprehensively.

'Well, this afternoon, as I was coming back from the shops, there was this man waiting by the garden gate, kind of looking up at your flat. And when he saw me go in, he gave me this really funny look.'

She smiles expectantly, for she is trying to help, and now I guess she wants some positive affirmation. But all I can do is stare at her. 'Oh,' I say dully.

'I don't know if it's connected or not. It's just this feeling I had. You know, female intuition, and that?'

I swallow. I wish I had never told her about the noises coming from the kitchen roof, for the man she saw was probably just an estate agent or a client of Jan's or any manner of innocent person. And, of course, she is only trying to help. But now, like all the other stuff, the image of some strange man watching my flat is going to stick in my already overheated thoughts, like a splash of burning fat.

'And it wasn't Matt?' I ask.

She shrugs, as if she can hardly be expected to remember what Matt looks like. 'To be honest I didn't get a really good look at his face.'

I cannot stop myself shuddering. 'Let's not give ourselves nightmares,' I say lightly. 'I'm sure it was nothing.'

'Probably not.' She chuckles, her expression buoyant again. 'I'm pooped,' she says, almost, but not quite, reaching out for my arm. 'Let's go to bed.'

22

We are standing on the cliffs again, waiting. The sky is clear, but below us, the sea is angry. This gives me a churning, queasy sensation, as if I am trapped on a boat I know is about to sink. I want to turn and run, but for some reason I am unable to move. Looking towards the bilious swell I see that, on the horizon, a ridge of water has started to gather in intensity, rising ever higher as it rushes towards the land. I watch the wave, transfixed. It is now so large that the whole ocean seems to have been sucked up into it, a tidal wave of water and froth that, any minute now, will be dumped back down, sweeping the beach and cliffs unforgivingly away.

The sky is black, the sun blocked out by the approaching wall of water. There is no point in running, no point in doing anything other than standing here and waiting. I can hear the roar, feel the wind rushing in my ears. A drop of water wets my forehead, and then another. Any minute now, I shall be engulfed. I squeeze my eyes closed, cowering against the inevitable impact, then suddenly open them again.

It is morning, and I am lying on the sitting-room floor, wrapped in a duvet. I feel chilled and unpleasantly damp. In fact, I realize, as a splash of water lands on my head, I am being rained on. Perplexed, I brush my fingers against my wet skin. Another drop of water has just hit my nose. Pulling myself up, I see that I am lying in a puddle, and being vigorously dripped on from the ceiling, where, directly above me, a pregnant lump in the plaster leads to a single bulging drop of water. 'Oh, no!'

I peer along the line of staining. A puddle of water must

have accumulated on the floor above; perhaps some of the roof tiles are missing and the rain has got in. My own carpet is damp too, not just where I have been lying but also beside the french windows, which have oozed rain in incontinent patches from their bottom panels. The building is like a leaking ship, I think in irritation, unable to withstand a minor autumn storm. What with this and the prowler, I really ought to gather my strength and move. Even if the man has only ever existed in my head, the way the fire escape leads down to the pavement seems like an open invitation. *Intruders! Come on up!*

Yet achieving anything other than the most basic tasks seems impossible. I must have had no more than three or four hours' sleep last night, and can feel the exhaustion pressing behind my eyes, an oppressive weight I must carry all day. Standing, I spread the duvet over the peeling radiator in a feeble attempt to dry it, and stumble towards the bedroom. I have just remembered that I am meant to be attending a staff–student teaching committee this morning, and, if my watch is correct and it is indeed ten to nine, I have only half an hour to get there.

Luckily Beth is still asleep. Apart from a sprinkling of rain along the window-ledge, the bedroom appears to be dry. I lurch blearily towards the wardrobe, grab some clothes and dress quickly. I shall have to call the landlord later about the ceiling. After that I am going to contact the university housing office, and arrange a room for Beth. I pick up a scholarly paper I am meant to be commenting on for a forthcoming issue of *Feminism and Oral History*, rip off the first page and scribble on the back: 'Beth! Could you meet me later today on campus? We need urgently to sort out your housing difficulties (sorry, but I'm going to have to reclaim my room for guests due to arrive this evening). Best, Cass.'

It's a lie, but better than telling the truth: *Sorry, but I can't cope with looking after you.* I pin the note to the front door, then snatch my bag from the hall table, slam the door behind me and leap down the worn stairs. I have forgotten my coat, I realize, as I reach the landing, as well as the landlord's number, but it is too late to go back: whatever calamities are taking place in my personal life, I cannot afford to be late for work again. With a leap of nerves I remember that in a few weeks' time I am due to meet the dean for a 'critical self-assessment' of the term's achievements, a bureaucratic chore for those lecturers who behave normally, but for me something that may be rather more challenging. The students will have turned in their course-assessment forms by then, and will surely remark on how I was late for every seminar, how I ad-libbed through each lecture and how often I launched into a sentence only to forget half-way through what I was trying to say.

It is now twenty past nine. Oh, God, ohgod, ooohgodddd. I turn the final corner of the stairs and stop in my tracks. In the hallway, Jan is wading ankle deep in water, a bucket in her hand. As she hears me approach, she turns, grimacing. She is wearing a waterproof yellow cape, a baseball cap, and her camouflage combats, rolled to gooseflesh thighs. 'I've been waiting since six this morning,' she says, in answer to my unasked question. 'Apparently every emergency vehicle in the county is busy.' Placing the bucket on her hip, as if she were an African woman at a waterhole, she shakes her head at me, presumably in despair.

I stare at her, taking in the sodden hall walls, the bits of newspaper floating by the door. 'What happened?' My voice sounds small and weak.

'Worst storm in two hundred years, according to the news. There's cables down all over the place, trees across the roads. I could've told them all about it after those cards last week, not that they'd have listened.' She chuckles wryly, turns back to the water and scoops at it ineffectually with her bucket.

I take a deep breath. 'Do you need help?'

'I've only got one bucket, so what's the point?'

Thank God for that. Simpering guiltily, for I am about to splash through the hall and escape down the front steps, I add, 'Is it all in your flat too?'

'Only a little bit in the hall. It's this blocked drain that's done it. Some clever dick left the front door open so it all overflowed in here.'

'God, I hope it wasn't me.' I roll up my trousers and hop from the bottom step to what looks like the shallowest patch of water in the middle of the hall. With one more leap, I shall have reached the door.

'Not unless you came in after midnight,' Jan says, not looking up from her sploshing. 'That student of yours kept ringing the bell, and in the end I had to go to the door and tell him to get lost, so it was probably me.'

She says this just as I am taking my leap for freedom. I land badly, the muddy water splashing over my legs as I slip on the slimy mat. Steadying myself against the door-frame, I turn and gape at her. 'What student?' My legs have gone all weak, and it is not from the jumping.

'The lad with glasses that's been hanging around. He wanted me to let him in, but I said if you weren't answering your bell he should shove off.'

My stomach plummets. 'He wanted you to let him *in?*'

She nods, as if it was obvious.

'And he was young, with glasses?'

'A blue kagooly thing. He was in a bit of a psychic mess, to be honest. Very troubled. I could see it in his aura.'

'But I didn't hear a bell. What does he want?'

Jan looks at me for a moment. Then she shrugs. 'Ask him yourself,' she says. 'He's still outside.'

I goggle at her. What on earth is Alec doing hanging around my flat? I lurch out of the door and skid down the front steps, looking around cautiously. It is ridiculous, but I am now so tense that I am almost expecting him to leap out from behind a lamp-post and hold a knife to my throat.

But now I am outside, the front door crashing thunderously behind me and cold air blasting my face, what I see is something else. I survey the scene with shock. The street appears to have been hit by a hurricane. The square gardens where I stood last night with Matt are devastated: the lawns are covered with twigs and leaves and the now bare-branched trees are smashed and broken, with branches lopped off or, in several cases, completely uprooted. As I peer along the side of the building I see the source of last night's knocking: my fire escape has come away from its rusted braces and now hangs perilously down the side of the building, the metal steps clanging softly in the wind. Even more dramatically, one of the cars parked by the railings has been squashed by a capsized oak, which now lies tragically across what remains of the bonnet. Twigs and roof tiles are strewn over the road. Over the sea another front of swollen pewter clouds is blowing in fast across the Channel. Even with the wind crashing around me, I can hear the roar of the waves.

There is no one around: it is as if Armageddon has arrived and I am the sole survivor. I hurry across the pavement and reach my car, which, considering the fate of the vehicle on the other side of the road, is miraculously intact. When I unlock the driver's door, it swings open violently, caught by a gust of air. As I wrestle with it I notice a tall figure hurrying towards me. My heart sinks, for it is unmistakably Alec.'

I am desperate to get away before he reaches me. Shoving my briefcase on to the back seat I try to climb quickly inside the car, but it is too late. His hand lands on my arm.

I jump back in consternation. Next to the car, he has pulled back his hood and is gazing at me through misty glasses. 'Dr Bainbridge?'

I swallow hard. 'What do you want?'

It may be an overreaction, but I am gripping my keys between my knuckles, just as I was taught in the women's self-defence classes. Alec regards me gravely. He is just a boy, really, with a soft sheen of hair on his upper lip and a bony leanness, like a young dog, yet just being close to him ties me into a tangle of distress.

'I need to talk to you.'

He says this with an urgency that sets my teeth on edge. I look away from him, towards the buffeting door of my car. Is this still to do with Beth and her essay? Is he some kind of obsessive, unable to let the matter rest? Or is it something worse?

'How did you know where I live?' I say coldly. I do not want him to see how much he is scaring me.

'I've got a room on the other side of the square. I see you coming and going every day.'

I gaze at him incredulously. Could it be him whom Beth saw yesterday, standing outside my flat? When I speak, my voice is shrill. 'Just leave me alone!'

Steadying himself against the horizontal wind, Alec blinks back at me. Around his face, the nylon hood of his kagool flaps and balloons in the gale. Then, suddenly, he glances away from me to the sky, where the seagulls are flapping hopelessly in the wind. Swirling around his feet are the pages of a discarded newspaper. 'Flood Chaos Hits Sussex,' I read distractedly. He kicks forlornly at the damp pages. There is a long pause, in which I turn back to my car, then he appears to decide something. 'Beth isn't what she seems,' he says. 'That's all I wanted to tell you. I know she's been staying here and . . .'

'Oh, yes? How did you know that?'

His drawn face twitches and I remember his assumed superiority in class, the way he belittled the other students. 'I've seen her here,' he says.

'Spying on us, are you?' I snap.

He frowns grumpily, stuffing his hands deep into his pockets.

'I don't like what's going on,' he mutters. 'I've decided to take matters into my own hands.'

This sounds like another threat. Despite the wind, which gusts so hard I can barely keep my feet on the ground, my face has grown hot.

'Mind your own business!' I shout over the buffeting gale. 'You can't just —'

I do not catch the rest of what he says for the wind smothers his words. I climb into the Beetle. I want to be in my car, driving past the smashed-up trees to the refuge of my office. 'Leave us alone!' I shout. 'If you've got some kind of problem then go and see your personal tutor!'

Then, slamming the door in his face and staring resolutely in the opposite direction, I turn on the ignition.

23

Alec's presence outside my flat has left me shaken and tearful. I dab at my eyes, telling myself to toughen up as I drive round the square and turn towards the dual-carriageway that runs along the cliffs then cuts north towards the university. Why is he plaguing me like this? He wraps everything in terms of his fanatical concern with classroom procedure, but it feels as if he is trying deliberately to rile me. There are other things too. I try to pull the threads of various thoughts into something more substantial but, like the wind, my mind refuses to settle, leaping twitteringly from one topic to another. What I do not want to think about is the face on the roof.

If only I was not so exhausted I would be able to work it out, but now I am picturing Matt as he stumbled back over the muddy grass, his face closed against me. A renewed surge of weepiness prickles my eyes. He was my partner for ten years, the man I assumed I would spend the rest of my life with. Yet in those awful seconds everything we ever had was violently uprooted and cast aside.

Away from the sweep of sea-front crescents, the road stretches past golf courses and retirement homes. I press my foot on the accelerator as the Beetle stutters unsteadily along the highway. Below the chalky cliffs I glimpse the crazy crashing waves; occasionally a finger of froth reaches up over the edge and sprays the passing cars with salty water. Beside the road, the lamp-posts rock and creak precariously, drunk sentry-men, pretending to be sober. The bullying wind buffets and prods my little car. It is so stormy that I am not altogether confident that the wheels can remain on the road.

What a fitting end, to be whirled up and smashed down by a twister. From now on, I will always be alone: there is no returning from this empty place.

Dourly I grip the steering-wheel. Why am I so surprised? I should have seen it coming a mile off. In spite of their better judgement, people are meant to grow restless in their thirties. Rationally no one of sound mind would welcome the prospect of sleep loss, career disruption and domestic chaos. But gradually they feel that something is missing, wonder why they are leading such self-indulgent lives. And before they know it, they're going googly over babies in supermarket queues, the contraceptives are in the bin and they're lying in bed together picking out names.

But not me. Not ever. And that means no man will truly want to stay. For despite all his self-consciously constructed individualism, Matt is tied more closely to the dictates of society than he cares to acknowledge. And what our culture decrees is that we have reached the time when we should be producing children. For a split second I picture the beach and the boat, then suddenly there is a loud slap and a sploosh of seawater souses the windscreen. I curse loudly, swerving and clicking the wipers to full. The sea is reaching out and grabbing me, just like my dream.

It's to do with your family, isn't it? That was what Matt said last night. As the car rocks unnervingly in the wind and the wipers work themselves into a frenzy of scraping, I recall his mystified expression. We have been together for all these years, but I have never told him anything beyond an incomplete account of my father's death and the subsequent rift with my mother. He would not understand – how could he? His parents still live together in cosy late middle age, with their cottage in the Lake District and ramblers' trips to Provence. He had a happy, uneventful childhood. He has had no experience of death and loss. And now, without warning, I remember the summer after my father died, self-pity squelching through me.

This is not the first time I have been here looking out at this sea, that is the problem. And now I cannot stop these memories reaching out and engulfing me.

August 20, 1980: it was my mother's wedding day and she had only just told us. 'I'm going to marry Don,' she said, that morning, folding her arms and glaring at me defiantly. 'We're doing it in two hours' time and we expect you to be there.'

I was gobsmacked. She had told us it was to be a family weekend at the seaside, not a sodding *wedding*. With hindsight I see that she must have planned it that way, hoping that once she had us safely installed in the hotel we would put up less resistance. How wrong she was.

It is now many years ago, but I remember everything: the hot morning sun, the way I felt so sick. I watched her prepare herself for the register office in silence, slouched sulkily on her 'Pavilion Suite' double bed in an agony of resentment. She was wearing white high heels, a silky cream shoulder-padded suit and clip-on pearl earrings. Her hands trembled a little as she pushed them on to her lobes. I suppose she must have had fantasies of me as a cute little bridesmaid, for on making her announcement she had whipped out a hideous taffeta dress from Laura Ashley that she must have secreted in her bags when we packed for the weekend. It was about three sizes too small, but I would not have been seen dead in it even had it fitted. I pulled myself off the bed and told her to piss off.

Another wave sploshes over the cliff, narrowly missing my car. Pulling over, I unclick the door, which the wind flings open, and climb out. Up here the gale is so ferocious I can barely stand. Steadying myself against the Beetle's bonnet, I peer over the edge of the cliff at the bucking white horses. It is not a safe place to be, but I do not care. I never intended this to happen, but returning to this place has loosened the foundations of my life, and now I am unable to escape the consequences. I wish I could change what happened; I wish I could reach back, with the sensibilities of an older woman, and rescue myself from that calm summer day.

But it is impossible.

After swearing at my mother I lumbered out of the sea-front hotel and across the road to the beach, where I sat throwing pebbles at the listless waves. It was going to be another baking day: the few shimmering clouds lying low and pink across the pale water at breakfast had long since evaporated and already sunbathers were stripping off and staking out their patches on the stones. Over by the pier a couple of young guys were placing deck-chairs seawards on the promenade. I could hear the snap of canvas as they unfolded the chairs, their cheery voices and the tinny electronic music from their radio: 'Love Will Tear Us Apart,' they sang, and I felt sicker than ever.

How could she do this? My mother knew how David and I hated Dr Death. He had been creeping around us ever since Dad died, crunching into our drive in his red MG and crowding the sitting room with his large, ramshackle body. He was obsessively protective of the car, driving it pitifully slowly and shouting at David that time his football had landed muddily on its windscreen. It was the only occasion he had allowed his obsequious front to slip. Until their marriage, he had remained fastidiously friendly, chuckling meaninglessly and ruffling our hair every time he saw us, as if that was what was required with young people. My main memory of this period is of him waiting for Mum with us in the lounge, humming in the pretence of pleasantness while we ignored him in front of the TV. When Mum appeared, flustered and red-faced with expectation, he would jump up with relief, guiding her out of the room and towards his waiting car, his hand placed protectively on her shoulder. 'Your poor mother,' he would say, and she would sigh and place her head mock-mournfully on his shoulder.

It made us ill. Whenever he turned his back, David and I would stick our fingers down our throats and pretend to puke. We wanted Dad, not this sixty-year-old fogey, with his silk cravats and golf clubs. Despite their bickering and sour tempers, I had always assumed that my parents loved each other. But as I watched Mum and Dr Death fooling around in the kitchen, I saw that I had been wrong. And now he was going to become my step-father. Mum had told me that, 'on pain of death', I had to attend the ceremony, due to take place at twelve in the register office across the road from the pier. My watch told me it was half past eleven. I tossed a final stone into the water, hauled myself up and walked in the opposite direction.

It was mid-afternoon by the time I returned. I had stomped along the entire length of the beach, through the marina, past the clicking boats that jostled for space in its waters and out, under the steep, chalky cliffs that rose abruptly from the shore. I would run away, I thought, escape to somewhere no one could find me. Or perhaps I would simply cut my wrists, splattering blood all over the newly-weds' marital bed. That would make them sorry.

The tide was out, the sea shrunk back from the beach to reveal acres of slippery green rock. Beneath the path, children pottered with buckets and nets while their parents huddled in the shade of the groynes. I was filled with hatred, not just for Mum and Dr Death but for every single person in this horrible holidaying place. My legs ached too, and my back was starting to hurt. After a while I had to stop and rest, placing my hand against my spine as I tried to rub it better. By the time I got back to the hotel I was so exhausted I could barely walk, and my head was throbbing from the merciless sun. The wedding was long over, but thankfully there was no sign of Mum or Dr Death. I collapsed on to my bed, curled up and fell asleep.

I awoke to the sound of my mother's voice berating me. On opening my eyes I saw that she was standing over the bed, shaking my shoulder. Her face was flushed, her breath rancid with champagne. Dr Death was hovering next to her. I guess David was downstairs in the TV lounge. Slowly I became conscious of what she was saying.

'You're a selfish little cow,' she whined. 'I asked you to do something that was incredibly important for me and Don and you deliberately went against my wishes. We waited outside for you for over half an hour. We nearly missed our slot!'

Rolling over, I stared into her face. Once, she had been the centre of my world. I would do anything to be allowed to sit on her lap and put my arms round her soft, warm body. She would read to me and tickle my toes, and I would smother her with sloppy baby kisses. But now all that was over. I was a fully fledged teenager and I loathed everything about her: the martyred tone of her voice, the cheap Marks & Spencer power suits she had taken to wearing, the way she referred to herself in front of Dr Death as a 'little girlie'. As our eyes met, she almost flinched. I suppose she still loved me, and it was shocking to see the hatred in my face.

Reaching out for her revolting husband's hand, she took a deep breath, as if making a saintly effort to keep her temper, and said, 'Now will you please get up and get ready to come out to dinner? We have a table booked for eight and it's already after seven.'

I sucked in my cheeks and flicked away my eyes. 'Fuck off,' I replied.

Snivelling like a little child, I turn back to the Beetle and climb inside. Last night Matt had asked me about my family, but I was unable to reply. Perhaps I should have told him everything. If I had, could he ever forgive me?

24

Miraculously, I arrive at work with five minutes to spare. I do not want to look at my emails, or even be alone in my room with the possibility of Alec lurking around, so I proceed to Maggie's office and make a pretence of looking through my in-tray. As I walk through the door, she regards me over her pince-nez. She's a heavy woman, with her grey hair piled in a bun and her bosom laden with strings of wooden beads. With her withering stares and aptitude for putting overly cocky academics in their place, our departmental secretary has a somewhat frightening reputation. 'Bit breezy,' she says, raising her eyebrows at my hair, which no doubt resembles a haystack in a hurricane.

'You said it.' I rifle half-heartedly through my mail. It's the usual guff: a thick wad of files from the postgraduate office, a wodge of essays, a couple of flyers concerning academic publications. When I reach the top item, I tear it open without thinking, only vaguely noticing that my address has been written in capitals and that it has been posted from outside the university.

Yet as I pull out the contents, I feel the familiar plunging sensation. I gawp at what I am holding between my fingers for five seconds or less, then stuff it back into the envelope in shock. It is another colour photograph of me, blown up large. The background is indistinct but could be the campus, for there is a blurring of figures behind me, and a row of steps, perhaps those leading to Block D. I appear to be alone and am looking particularly harried, my forehead crumpled in what I can only interpret as agitation. My hair blows messily around my face. On the top, someone has written in thick red felt tip:

It's not her. It's YOU.

The felt tip smudges my fingers. I wipe it on my jumper, but it does not stop me feeling soiled. I feel woozy with alarm, my insides tipping as if I were on a white-knuckle ride at Alton Towers, but with none of the pleasure. Did Alec send this too?

'Are you all right there, Cass?'

When I eventually get my voice to work it is taut with repressed hysteria. 'Yeah, fine, thanks.'

It must be from Alec. He's got into some kind of obsessive vendetta with me and is trying to intimidate and harass me, just as he bullied Beth in class. I stand by the rack of metallic in-trays, swaying as I try to figure it out. If only I was not so tired I would be able to get it into focus. The 'her' clearly refers to Beth. There was something else he said this morning that bothered me, but I cannot remember what. All I know is that since the beginning of term he has systematically undermined and threatened me, and now I have reached the stage where I have to do something about it. I place the envelope back in my tray and turn to face Maggie, who is tapping calmly on her keyboard. 'Do you have the third-year Humanities files?'

Without looking up, she gestures towards a large cabinet. 'Second drawer down.'

I have only a minute or so to do this. Squatting by the cabinet, I pull open the drawer and start to rifle quickly through it. If the handwriting on the picture matches that on Alec's application form – which must surely be on the file – then I can take my case straight to the university authorities, or even the police. I am not sure what my case is, but I am increasingly determined to grasp some control over the situation.

Alec's surname is Watkins. I leaf through the Ws, finding three. Lila Washemi, Jonathan Welborough and Alec Watkins.

'Hmmf.'

I pull out the file and glance quickly through it. He attended a sixth-form college in Potters Bar, I note, skim-reading the excellent reference the head teacher gave him, got five As at A level, and has left blank the section under 'Next of Kin'. Like his essay, the application form has, irritatingly, been typed. I shove the folder back into the cabinet and haul myself up. According to the clock on Maggie's wall, the staff—student meeting has just started. I should be hurrying along the corridor towards it, but something else is niggling me. 'Maggie, look, I'm sorry to keep disturbing you, but are those *all* the files?'

She turns from her typing, her face pained. 'That's what it says on the drawer, isn't it? If any are missing somebody has taken them without my permission.' She looks at me sharply over her pince-nez, a rebuke already forming on her lips.

Not daring to press the point, I turn and hurry down the corridor towards the meeting. As I do this, I hear my mobile trilling sharply from somewhere in my bag. I didn't even know I had it with me, let alone remember turning it on, but now I am putting down my bag and groping crossly for it. Why do they make these things so bloody small? Finally I locate it, tucked between my Filofax and a pair of laddered tights. I'm surprised it was even switched on. Stuffing my bag under my arm and holding the phone with the other hand, I continue to pace towards the meeting.

'Hello?'

'It's me.'

My heart flops dismally. Please, *not now!*

'Hi, Beth,' I say flatly.

'I'm sorry to call you, Cass,' says the little voice at the other end of the line, 'but I'm scared.'

The screws tighten a notch. *Oh, God, what now?*

'What is it?'

'There's a man standing on the roof.'

I gasp and stumble a little, steadying myself against the wall. Students push past. Maggie, almost buried under a huge pile of files, does a little skipping dance to one side of me. Then, having successfully completed her manoeuvre, she overtakes me and hurries down the corridor.

'He was knocking on the window,' Beth goes on. 'I saw him standing there.'

'Oh, God!'

Down the phone, she is silent.

'What did he look like?' I croak.

'I didn't see his face, just the back of him.'

'You *have* to call the police!'

Perhaps she nods. What she says, with a shuddering breath, is, 'Will you come home, Cass? Please? I'm too scared to go out.'

I can hardly breathe. How can I possibly go back to the flat now? I am far too much of a coward to face what is waiting for me there. 'Get the police!' I screech.

Either I have gone out of range, or she has put the phone down, for it crackles, then goes dead. I stare at it, stunned. So I did not imagine the prowler, after all. There really was someone there, who either wanted to get into the flat or who wanted to scare me. And now he is back.

But this time I know who he is. He must have gone straight to the window after our confrontation by my car, wanting, for whatever perverse reason, to terrify poor Beth. It was, as I suspected all along, Alec who sent the emails,

Alec who posted today's photograph, and Alec who has been behind the creepy calls.

'Good morning, Cass! Coming to the meeting?'

I spin round. Behind me, Bob Stennings is fast approaching and I am not agile enough to dodge out of his way. He sweeps me along, his arm almost but not quite around my shoulders, and burbles on about the curriculum-restructuring committee he is hoping I will join. 'So it really would be a terrific help if you were to get involved,' he enthuses, as he virtually pushes me into the seminar room where the meeting is being held. 'What we need is new ideas, new energy, new blood!'

I gawk at him, too dumbfounded to speak. I should be making my excuses and calling the police, or dashing back to the flat to see if Beth is safe but, like a car that has overheated, I am in such turmoil that I am unable to take action. It is as if I have fallen from a great height and, while my external structure has remained intact, everything inside has broken: I may look unscathed, but my normal responses no longer work.

The room is full. The chairs around the large rectangular table in the middle are mainly occupied by my colleagues, who are variously sipping cups of tea, chatting in a low mumble of conversation, and studying the sheaves of papers in front of them. Around the edges of the room are ten or so students, most already doodling and looking bored. As I slump into the nearest available seat I am aware of people turning to look at me. Julian, for example, who is sitting directly opposite the door, glances up and a bemused expression passes across his face. Then, surely too hurriedly, he looks away again.

'Right, then, right, then, right, then!' Stennings is exhorting, waving his arms around like a lunatic PE instructor. 'Let's get going!'

He starts to drone on about the forthcoming curriculum

restructuring. I can hear my name being mentioned, and manage to smile and nod in what I hope are the appropriate places, but I do not hear a word of what is said. All I can think of, over and over and over, are Alec's words: *It's not her. It's YOU.*

I must contact the police, or go to someone in authority – who? – and report it, but now that the meeting has started, I am unable to move. None of this should matter so much. I should be able to deal with a weird, obsessive student without falling apart; I should not get so scared. But now that Madge Wernski has taken the floor and is speaking at length about the importance of inter-disciplinary courses, I am hurtling back in time, no longer able to stop myself.

The trouble is, I was hunted once before. And now, finally, I can no longer stop myself remembering 11 November 1979: the night that everything changed.

I was sick the moment I reached the alley, leaning against the damp breeze-blocks and throwing up over a municipal bin that had been pushed there. For a minute I thought my head would explode, that I would empty my entire insides on to the refuse of tin cans and styrofoam burger cartons, but after a while the convulsions stopped and I felt slightly better. Straightening up, I tried to focus on the graffitied wall and the thin patch of city sky above me. The winter night was freezing and I had started to shiver violently. I should return to the gig and retrieve my coat, I thought vaguely, then try to get home. But the idea of returning to the heaving mêlée was preposterous. Staggering, I managed to turn round and take a step or two towards the main road.

It had started to sleet, in an uncommitted, sporadic way. Ahead of me, the street was surprisingly empty. Even the bouncers, who a few minutes earlier had been smoking fags and laughing on the steps of the Odeon, had disappeared. Thinking, in a confused way, that perhaps I could find a bus to take me back to the station, I wove drunkenly along the pavement. I was aware even then that someone was walking behind me, but I was only fifteen and, despite my pretence at hard-girl savvy, completely naïve.

I threw my arms around myself and continued to totter down the road for perhaps another three or four minutes. I was accustomed to the bland safety of the suburbs, but this was Peckham and, pissed as I was, I was beginning to grasp that it was not a good place to be wandering around late at night. The large Victorian houses on the other side of the road were mostly derelict, their front gardens thick with brambles; on this side the shut-up shop fronts, with their security grilles and padlocks, had come to an end and I had just entered a large expanse of wasteland, bordered by the broken pavement.

I started to walk faster, rapidly sobering up. The person behind me was still there and I was growing increasingly tense. If only I could reach another stretch of lively street, with pubs and people and lights, but the road was plunged into darkness. When a beaten-up saloon with blacked-out windows drew alongside me, my heart knocked hard. The car hovered, its occupants taking a good long look. From inside, reggae music pounded, the low-slung vehicle visibly reverberating. Staring snootily ahead, I marched on, only daring to breathe as the car finally accelerated past.

Oh, my God! I clamped my hand over my fetid mouth. I had suddenly remembered that my quest for a bus was hopeless: I had no money. Everything I needed to get home, including my return train ticket, was in my bag, currently stored in the Odeon cloakroom. And that meant I had to turn round and walk back past the dark wasteland. I whirled unsteadily around, and started to stagger back along the increasingly slippy pavement. But what I saw now made my legs sag at the knees. About a hundred feet away, leaning against the security fencing that separated the pavement from the wasteland, was a man.

I knew immediately that this was the person who had been following me. And now, I was sure, he was waiting for me. It was too late to turn back, for I was almost upon him; certainly, it was too late to run. And so, staring hard at the boarded-up houses on the other side of the road I took one step after another, walking unstoppably towards him. Surely, I kept thinking, a car would pass. Or even a policeman. Didn't they have policemen in Peckham?

But now he was stepping away from the fencing and standing in my path, his arms folded. And with jagged relief, I saw that it was not some hooded attacker but the man I had been dancing with at the gig.

'Hi,' he said. 'Got lost?'

It was the first time we had spoken. He had a surprisingly posh accent and was smaller than I remembered, his physique thin and wiry.

I giggled nervously, still not entirely reassured. 'Forgot I didn't have any money on me.'

'Going home?'

'Yeah.'

He was still standing in my path, almost blocking it.

'Want a lift?'

I shook my head. What I wanted was a gentlemanly offer to escort me back to the Odeon, and then to be left alone. 'Nah, it's OK.' I shrugged, trying to appear grown-up. He must have been a good ten or even fifteen years older than me. Not knowing what else to do, I giggled again. It must have been the cold, for I could not stop myself shaking.

''Scuse me.'

But still he did not move. 'It's so cold,' he said. 'You need to warm up. Why don't you come and sit down with me?' He gave me a cracked smile, his eyes not moving. I was feeling scared again, almost wishing the souped-up saloon would return.

'I need to get back,' I said, trying to sound polite but firm.

'Nice little dancer, aren't you?'

I took a step away from him, still gurning, still trying to appear cool. 'I need to get back,' I repeated, but this time I could barely get the words out.

'Do you, now?'

'You're standing in my way.'

It sounded like a challenge. The moment I said it I knew I had made a mistake, but it was too late, because he had grabbed me round the waist. 'Come on, darling,' he was saying, and already he had pushed me back towards the fencing, his iron-hard arm placed unbudgingly around my waist, and we were tripping backwards. 'Don't be shy.'

'No, please,' I whispered. 'I don't want to.'

But he had me now, and there was nothing I could do. We stumbled back through a gap in the fencing on to the muddy grass and he climbed on top of me, shoving his boozy face so close to mine that I could hardly breathe. I could feel the icy slush soaking through the seat of my jeans; my left cowboy boot had somehow got kicked off.

'No,' I kept saying pathetically. 'Please don't.'

'All I want is a little kiss and a cuddle. You were all over me a minute ago.'

'Please stop . . .'

But of course he carried on. My useless remonstrations were lost, buried under the urgency of his desire. Pushing his knee between my legs, he parted me with workmanlike efficiency, the way a butcher might splice meat from a joint. His hands were on my breasts, too, pulling apart my light-weight teenage bra as if he was an impatient child tearing a sweet from its wrapper. He squeezed my tits so hard that I yelped with pain, while he groped with the other hand at my jeans and pants. I kept trying to swivel to one side, in the hope of dislodging him, but it was too late, for he had managed to rip them down and was holding me firmly, his knees still pushing my legs apart.

'Get off me!'

I could feel his erection, hot and springy, on the inside of my thigh, and suddenly he was shoving himself up, inside me, with a violence that made me yell out in shock.

'So, does anyone want to add anything?'

I look up with a start and see that I am not being raped on a muddy path in Peckham, but attending a teaching committee in a university seminar room in Sussex. I must have been sitting there for over ten minutes, as the meeting proceeded around me, lost in a blur. But now that I have started to remember it is all coming back, and there is nothing I can do to stop it. Over all these years I never told a soul. But I have never forgotten, for it has always been a part of me: Part One of my unspoken history.

If only I had told Mum the next morning what had happened, but I never did, for she was angry about the vomit on the carpet and I was unable to stop myself slipping into my default mode: moody silence. If I had managed to break through to her, what would have happened?

Behind me the door opens and closes with a quiet click, and someone shuffles past, a late-comer looking for a place to sit. I move my chair a fraction to let them pass and glance up, then turn cold.

It's Alec. I scrutinize him, wishing he would disappear in a puff of noxious smoke. Now that he is padding around the room, the terror I felt at Beth's call is turning into something closer to anger. Is he deliberately following me? How dare he try to scare me like this? And how dare he bring these memories back? Finally he has found a chair on the other side of the room, and perches on the edge of it, picking up his papers and staring at them intently. His dripping kagool is lying in a heap on the floor. I suck in my cheeks, trying to breathe normally. Somewhere close to my ear a student is talking at length about how his library card has stopped functioning.

'Right then,' Bob Stennings says, when there is a brief lull. 'Let's put that down for the student-resources committee and move on to item six: Student Concerns.'

He glances hastily around the room, clearly hoping that we can tick item six off the list and move on. I stare at my feet, wondering if I should simply rise from my chair and leave. With Alec so close I doubt I can remain sitting here. But it is too late, because now he is coughing and raising his hand and the violent knocking in my chest tells me that whatever happens I will not escape him now.

'Alec?' Bob Stennings says. 'You're the second-year rep. Do you have a matter to raise?'

Alec clears his throat and pushes his hand through his damp hair. He looks ill, with dark shadows under his eyes and an unhealthy glow to his cheeks. Could he really have been the person staring in at me that night? At the head of the table Bob Stennings is still studying his papers. 'Is it concerned with teaching? I'm trying to keep to the agenda here.'

'It's about the historical-methods course,' Alec replies, turning now to look at me. He seems to be having trouble getting the words out, his speech slow and laboured.

'Go on.'

'Well, the problem is that I'm highly concerned that basic administrative procedures aren't being followed.'

He sits back, fiddling with his glasses, and the entire room turns to stare at me. I swallow heavily, feeling my cheeks turn scarlet. He is obviously going to say something about Beth's essay. Clutching my clammy hands, I try to speak but my throat seems to have seized up. Meanwhile Bob Stennings is humming and hawing and saying, 'Perhaps this is something best taken up directly with the tutor concerned.'

'The tutor concerned is refusing to make herself available.'

'Hum . . .'

'Can I elaborate?'

Interpreting the silence around the room as assent, Alec continues, 'The basic situation is that since the beginning of term, despite my attempts to raise the matter with her, she refuses to see me. In fact . . .' he pauses, perhaps gathering courage '. . . in fact, she has recently informed me that she wishes I would leave her alone.'

Bob Stennings looks at me, perplexed. Around the room, the low-level muttering of voices and shuffling of papers has ceased. The meeting is hushed, the bored students at the back now leaning forward expectantly. 'I really think these matters should be raised elsewhere, Alec. Perhaps with your personal tutor?'

Two chairs down from me, a hand is raised and someone says, 'I think it should be raised here, if that's what he wants.'

It's the ginger side-burned Fuck Capitalism twerp. I sit frozen in front of the assembled audience. I can feel everything gathering force inside me, about to burst out.

'Perhaps we should allow the course tutor to explain herself,' Fuck Capitalism continues, looking meaningfully at Alec. He's obviously been primed to be supportive.

'No, Nick, I don't agree. It isn't appropriate here. Alec and Dr Bainbridge need to set up a meeting to sort it out later.' This is from Julian who is glancing sympathetically in my direction.

I am trying hard to control myself, clutching at the sides of my chair and pressing my lips tightly together to prevent the bubble of speech escaping, but it is becoming increasingly hard. I did not want this to happen, not in so public a venue, but now that Alec is sitting opposite me, my emotions are rising dangerously, like a river about to flood. 'Actually,' I hear myself say shrilly, 'I'm quite happy to answer Alec here. If that's OK?'

Opposite me, Julian raises his eyebrows. I get the sense he is trying to warn me to shut up but I am too upset and angry to pay any heed. 'You're right, Alec,' I say, turning so that I am facing him. Considering the way my heart is pumping, I am surprised at how insouciant my voice sounds. 'I *do* want you to leave me alone.'

Alec blinks. He has gone very pale.

'In fact as soon as this meeting is over I plan to go to the police and report your behaviour,' I continue. 'I'm sure there are all kinds of things they would be interested in.' I stop. The palpitations are easing, but my hands are shaking uncontrollably. So that no one will notice, I grip them in my lap. I feel like a bungee jumper, about to leap off a high building.

'What kinds of things are those?' Alec says frigidly.

I can see his Adam's apple moving up and down his throat. The room is so quiet that I can hear the tick of the radiator and the whistle of wind through the windows.

'You've been harassing me, ever since the beginning of term,' I say, still staring at him. 'You've sent me abusive emails, plagued me with nuisance calls and tried to break into my flat.'

There! I have said it. I am plummeting through the air, the elastic about to jerk me back up. I take a breath, trying to pull myself into shape. Around me, everything other than Alec and me seems to be spinning into the distance, leaving us centre-stage.

'I've got witnesses and hard evidence.'

'It's a lie,' he whispers.

'I don't think so. You door-stepped me outside my flat this morning, and I've just had a call from Beth Wilson saying she saw you standing on the flat roof of my flat. You were trying to break in.'

My voice sounds unfamiliar, like that of someone scared and bitter. I look at the shocked faces of my colleagues. I should be feeling vindicated, but instead I am so tense I may possibly explode. Of course Beth did not actually *say* it was Alec, but who else could it have been?

Alec's mouth is opening and closing like a beached fish. At the head of the table, Bob Stennings looks horrified. There is a stunned pause, then he coughs. 'Sorry, Cass,' he says, ever keen for administrative clarity. 'Who is this Beth Wilson?'

'A third year, majoring in gender studies,' I say sharply. 'She's been staying with me.'

'And when was it she was meant to have seen me?' Alec asks.

'Just now. I had a call from her about half an hour ago. She's scared out of her wits.'

'So how could I have cycled all the way here if I was breaking into your flat?'

I pull a face at him, not giving a damn how he got here. I was about to say more, about the photograph, and the emails, but I have just remembered something else. *The fire escape had blown down.*

'Hang on a minute. Please may I say something?'

At the back of the room a girl is hesitantly putting up her hand. She's one of the Ph.D. students, a bit podgy, with a tendency towards Goth makeup and long black dresses. Pushing the agenda aside, Bob Stennings nods at her defeatedly. Student concerns is clearly going to take longer than anticipated.

'Go on.'

'It's just that I passed Alec in my friend's car on the university road about forty minutes ago. It was like he said, he was cycling, but it was so windy he was going incredibly slowly. We were all waving at him.' She laughs apologetically. 'Sorry, Alec, but it looked as if you were about to take off.'

There is a brief, uncomfortable silence.

'Well, what about all those emails then, and this?'

I scrabble through my pile of mail and pull the photograph from its buff envelope, holding it up so that Alec can see. Around me, people strain forward, peering at the odd picture and sloping writing. I am expecting Alec to balk, or look contrite, but he furrows his brows. 'I have absolutely no idea what you're talking about.'

'Look, Cass, perhaps it would help clarify matters if we could check when this thing was posted,' Julian interjects.

I glance again at the postmark: 14 Nov. 'The day before yesterday, from Brighton.'

'Well, then, you have your answer. Alec couldn't have posted it because he spent the first three days of the week with me at the British Library in London. He's working as a research assistant on my British Academy project.'

There is a long and terrible silence. So the elastic was rotten: I jumped, but did not bounce back up. Bob Stennings turns back to me. For a moment he regards me with avuncular pity: despite his jocular bluster he is intelligent enough to see what a mess I am in. 'So you must be mistaken, Cass.'

'But who could have sent it?' I gaze around wildly. My heart is bashing unhelpfully against my ribs, my lips are dry. All I can think is that I have got everything completely wrong. If Alec did not send me this picture, and was not on the roof, then it must have been someone else. But to confuse matters further, the fire escape was blown down this morning, so how could anyone have climbed up it?

Meanwhile everybody in the meeting is gawping at me as if I had just grown horns on my head. Julian has risen to his feet and is saying something, but a whistling sound in my ears is blocking it out. Finally I manage to stand. Forcing myself to look at Alec, who is sitting on the edge of his chair peering intently at the floor, I force the words from my cotton-wool mouth: 'I'm so sorry. I've clearly misjudged the situation.'

Then, trying and failing to look as if nothing much has happened, I slump back in my chair.

25

The next hour passes in a blur. I remain motionless, strapped into my seat by a disabling mixture of mortification and panic. My hands are folded tightly in my lap, I stare blankly at the floor. I am determined not to raise my eyes and see the curious glances of my colleagues. When the meeting ends, I am the first to stand and hurry out of the door. Back in my office I sit down woodenly and try to reel in my spiralling thoughts. I thought I understood what was happening, but it seems I was wrong. Squeezing my eyes shut, I try to remember the order of events: Alec was antagonistic and unpleasant; there were the odd emails and phone calls. Every time I turned round, he seemed to be hovering accusingly behind me. And each of the emails followed a confrontation with him. Yet he could not have been the man standing on the roof, for not only was he cycling the six miles to campus but with the fire escape damaged only Spiderman could have scaled the wall.

Why would Beth lie? Was the story about a man watching the flat from the garden gate a fiction too? As I ponder this, the phone rings. I pick it up instantly.

'Hello?' I say, feeling about five years old.

'It's me,' Matt replies.

I go all giddy, my heart thumping in my ears as if I were standing on the edge of a precipice. Last night in the gardens it all seemed so clear: our relationship was over because I can never give him what he wants, but now, as I hear his voice, I am desperate for a reprieve. *Please!* I want to beg. *I can't bear for this to be the end!*

'Hi.' Can this feeble little voice really be mine?

For a second or so Matt says nothing. Perhaps he is going to give me another chance, I think madly. Perhaps he has decided that he doesn't want a baby after all and we can start again. 'I'm coming to London –' I start, but he butts in.

'I want to fix a date for moving your gear out of the house,' he says tersely. 'Your things are getting in the way. I'm going up to Manchester tomorrow and I need them out by the time I return.'

I gasp, winded by the finality in his voice. 'What do you mean?' I stammer. 'I live there!'

'You live in Brighton now, not here.' His voice is cold and hard, all emotion sealed off.

My body feels numb, as if it has suffered a total systems failure. 'You can't do this!'

He actually laughs, the cold chuckle of contempt he reserves for the work of stupid colleagues or dishonest politicians being grilled on *Newsnight*. 'I think you'll find that I can. Since the house is legally my property I can do exactly what I like.'

After a moment I stammer, 'Can't we at least discuss it face to face?'

'Discuss what? You dumped me, remember? Your new friend made that totally clear. All I want now is for you to clear your stuff out. OK? Oh, yeah, and I'd be grateful if you could stop all these hysterical messages, too.'

Before I can ask him what on earth he means, he puts the phone down. I sit, staring at the humming receiver lying limply in my hand. What hysterical messages? Is he referring to my attempts to contact him last night? And why does he attach so much significance to Beth being in the flat? I stretch my fingers over the grimy green phone, feel the weight of it in my hand: such a functional piece of plastic, which has brought such devastation. Whatever, I think, rolling it dejectedly between my palms. None of these details is important for everything is over.

I put the receiver back. My hands are trembling. There is a chance I might throw up. I do not know what to do or where to go. I stare blankly at my watch. Yes, I do. I am going to stand up, open the door, and go back to the flat to pack. Then I am going to call in sick at the university and escape to Sarah's house in Highbury.

I gather up my things, barely aware of what I am doing. I shall leave academia, I think, go and stack shelves in Sainsbury's. How can I possibly continue without Matt? He was my coach, my mentor; the rational voice who goaded me on. He rescued my Ph.D., helped me profoundly with my book. I only wrote the damn thing to please him. What, now, is the point in anything?

I push a stack of essays on to the floor and rootle half-heartedly for my glasses. I feel as if someone has blown a vast hole through the centre of my body with a cannon. *Why are you surprised?* screams the voice in my head. *Isn't this what you deserve?* And then, before I can stop it, the image is with me again. *Spindly legs and dozy, blinking eyes; a soft, damp head.*

But now the phone is ringing again. My mind fuzzy with shock, I grab it, pressing it tightly to my ear.

'Hiya, Cass,' Beth says, in a whimsical little voice. 'Only me.'

The moment I hear her voice I snap back to the present. For someone who, only an hour earlier, rang me in panic, she sounds remarkably composed.

'What is it now?'

Down the phone I can sense her expression change, a quick shift in gear as she registers my displeasure. 'Just calling to see what you wanted for dinner,' she says sweetly.

The receiver feels hot and slippery. Surely she must have seen the message I pinned to the door. Why is she asking me about dinner?

'Why did you tell me you saw someone on the roof?' I say abruptly.

'I was scared, Cass.'

Her voice is whiny and petulant, and suddenly I can no longer remember why I ever liked her. She was lying this morning, I think, with dislike. And I wish she would stop using my first name, too. It makes her sound like a smarmy telesales representative, attempting intimacy when none exists in order to get her own way. 'You're lying,' I say flatly. 'There couldn't possibly have been anyone there because the fire escape blew down in the night. That was the noise I heard yesterday evening.'

The pause is so long that I wonder if she is still there. Then, very softly, she says, 'I only told you what I thought I saw. I never said it was real.'

'What's that supposed to mean?'

'Just that I was feeling scared.'

'And you didn't phone the police?'

She laughs, softly and sweetly. 'Of course not, Cass.'

Suddenly I can no longer contain myself. My mind is too crowded and I am too upset without having to deal with the additional complications of this silly little girl and her manoeuvrings. 'Look, I'm sorry, Beth,' I say curtly, 'but I'm afraid you're going to have to move out of my flat today. Like I said, I've got friends coming this evening. You're going to have to make alternative arrangements, OK?'

She starts to say something else, but I cannot bear to hear it. I have to be firm and not listen to any more sob stories: I have done what I can to help and now I have to focus on myself. In a way, discovering the culprit of the emails and photograph is irrelevant. All I know is that I must go back to the flat, pack my belongings and get away before the memories, which are now crowding in so fast and furious, engulf me.

'Go and see the housing officer on campus,' I say briskly. 'They're open all day.'

Then I put the phone down.

I drive back erratically, my brain hardly registering the scenery. Despite the fallen trees and relentless wind, it does not take me long to return to the square. Inside my bag, my mobile is trilling frantically but, not wishing to hear Beth's predictable pleadings, I do not answer. After I have parked the car, I walk heavily towards number sixteen. The early-afternoon light is so dim it feels like dusk, and freezing rain is beating on my forehead. In the garden, the trees are cavorting madly, dark puppets jerking to an unseen hand. Just ahead of me, a tile shoots off a roof and smashes on to the pavement. I step over its shattered remains. The sky ahead is battered and grey.

As I approach the building, I am feeling irrationally anxious again, even though everything bad that could possibly happen just has. There is something more I need to think about, before I go inside my flat, but already it feels too late. I unlock the front door, push it open and step into the damp hall, suddenly remembering Jan with her buckets.

Most of the water has gone; all that remains of the deluge are some squelchy puddles and a stack of sodden newspapers, piled by the inside wall. I pick my way across the ruined carpet and creep past Jan's door. I want to bound up the stairs, grab my things and escape as fast as possible, not stand in the freezing hall and make polite conversation with some flaky New Ager. But it is too late. Perhaps she has been listening out for me for her door opens and she steps into the dingy light. 'Open Sesame,' she says, wincing at the cold.

I try to smile at her, but only manage a ghoulish grimace. 'Quite a storm out there.'

'Mmm.'

'It's global warming that's doing it.'

'Yeah.'

She gives me a long, cool stare. Perhaps she is irked that I did not help this morning. 'Got the removal men in, then?' she says suddenly, inclining her eyes to the ceiling.

I blink back at her. Perhaps her cards have predicted my forthcoming move. 'Not yet.'

'You could have fooled me.'

I do not understand what she means. She is about to say something else, but I interrupt. 'Look,' I blurt, 'I'd love to chat but I'm really cold and tired.'

Before she can add anything else I turn from her and bound up the stairs. I have been rude I know, but I am yearning to get away. When I reach the landing outside my flat, I pause, trying to pull myself together. I am breathing too fast and my legs are unsteady. Leaning against the wall for support, I slide the key into the front door and push it open. Please, I am thinking, let Beth be gone. I cannot bear to deal with her problems, not at the moment.

As I step into the hall I look around with relief. Since the brief rule of order yesterday, the flat has reverted to its usual mess: coats are piled haphazardly on a chair, unopened letters and bills are scattered on the floor; there is no sign of either Beth or her obsessive tidying. Even more promisingly, the note on the door has gone. The place is quiet. I can hear the clank of pipes, the rattle of windy windows, but no sign of occupation. The flat smells stuffy, as if it has been shut up for weeks.

From its place on the hall table, the telephone is ringing. I hesitate. It will probably be Beth, but the tiny chance that it might be Matt is irresistible. In spite of everything that has happened, I am desperate to hear his voice, desperate for some hint of softness, the hope of a future. Without further prevarication I lunge at the phone. Gripping the smooth plastic with my icy hands, I press 'talk'. When it comes, my voice is an unrecognizable croak. 'Matt?'

The pause is long enough to tell me I have made another mistake. Instead of Matt's abrupt voice I hear another, younger and more upper-class man clear his throat and say hesitantly, 'Cass, is that you?'

It is a second or so before I can reply: I am winded with disappointment. Eventually I clear my throat and rasp, 'Yes?' My hands are so cold I can barely grip the receiver.

'It's Julian here, Julian Leigh.'

'Uh-huh . . .'

'Are you all right?'

'Kind of.'

'You seemed in quite a state earlier. I guess that photo must have really freaked you out.' He sounds genuinely concerned.

I hold my breath, determined not to give vent to the howl of anguish that, at the merest hint of sympathy, builds in my lungs. Why have I been so hostile towards him? All along, he just wanted to make friends.

'Anyway, look, I don't want to pour oil on your fires, so to speak, but there was something else I wanted to discuss with you.'

I stare at the phone, unable to make sense of what he's saying. What could he possibly want to discuss?

'It's about your student,' Julian continues. 'The one you said was staying with you?'

My chest goes tight. 'What about her?'

'I've been looking her up. Beth Wilson's her name, right?'

'Yup.'

'And she's doing gender studies as her major?'

'Right.'

My eyes scan the hall and empty sitting room. She has

definitely cleared out, I keep telling myself. So why am I so edgy? Downstairs, I can hear Jan moving stealthily around her flat.

'The thing is, there's no such subject as gender studies,' Julian continues.

I clutch the phone a little tighter. 'No such subject?' I echo.

'I guess you wouldn't have picked it up because you're new to the system, but we've never run gender studies as a major. That got me intrigued, so I went to check your young lady's file.'

The line crackles. I want very much to hear what he's saying, but something is distracting me. The sounds I thought were coming from Jan's flat are nearer, I realize. In fact, they seem to be on the other side of my bedroom door: the soft shuffle of footsteps, the scrape of objects being moved.

'Basically, there's no file for a Beth Wilson. That's why none of us had ever heard of her.'

From the direction of my bedroom there is another muffled thud. I am feeling increasingly dizzy. So that was why this morning there was no Wilson under the Ws.

'What do you mean?' I whisper.

At the other end of the line, Julian chuckles, presumably at my feeble-mindedness. 'That she isn't one of our students. For all we know she just wandered into your class off the street. Until they insist we all have these ID cards it's perfectly possible, although I suppose she wouldn't be able to check books out of the library. The only thing I can't work out is why you didn't rumble her when you took the register in the first week.'

I swallow heavily. 'I don't think I ever took a register. I lost the computer printout.'

Julian pauses, too polite to state the obvious: Cass, you have messed up big time. 'But wasn't it evident?' he says eventually. 'That she didn't fit in?'

'She seemed fine.'

But no sooner have I said this than I remember that on the two occasions she was forced to perform, she faked it: copying my thesis for her essay, and the *Society and History* article for her presentation, all perfectly possible to photocopy in the library without a card. And, like the fool I was, I allowed her to get away with it.

'So this girl is clearly an *impostor*,' Julian is saying jocularly, and I imagine him wiggling his fingers in the air in ironic inverted commas, a trademark gesture. 'That's what Alec was trying to talk to you about. He's just been telling me how he realised from day one she wasn't a proper student.'

The thudding has stopped but, very clearly now, I can hear footsteps pacing my bedroom floor.

'So we're going to do a little more checking out and then get back to you.'

'Thank you for telling me this,' I rasp down the phone. 'I have to go now.'

'Cass?'

I do not let him finish. Pressing 'off', I slowly put down the phone. Across the corridor, there is sudden silence. Slowly I move towards the bedroom. My chest feels as if it is going to explode. *Jesus*, I am thinking, *what's going on?* When I reach the closed door I stop, trying to pull myself together. I still cannot hear anything on the other side. But then there is a definite crash: a window that I know for sure I did not leave open banging against the wall. As the blood drums in my ears, I push open the door.

My bedroom has been transformed. It was hardly tidy before, but now my entire wardrobe appears to have been emptied on to the carpet, as if somebody has been frantically searching through it, my clothes hurled into heaps of discarded fabric corpses. Stacked around the walls are mountains of books and newspapers, piled so impossibly high that many have slithered to the floor in avalanches of print. As I stare at them, I realize they must have come from the boxes in the spare room. The curtains are drawn and the main light is off, but in the corner by the window a child's night-light, which I recognize from the cupboard in the spare room, has been plugged in. Round and round it spins, pictures of Humpty Dumpty and his broken head illuminated on the ceiling.

I turn slowly towards the bed. For a second I think I am mistaken and that the occupant has already left: all I can see is the lumpy shape of my duvet, a pillow tossed carelessly aside. But then I see a foot protruding from the end, and as I whisper her name, Beth sits up and looks at me.

Brighton, 23 November

Dear Mum

Everything is finally kicking off — stuff is happening, the proverbial shit hitting the fan. So I've decided there's things I need to do. All my life I feel as if I have been standing outside the window of some other child's house, my nose pressed up against it, and it has to change. How can I progress when I do not know who I am? And how can I let other people in when I do not know why you shut me out?

Life's got more complicated than I had hoped, you see: people have done and said things I've found hard to understand. I always thought I was a good person. I have never wanted to hurt anyone. But recently all that has been spiralling out of control.

And now I am certain that I have to act.

26

On seeing me Beth has pulled the duvet over her chest, and is gripping it with the surprised look of a child caught in the midst of a naughty game. She is wearing my red dress again but must have taken scissors to it, for in place of the long velvet sleeves there is an uneven mass of cauterized threads from which her mottled white arms appear, like bones protruding from shredded skin.

'Hi, Beth,' I say, as if she was doing something unremarkable, like reading a book or having a nap. 'What's up?'

'Just sorting some stuff out.'

She smiles in what I interpret as embarrassment, her brown teeth showing. I step over the papers and clothes into the middle of the room. After the initial spurt of adrenaline by the door, I am feeling calmer. So, she has told some lies. There may still be a sensible explanation.

'You're in my bed,' I say slowly. 'And what have you done to my dress?'

She shrugs, as if her behaviour was normal. My fists clenched, I stand by the side of the bed, trying not to look directly into her eyes, which are rheumy and distracted, and keep shifting to the door behind me as if she is expecting someone else to walk in, the final guest in our impromptu party. She seems transformed from the sunny presence that filled my flat that morning five weeks ago. And now that I see her like this, in such obvious confusion, I realize that her behaviour is not as unexpected as it might seem, for she has been behaving more and more strangely all week.

'Did you get my note?' I ask.

She looks up at me with wide, surprised eyes. '*What* note?'

'I wrote you a little note, asking you to come to the campus so that we could arrange some emergency accommodation for you.' I am trying to keep my voice light and carefree, but the way in which she is staring at me is making it increasingly difficult.

'*Did* you?'

My heart palpitates unpleasantly. Of course she got it, but any authority I might once have had over her was clearly a mirage. Now she is giving me a coy smile. 'You really like playing these games, don't you?' she says slowly.

'I don't know what you mean.' I purse my lips, trying to keep the wobble of fear from my voice.

Beth flutters her eyelashes flirtatiously. 'You don't expect me to take this grumpiness seriously, do you?' Flashing me a knowing look, she tosses aside the covers and swings her legs purposefully over the edge of the bed. My dress has been ripped down the front, I see, and she is wearing my high-heeled boots. They are too big for her and the effect is comical: a little girl caught rifling a grown-up's wardrobe. Nodding enthusiastically, she hoists herself up. 'We both know what's really going on, don't we?'

My face crumples with incomprehension. I feel like a word-perfect actor in the wrong play. Rather than playing the grown-up in control I am rendered passive and do not know my lines. 'I haven't a clue,' I say calmly. 'I want you to explain it to me.'

'What is there to explain?'

She is still standing in front of me, fluttering her eyelashes, and I have to fight the urge to scream at her to get out. Tread carefully, Cass, I tell myself. This situation needs care. 'Why aren't you registered at the university?' I say, as if I am asking why her hair is long rather than short.

She laughs, as if the question were irrelevant. 'They

249

would never have let me in. Not after what happened in Leeds.'

I have no idea what she means, but I am feeling more and more tense. She takes a couple of tottering steps, then stops in the middle of the bedroom, her eyes shining as if she is anticipating the most marvellous surprise. I fold my arms, trying to reassert my authority. This is *my* flat. And even if she is not a proper student, I am still her elder. But even as I tell myself this, I am reaching into my pocket and fingering the reassuring metallic cool of my mobile. How long, I wonder, would it take for the police to arrive? 'Why did you tell me you saw someone on the roof?' I say sternly.

She blinks at me woefully. 'I was feeling lonely! I wanted you to come home and be with me.'

'So you lied to me?'

'You see, I wouldn't put it like that. I would say I *constructed* a certain kind of truth. Isn't that what you've been teaching us all term? That there is no objective truth?'

I shake my head. I have just noticed the way she is gripping her arms, her fingers digging hard. Her sleeves are pushed back to her elbows, and already the soft skin on her inner arms is red and smarting, the bruising taking hold. 'Not really,' I say. 'No, not at all.'

'But we mould it, don't we? All you have to do is listen carefully, and the truth will be revealed. Isn't it something like that?' She laughs, throwing back her head to show her stubborn little chin.

She has clearly missed the point of the entire course. 'What's your truth, Beth?' I ask quietly.

'Different from what you think, and yet the same.'

She stares smugly at me, so different from the girl I took for tea on that first day of term. Was that just a charade? A performance to charm me, and reel me in? 'What's that supposed to mean?'

'You know as well as I do.'

If I have to look at her smirking face any longer I shall slap it. I glance away, and say evenly, 'What about your foster-family? Did you mould the truth about that as well?'

She grins goofily, reaching up and pushing the limp hair from her pimply forehead. 'What foster-family?'

'The people whose daughter died? Or did you make that up as well?'

As I say this, she pulls her face into a mockery of apology, like a teenager being reprimanded for a crime she does not take seriously. 'Is that what I told you? Does it really matter?'

'Of course it matters! If you never had a foster family then why the hell did you make such a big deal about them kicking you out?'

For a second something ugly comes into her face, anger perhaps, or even hatred. Then she seems to fight it back.

'I just wanted to be with you, Cass. Is that so very bad?' She gazes at me and does the irritating bird thing with her head, cocking it to one side coquettishly. As I regard her standing in the middle of my wrecked bedroom as if she owned it, I am filled with revulsion so strong that I shudder. I can feel the anger rising in me; my fingers tingle, and its bitter taste is swilling in my mouth. Why did I ever let her get so close? I am meant to be an oral historian, an expert in listening to the nuances and hidden meanings of people's stories, checking and cross-checking the verifiable facts. Yet I believed everything she said, with almost childlike innocence, failing to investigate even the most basic elements. Would it really have taken much expertise to rumble that she was not a real student? And the story about her family, it never rang true, especially not the dead daughter. Yet, fool that I was, I thought she needed my help so I took her in and did everything I could for her. But now I see that her vulnerability was an illusion, that despite the mirage of innocence she

251

revels in deception. No, it is not my help but something else – which I still do not understand – that she wants from me.

'None of this is really important,' she says softly. 'You know that. Why don't you just acknowledge it?'

'Acknowledge what?'

'Our real relationship, of course.'

I stare at her. My jaw has gone slack. What does she mean, 'our *real* relationship'? How could anyone know about my past?

'That very first seminar, when you gave me that little wink? That was my signal.'

Her self-satisfied expression shows that she believes it to be obvious. Making a conscious effort to control myself, I snap my mouth shut. What little wink? My mind leaps and jumps, the memories whirling in a blizzard of fragmented images. *Your raw black eyes; the warmth of your skin against mine. I could feel your heartbeat, as fast as a galloping horse.* But Beth does not appear to have noticed my confusion for she is still speaking.

'Don't worry,' she says, almost soothingly. 'I got your signals, each and every one. Like the way you only picked up the phone after five rings? And leaving your mobile for me to take from your bag that first day we were together?'

I shake my head at her. I am finding it increasingly hard to concentrate on what she is saying. *A soft fluttering sensation. It was both the beginning and the end.*

'I don't know what you're talking about,' I say weakly.

'Oh, come on, Cass. Isn't it time to stop pretending? I knew you'd never have the guts to admit to everything so I did it for you. That was what you wanted, it was obvious. All it took was a couple of text messages to get rid of all those so-called friends of yours. And when I gave the mobile back to you, you were so relieved I'd made the break for you that you blew me a kiss.'

I cannot make head or tail of this. I keep trying to concentrate on the present but, as if on elastic, my thoughts keep snapping back to the past. *I left you there, perhaps to live, perhaps to die. And ever since you have haunted me.*

'Who are you?' I rasp. 'What do you want from me?'

'You know who I am,' Beth says, taking a step towards me. 'And you know what I want.'

I have started to edge towards the door, my mind spiralling into a little jig of panic. Surely, it could not possibly be?

'Just admit it,' she whispers. 'Go on, you'll feel better once you do.'

I gaze at her, remembering the emails. *I know.*

'You sent the emails,' I say faintly.

'Of course I did, silly!'

I know. She wrote it again and again and again. But how can she possibly know about my past? No one knows except me. *Maybe you lived and maybe you died.* Suddenly she lurches towards me, her arms outstretched as if she expects to land in mine. I step aside quickly, and she trips, blundering into the side of the door as she steadies herself. Her forehead is slimy with sweat and damp patches are spreading from the underarms of the red dress.

She looks up at me beseechingly. 'I know it's hard, but you just have to be honest. We both know the real reason why you don't want to marry that boyfriend of yours, why you haven't had kids. You've kept it secret too long.'

She is on the verge of reaching out and touching me but the idea of making physical contact with her is repellent. Could she somehow have discovered my history? Is this scene heading towards blackmail, or something worse? As I gawk at her in confusion, I know that the wave has reached its apex, that it is all about to come crashing down. 'It's none of your business,' I say faintly.

'That's not true.'

Pressing her palm against my cheek, she forces me to return her gaze. I can smell the faintly rancid scent of her breath, see in vivid detail how her acne pokes through the foundation she has smudged into her skin. I feel as if I am in a dream, moving clumsy and disoriented through a distorted landscape of things that are not as they seemed. *I was still alive, but only just. This is the end, I was thinking as I walked away. Now nothing will ever be the same.*

'Just say it,' Beth implores.

'I can't.'

'Yes, you can. You have to.'

The room is so quiet. Beside me, Beth keeps breathing, and I can hear the lumpen pounding of blood in my ears and, if I listen very hard, the distant rage of the sea. So, somehow she has found out the truth. All my adult life a part of me has craved for this to happen, and now that it has I am woozy with terror. But it is too late now. I have to do as she says.

'I had a baby,' I breathe. 'I left it on the beach to die.'

And now that I have said it aloud I know that everything has changed and that it will never be a secret again. *The baby was mine. I held it against my skin for no more than a minute, but it was mine. And then I walked away.*

I stare, glazed, back at Beth. She is the first person I have ever told. Although I still cannot work out how, she has caused the truth to come flooding out. And now I am expecting her face to register recognition or even relief. But she does not seem interested. Instead she is frowning at me with the irritation of a supreme egoist whose moment of glory has been interrupted, her feet tapping impatiently in the over-sized boots. 'What are you talking about?' she says crossly.

'The baby. I mean, that's the secret. Isn't that what you're talking about?'

She laughs and says something more. But I am no longer

listening, for now that I have come this far I cannot stop thinking about my child as it lay there on the stones. The baby was perfect, each tiny fingernail, each stubby eyelash. Feet the size of my little finger, ears that coiled like shells. A sea creature, curled and mysterious, to be given back to the waves.

'I'm not talking about a baby,' Beth sneers. 'I'm talking about you and me. About the fact that we're in love.'

'*What?*'

I feel so dizzy that, for a second, I have to close my eyes. Have I completely misunderstood everything she has been saying? I try to reel in what has just taken place, but it has already slithered away. Anyway, none of this matters, for I have finally said the thing that for so many years I have kept locked tightly inside. I was fifteen, almost an adult, almost a child, but over the months I had felt the fluttering change to something more purposeful: the flopping of a fat fish, the life waiting to burst free. I knew about biology, even if at first I had denied it. I had done my calculations: I knew what to expect.

When I open my eyes again I see Beth's hot looming face, staring angrily into mine. 'Cass!' she whines. 'Why aren't you listening to me?'

I shake my head, trying to break the trance.

'What's the matter with you?' she mutters petulantly.

Slowly, I force myself to look at her. 'I want you to leave,' I say quietly.

'No . . .'

I swallow my agitation, reach out and put a steering hand on her forearm. It feels clammy and hot, as if she has a fever. She has calmed slightly, but her breath is coming in short, shallow gasps. In the background, I can hear my phone ring once and the answer-machine pick up. *Hi, this is Cass Bainbridge. Leave a message and I'll get back to you . . .*

'We were meant to be together, Cass,' she says, shaking her head at me in admonishment. 'You promised me you were going to look after me for ever. Like I said, that woman in Leeds doesn't matter any more. It's only you. But now you're throwing it all back in my face.'

I look into her bloodshot, confused eyes. Then I take a deep breath. No, she cannot possibly be connected to me. 'Get out,' I say.

It is incredible how calm I feel. I straighten my back, regarding her composedly. On the other side of the door I can hear the crackling of a male voice coming through the machine. It sounds urgent, the words coming in staccato blasts, then cutting off as the phone is put down. 'If you don't leave immediately,' I say matter-of-factly, 'I'm calling the police.'

'All those promises. And now it has to come to this.'

Despite her attempt at menace, she sounds young and girlie, as if she is playing a role in a school play.

'I never made any promises.'

She grins, about to produce her trump card. 'You wanted to kiss me that night in your bed, but you didn't dare.'

I inhale sharply, glancing away from her small, determined face. So she had been awake all the time. For a second my cheeks become warm, but then the emotion dissipates. It no longer matters what I did or what she thinks, for I have said the words: *I had a baby.* I turn the phrase over and over, feeling the shape and weight of the strange words in my mind. I feel stunned, in a strange liminal state where their meaning has not yet sunk in. When I eventually speak I sound different; older, perhaps, but also less afraid. 'I want you to leave me alone.'

My hands close over the brass knob. I am on the verge of escaping, but suddenly it is too late.

'Don't go!'

She is upon me, pouncing with a soft, feral growl and pushing me on to the carpet with a force I would never have suspected. Although I must be at least four stones heavier, I am so surprised that I am momentarily unable to defend myself. I try to release my torso from her grip, swivelling round and prodding my fingers into her eyes, but before I can lever myself into the right position she has climbed on to my back and is pushing my face down. I give a stifled yelp, my mouth squashed into the fluff-scuffed carpet. From my new position I can smell the mouldering aroma of damp flooring, and hear the muffled tones of Jan's TV.

I move my head a fraction and manage to glance at her. She is sitting astride my back, the lunatic rider of a fallen mare. I can feel her cold fingertips at my neck, smell the warm musk of her body. When I speak, my voice is small and wheezy. 'Who are you?'

'I'm not anybody.'

She purses her lips, a little girl in a huff. If wanted to I could surely push her off my back, for she is so small and light, like a Lilliputian attacking a feminist version of Gulliver. 'Beth,' I say slowly, 'this really is very silly.'

She does not reply, but I feel a sharp tweak at the back of my neck as she digs her nails into my skin. I am concentrating hard now, trying to keep my voice as low and soothing as possible. 'I know you're upset,' I carry on. 'That's OK. You've had a horrible old time.' I sigh, pausing for effect. I am not sure why I have started to talk like this, but it seems to be working. Behind me, the pressure of her fingers on my skin eases.

'So I'm not going to say anything more about it. What we're going to do is clear this mess up, then sit down and have a cup of tea together. How about that?'

My tone sounds deeply familiar. It is as if I have redis-covered an ancient store of knowledge, something so deeply

257

engrained I did not even realize it was forgotten. I rummage wildly through my memories, clasping their wispy tendrils.

'Come on, love,' I say gently. 'Let's try and calm down.'

And then I remember. This was the way my mother used to speak to me, before she stopped looking me in the eye and I started to hate her. Cassie-baby she used to call me when I was little. Come and cuddle Mama, Cassie-baby, lay your head on my shoulder, everything is going to be fine. Sometimes, after some fall or conflict, I would sob so violently it made my tummy hurt. She was the only person who could console me then. She would scoop me on to her lap, hold me there against her soft belly and stroke my hair until my shoulders stopped heaving and my eyes began to close. I loved her so much. And now, as I feel Beth relax her grip and shuffle off my back, I know that whatever happened between Mum and me all those years ago I must forgive her.

'I just want you to look after me,' Beth says, in a little voice. 'I'm feeling so tired.'

'I know you are, love.'

'Everywhere I go, people hate me,' she whimpers.

'Of course they don't . . .'

I turn round, sitting up and slithering my bottom slowly towards the door.

'They do,' she mutters. 'I've never had any proper friends.'

'I'm sure lots of people like you,' I say, in the same sing-song voice. Taking her hand, I give it a duplicitous squeeze. The anger is draining from her face, but her eyes keep flitting round the room, as if she has forgotten why she is here.

'In the seminar you're great – really helpful and fun . . .'

'But I was thrown out because of that woman. And none of the other places would touch me with a barge-pole.'

I do not enquire what she means. She frowns, as if she is trying to work something out, her eyes hazy. I take her free hand and stroke it gently. She is slumping against me, leaning her entire weight against my upper body. She is barely out of childhood, with her baby-smooth cheeks and sweet honey-coloured curls. What happened to her? Were the seeds for this scene sown in the womb, a genetic predisposition to obsessive-compulsive behaviour? Or was she abused in some way, her chances wrecked by parents who were unable to give her what she needed?

'Your mum and dad aren't really dead, are they?' I say gently. She shivers, clutching at her bruised arms.

'They might just as well be.'

'Do they know where you are?'

She flinches. 'They've never given a shit.'

There is a long pause. All I want now is to get away.

'Shall I make you a camomile?' I say eventually. 'That would make you feel better.' She nods mournfully. Very gradually, I start to edge away from her. 'Then perhaps you can cook another meal?'

She glances up, her face clouding at some memory.

Gingerly, I stand and turn towards the door. I do not want to move too quickly, in case she recognizes the urgency I am trying so hard to disguise. If only I had a key to my bedroom, so that I could lock her in. She has collapsed back on to the floor now, and is lying crumpled on the carpet, her arms covering her head so that all I can see of her face is an unruly tangle of damp curls. Smiling as serenely as possible, I open the door a crack.

'Cass?' I hear her mumble.

'Yes, love?'

'You won't be long, will you?'

'Of course not.'

As soon as I have stepped out of the room, I hurry across the hall. My legs are quivering like those of a landlubber caught on a stormy ship, my heart flops heavily in my chest.

When I reach the door to the landing, I yank it open. I am trying to be as quiet as possible but it is draughty out here and as I walk through the door the wind snatches it from my fingers and slams it hard behind me.

Outside, the wind blasts my face with a force that moment-arily takes my breath away. Across the road, the trees are dancing crazily, their branches whipping back and forth like pissed-up, pogoing punks. At the bottom of the square, on the other side of the dual-carriageway, I can hear the thundering of the waves. I run across the road, hurrying towards the gardens. The scene with Beth has already acquired a blurred, dream-like quality, irrelevant and in the past. All I care about now is my baby.

I push open the gate and splash heavily across the muddy lawn. In the twenty-four hours since Matt and I had our fight, the garden has been violently altered. The grass is strewn with bashed-in branches and twigs, and at the bottom a large tree has been completely upended and now stretches across the path, a sleeping giant. As I approach the bottom of the enclosure I can hear the relentless roar of the sea. I start to sob, running wildly towards the dank tunnel, which burrows underneath the road towards the beach. *You pulled me away from you*, the voice is screaming. *Put me aside, like a parcel delivered to the wrong address. And then you left me to die.*

But that is not true – surely I did no such thing. I clatter through the tunnel, wrapping my arms around my body in a hopeless attempt at comfort. In a moment I shall burst out on to the seashore, the place where it all ended and all began. For a few muffled seconds there is silence, just the drip of water from the mossy ceiling and the clanking of the gate at the end. It is almost completely dark in here; it smells of stagnant water, salt and a hint of urine.

Then, suddenly, I have reached the end. I throw open the gate, stumble on to the pebbles and run towards the sea. Rain slams into my face and I am almost knocked down by the wind, but finally I am here. For a moment I stop, staring frenziedly at the dirt-green waves, which splatter the sides of the marina wall and crash on to the shingle.

The stones are piled high in this part of the beach, sculpted by the wind into a strange undulating landscape of hills and hollows. I stumble over them, rushing ever closer to the water. I have been living so close to it since the summer, the waves and strip of blue beyond the beach my constant backdrop, but this is the first time I have dared face it. And now I am back at the scene of my crime, the place which I have never really left.

Where exactly did it happen? I peer frantically through the mist, wiping the spray from my eyes with my sleeve. Not this far east, surely, but closer to the pier, because that was where the restaurant was. For a split second I picture myself lying on the stones, the bloody water splattering down my thighs. I thought I would die, that in the morning they would find me laid out on the pebbles, bleached and baked in the dawn sun like a cuttlefish. I did not want to conceal it by then, I was desperate for help. But it was the most deadened part of the night and the beach was empty.

And then it was coming, pushing its way out so fast that even had I tried to drag myself back up to the road I would not have made it. It must have been as desperate for life as I was to contain and stifle it.

My stomach lurches at the memory. I swing back sharply to face the sea. I am so close to the waves that the froth is splashing me, but I hardly notice. All these years I have carried it secretly inside me: not a swelling expectant life but the deadening knowledge of what I did.

27

Mum threw me one of her I-dare-you-to-disobey-me looks and stalked out of the hotel room. It was against all my principles to do as she said, but I was feeling too ill to resist any further so I pulled myself out of bed, changed into a long, fringed tent I had bought from Kensington Market in my heavy-metal stage and an outsize Afghan jumper, then staggered down the stairs. The backache had shifted now, lodging in the front of my tummy, like a bad period pain. It kept coming and going, making me wince in discomfort, then fading away. Sitting in the back of the taxi they had ordered, I whistled through my teeth at an unexpectedly strong twinge. It was from the walking, I was telling myself, I must have strained a muscle. It could not possibly be *the thing*.

At the restaurant I could not bring myself to eat the plate of pasta that was ordered for me. I was feeling sick again, and the pains were growing steadily stronger. Mum and Dr Death kept ordering bottles of sparkling wine and clinking their glasses in smug celebration. I, however, could not bring myself even to have a sip. It tasted of disinfectant, and made me heave. In fact, as the waiters cleared my untouched plate away, I realized I was about to throw up. Clutching my belly, I ran for the toilets and retched into the nearest available cubicle just as another gripping pain struck.

When I emerged, I found Mum waiting for me by the wash-basins. 'Have you been drinking again, Cass?' she said, looking me slowly up and down.

I stared dumbly back at her. I should have grabbed her

hand, placed it on my swollen stomach. I'm in labour, you stupid woman! But all I could manage was a small shake of my head.

'Because that's what it looks like to me,' she said, her voice rising dangerously. 'I thought you'd stopped all this juvenile behaviour, but no. That's what you've been doing all day, isn't it? Hitting the bottle.' Her over-made-up and increasingly bloodshot eyes squinted at me disapprovingly. 'No wonder you're being sick.'

The way she was looking at me made me want to burst into tears. If only she was not always so critical of me. If only I could tell her the truth. Yet despite my horror at what, since the spring, I had been increasingly unable to deny, I had found talking to her impossible. In the first months, when my body had been rocked with sickness and exhaustion but nothing showed, my approach had been simple: total and absolute denial. So I had missed period after period, but it didn't mean anything, I told myself. Like it said in that doctor's column in *Cosmopolitan* magazine, it was probably the result of stress, or a sudden change in diet. Amenorrhoea: they even had a medical term for it. At that stage Dad was still critically ill, so it remained a small, nagging fear, hanging around uneasily in the pit of my stomach, not exactly forgotten but ignored, like a neglected dog that is growling but not yet baring its fangs and attacking.

Yet later, after he had died and life was, in my mother's tight-lipped phraseology, 'back to normal', my fears became harder to suppress. My belly had swollen into a hard, tight mound by then, and I could feel the thing inside kicking and shifting around. I never thought of it as a baby, just this alien thing that was taking me over and from which there seemed no escape. All winter I had forced the memory of the sleety wasteland in Peckham from my head. The whole thing had been my fault, of that I was sure, a violation so vile and so humiliating that I would never, ever tell anyone, least of all my mother. Yet despite my fevered efforts, sometimes my brain could no longer contain it and, like a monster grabbing me from under the bed, it kept popping out at me with a ghoulish shriek. It was my fault for dancing like that, the monster jeered. I had lurched off from the gig like a lunatic, and he had followed me and grabbed me and done it to me, tearing my jeans and my bra, and leaving me hobbled and bleeding. I had been dancing with the guy like a strumpet, I recalled, in an agony of shame, so I must have deserved it. And now, as I lay awake, gazing across my room at the mess of records and discarded clothes that, as a matter of teenage policy, I refused to tidy, I knew that the thing all schoolgirls most dread was indeed taking place, right now, inside me.

When I did sleep, I had nightmares: terrifying ordeals in which I was trying to escape from some faceless pursuer, but could not get my legs to move. During the days I would lurch from blank-headed pragmatism to a terror so engulfing that I could barely remain standing. It could hit at any time: in the middle of a lesson, waiting for the school bus, sitting surly-faced and silent with Mum and David at tea: a sweeping sensation of panic that would leave me vertiginous and gasping for air. If anyone noticed, I suppose they assumed it was grief. Poor child, of course she's behaving strangely. It's only a matter of months since her father died.

But mostly no one did notice. And I was far too scared to tell Mum. It was not that I feared she would beat me and throw me on to the streets: she was a surgery receptionist in the Home Counties in 1980, not a Victorian patriarch. It was more that I could not bring myself to form the words into a comprehensible announcement for in doing so it would become irrevocably real. Have you heard the news? It's such a shocker . . . Cassie Bainbridge is up the duff!

Looking at my mother now, I could feel the words forming

in my mouth, my surprise wedding gift. *I am going to have a baby.* But the way she was eyeballing me made me swallow them back, too cowardly for the reaction I knew they would evoke. 'I haven't been drinking,' I muttered.

And now she was grabbing my wrist and pulling me closer to her. 'There are going to be some changes, now that Don is here to look after us,' she breathed. 'It's time you stopped being such a bloody little handful.'

Nine months ago I might have attempted to punch her in the face, but now I hardly had the energy to speak. I jerked my wrist out of her hand, turned and stumbled out of the toilets, heading across the restaurant floor to the exit. When I got there I stopped, glanced over my shoulder to see where she was, like a recalcitrant toddler. I was furious with her but I did not want to be alone. What I saw was that she had returned to the table, was saying something dismissive and sitting down next to Dr Death. She was not even looking in my direction.

Why didn't she follow me? I have never understood it. I was her daughter, and she must have known something was wrong. Was she trying to teach me a lesson, showing that what she called my 'attention-seeking behaviour' would never work? Or had she simply given up? I keep trying to put myself in her position: it was her wedding night; she had already endured years of teenage aggro; she had no idea how bad things were; her unhappy marriage had ended four months earlier with her husband's unpleasant death. But even as I try to imagine how she felt, my sympathy evaporates, like water in a desert, and all I can remember is that, right then, I needed her more than ever. How could she not have noticed? I had left enough clues: all I needed was for her to question me and then it would all have come spilling out. Yet despite the unopened packets of sanitary towels and the Rennies I kept in my pocket and ate like sweets, she had never said a word. She was busy with Dr Death by then, rushing in and out of the house with her makeup on and a high-pitched giggle I had never heard before. 'It's time for *me*,' she would say, if challenged. I overheard her on the phone to my grandmother one evening, her voice rising defensively: 'I've been through enough. This is the only chance I'll get.' As for her adored doctor, he clearly wasn't very medically observant. Most of the time he pretended I wasn't there. When he did glance in my direction, I suppose that all he saw was a fat, bad-tempered teenager, whom he would rather not engage with.

Or perhaps, deep down, Mum knew the truth but, like me, was foolishly hoping that if the problem was ignored for long enough it would go away. Whatever, it was now too late for her to guess or me to confess. The swing doors expelled me on to the promenade with a *phut* of stale restaurant air. It was after nine by now, and the pavement was filled with people enjoying the warm night. I did not know where I was going, only that the pain was about to start again. As I staggered towards the iron railings that led down to the beach, it hit more quickly than I had expected. I doubled up and almost fell, stumbling straight into the path of a group of teenage lads. They must have been about my age, clutching cans of lager and strutting drunkenly towards the town centre.

'Whoa, babe!' they shouted, as I sheered in the opposite direction. 'Keep yer fucking hair on!' As I fell against a bench, trying to breathe through the agonizing beats of the contraction, I heard one sneer, 'Fat bitch.'

For perhaps ten seconds I thought I would die. The pain clutched me tightly with its evil pincers, then gradually receded and was gone. Snivelling to myself, I climbed down the steps, heading for the sea. It would be cooler down there, I was thinking, I could wash my face. My jumper was

266

suddenly suffocating me, so I pulled it off and wrapped it loosely around my enormous middle. Ahead lay the expanse of shingle and then, glistening under the moon, a flat strip of water.

I looked around desperately. Closer to the neon lights of the pier, the shore was scattered with fires, their embers glowing in the dark. There were couples too – I could make out the horizontal figures, rolling on the stones. Heading east, I started to lumber towards the darkest part of the beach, away from the lights and eyes. Odd things were happening to my sense of time. I lurched from one hummock of pebbles to another, resting as I went. It seemed like only moments since I had been there, but as the fiercest pain yet was slowly passing away I realized that the fires had gone out, and I was alone. For a moment of fleeting lucidity I understood my predicament exactly and was overcome with panic. The thing was coming. I could not stop it now, and nor could I get help, for the incline of stones I had slithered down so many hours earlier was too steep and I was too weak to climb back up. As I gazed back at the Victorian street-lights, which swept gracefully along the front, they seemed to have moved miles away; another reality, impossible to reach. Then the pain returned and I was lost to it, my mind feverishly counting out the beats of its grip, my body writhing as if I was no longer the person inside.

It was about this time that I tried to stand. I had been crouching down, my face pressed into the sand, my knees grazed by the stones, and was so stiff I could barely move. I had about five seconds left before it hit again. I pulled myself up, turned to face the sea and suddenly felt water pouring down my legs. As I put my fingers to my dress, I found it was soaked with what could only have been pee. But the stuff was bloodied too. I sniffed at it, growing more and more afraid. The liquid was pouring out of me as if my insides had burst.

As yet another surge of pain sucked me in, I knew only one thing: I was going to die, right here on this stupid beach.

But it was not death that was overcoming me, it was life. And now I was overtaken not just by the staggering pain but the desperate need to shit, or do something to expel this thing from my body. Perhaps it was a stomach upset, after all, I thought wildly. Perhaps this was just an attack of diarrhoea. I pulled down my knickers and squatted among the stones. I can remember the sweat running down my face, the horrendous sensation that I was about to burst apart, like a squashy fig. I could smell the rotting cuttlefish and the salty water that licked languidly at the beach and the stench made me gag. Ahead of me, the sea was slick and glazed, oblivious to what was happening.

There was no going back. As the dawn light spread across the sky, and I squatted on the stones, I could feel the bulk of something huge and hard pushing against my bottom. The pain was unbearable, and I was panting with fear. I would be torn in half and die, I was sure: tomorrow the sunbathers would find my body, split into gruesome bits. Then there was another contraction and, unable to stop myself pushing down, I felt a sodden lump of something emerging from between my legs. One more, just one more, my body told me, and it would be over. Then, suddenly, I felt it drop from me, plopping like an overripe fruit on to the ground between my legs.

I lay down after that, placing my cheek against the stones and weeping. The pains had stopped, receding to just the faintest tremor when I had felt something else, warm and jelly-like, slide from me to join the thing I had produced on the stones. I did not want to turn round and look at it, but I could feel the warmth of skin brushing against my slippery thighs and hear a faint, bleating cry. Eventually I pulled myself up and looked down.

268

It was a baby. I had known all along, but now, as I leant down and placed my hand gently against its bloody face, I was overcome by wonder. How could this have happened? All those months of fear and dread and all the time it had been quietly taking form inside me: a minute, yet fully formed person, with dark wet hair and tiny hands that punched the air. It was amazing, and so completely perfect, too. As I stared down, two black eyes gazed dreamily back. I brushed my fingers against its wet mouth, and it opened expectantly: a baby bird, waiting to be fed. I glanced along its skinny body and saw that a rubbery purple length of cord protruded from its belly; attached to this was a disgusting, gelatinous mound of flesh, which rested between my legs like a horror-movie prop. Somewhere in my mind, the phrase *umbilical cord* echoed, like a biology lesson, learnt by rote. Groping among the pebbles my fingers found one of the bleached white cuttlefish, its bony remains dried hard and sharp at the edges. I sawed at the cord and razed it in two, like a portion of calamari. When it came apart I kicked the bloodied mess of placenta into the sandy pebbles. Then I picked up the baby, its head flopping against my shoulder.

It was as cold as alabaster, but I could feel its heart pattering against my skin. Reaching behind me, I located my jumper, which many hours earlier had dropped to the ground, and wrapped it around the tremulous body, holding it tight against my chest as I stared down. It was so beautiful, my little child, its dark eyes so sentient and filled with trust. And as I tried to warm it up, I knew what I had to do. I would give anything to reverse that now, to return to that sultry summer night and guide my fifteen-year-old self back up to the road to the safety of the hotel, but I was half deranged with shock. It seemed the only way out.

And so I stood up shakily, and began to stumble along the shore. I was getting scared again for soon it would be day, and we would be discovered. The baby nestled into my crooked arm, as silent as a doll, its half-blind eyes blinking at the strip of sunlight that now gleamed over the top of the pier. After a few minutes I stopped, looking around in mounting panic. I could feel blood dripping down my legs, and my sight kept going in and out of focus.

A short distance from where I was standing a fishing-boat had been dragged to the top of the shingle, and was resting alongside a heap of plastic buckets and thick coiled ropes. I blundered towards it, knowing only that it might provide some kind of refuge. When I reached it, I stopped, peering inside. I wanted somewhere warm and dry, for although I was desperate to hide it, I did not want any harm to come to the baby. Today, of course, it seems murderously careless: the obvious thing would have been to carry the child to the road, or even leave it on a front doorstep, anywhere but in an old boat on the beach. But I was far from rational thought.

Apart from another bucket, a bundle of blue nylon netting and a wooden slat that served as a bench, the boat was empty. It had clearly not been to sea for a while, for the floor was dry. It was a good place, I was thinking: the sun and sea could not touch my baby here. Leaning over, I placed the bundle under the bench, pushing it far back so that it was out of sight. The baby was sleeping now, its lashless eyes closed tight against the new world: part of me, and yet already no longer mine. I would like to tell you that I kissed the child goodbye, or breathed a final prayer into its ears, but I did neither. All I could think was that no one should ever know what had happened. So I put it down gently, making sure that the jumper was tucked in around its chilly skin, then I turned and stumbled back across the stones.

I know that what I did was wrong. I should never have left the baby like that. I should have kept it close to me, huddled against my body. I should have carried it back to the warmth of the hotel, fed it with the thick white stuff that was now filling my breasts and not cared what anybody said. I should have been a mother to it, and today my child would be an adult. Perhaps we would be friends; I would certainly be free.

But I did none of those things. I was fifteen, terrified and in shock. So I put the baby into the boat and returned to the hotel alone.

When my mother woke me five hours later I told her I had a heavy period and wanted to stay in bed. She did not ask any further questions; if anything, she seemed relieved. I suppose she had been dreading spending the first day of her marriage with the delinquent drunk she had for a daughter. And if she noticed the bundle of bloodied clothes that I had stuffed into the bin, or wondered why, after all these months, I was suddenly bleeding so heavily, she did not comment.

It was not until the next morning that I saw the front page of the local newspaper. A new-born baby had been found on the beach by a dog-walker, I read. While it was a criminal offence to abandon a baby, they were appealing to the mother to come forward; she would need medical attention. It was imperative she get in touch.

I scrunched up the paper and threw it into the bin. Despite the blood that was still pouring from me, I would never come forward, for it was clearly a trap that would end in gaol. Instead, what I would do was simple: I would go back home with Mum and David and Dr Death. I would work and work and work, just so I could block the thoughts of the baby from my head. And then, when I had got three As at A level, my place at Oxford guaranteed, I would sever all contact with my past.

28

Please stop. I cannot bear to think about this any more. Closing my eyes at the pellets of rain that pummel my face, I start to run along the edge of the shore. Everyone thinks I am such a good, caring person: kind, motherly Cass, with all her waifs and strays. Even Matt wanted a baby with me. He thought I'd be a lovely mum. *Don't ya know she's already had one? What a mother she turned out to be!* I start to sob with self-hatred. I do not know what I am going to do when I get there, but I am heading for the marina.

Once I get to the edge of the concrete walkway that circles the moored yachts and dinghies, I climb the steps leading to the path. On dull weekends when the sea is grey and calm the place is filled with pudgy-faced fishermen and kids on skateboards, but tonight it is empty, for only a fool would brave the waves that splash playfully over the walls. I am already half drenched, but am hardly aware of my damp, clinging clothes. Ignoring a sign that reads: *Danger! Do not enter this area in bad weather!* I start to run along the narrow path.

When I get to the furthest point, I stop, staring out at the violent sea. I am imagining what it will be like to be in the freezing water, its darkness closing irrevocably around my head. I will be weighted down with it, sinking slowly to the bottom, for ever devoid of direction, like a ship that has been battered to shreds by the ferocious white horses. As a vast plume of water reaches over me, I close my eyes, giving in to it, knowing I can never return.

The surf smashes into me, forcing me back against the

concrete balustrade as I splutter at the salty water. I try to regain my balance, but another even larger wave rises up over the wall, its icy fingers splattering the breeze-blocks. As I crouch there, waiting for the inevitable, it seems the wind is roaring the words at me: *Dr Cassie Bainbridge: her cosy life is a lie!* Now another surge is reaching right over me, as if it is deliberately trying to pull me in, and all I can do is listen to the slap of water against the wall and wait for its freezing touch. *Haven't you heard? She had a baby, left it on the beach to die!*

Here it is at last. The wave rams into my torso, bashing me violently back into the marina wall, where I slide down on to my bottom, gasping at the shocking cold. I have been waiting for this: each and every time I pass a baby on the street or hold a toddler on my lap, I remember the child I left behind, and wish that I were dead. And now the few seconds between the wave hitting me and pulling back have elapsed, and even as I try to stagger to my feet, another reaches out and slaps me hard in the face.

As this happens, as I feel the water going over my head and screech at the cold, I remember something else. *The baby did not die but was saved. There was an old man, a dog. They found the bundle just in time.* And now that I am so close to being sucked into the sea I understand that this was never what I intended. I did not return to this place to die. I came here because beneath the surface of my foolish denial I have always dreamt of finding my child, and to do that I had finally to face this place. And now, more than anything, I want to live.

Gripping the concrete with my wet fingers, I edge along the walkway. It is so windy here that I am in danger of being blown down into the maelstrom so I keep my back to the wall, creeping slowly along. All around me, the wild waves crash mockingly over the concrete. I need to retreat about a hundred metres, back to the sanctity of the moorings, where the sea slaps vigorously against the clicking boats but at least is caged by the walls.

A giant wave has just landed behind me. Closing my eyes against it, I take another two or three steps, bracing myself against the wind, which batters me in unpredictable blasts. In another twenty-five metres, where the walkway turns back towards the shore, there is a niche built back into the wall where the fishermen sometimes shelter from the rain. Perhaps I can wait there until the storm abates. Around me, the sea suddenly calms, as if gathering strength for its next onslaught. I wrap my arms around my waist and make a dash for it. It has started raining hard again, reducing my surroundings to an impenetrable, misty grey.

I am nearly there. My clothes are soaked, my hair slicking wetly over my cheeks. I have almost lost sensation in my fingers. But for the first time in over twenty years, I think I may truly be alive. I scuttle towards the niche, almost whooping with relief to be so close to safety. It does not matter how long I have to wait there, for eventually the storm must pass and then I can venture forth again. I can dimly see its outline, strong and upright, like a sentry-post. Yet as I take my final steps and the niche emerges through the fog, I stop, my heart jolting. I can feel the hairs on my arms bristle like those of an affronted cat. It is already occupied, I realize, with plunging horror. And that means I am trapped for just as retracing my steps along the wall to the homicidal waves is inconceivable so is any advance. For now, stepping directly into my path is Beth.

For a moment we stand facing each other, the waves sploshing around us. She must have heard the door slam and followed me here, her fragile trust in me shattered. And now, as I peer through the slanting rain at her small, strained face, for the first time I am truly afraid of her. While I was imagining a male prowler, all those different, nightmare versions of the man waiting in that Peckham street, it was a young girl with acne, baggy jeans and trainers who was stalking me.

'What do you want?' I shout, above the roar of the sea.

She takes a step towards me. It was her who made all the calls, her who I saw standing on the roof that night, and her who, after stealing the keys from my bag, let herself into the flat to fiddle with my computer. And now she is standing perilously close to the edge of the path. 'I love you, Cass,' she says softly.

The ominous foreboding is rising inside me in a sharp peak. 'No, you don't,' I yell back. 'You don't know anything about me.'

'You said you'd look after me.'

I gaze at her. My heart is punching so hard I can no longer speak, so I just shake my head.

'Why are you doing this?' Her voice rises, no longer petulant and sullen, but strident and demanding. She is breathing faster too: through the mist I can see the rise and fall of her chest, the agitated way her fingers are flicking at the rain.

'Beth,' I mouth at her, 'you have to calm down.'

But that just makes it worse. Blundering towards me, her eyes dull with rage, she gives a roar of fury. 'Why can't you love me?' she screams.

Then, before I am able to step to one side, she has grabbed me and, grasping my waist, is pulling me to the side of the walkway. I am much bigger and stronger than her, but have been caught off balance, and suddenly we are right at the edge, the waves waiting below, like a pit of hungry lions. I think I may be screaming: it is hard to tell, for the sea and wind are both so loud, and Beth herself is shouting something about how people always let her down, and my chest is banging uproariously. Anyway, now it is too late for both of us for, as we grapple, Beth pushes me backwards and, like a cartoon character in a comedy fight, there is nothing beneath my feet and I am falling, my arms cartwheeling in the air. And since Beth is still holding on to me, she is falling too.

For perhaps a second there is nothing, just the whizzing sensation of falling fast and far and the desperate grip of Beth's fingers on my arm. Then we hit the water and, gasping at the icy temperature, are propelled helplessly down. I am so shocked at the cold that my reactions cut out. I sink, deeper and deeper, into the cloudy water, my mouth tasting salt, my hair floating around my head like a halo.

The sinking seems to take minutes rather than seconds. And, oddly, now that I am here I am no longer afraid. It is dark at the bottom, and after the relentless wailing of the wind, blessedly quiet. Despite the freezing water, my body is so numb that I almost feel warm. I could stay down here for ever, I think dreamily; I need never remember the child again.

Then suddenly Beth's hands are scrabbling at my shoulders, groping maniacally at my arms. As I feel her pulling me down and the last molecule of oxygen is expelled from my chest, I am returned to the reality that I am drowning. I have to reach the surface: I am desperate to breathe. As I twist myself vigorously around, I shove her fiercely away, then push down as hard as I can, straining upwards, towards the light. Perhaps she is clasping at my feet, or perhaps they have simply become entwined in seaweed. Whatever it is, I kick it savagely away, my arms thrashing at the water.

Then, suddenly, my head is breaking through the surface and there is light and air and I take a deep, hiccuping breath. But even though I have risen up this far, I have not stopped panicking. As my heavy limbs thrash ineffectually in the water, I am a child again, gulping at the air, my head bobbing under. *Just reach out with your arms,* Mum used to boss me, half laughing, half irritated. *Make those froggy movements with your legs. It's so easy!* And then she would let me go, standing back expressionlessly as I spluttered and flailed around. *Please, Mum!* I would wail. *Don't!*

But of course she did, and now I am alone, and can only just manage to stay afloat. I kick desperately at the water, remembering her instructions. *Keep your arms under the surface, that's it! Come on, reach out for me, good girl, now you're doing it . . .*

My waterlogged clothes are too heavy. I pull at my coat and release myself from the sodden material. Then, arms and legs freed, I take another deep breath. I keep swallowing water, and my sight is obscured by the breakers that splash over my head, but I am determined not to drown. *Keep kicking, Cassie!* my mother implores. *Don't give up!* And to my amazement I am making progress, managing to keep my head out of the water and pull myself along, even as the choppy waves splash into my face. When there is a lull in the battering, I tread water and look around. As I do this I see that I am not far out to sea, as I had imagined, but only about a hundred yards from the beach. Then another wave smashes down and I am spun endlessly around as the backwash pulls me under.

But this time I come up fighting. And now I see that the tide is in my favour. Rather than dragging me out, it is coming in, sweeping me resolutely towards the beach. So I give in to it, stop fighting the rolling crests and allow my weight to be taken by them, pulled back towards life and hope. When my feet hit shingle I think I am safe, but then the undertow is dragging me back, my head going under the water again, my body whirling. I am caught on something, too. It is tugging at me, pulling me backwards. I push it away in confusion, twirling around, and suddenly realize that somebody else is in the water beside me. They have placed their arms around my middle, and are dragging me to safety, pulling my head clear of the foam as we reach the shore.

And now I am clear, lying on the stones, hiccuping after the mouthfuls of foul liquid I have swallowed, gulping at the air. Next to me, a drenched figure is staggering up and shouting, 'Get back from the waves!'

The arm goes round me again and I struggle to my feet. Slowly we clamber up the steep hillock of pebbles, puddles of water flowing in rivulets from our soaking clothes. I am huffing with exertion and shaking with shock, my feet tripping over the piles of driftwood and rubbish thrown up by the storm. What I feel, at least in these first minutes, is a raw blast of exhilaration. It is incredible that I was spotted, a miracle to be alive. Looking down, I see that, amazingly, my shoes are still on my feet. They squelch frigidly as I move. I have been given a second chance.

Finally, we make it to the top of the pebbles. I sink down, too exhausted to go further, my initial joy at being rescued already fading into something else. A minute ago I had not noticed the cold, but now I have started to shiver uncontrollably, my teeth chattering in my jaw like a joke-shop skeleton. Gazing back at the wild waves, I remember Beth, and how I kicked away her hands. Next to me, my companion squats beside me. I still have not seen his face, but I know who he is. 'We have to get you an ambulance,' he says.

'Beth's still out there,' I reply flatly.

'I know. I followed her to the beach. I saw the whole thing.'

And now I turn and, looking into his pale, distraught face, I reach out for Alec's hand.

29

After that, a lot of things happen at once. Alec locates his rucksack on the shingle and, producing his mobile, calls the emergency services. There is an ambulance and the police, and a short while later a helicopter, which sweeps searchlights over the stormy dusk sea. The paramedics fuss around me, but I do not need their ministrations and refuse point-blank to go to hospital. I accept a thermal blanket and a cup of tea and sit with Alec on our ridge of stones, facing the waves, which have now started to recede. Despite his soaking and the earlier traumas I inflicted on him, he is as sharp-witted as ever. When the police question us he interrupts my fumbling attempts at explanation. He saw it all, he says. Beth pushed me off the marina wall, then fell herself. She had an obsession with me, was mentally disturbed; if they need verification they could speak to Dr Leigh. The police jot things in notebooks, stand aside from us, making calls. Later, there will be formal interviews and statements, but now all we can do is wait.

Beth will not return alive, that much is clear. As I gaze at the churned-up sea, I know that, unlike my incredible escape, she must have drowned. I keep asking myself if there was something I could have done to avert her terrible end. I should have stayed with her in the flat until she had calmed down; I should have rung for help; somehow I should have averted the fight on the marina wall. Yet even as I try to picture these different scenarios, I know that whatever happened I would never have been able to give her what she needed. It was her overwhelming, fanatical desire to be loved that propelled her into the water, not me.

But despite these reassurances, I also know that I have been a fool. I have been like the worst sort of amateur researcher, focused only on a single, predetermined argument, ignoring all evidence that does not fit. My methods have been appalling, my analysis corrupt. Seeped in subjectivity, since meeting Beth I have followed only one narrative: that of my own past. In every exchange we had, I was so blinkered by my own history that I was unable to see her for what she was. Why did I not question her more closely? Why was I so prejudiced against Alec? He tried to warn me about her, Julian had said on the phone, but I refused to listen.

As the afternoon dusk deepens and the sky darkens, I barely move. The helicopter still chatters above, but we all know that Beth is dead. It seems only a short while since I was pulled from the waves, but I suppose hours have passed for when the racing clouds occasionally pull back, the moon is high and bright. The sea's mood has changed too, the waves rolling in more calmly, the tide sweeping away from the beach in a wide arc. The rain stopped some time earlier. In fact, I am neither cold nor wet. I am wearing a man's jumper, I notice, with a slight start, and more blankets have been piled over my shoulders. When I glance up, I see that Alec is standing beside me. 'Do you want another cup of tea?'

'No, I'm fine.'

'They're going to call off the search until morning.'

'Right.'

He shifts from foot to foot. Despite what we have just been through together, he remains visibly cautious of me, his arms folded, his eyes fixed on the horizon; perhaps he fears another fevered denouncement. I turn so that I can see his face. He looks better than before: his cheeks are pink with cold but he has changed into dry clothes and is clutching a steaming polystyrene cup in his hands.

'They think you might need treatment for shock,' he says falteringly. 'They want to take you to hospital.'

I shake my head, not allowing him to finish. The paramedics are wrong. I am not in shock, but instead have been overtaken by a clarity so striking that I feel as if I can see for miles. It is as if all these years I have been becoming increasingly myopic, my sight blurring by increments so that the haze seems normal. But now I have been fitted with the most wonderful spectacles and my surroundings are zooming into focus.

'Where did you get the clothes?' I say, interrupting him.

'They let me go home and have a bath.'

He frowns at some unpleasant memory, perhaps recalling how he witnessed Beth disappear into the sea. He has really suffered, I think, and all because of me.

'Won't you sit down?' I say gently.

He lowers himself obediently on to the wet stones, his arms still tightly folded. I want to take his hand again, and squeeze it, but too much time has elapsed since those first exhilarating moments on the shingle and now we have reverted to awkward formality.

'I'm so sorry, Alec,' I say quietly. 'I misjudged you. And now you've saved my life.'

He looks down, picking up a stone and weighing it in his hands. 'It's fine.'

'You could have been killed yourself, plunging into the sea like that.'

He shrugs, not allowing himself to be a hero. 'It wasn't a big deal. I'm a strong swimmer. I go into the sea almost every day.'

I want to say more, to extend my apology over him like the comforting blanket he has placed over me, to warm him with my praise. But he does not allow it.

'I saw the whole thing,' he says despondently. 'Julian was really worried about Beth staying with you so I was coming over to your flat. Then you came running out and she was following you.'

He skims the stone across the pebbles. It bounces twice, then lands with a *ping*. He watches its progress, his lips turned down. He still does not want to meet my eyes.

'So,' I say, 'it seems you have a thing or two to teach me about veracity.' I hold my breath. It hardly matters now, but I am waiting for the put-down.

But rather than sneering at me – the contemptuous student I had always imagined – he shuffles his feet, as if embarrassed at having proved me wrong. 'I knew she wasn't a proper student from the first seminar. Like Julian said in the meeting, there's no gender studies. She didn't even know where the library was.'

'I should have spotted it,' I mutter.

'She tried to befriend me,' he continues. 'She kept asking to borrow my notes from last year and trying to wheedle information out of me about Julian and you, but I wasn't having it. In the end I had to tell her to get lost. And then today, after that meeting, I remembered that she'd said something about being at Leeds. So Julian rang his friend who teaches there.'

He pauses, picks up another stone. Something about the crease of his eyes, his pensive expression reminds me of my father. He doesn't want to continue, but I force him: 'And?'

'He remembered her all right. She had a different name, but the girl he described sounded just like her. She got into this mad stalking thing with this lecturer and ended up trying to attack her in her office. She got a two-year suspended sentence and a court order for psychiatric treatment.'

So that was what she was talking about in my bedroom. I shudder, pull the blankets closer round my shoulders. 'Oh, my God.'

'Exactly.' He stops as if there is nothing else to say.

I want to drop my head into my blue fingers, give my hair a punishing tug. Instead, I place my hand on his bony knee. 'I'm so, so, sorry.'

He turns so that I can see his pained expression. All the time I was judging him arrogant and cruel, he was struggling with this troubling knowledge that I refused to hear. No wonder he laid into Beth in the seminar: she deserved it. 'It wasn't your fault,' he says.

My eyes are prickling. If only that were true. 'Yes, it was.'

Ever the stickler for historical accuracy, he does not contradict me. Yet the tension between us has eased: perhaps he just needed to hear my apology. We sit for a while in silence, regarding the landscape the tide has left in its wake. The clouds have drawn back even further now and the moon lights our surroundings with calm iridescence. The remnants of the storm lie all around us: oily planks and driftwood so polished by the waves that it is as smooth as stone; plastic containers, little bits of rope; line after line of tangled seaweed; bottles and lumps of broken glass. I would like to gather it together, build a mad monument of sea litter and dedicate it to all children who believe themselves lost. But instead I sit self-consciously next to Alec, digging at the shingle with my foot.

'Your parents must be proud of you,' I say eventually. 'You should give me their address so I can write to them and tell them what you've done.'

For a moment I am not sure that he has heard. Then he says, very softly, 'I don't have any parents.'

My head jerks up. 'No?'

He snorts in an attempt to make it sound like a joke affliction, something to be ribbed about by one's mates. He has acquired Julian's habit of speaking in inverted commas, too. 'My mum "abandoned" me. Spent my childhood in so-called "care".'

I feel as if I have just stuffed my fingers into a plug-socket and turned the power on. I gasp, struggling to make connections, for I have just remembered something else: my baby was a boy. Of course he was – I knew it all along. And now this young man is sitting here, telling me that his mother abandoned him! He is just the right age, and tall and studious, just like me! He even looks like Dad! I must be goggling at him like a crazy, because he flushes and looks away. He is so like me, I think, my thoughts leaping and bounding. Could it possibly be . . . ? Very slowly I bend down and pick up my own stone. I can feel it, round and cool, in the palm of my hand. The blood is rushing to my face.

But as I am imagining a tearful reconciliation, with us collapsing into each other's arms as we joyously call out each other's names, Alec is glancing away and lobbing another stone, hard, into the line of debris that marks the sea's retreat. 'As a matter of fact I've recently decided to try to trace her.'

My hands squeeze the cold stone, my nails digging into my palms. I want to say something meaningful, but can only manage 'Yeah?'

'It's one of those odd things. All this stuff . . .' he pauses, and I know he means with Beth and me, but is too polite to spell it out '. . . it's made me realize how much I need to know about her. Forming relationships and communicating isn't exactly my forte. As you've no doubt noticed. I've been trying to work out how to change that.'

'You sound like you've been through a lot,' I choke.

But he is not interested in what must seem like platitudes. 'Apparently there'll be an address on the birth certificate, and all the stuff surrounding the case . . .'

I can feel my eyebrows knot. I lick a fleck of salt from my lips, digging my fingers into my spare tyre in consternation. What is he talking about? How could there have been an address on the birth certificate? 'You have a file?'

The gulls above me are squawking so loudly I can barely hear Alec's soft reply. 'Of course. There was a court case, when I was taken into care. And apparently there'll be an address too. I mean, I just want to find out why my mother did it.'

'Did what?' I stutter. I am still wildly holding on to the notion that he is my child, but already it is slipping away.

'Left me on the train. Apparently she was drunk. I was eighteen months old. She came back to find me after she'd sobered up, but they'd already decided she was an unfit mother. I think she might have kept in touch when I was still little, but then she sort of drifted away. They tried to get me adopted, but I was too old by then and getting difficult . . .' He trails off.

It is lucky that he is not looking at my face. I swallow incredulously, watching the birds swoop and dive at the water. Alec scoops up another pebble and flicks it across the water; it hops three times before disappearing.

'It's all I can think about, to be honest,' he says. 'I keep writing her these stupid letters, trying to work out what I would say to her if we ever met.'

I gaze blankly at him, this lonely young man who has become entangled in my life. I can feel the disappointment pouring through me, a heavy, seeping craving for the child I thought I had found. *Where are you?* I want to scream at the sea. *Who did you become?* And then this startling thought, that even now, as the rescue helicopters chatter above, is starting to take hold. *I am going to find you.*

'It sounds as if she should be the one doing the talking,' I say.

'Yeah, but that's the bit I can't imagine.'

We are silent. Alec is still chucking stones at the water and I have turned away from the sea, looking beyond him towards the pier, which despite the bad weather is lit up expectantly,

285

like an overdressed prostitute waiting for customers in the rain. Of course he is not my child, I think, as the disappointment fades and something else takes over. It would have been a preposterous coincidence. No, I will have to work harder to get what I want.

I stand up, letting the blankets fall to the stones. What I feel, I note with surprise, is burgeoning excitement. Everything has changed, and in an odd way Beth has helped me change it. For while I could never have saved her, perhaps her obsessive needs will ultimately help me to save myself. I am no longer like the restless waves, endlessly drawn towards and repelled by the beach. Over the years I have studiously avoided it, yet ironically I have never really left this beach. But all that is going to change. I have come clean, owned up.

And now there are things I have to put right.

Two days later Alec comes to see me. I have been having an eventful time, what with dealing with the police and explaining everything to Bob Stennings. In fact, ever since I was pulled from the sea, I have been surrounded by people and offers of help. Sarah wants to come down, and this morning Julian arrived with flowers, as if I had been taken ill. I appreciate their support, but I am not ready yet for talk. I am still reeling, still trying to make sense of what has happened. How did I fail to notice Beth's lies? She stole my mobile in the café, I realize now, and must have gleaned my address from those bills in my bag. The story about foster-parents, of course, was a complete fabrication. Instead, it turns out that she was staying in a back room at the bar where she worked. Her parents, who had reported her missing three months ago, live in a small village near Leeds. And, fool that I was, I picked up none of this.

The main reason I don't need company is that I have Jan

here, making me cups of tea, moving the buckets in the sitting room and, best of all, asking nothing. I am finding her company surprisingly therapeutic: stuff happens, that's her view. Later, she's promised, we're going to do my cards.

The flat no longer scares me. One of the few things I have decided, among so much debris, is that I am going to stay here after all. The landlord has promised to fix the leak, and then I am going to redecorate. Jan is going to help me; she assures me she's a dab hand at DIY. We have already decided on the colour: a deep, generous terracotta, a tone to warm us up.

So when Alec announces his name at the intercom I'm more composed, if not recovered, pleased he's here, though not surprised. I let him into the flat and, after giving me a shy hug, he walks across the hall to the french windows in the sitting room, which I have opened wide despite the cold. He seems different: less hesitant, perhaps, certainly less distant. I still hardly know him, but I think we both feel a burgeoning closeness, a sense of sharing something big. Now he is gazing out at the gardens and the strip of sea below.

'I've got something to tell you,' he says, as I bring him some of Beth's camomile tea. 'That's why I'm here.'

I look at him enquiringly as I set the steaming mugs on the floor. Every second or so, a drip lands in one of the buckets with a loud plop. 'Oh, yes?'

'I've decided to leave.'

'Oh!'

I am more taken aback than perhaps I should be. He is so obviously studious that I cannot imagine him without the university. He stares back at me with his intelligent brown eyes, taking in the bemusement in my face.

'But what about your degree?'

'I'm taking a year out. I don't know what I'll do after that.'

'God, Alec, isn't that a bit radical?'

He shrugs, as if it no longer matters. 'It's not just because of what's happened. It's something I've been building up to all term.' He clears his throat, almost apologetically. 'It was one of the things I wanted to talk to you about.'

'Ah . . .'

'I mean, it was your course that really did it.'

I gulp. On seeing my expression, he flashes me a fleeting, rueful smile. If only he smiled more, the guy would be really handsome.

'It's nothing personal,' he says. 'It was just the exercise of having to make the connection between, you know, big histories and personal histories. I couldn't really cope with it.'

'But your work was so brilliant.'

His mouth twitches. Possibly he is irritated by such an obvious statement. 'It's not that,' he says off-handedly. 'I can always do the work. It's the other stuff.'

I pick up my tea. I have not taken my eyes from his face. I know exactly what he means.

'I want you to have these,' he says. 'That's the basic reason I've come. They're for my methodologies project.' He pulls a large padded envelope out of his jacket and hands it to me, his face grave. The way he does this, with such solemn ritual, makes it clear that it contains something important.

'This is your project?'

He gives his head an impatient shake. I am obviously missing the point.

'I know it's not what you want, but I couldn't write a five-thousand-word paper on some project I'd dreamt up just to pass the course. In fact, I'm not expecting you to pass it. If I'm honest, I don't even want the other examiner to see it.'

I turn it over questioningly.

'It's really only for you,' he adds quietly. 'I want you to see it as a sort of explanation, about me dropping out, I mean. It's photocopies of some letters I've been writing, those ones I told you about on the beach.'

I nod. There doesn't seem to be any point in doing anything else, for he has made up his mind to leave and now all that remains is for me to read what the envelope contains. 'So what are you going to do?' I ask.

He takes a breath. 'Find my mum,' he says, tossing his head, not with arrogance, I now see, but nerves. 'I've been dreaming about it for years, and now I'm going to try to do it.'

The blood rushes to my face. I want to throw my arms round him, smother him with congratulatory kisses. 'That's fantastic!'

His face clouds, as if for the first time he acknowledges the possibility that I might have reacted differently. 'It might be a massive mistake, but I want to know more about what happened, why she drank and everything. I mean, what it was about me.' He stops, looking at me appealingly. 'Perhaps I was just a total brat or something.'

'I bet you were gorgeous,' I say, trying to chuckle and wiping my eyes casually with my sleeve as if they have simply got something in them. I mean it, too, for now that I have learnt the truth about Beth, I can see the truth about Alec. More than coldness or haughtiness, it is his insecurity that makes him how he is. And just as I responded to Beth's little-girl neediness with open arms, his taciturn refusal to charm propelled me into a baseless and much regretted prejudice.

'Do you?' he says anxiously, and I realize that, despite his shyness, he longs to share this with someone. He is so withdrawn and private, but now that he has started to talk, it is spurting from him like blood from an arterial wound.

'Of course. It's like I said on the beach. If she knew what you were like now, she'd be really proud of you.'

'So do you think I'm doing the right thing?'

'Yes,' I say, and my eyes feel hot and scratchy. 'I do.'

'I mean, she might not want to see me, might she?'

I gaze at him.

'She might want to forget about me,' he says, trying to smile.

'I doubt very much that what your mum did was anything to do with you,' I say quietly. 'She was probably in a terrible state.'

He nods, as if this was what he wanted me to confirm. 'I was told she was very young.'

'Look, Alec,' I say, 'whatever happened and for whatever reasons your mum got drunk and left you on that train, I bet she thinks about you every single day. She's probably longing to find you.'

He glances at me, his face lightening. 'Do you think?'

'I'm sure.'

He swallows. I hear myself say slowly, 'What if it was the other way? If she came to look for you?'

And now he smiles, showing his white teeth. 'Are you kidding? I'd be ecstatic.'

'Even after what she did?'

'It wouldn't matter. Perhaps we could make it right. I just want the chance to try.' He stares back at my doubtful face. 'It's not about forgiveness, that's what I'm trying to say. It's about finding out who you are and where you come from. I suppose to you it sounds mad, but right now, at this moment in time, it's the only thing I care about.'

I look at him, still so young, on the verge of his life. 'No, Alec,' I say, and I don't know whether he hears the emotion in my voice or not. 'It doesn't sound mad to me at all.'

After this brief but intense exchange, he doesn't stay long.

We drink our tea, comparing notes on our experiences at the police station, and then he lopes off. Whatever happens, we both agree, we will stay in touch. 'Write to me,' I say, placing my hand on his shoulder as he disappears through the door. 'If you need any help, just ask.'

As I watch his solitary figure cross the square, I think that maybe there is a reason why he and I were linked this way. Perhaps it was our shared need to learn about our past, our yearning for what we have lost but never known, which Beth sensed in us and which made us vulnerable to her. And perhaps she, too, suffered from something similar: a different configuration of circumstances, but like Alec and me, a history that was somehow distorted, a narrative filled with silence, its main characters missing.

One day, I would like to sit with Alec and tell him everything. One day we may even be friends.

Dear Mum

So much has happened. Bad things, as well as (perhaps) good. I'm not going to go into it all now. Maybe I'll tell you one day.

This is the last letter I am going to write, because I have reached a decision. I am going to leave the university, and I am going to find you. I've done something that feels like a really big step, you see. I've made contact with the social services, and they have promised to show me my file. I'm going to meet the counsellor next week. And so I'm going up to London, to stay with one of the postgrads who I made friends with last year. I'm telling myself to expect nothing. But I'm sure I'm going to find you.

I've packed up my room, stuffed some clothes and books into a rucksack, and now I'm finally off. In the back pocket of my jeans is the address of the place where they have the files. I keep reaching back, to check that it's still there, the key to my past. Perhaps I am making a mistake. Perhaps there will be nothing to find. Perhaps I will arrive at your front door, and discover that I'm too late and you've moved. But the fact I'm clinging on to is what the social worker told me over the phone, that on my eighteenth birthday you left your details on my file. So you must want me to contact you, mustn't you?

So this is the last letter I shall be writing. Hopefully in just a matter of days, I shall place this whole bundle of communiqués into your actual hands. Will it be a happy ending for us both? Who knows? You are both my mother and a stranger. I want terribly to know you, yet I am afraid of what that may involve. So, naturally, I'm scared. There's been a lot going on recently and I have not slept or eaten for days, I probably look a wreck. You may open the door and wish to hell you hadn't given me your address. You may simply pretend not to know who I am.

But whatever happens, I do not think I will regret it. It's a matter of identity, you see. All my life I have wondered who you are and what you are doing. And now I am going to find out.

Here's to our future.

Your son,

Alec

30

I find her house at the end of a sunken Dorset lane, which winds teasingly through the West Country fields. It is spring now, and the hedgerows have exploded into glory: steep banks of cow-parsley and primroses line the route, as if cheering me on. On the passenger seat I have my map, spread at the correct page, and next to that the address, which I have scrawled beside my list of directions. Although it is still early April, I am hot, and have wound down the windows, allowing the fresh scent of blossom and new grass to blow through the car. I switched off the radio many miles ago: I no longer wanted my thoughts clogged by mundane chatter or the background buzz of music. Instead, I need to concentrate on this final period of transition, the strange freedom of having left but still not arrived.

I am nervous, but not afraid. When I reach the crossroads, the last direction on my list, I take a left, then immediately see the house sign: 'Oak Tree Cottage'. I turn off the road, staring curiously around. It is not what I expected: the house more secluded, the front lawn, which is sprinkled with daffodils, less well tended. I grip the steering-wheel, every muscle tensed as the Beetle's tyres crunch the gravel drive. For a panicky moment I think I have made a mistake. It is so different from what I had imagined – a mock-Tudor monstrosity with stone lions on the gate, perhaps, or a double-glazed bungalow with a fussy water feature, not this tumbledown cottage with its overgrown garden. Then I glance through the ground-floor windows, see the photographs on the wall, and know that I have come to the right place after all.

By the time I have parked the car, my mouth is dry. I have been anticipating this scene for so many months now, imagining and re-imagining how it will be, but now that I am finally here, my careful preparations have dissolved and I am struck by the urgent desire to reverse back down the drive, never to return. But of course it is too late. She must have been waiting for me, for even before I am out of the car she is standing expectantly on the step. Fumbling with the rusty car door, I push it open, breathing in the sweet rural air. For a moment, too cowardly to look directly at her, I busy myself with my arrival, leaning over the back seat and tussling with my bags and the flowers I have brought, anything but face what I have driven all this way to find.

Then, finally, there are no more excuses left, and I am stepping across the drive, looking into her face and saying, 'Hello, Mum.'

Her appearance shocks me more than it should. I have not seen her for nearly fifteen years, so should have been prepared for her transition from forty-something woman to a senior citizen in her sixties. And yet for a moment I hardly recognize her. The intervening years must have treated her badly, I think, with a surprising jump of pity. Her face has sagged, she has thick jowls around her jaw, which she is now stroking anxiously with gnarled, arthritic fingers, and she seems smaller than I remember, as if life has literally ground her down. She looks, I realize with a little thrill of recognition, like my grandmother.

Yet when she smiles, holding out her arms like the text-book mother she never was, I see the same uneasy mix of hope and disappointment in her eyes that I had forgotten but now remember so well, her still good, even teeth, the frown line on the bridge of her nose, and I know that while she has grown older, she has not changed.

'Well,' she says. 'Here you are.'

I step awkwardly into her embrace. We are not sure how to do it, for we have never established a family convention of adult greetings. I attempt to brush both her cheeks with my lips, a polite and possibly overly cosmopolitan greeting that signals neither hostility nor warmth, but she moves back too quickly and I crash embarrassingly into her hair. I cannot get used to the fact that she is shorter than me.

'Are you wearing heels?' she says, disengaging herself and looking me up and down. 'I must say, I wasn't expecting you to look so good.'

I grimace, unable to respond to such a mixed compliment. So I was right in my recollections. I have only just arrived and already we have plunged into the old ways: she, sharp and critical; me, defensive and rude. What did she expect? Ripped jeans and cheesecloth? For a moment I am subsumed with irritation, my mind scrabbling for a sharp, fifteen-year-old's rejoinder, 'Yeah, and I wasn't expecting you to look so bloody old,' but I rein myself in. I have not come all this way for a teenage fight.

I follow her meekly into the house, my throat clogging with emotion. I have never been inside the place before, yet it feels like my childhood home for she has filled it with herself. There, hanging on the wall, is the Monet print she used to have in her bedroom, and crowding the small sitting room is the old brown three-piece suite. On the mantelpiece is the china cat I used to pretend to feed when I was small, and next to that, my grandfather's carriage clock. Even the rug is the same. It feels as if my childhood has been tossed haphazardly into the air and tumbled back into this unfamiliar setting.

'Shall I make some tea?' Mum is saying.

I am gazing at the framed photographs on the far wall. Like so much else in the room, I have seen many of them before: the black-and-white wedding picture of my grandparents taken on the steps of Kensington Register Office in 1934; the school portraits of me and David; the holiday snap of us in 1975 eating ice-cream on the beach. There are more recent additions, too. The first is of Mum and Don posing in a studio some time in the 1980s. My mother is dressed improbably as an Edwardian lady with an Eliza Doolittle boa and straw bonnet, my step-father in a top hat and tails, as if they were in the chorus line for *My Fair Lady*. Like the Gilbert and Sullivan productions they performed in as I studied for my A levels, it is the kind of thing Don would have relished. Next to this is a large picture of a beaming couple, sitting in a sunny garden. The woman is small and pretty and cuddles a baby on her lap. The man has a beard and his face is brown and slightly lined, as if he spends a great deal of time outside. Although grown older, it is a face I know intimately.

'That's David and Clare, and little Izzy,' Mum says behind me. 'I took it when I was visiting last year. Isn't she great?'

'Yes,' I say faintly. 'She's gorgeous.'

For a moment I think I might burst into tears. I close my mouth tightly, fighting the swell. All the time that I had imagined this scene, I had never anticipated being confronted by my perfect brother's perfect baby.

'She's nearly four now,' Mum prattles on, 'and they're expecting another little babba in July! We all wanted to let you know, but you didn't reply to any of our letters so we didn't know where you'd got to. You are silly, getting so out of touch.' She touches my arm almost affectionately, as if she is berating me for not calling regularly enough, or missing some family celebration. 'I'm sure he'd love a visit,' she says. 'He and Clare have got a terrific set-up out there.'

I stare at the picture for a few moments more. Good old David, always the success story. And I can just picture Mum as Grandma too, coming to see little Izzy with pressies and cuddles and trips out. All the things she never did for me.

When I turn back to the room, she has disappeared. I sit down heavily on the settee, which has faded from deep brown to a washed-out beige. She has let her standards slip, I realize, as I look around. There are wisps of cobweb in the corners of the ceilings, and the top of the bookshelf is distinctly dusty. Yet the place does not feel unloved. In fact, it is the reverse of our family house, which she would spend all day cleaning, togged up in yellow rubber gloves and her blue nylon housecoat, yet which remained strangely characterless. It was as if her whole identity depended on keeping her house clean. Or, rather, like the hard rock cakes and sunken sponges she would dutifully produce every Sunday, it was as if she was trying to prove she was something she was not. And this ramshackle room, with its bunches of wild flowers arranged artfully in cracked vases, its library books, stacked just like my own, in piles around the floor, and its eclectic pictures covering the woodchip wallpaper, is probably so much closer to the person she really is.

'Here you are.' She has returned with a tray of tea and biscuits, which she sets down on the coffee-table that, all those years ago, I used to skate on in my four-year-old's socks. She pours the tea, her fingers grappling with the large pot. 'Look at my silly hands,' she sighs, 'they're such a bore.'

'Poor you.'

She tuts, more at the task of pouring the tea than at me, then says, almost reproachfully, 'You must be tired. It's such a long drive.'

'It was fine.'

I balance my cup on my knee, not knowing what to say. It is as if she is my great-aunt. I clear my throat. 'I'm sorry about Don.'

She glances up, apparently surprised at the reference to his name. 'Yes, poor Don.'

'David told me about it when it happened. I should have written to you.'

Something passes across her face, a shadow of grief or an old hurt she has grown used to disguising. 'It's a long time ago now,' she says emotionlessly, nodding at the wall. 'I gave all his clothes and the furniture to his children. You never met them, did you? They're ever so nice. All with their own children now, of course. The only thing I've got left of him are his golf clubs.'

I sip at my tea, munch the chocolate biscuit she has placed on my saucer. I hadn't even remembered that Dr Death had kids. Mistrust hangs thickly between us, like an old curtain that needs taking down and dusting.

'If it wasn't for that photo I wouldn't even be able to remember what he looked like,' she says dismissively, 'but thank you for mentioning him.'

I suck at my cheeks. The task of reaching her seems gargantuan, but while twenty years ago we were separated by the raging torrents of adolescent anger and maternal unhappiness, what now lies between us in an unbreakable pane of polite formality. And after everything that has happened I am not sure I have the strength to break it down.

'Have you still got the same boyfriend?' she asks. 'David told me he was a lecturer, or something.'

I give her a frigid smile. It still hurts so much. 'We finished it.'

She shakes her head at me, as if I have been carelessly irresponsible. 'What a shame. Anyone else on the horizon?'

'No.'

For a fleeting moment I picture Julian in the cinema, our knees carefully not touching, the shared armrest a no-go zone. The walk and pub lunch we had the week after came to nothing: it was too soon, my heart still too raw.

'Gosh, dear, don't leave it too late, will you?'

I am struggling so hard to control myself that my cup rattles in its saucer. I did not choose this, I want to snap. Do you think I want to be alone? I gaze around the room, blinking back the emotion as I remember the last time I saw Matt, the way we cried and hugged goodbye. Even after we had unravelled the tangles we were in, Beth's lies and my truths, we could not return to the place we used to be. It is for the best, we wanted different things: I repeat this over and over, like a dirge.

I eye my mother bitterly. OK, I am thinking, so nothing has changed. For a moment I want to put down the blasted tea, and walk out, but I stop myself. This is not what I've come here to discuss.

'Mum?' I say.

She looks up, and her expression is suddenly so fragile that, for a moment, I am ten again and she is as brittle as a splint of wood, about to snap. 'Yes?'

I hesitate, then plunge in. 'I'm sorry I didn't reply to any of your letters.'

She glances away quickly, busying herself with the teapot. 'You were busy . . .' she mutters. 'You've always worked so hard.'

'It wasn't that.'

Her hands fly to the jowly flaps, fingering them nervously. 'Let's just put it behind us,' she says.

'No,' I say. 'Let's not.'

She swallows hard, still gazing at me as she puts down the teapot. As I look at her, with her arthritic hands and stooped shoulders, I remember the mother I once had, who would jog across the sand towards the sea, and dive into the icy Cornish surf without flinching, and am subsumed with regret. I loved her so much, just because she was my mum. And of course I longed for her to love me too. But over the years we became set in combat, our roles solidified.

And even though part of me wanted badly to change, I was unable to break the mould. And now, although I do not want to hurt her any more, I have to see this through. 'The thing is,' I say slowly, 'the reason why I've come, is to ask you something.'

I am finding it hard to breathe. I am an adult, for God's sake, but still have a child's terror of being found out.

'Go on, then.' She folds her hands in her lap. 'I'm waiting.'

'And there's something I want to tell you too.'

'Gosh. We are going to be busy.'

I suck at my lips. So she is still sharp as paper, seemingly flimsy but with the ability to draw blood.

'Please don't put me down,' I say quietly. 'I don't want to fight with you any more.'

Behind her glasses her eyes seem steely. 'Just say whatever it is, Cass. I know you haven't come all this way to drink tea.'

'All right, then.'

I fold my arms. I have rehearsed this so many times, and never found the right phrasing. Whatever I say makes me sound like a plaintive little girl. I run the questions through my mind, like a multiple choice: Why didn't you, why couldn't you, why wouldn't you . . . Then I just open my mouth and say it. 'Why weren't you able to love me?'

For a moment her expression is blank, as if she has not understood the question. Then, almost in slow motion, her face seems to collapse. Her eyes water, her skin turns pink and puffy, her mouth droops. She takes off her glasses, puts her fingers to her eyes and rubs them. 'What do you mean?' she says, her voice so low I can barely hear it.

'You know what I mean.'

The silence is devastating. I perch on the settee, my teacup still clasped in my hands. If only she would say something, but she just stares vacantly across the room, as if conjuring up the ghosts that inhabit her photos. I am so afraid of what she might say that I keep repeating it over and over again, an incantation to magically prevent the words I dread: *Love you? It was impossible!* How perilous my history must be, to depend so completely upon the utterances of one person, how fragile my sense of self. But rather than the contemptuous snub I dread, Mum shakes her head. 'But I did love you, Cass,' she whispers. 'You were my little girl.'

I study her face, chewing my lip. This is almost impossible, but I have to carry on. 'I never felt you did,' I say slowly. 'I'm just trying to work out why.'

She does not like my tone, I can see, for her expression changes, the shutters falling with a rattle. I am longing for her to say more, but now she pushes her glasses back up her nose and says tautly, 'I think you're projecting things.'

'I don't think I am.'

She glances away, examining her nails. 'You became very difficult,' she mutters. 'As a teenager . . .'

Again, the little-girl voice: *Why do you always blame me for everything?* But I push it away and say instead, 'It wasn't a good time for me . . .'

'What can I tell you, Cassandra?' Mum mutters, fingering her glasses and still not meeting my eyes. 'David was always so much easier.'

Yes, I know David was easier. You've told me a thousand times! The girl was difficult, the boy a cinch. The history of Cass, chapter one, first paragraph. Now, please, help me rewrite the rest.

'That is not useful,' I say.

There is another long pause, and I think she is not going to reply, dismissing my question as the silly probings of a demanding child. Then she stands up and walks across the room, reaches into the bookcase and pulls out a thick, leatherbound album. She holds it to her bosom, as if afraid of letting it go, then hands it to me. 'You can have this, if you like,' she says. 'David has his.'

I take it from her, feeling the warm leather between my fingers. It smells musty and old, but there is no dust and the creases along its spine imply it has been opened many times. As I turn the first page, I remember where I have seen it before. It is my baby album, filled with pictures and mementoes from my infancy.

I leaf through it, my breath catching. There I am, round and jolly, harnessed into a vast perambulator; it is perhaps a year later and I am sitting in the old high-chair, which I suddenly remember as acutely as if I was tied into it yesterday, with its scratchy wooden seat and Formica table, holding a spoon in my fist. Here, secured between the leaves, is a lock of my hair, chestnut and curling, tied with a pink satin bow; there is even a paint-splashed footprint. Later I graduate into embroidered smocks with matching pants; I push a little truck filled with bricks, my fat face split by a toothy toddler grin; I even kick a ball in our small back garden with my father. There are no pictures of Mum, and now I understand why. It was her behind the camera, snapping away, like any other devoted parent.

When I have finished looking at the book, I place it gently on the table, next to the teapot and biscuits. I feel as if everything that has happened in the last months is about to burst out of me, spilling through the room and washing everything away.

'I wasn't able to be the mother I wanted to be, Cass,' Mum says quietly. 'I did love you, but when you were growing up I was so unhappy.'

I look up at her in surprise, searching her lined face for further information. I have never heard her talk like this before, and hearing her say these words, so sad and resigned, is a shock. 'Why?' I say. 'What went wrong?'

She shrugs. 'Perhaps I just wasn't cut out for it.'

I glance away from her, disappointed. *That's too easy; it's never so simple. How could you have been 'not cut out' for loving me?* 'But why not? Everyone else's mothers managed.'

I do not meant this to sound so accusatory, but rather than snapping something equally hurtful back, she says, 'That's what I used to think. But looking back I doubt if it was the case. What you'd probably find, if you asked, is that lots of us were dreadfully depressed. But we never talked about it, we just spent all our time trying to live up to some ridiculous ideal. It wasn't like it is now, with all this new touchy-feely stuff, we didn't express our emotions. You've got to remember that Women's Lib hadn't really made much impact in the 1960s, not among ordinary people, at least.'

'I know,' I murmur. 'I wrote a book on it.'

'Yes,' she says, abrasive again. 'I've got it.'

'You read it?'

'Of course I did. You are my daughter, you know.'

I bite my lip, surprised at the force of her rebuke. But when she next speaks, her voice is gentle. 'The thing is, Cass, I should have been out there, like you are now, having some kind of career. But it wasn't like that then. When women like me got married, I mean, the ones who weren't posh or hadn't been to university, they were basically expected to make that their first priority. Of course I had a job, but that was just to help make ends meet. Your father was very incautious, you know. He went and got himself sacked and then I had to be the one bringing in the money . . .'

'But that wasn't my fault,' I mumble.

'Of course it wasn't. And you were the sweetest, most adorable little girl.'

I stare at her. More! I want to hear more!

'But I got so depressed,' she continues. 'And I suppose I found it hard to . . . connect.'

I peer down at my hands. I am not going to attempt to speak.

'And later,' she goes on, 'when your dad and I weren't getting on and everything was coming to a head, well, maybe you picked up on it . . .'

I cannot stop myself. I hear myself say, 'You were unfaithful to Dad with Don before he died.'

I am almost expecting her to yell at me for being impudent, but she does not flinch. 'Yes, I was,' she says simply. 'But he was unfaithful too.'

The statement hits me with a dull thud: I can feel it slowly penetrating my skin, digging deep. As yet there is no pain, just a numb realization that everything I remember about my childhood will have to be sifted and sorted and made sense of anew. It is just as I have always taught my students. We like to make things simple, to have a linear narrative with a beginning, a middle and an end, but there are so many different versions of the past and time twists our memories in such strange ways that the truths sink, like different layers of sediment, and turn into something else again. There is more too, a thought I had not expected, but which now feels like the unexpected easing of a sore borne for so long I had forgotten it was there. *We have so much to discuss.*

And now I have the courage, which all this time I have been trying desperately to find. 'I need you to tell me about it,' I say. 'I'm trying so hard to make sense of it all.'

'Well,' she says briskly, but not unkindly, 'I shall.'

I take a breath. 'But, first, there's something I want to show you.'

I bend down, rummaging in my bag. I feel wired, like a cable pulled so tight that even the smallest movement causes a ricochet of anxious tremors, all down the line. When my fingers close around the plastic folder I pull it out and hand it over. This is the only way I can possibly tell her.

She looks at me, pushing her glasses up her nose again. 'What's this?' she mutters, furrowing her brow as she scans the smudged photocopy she has now pulled from its casing. 'Is it something you've published?'

'Just read it.'

I watch her read it, my heart flopping over. I found it in the British Library without much difficulty, for I knew the date and place. All I had to do was look up '*Evening Argus*, 21 August 1980'. And there it was.

BABY FOUND

A man walking his dog discovered a new-born baby on Brighton beach early this morning. It is thought that the infant, which was concealed in a fishing vessel, was less than an hour old. Jim Wright, who is seventy-one and lives in Carlton Hill, told the Argus *today how his dog, Queenie, first found the baby in the boat. 'I couldn't believe my eyes,' says Mr Wright, whose quick actions in wrapping the child in his sweater are thought by paediatricians at the Royal Sussex Hospital to have saved the child's life. 'I thought at first he was a doll, but then I realized it was a real live baby. Who would dump a tiny child in an old boat like that?'*

The infant, who has made a good recovery from his traumatic first hours, is currently being looked after at the Royal Sussex. Meanwhile the police are appealing for the mother to come forward. While abandoning a child is a criminal offence, the police have issued an assurance that she will be treated sympathetically.

Mum is spending a long time scrutinizing the paper. She keeps reaching the end, then going back to the beginning, as if trying to force sense into it.

'But I don't understand,' she mumbles. 'Why are you showing me this?'

Suddenly she stops looking at the article. Very slowly, she puts it down.

'August the twentieth was our wedding day. We were staying in Brighton.'

I nod.

'Somebody left a baby on the beach . . . a young mother or something . . .'

I am unable to respond: too many conflicting emotions are fighting for space. I am still angry, both with myself and with her for what happened that day. But it is making me so exhausted, this sense of being trapped for ever in our respective roles, and I long for change. Where will my anger get me, after so many years?

'You ran off,' she murmurs. 'You were in a terrible mood. And you didn't come back all night.'

'That's right.'

Something new is moving across her face as she struggles to fit the pieces together. 'You'd put on so much weight. And you were sick in the restaurant, too . . .'

Our eyes meet, and in that moment, as the understanding of what happened that night slowly takes hold of her features, I find what I came here to discover: this information is new. If she suspected my pregnancy she never allowed it to rise to the surface of her conscious thoughts. Her crime was simply that she was too preoccupied and distracted to grasp what was happening, not what I have always darkly suspected: that she knew but did not care. And now I realize something else too: I still love her.

'Goodness, Cass,' she whispers, and she drops her head into her hands.

'It was mine . . .' I say. 'My baby. I had him by myself on the beach. And then I hid him in a boat. I was scared you'd find out and be cross.'

I stop. If I listen very carefully, I can almost hear the sound of the waves rushing over the stones. Mum is trying to say something now, but her voice is muffled. As I look across the room at her, I know that everything between us has changed. So she was cold and distracted at times; so she did not love my father; so she found being a housewife hard. And, most difficult of all for me to stomach, so David was always her favourite. So what? I have to put all this behind me. It is time to rework my childhood, to cast myself in a different role. Mum loved me, or she tried to, but our relationship got snagged on rocks we never saw were there: the collective history of her generation, the story of her marriage, and my own secret past. But now there is a new narrative to be forged. Perhaps it is one we can eventually tell together.

'I've had enough of it messing up my life,' I say quietly. 'I want to try and find him.'

After that, we spend the rest of the day huddled together, talking. I was meant to be staying in a bed-and-breakfast, but after what has happened it seems preposterous not to stay with Mum, so I bed down in her spare room, tucked into the worn flowery sheets I remember from infancy. There is so much to say, all those years to fill in. But we both know there will be time for that later. Instead, we spend most of the long afternoon and evening discussing how we are going to make amends.

This is what we have decided. Tomorrow, after breakfast, we are going to drive back to Brighton. When we get there we are going to go to the police and I am going to tell them everything I have just told her. We do not think they will prosecute me, not after all these years. But they might have some record of what happened to my child, or at least the names of the social workers involved. And then maybe, just maybe, I might find him.

It is night. Mum has put out the cat and switched off the downstairs lights, and I have changed and washed in her small bathroom, peering through the leaded windows at the dark fields that surround the house as I brush my teeth. She has retreated to her bedroom now; from inside it I can hear her sighing and moving around, then she finally clicks the door shut.

The house settles into silence. Alone in my small room, I push open the window, and the night air pours in: sweet and damp and hinting of the summer soon to arrive. There is no moon and the night is inky black, an all-encompassing darkness that does not exist in cities. I can hear the gentle lowing of cows from the field behind the house, their misty sighs and the creak of their hoofs on the new grass. A little further away, sheep are bleating to their lambs, a deep, guttural cry echoing through the night.

I am tired in a way I have not experienced since I was a child: my limbs ache as if I have been running all day through fields, or racing my bike along the hilly country lanes. I lie down on the bed, burrowing under the blankets with relief. I feel as if I am sinking deep into the soft, saggy mattress, possibly never to return; through my exhausted body, a new warmth is spreading. Perhaps I will sleep for ever. But before I close my eyes and give in to the rest that, in all these long years of guilt and regret, I have never had, I hold one image in my head.

I am standing on the cliffs again, looking down at the crashing sea. The rockface falls, sheer and lethal beneath my view. Further down, seagulls nest in the jutting crags; impossibly, flowers are growing there. Out over the water, gannets circle the Atlantic breeze, then take aim and dive.

I am so close to the edge that my legs sway beneath me. When I peer over, I see the stony beach with its seaweed fringe, the foamy tide. This time, though, I am not afraid. And this time, rather than turning from the edge and running lumpenly away, I face the rocks and waves and cruising gulls beneath me.

And then I jump.